Death's Enemy

George Rosie

Death's Enemy

The Pilgrimage of Victor Frankenstein
A novel

WILLIAM HEINEMANN : LONDON

First published in the United Kingdom in 2001 by William Heinemann

1 3 5 7 9 10 8 6 4 2

Copyright © George Rosie 2001

George Rosie has asserted his right under the
Copyright, Designs and Patents Act, 1988 to be identified
as the author of this work

William Heinemann
The Random House Group Limited
20 Vauxhall Bridge Road, London SW1V 2SA

Random House Australia (Pty) Limited
20 Alfred Street, Milsons Point, Sydney,
New South Wales 2061, Australia

Random House New Zealand Limited
18 Poland Road, Glenfield
Auckland 10, New Zealand

Random House (Pty) Limited
Endulini, 5a Jubilee Road
Parktown 2193, South Africa

The Random House Group Limited Reg. No. 954009

www.randomhouse.co.uk

A CIP catalogue record for this book
is available from the British Library

Typeset by Deltatype Ltd, Birkenhead, Merseyside
Printed by Mackays of Chatham Ltd, Chatham, Kent

ISBN 0 434 00827 3

For Eilidh Vaughan, first of the next generation

Acknowledgements

One of the best parts of writing any book is the research. The research that went into this book owes a great deal to the assistance of people across Europe. My thanks, therefore, to the ever-helpful librarians of the National Library of Scotland in Edinburgh, and the Mitchell Library in Glasgow. And also to librarians, museum curators, church wardens and municipal officials in London, Gravesend, Geneva, Coppet, Ulm, Landshut, Donauworth, Munich and Ingolstadt. None of the travel and research work would have been possible without a Writer's Bursary from the Scottish Arts Council, for which I am more than grateful.

This book has been a long time in the writing. Encouragement from friends, colleagues and family has been vital. My thanks for that encouragement go to Neal Ascherson, Allan Massie, Les Wilson, Ross Wilson, Dr. Jim Dyer, and especially, to Alistair Moffat who nagged and cajoled me into completeing the work. Thanks also to my agent David Godwin (who saw the potential of the story long before he was an agent) and to my editor Ravi Mirchandani of William Heinemann who took the book on.

I owe an especial debt of gratitude to my wife Liz for being so patient for so long with my fascination with the science and electrophysiology of the late 18th and early 19th centuries. It could not have been easy. My offspring Paul, Scott and Jennie helped too by being interested. To all of them, many thanks.

George Rosie
Edinburgh
May 2001

BRAUNAU-AM-INN, AUSTRIA: NOVEMBER 1819

As I washed down the huge corpse that dreary night in November I knew that my journey was almost over. It had been more than a journey; it had been a pilgrimage. My hands trembled and my stomach quaked with anticipation as I laid out my instruments. I, Victor Frankenstein of Geneva, was about to achieve the goal I had pursued for the last quarter century: the restoration of a human being to life. I had acquired the skill, the knowledge and the cunning to infuse the spark of being into the lifeless thing that lay in front of me.

But that knowledge had been hard won. My pilgrimage had been long and weary. It had cut me adrift from home and family. It had left me wifeless and, so far as I knew, childless. I had few friends. It had taken me into almost every corner of Europe, from the glaciers of the Savoy and the neat towns of Austria to the ugly, rain-battered cities of Scotland. Like my mentor, the great Paracelsus, I had wandered most of the Continent asking questions. I knew now that there would always be more questions than answers. Only the Godly had answers.

My hands were shaking as I arranged the electrodes on The Creature's body. I worked as fast as I was able but I was tired and almost unnerved. And as I stared down at the huge corpse another figure rose in my mind's eye. It was one I had not seen for many years. It was the Man of Light, a figure who had eluded me since I first conjured him up many years ago near the mud flats of the River Thames in the town called Gravesend.

He was as vivid now as he had been then. He hovered somewhere between the huge creature's bone and flesh. He was a shimmering, elusive being of pure energy. He was not so much a skeleton as a kind of internal shell. He flickered through tissue and muscle, kidney and bowel, eye and brain. His shifting, luminescent form was as rooted in the flesh as were the bones of the skeleton. He was as insubstantial as a ghost and as powerful as lightning.

I could see him glimmering in the recesses of The Creature's heart, chamber by chamber, valve by valve, artery by artery. Without him we were so much fleshy rubble. We were nothing but a tangle of muscle and bone, flesh and entrail. The Man of Light was whatever strength we had. He was what held us together. When he guttered and was extinguished there was nothing for us but the grave. He was life itself.

And like me, Victor Frankenstein, the Man of Light was Death's sworn enemy.

SON

THE REPUBLIC OF GENEVA: 1790

In the *grand salon* of our house in the Cour Saint-Pierre there is a portrait of my mother. It is clumsily done, by a young portraitist who was fashionable among the ladies of Geneva before he debauched one of his sitters and had to flee to Paris. It shows a woman in her thirties wearing a low-cut dress which displays an inadequate bosom, bony shoulders and freckled, wiry arms. Her thin, light-boned face is wreathed in fairish curls and the painted mouth is fixed in a tight smile. Grey eyes look out under heavy brows. Their expression is direct, but wary. Her right arm is resting on a pedestal on which sits a marble bust of my father: grey, hard, implacable. The stone face looks disdainfully down at his wife.

In his incompetence (or perhaps it was insight) the young painter made the marble bust too big, too dark. What was meant to support, dominates, overwhelms. Instead of providing an affectionate backdrop to my mother, the grey marble figure broods over her like a thunder-cloud. Where my mother was meant to look quietly joyful in his presence, she looks threatened. The fingers of her left hand are slightly curled, as if in the process of making a fist. I have seen many people study the painting, but never heard anyone admire it.

As a child, the portrait fascinated me. I would stare up at it for minutes on end, trying to imagine it without my father's grey presence. Would the sky mysteriously lighten? Would my mother's smile widen? Would her eyes glitter with happiness? Would her left hand unclench? Would the tension go out of her shoulders? Would her bosom swell, become creamy and ample? In short, would our lives lighten if Alphonse Frankenstein was no longer there?

I suppose that I hated him and loved her, a common enough conjunction of emotions. She was the centre of my universe, while he was a harsh presence which swiftly came and as swiftly went.

Alphonse Frankenstein was Genevan to the bone. He was one of The Two Hundred, that all-powerful *haute bourgeoisie* which formed the most successful oligarchy in Europe, the Republic of Geneva. As a member of the twenty-five-man Senate or Small Council, Noble Alphonse Frankenstein was at the very heart of power in the Republic of Geneva.

My mother was a disappointment to him. Even as a child I could see that. What he wanted was a wife who would run the Frankenstein households in Geneva and Bellerive with a deft touch. Someone to ensure that the children were content and the servants biddable. Someone who would take a ladylike interest in poetry, perhaps, sketch a bit and play a little music badly. Someone who would accept his view of the world without question. There were many such women in the *haute ville* of Geneva and he was unlucky not to have found one.

Instead he married Caroline Beaufort, a clever, strong-minded woman some fifteen years his junior. She was a Protestant among Protestants. Her ancestors were among the

Huguenots who had flooded into Geneva after Louis XIV of France revoked the Edict of Nantes in 1685. Her father (my grandfather) had made and lost his fortune manufacturing and selling textiles. But like all good Huguenots, Grandpa Beaufort had made sure that his children – all his children – were well educated. My mother was fiercely interested in everything.

She was also one of Geneva's most energetic hostesses. Her *salons* at our town-house in the Cour Saint-Pierre or at the Frankenstein *campagne* Bellerive were among the finest in Geneva. The *literati* of the Republic trooped in and out of her drawing rooms in a seemingly endless procession. Poets, philosophers, painters, politicians, lawyers and playwrights: they came to dazzle one another with their opinions or impress the literary-minded ladies. Not even Geneva's renowned English Club shone more brightly than Madame Caroline Frankenstein's gatherings.

It was a heady atmosphere for a bookish boy. Money was spent on my education. Books came from all over Europe. Our libraries were filled with the texts published in Geneva which the rest of Europe disdained (or feared) to print. My mother hired only the best of tutors. Those who did not meet her exacting standards were speedily dismissed.

I suppose I was something of a prodigy. By the age of ten I was fluent in Latin and German and spoke decent English and Italian. Classical Greek, for some reason, always proved a challenge for me. I had a good memory and could recite poetry by the yard. My mother's guests bravoed the ease with which I could recite Horace, Ovid, Virgil and passages from Calvin's 'Institutions'. I had a passable singing voice and had enough music in me to strum usefully on a harpsichord.

I was also good with numbers. In fact I was excellent with numbers. I could calculate faster and further than anyone I

7

knew. This talent developed into another of my drawing-room tricks. I would stand in the middle of the room while the guests fired arithmetical problems at me. They were usually simple and I was rarely challenged by them. I rather enjoyed my role as Victor Frankenstein, the mathematical dancing bear.

For his part, my father disdained my mother's little soirées and usually absented himself whenever he could. He accused her of trying to turn my head with 'addle-pated revolutionary rubbish'. She accused him of wanting to transform me into a 'brainless Genevan money-grubber'. He wanted an heir who would take over the Frankenstein business interest and assume his rightful place among The Two Hundred; she hoped for a genius who would set Europe alight. I thought that he was a plodding bore and that she was wonderful beyond measure.

She rejoiced in the French Revolution and relished Geneva's own tradition of radicalism. She claimed to regret the failure of Geneva's (minor) insurrections of 1707, 1734, 1763 and 1782. She believed in change, a new constitution, political power to the *natifs* and artisans & craftsmens. Alphonse Frankenstein regarded her ideas with unamused contempt. A wealthy woman holding such notions struck him as either hypocritical or naïve or both. Order and stability were the twin stars in his firmament. Only by their light could a man make money, in the pursuit of which he travelled all over Europe.

While she saw herself as an enlightened figure free from religious bigotry, she was nevertheless hugely proud of Geneva's Protestant tradition which she described as 'the light of Europe'. As a descendant of Huguenots, she regarded the Catholic states – and especially France – as lying in the outer darkness. She viewed Geneva's slogan 'Post Tenebras Lux' without cynicism. She viewed the

8

Protestant reformation as *the* turning-point of human history.

'When nobody, no priest, nor pope, nor saint, nor angel stands between a man and his God', she told me more than once 'that changes everything. Some day you'll see that.'

She instilled into me the notion of the greatness of Jean Calvin. His presence was everywhere. We lived in the shadow of the Cathedral of St Pierre, and a few dozen yards from the little *auditoire* where Calvin had hammered out the ideas of the Reformation, and where the Scottish reformer John Knox had shepherded his little flock of British exiles before returning to Scotland to wrench that land from the hands of Rome. So vivid did she make Calvin's presence that I would stand in the window and sometimes see the gaunt, bearded, long-robed figure slipping under the trees, across the Cour Saint-Pierre and up the steps into the cathedral.

I had two good friends of my own age: Henri Clerval, whose family lived in a narrow house in the Rue de l'Evèche, and Jean-Pierre Huber, who lived round the corner in the Taconnerie. Jean-Pierre was a cheerful boy who would spend hours pulling insects apart and examining their parts through a little eyeglass he always carried with him. He told me that he planned to make his reputation by learning more about *ants* than anybody in the history of the human race.

Jean-Pierre and I were both keen experimenters. We foraged far and wide for phenomena to examine. We would climb high up into the cathedral's towers to draw our own maps and plans of Geneva and Lac Leman, or sketch the formation of the clouds over the Jura mountains. Fat Clerval would stand on the ground below with his grandfather's pocket watch and register how long it took various objects to reach the ground: feathers, small stones, bits of wood, pieces of slate, a dead sparrow.

Clerval went along with our strange ways, but they were

not for him. He was fat and fanciful, an aspiring *littérateur* who relished tales from Geneva's past. The bloodier the better. He had a grisly imagination. He swore that once a year he could hear the revolutionary lawyer Pierre Fatio being shot to death by a ghostly firing squad in the old gaol in the Rue de l'Evèche.

When we were not sitting under the trees in the Cour Saint-Pierre discussing the woes of the world, or scrambling on the Salève in search of specimens, we prowled the old ramparts with wooden swords, ready to defend Geneva. Our favourite fantasy was to re-enact 'L'Escalades', that bloody skirmish of 1602 when our town guard butchered a force of Savoyards and Spaniards who tried to storm the city by night. Severed popish heads decorated the old walls of Geneva for months. We once hacked the head off a dead cat and impaled it on a stake to recapture the effect.

But this was all slightly more than a game. The 1790s were not the safest of times for sprigs of the Genevan gentry like Clerval, Jean-Pierre and myself. The *natifs* were restive and hostile and agitated by the turbulence of the French revolution. We were safe enough in the upper reaches of the town, but once down in the Place du Bel-Air or the Place de Fusterie things could turn nasty. We were liable to be jostled, harassed or stoned by Geneva's young malcontents.

So I became handy with my fists and feet. I took to carrying a silk stocking which could be quickly loaded with a stone and transformed into a useful club. I learnt to stab with a stick, and never slash. Three coins between the fingers of my right hand wrapped in a handkerchief made a useful 'brass fist'. I acquired a reputation for sudden violence and thus was usually left alone. The fact that I was Noble Alphonse Frankenstein's son helped.

While Jean-Pierre could run like a startled hare, fat Clerval was useless in a scuffle and took many a pounding. One thumping, in an alley off the Grand Rue, had him groaning in bed for a week. The more cuffings he got, the deeper he retreated into his imagination. It seemed to be a grisly place, in which Clerval was a blood-boltered, sword-wielding hero.

But the bane of our lives was my cousin and adopted sister, Elisabeth Lavenza. She was a year younger than me, thin, fair, pretty and my father's pride and joy. She was also his eyes and ears. Any remarks about 'Alphonse the Abominable' were likely to get back to him and result in a cuffing. Fat Clerval doted on her, and reddened whenever she sidled up to him. She would brush her little breasts against him just to watch the blushes spread across his face. She never missed an opportunity to lift her skirts on some pretext or another. Clerval danced whenever Elisabeth whistled. He was forever begging Jean-Pierre and myself to let her trail along. Whenever we did, the expedition would peter out in tears, recriminations, angry silences.

Elisabeth was a gifted troublemaker. She was the daughter of my father's sister and a Piedmontese banker who disappeared after his wife died in Pisa, coughing her lungs out. Out of pity my mother took in the four-year-old Elisabeth. Elisabeth's talent, which she developed very early, was to play one member of the household against another: my father against my mother, my mother against me, me against my younger brother Ernest, Ernest against the servants, the servants against my infant brother William. She had no friends of her own and she was seldom invited out.

But she had an impressive hold over Alphonse Franken-stein. She was pretty, coquettish and apparently biddable. It was an engaging mask, but behind it she was calculating and manipulative. I had long since stopped complaining to my father about Elisabeth. He always took her part and would dismiss me with a growl. My mother had Elisabeth's measure but would never entertain my grievances against her.

'She cannot compete with you Victor,' she told me once. 'So she uses, ah, other methods. Which is what women do. All women. Don't be so *harsh* with her.'

As the political fevers induced by the French Revolution ran through Geneva my mother grew increasingly nervous. My father took pleasure in telling her that she and her liberal *salons* were fostering the very unrest she feared. But the result was that we spent more and more time at Bellerive, about five miles from the city. Our *campagne* was a handsome, red-tiled house set in wooded grounds which ran down to Lac Leman. At Bellerive we kept a couple of milk cows, some sheep, three ponies, a few goats and a flock of poultry.

Jean-Pierre and Clerval were regular house guests. For weeks on end we turned amphibian. We swam, dived off the jetty, took potshots with our catapults at the ducks and gulls, fished for carp, built crude rafts, and on calm days spent hours skimming flat stones across the surface of the water. We became fairly expert with the Frankenstein sailboat, although once we had to fish Clerval out of the water, gasping, half drowned and sobbing for his mother.

We netted sticklebacks and minnows to see how long they could live out of the water. We trapped spiders, beetles and worms to see how long they could live *in* water. We inserted insects into sealed bottles to see which species could live longest without air (it seemed to be earwigs). We once caught a mole, tied a strong piece of twine to one of its back legs, then let the little blind creature dig for a few minutes before yanking it back. The idea was to see how deep it could go in the time available. Eventually the twine broke.

Alphonse Frankenstein liked to bait the attendees at my mother's *salons* with the boast that 'If I don't make it, mine it,

12

finance it or sell it, then I ship it'. This was no empty claim. The Frankenstein business interest extended into every corner of Geneva, and out into the Swiss Confederation. And one of its arms was a fleet of two-masted barques which plied Lac Leman.

They were sturdy, well-built boats on which I spent a few summers working as a deckhand. My mother was horrified, but for once Alphonse Frankenstein was pleased with me. He told her, 'it'll do the boy no harm to get some honest grit under his fingernails', and put me in the charge of one of his best skippers, a dour, leathery man called Thomas Josse from the lakeside village of Coppet.

Josse was a hard man but a good teacher. I learnt how to work the tough little boats: reefing the sails, working the helm, stowing the cargoes and manoeuvring into the little harbours that fringed the lake. I learnt which reefs and sandbanks to avoid, and which formation of cloud over the Alps or the Jura foretold sudden squalls. Under Josse's hard blue eye, we ranged the length and breadth of Lac Leman, from Geneva up to Montreux and back again, criss-crossing the lake from Nyon to Thonon, Thonon to Vevey, Vevey to Evian. We shipped beer, marble, trout, cottons, watches, wine, roof tiles, beef and anything else my father's network of customers wanted or needed.

By the end of every summer my skin was browned by the sun and wind, my hands were calloused and every ounce of fat had been burned off my frame. My mother (who, I now realise, preferred the *idea* to the reality of the labouring classes) regarded my appearance with alarm and told me that I looked 'no better than a Savoyard mountain herd'. All that I needed was a 'set of rags' to complete the picture.

But I enjoyed these summers afloat. The physical labour, the constant activity and change, the succession of new faces, satisfied something in me. At the end of summer I always

13

felt ready for anything that the world – and Alphonse
Frankenstein – might throw at me.

THE REPUBLIC OF GENEVA: 1792

We are all the creation of others. Two people made me what I am – my mother, Caroline Beaufort Frankenstein, and Horace-Benédict de Saussure, the man I called Uncle Ben. Ever since he perched me on his knee and explained that the specks of light dancing around my mother's drawing room were particles of dust 'trapped in sunbeams' Uncle Ben has been my mentor.

He was everything I wanted to be: scholar, traveller, philosopher, mountaineer, political reformer, correspondent of the great. Uncle Ben was a man of huge reputation to whom everybody in Geneva – syndics, noble families, *natifs*, the Grand Council – listened. His walled house in the Rue de la Cité was the centre of an intellectual universe. And its doors were always open to me, Victor Frankenstein.

He was also everything that my father was not. Uncle Ben was steeped in the natural philosophy of his time; Alphonse Frankenstein never lifted his head from the trough. Uncle Ben explored the high ice-fields of the Savoy and calculated the height of mountains; my father haggled in the market over the price of Lac Leman carp. Uncle Ben discoursed with the great minds of Europe; my father gossiped with bankers and money-changers. Uncle Ben plumbed the mysteries of the world; my father counted his change.

They even looked like opposites. Uncle Ben was a wiry, slightly built man with a sharp nose and chin and bright blue eyes. My father was dark and heavy with a cold grey eye and a mouth like a rat-catcher's trap. Uncle Ben's speech was as light and fast as my father's was deliberate. Uncle Ben dressed colourfully and carelessly while my father invariably wore his banker's uniform of dark silk coat and breeches, brocaded waistcoat, and buckled shoes. Uncle Ben was light to the Frankenstein darkness. Or so it seemed to me.

To his twelve-year-old disciple he seemed to have done everything, been everywhere, met everybody. He was Professor of Philosophy at the University of Geneva at the age of twenty-two and the second man to climb the mountain in the Savoy we called Mont Blanc. In 1784 he had travelled to Lyons to quiz the balloonist Montgolfier about his flights, and returned to his estate at Genthod to experiment with his own hot-air balloons.

Uncle Ben had foraged all over Europe, from the volcano of Naples to the cotton mills of Manchester. He was fascinated by Britain, which he regarded as the strangest place on Earth, and regaled the *salons* of Geneva with accounts of the tramways of Leeds and the flint-glass factories of Cornwall. The ladies of the Republic delighted in his description of how his wife Albertine, in Spanish costume of silver and pink, had conquered the King of Denmark at a masquerade in London.

Horace-Benédict de Saussure was not, in fact, my uncle. He was an old friend of my mother's. Like her, he was a descendant of Huguenots, driven out of France by the

Catholic tyrants. They were close. I have heard it suggested that he was my mother's lover. I have no idea whether he was or not. He may have been. All I knew was that when Uncle Ben was around things tended to happen. They were things that demanded explanation. And Uncle Ben was a great explainer.

It was Uncle Ben who tried to explain to me the mysteries of lightning. We were standing in the grounds of the Frankenstein *campagne* at Bellerive watching the sky darken over Lac Leman. Lightning was flickering over the Jura mountains and being reflected in the lake. A strange, hottish wind was gusting around the house. Suddenly we were wrapped in a sheet of dazzling light, there was a terrible crack and roar, and an old oak tree a hundred yards from us was blown apart by a bolt of lightning.

It was the most beautiful thing I had ever seen. One minute the tree stood there creaking against the dark sky; the next it was flying apart in a burst of flame and sparks. Streams of fire seemed to issue from every crack. Shards of wood hissed over our heads while the rest of the tree drizzled down in fragments all over the house and garden. The whole elaborate structure flew apart in an expanding hemisphere of light that imprinted itself on the back of my eyelids.

My head was spinning and my ears were clanging as I clung open-mouthed and trembling to Uncle Ben. My parents, their guests and most of the servants spilled out of the house to discover what had shaken the building. All I could do was point and stammer. My mother rushed to us to make sure we were unharmed. While she threw her arms around me, my father glowered at Uncle Ben and me, as if we had conspired to bring down the lightning on his property.

He turned away from us, scanned the house to satisfy

himself that no serious damage had been done (three small windows had shattered) and then wandered disconsolately among the debris kicking at the litter of branches and leaves. My response was to giggle nervously, and he turned on me.

'What are you laughing at boy?' he growled. 'The ruin of a fine old tree amuses you, does it?'

He made me feel slightly ashamed. I had enjoyed that old oak tree. I had played under it, swung from it, climbed all over it, carved my initials on it and fallen out of it more than once. One memorable summer some years ago Elisabeth had helped me make a tree house in the branches, and there she had satisfied my curiosity about the female anatomy. That old oak tree had been good to me. But I could not help exulting in the high drama of its death.

My exultation lingered after my parents and their guests returned to the house. Only Uncle Ben stood with me over the smoking ruins of the old oak. A strange, sharp smell hung over the remnants of the tree.

'The only time I've seen something like that was near the summit of Mont Blanc,' he told me. 'You could feel it building up in the air. A kind of crackling, and tingling. One of us – young Jalabert – was wearing brocade on his waistcoat and hat. Sparks began to fly from his clothes. His hat started to hum. Imagine, a humming hat! Poor Jalabert. I think he expected to be burned to a crisp, right there in the snow. A biblical pillar of fire on the glaciers of Savoy. With a Genevan atheist in the middle of it. A nice irony, eh?'

'But what is it, Uncle Ben?' I asked. 'The lightning, I mean. Where does it come from?'

He shrugged. 'Who knows? It's everywhere. In the clouds, in the air, in the soil, in you, in me, probably in the old tree itself. Somehow, we don't know how, it builds up in the moisture of the clouds, then discharges itself into the earth in a huge spark. That's what we call lightning.'

18

That night I could hardly sleep. In my mind's eye I kept seeing the stream of fire run down the trunk of the oak before the whole tree exploded in a blaze of light and a blizzard of sparks. Time after time I watched the flame blossom and the tree disintegrate into fragments. The beauty of the moment entranced me. The power of it filled me with awe.

Over the breakfast table I badgered Uncle Ben with more questions. How did the lightning form? How long did it take? Why were there different kinds? Did it occur over mountains more than over flat ground? Were birds ever struck by lightning? Could it be predicted? Was there any way of measuring the power of the lightning bolt?

'That's been tried,' Uncle Ben told me, his mouth full of cheese. 'A Dutchman called Richmann, it was. Forty years ago, in St Petersburg. What he did was run a metal rod through the roof of his house to attract the lightning. Then he attached it by a chain to another metal rod standing in a glass jar on a table. To *that* rod he tied a linen thread, eighteen inches long and weighted with lead.'

'I don't understand,' my mother said.

'Normally the weighted thread hung perpendicularly,' he told her. 'But when the rod was suffused with electricity it was animated and began to rise.'

'Like hair standing on end,' she suggested.

'Exactly,' Uncle Ben said. 'So the more electricity that passed down the thread, the higher it would move up a marked scale . . .'

'And the more powerful the bolt of lightning,' my mother intervened 'the further the thread would move up the gauge. I see. And did it work?'

'After a fashion,' Uncle Ben said. 'A thunderstorm duly arrived. A bolt of lightning duly struck the rod. And the electricity duly ran down the chain. But when Richmann was leaning forward to see if the thread *was* moving up the gauge, a ball of lightning leapt out of the apparatus – and killed him stone dead. Dropped him like a felled ox.'

'Good God!' my father exclaimed. 'Is this true?'

'True as the cheese on your plate,' Uncle Ben said. 'Richmann's assistant saw the whole thing. And wrote a very complete account of it.'

'Good God,' my father repeated.

Uncle Ben knew how to tell a story. Everyone at the table was staring at him with fascination. 'The odd thing was,' he went on, 'Richmann was practically unmarked. The doctors found a burn mark on his forehead and a hole in his left shoe. The lightning – the electricity – seems to have gone right through him. From head to toe. Turned his insides to mush, though, if you'll forgive me ladies.'

'Bloody idiot,' was my father's judgement. 'Messing about with things like that.'

'Perhaps,' Uncle Ben said. 'But some knowledge is hard won. Philosophy has its martyrs, Alphonse, and poor Richmann was one of them. Anyway, Victor. I'm going back to Geneva today. I'll see what I can find in my library. I'm sure I've got something there that'll take your fancy.'

'No doubt,' my father grunted, and changed the subject.

Uncle Ben was as good as his word. Next day a messenger arrived from Geneva with a package for me. I unwrapped it to find a well-thumbed volume from the Saussure library entitled *The History and Present State of Electricity* by the Englishman Joseph Priestley. Attached to the flyleaf was a note.

'I hope this interests you,' he wrote. 'Doctor Priestley is a fine fellow. He's a Protestant clergyman by trade but a political radical by inclination. A mob destroyed his house in Birmingham, forcing the poor philosopher to flee for his life. Which is something that might happen to any of us in these troubled times. He now lives in London, but I understand that he's considering the safety of the Americas. Things have moved on since he wrote the book, so it may be out of date. If it is, my apologies.'

The apology was entirely unnecessary. The book was a compendium of wonders. 'The electric fluid is no local or occasional agent in the theatre of the world,' Priestley informed me. 'Late discoveries show that its presence and effects are *everywhere,* and that it acts as a principal part in the grandest and most interesting scenes of nature. It is not, like magnetism, confined to one kind of body, but everything we know is a conductor or a non-conductor of electricity.'

The words leapt off the page. Electricity! Its presence and effects are everywhere! A principal part in the grandest and most interesting scenes of nature! From this all-embracing notion Priestley ranged far and wide. All the world's electricians and their work seemed to be contained in its pages. I plunged into them. There are few appetites so voracious as the curiosity of a bookish, twelve-year-old boy.

I was most taken by the 'experiments on animal and other organised bodies' carried out by the Abbé Nollet, and, quite separately, by Priestley himself. So far as I could understand (which was not very far), Priestley calculated the power at his disposal from the area of 'coated' glass in each of the Leyden phials in his 'battery'. The electricity from eleven jars was enough to kill 'a pretty large kitten' which Priestley then tried to bring back to life 'by distending the lungs, blowing with a quill into the trachea, but to no purpose'.

But I kept circling back to the descriptions of lightning. With the vision of the exploding oak tree still etched in my mind, it was *that* phenomenon that interested me most. So I read avidly of Benjamin Franklin's 'discoveries concerning the similarity of lightning and electricity'. And I was

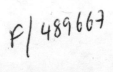

intrigued by Priestley's account of 'some of the more unusual appearances in the earth and heavens by electricity'.

I learnt that in the year 1749 the British Admiral Chambers reported 'a large ball of blue fire rolling on the surface of the water' which, when it struck his ship, 'went off with an explosion as if hundreds of cannon had been fired at one time'. One crewman was badly burned, the ship's main topmast was shattered 'into a hundred pieces' and marlin-spikes were driven into the deck by the blast. The lightning ball 'left so great a smell of brimstone, that the ship seemed to be nothing but sulphur'.

In my mind's eye I saw a ship adrift and burning on the high seas. Stricken by a spark out of hell.

THONON, FRANCE: 1792

I was twelve years old when I became the last Paracelsian. I was the solitary custodian of a great intellectual empire that had once stretched across Europe from Russia to Scotland. I saw myself as the last sentry on the parapet, the Paracelsian world's sole defender against the armies of darkness and ignorance. Let the rest of the world regard the Lord of my Imagination as an obscure and discredited warlock. To me, Philip Theophrastus Bombastus von Hohenheim – the man who called himself Paracelcus – was the world's greatest genius.

I found him one rainy afternoon in the spa town of Thonon, across the border in France. My mother had persuaded my father that the health of the Frankenstein family would benefit from a few days in the clear air and mineral waters of the French resort and he, surprisingly, agreed. We had no sooner settled into an inn on the edge of Thonon when the clouds descended and the rain settled in. So I spent the next few days plundering the books on the drawing-room shelves. One of them was a biography of Paracelcus.

Thus I vaulted into the plague-haunted, war-racked Europe of the early sixteenth century. Wherever Paracelcus went, Victor Frankenstein of Geneva was at his elbow. Together we sweated and choked in the silver mines of the Tyrol to make the Fuggers of Augsburg even richer. I laboured with him in the fierce heat of the smelting vats. And I sat with him in the darkness as he explained to the black-faced miners that what was killing them was the dust from the mine-workings and the greed of the Fuggers, and not the spirits of the mountains.

Rumours and legends swarmed around Paracelcus like blowflies around dead meat. He was, the ignorant said, a eunuch whose genitals had been devoured by a rooting pig. He had been mutilated by a Swabian soldier. His sword 'Azoth' could bring the dead back to life. Azoth's crystal pommel allowed Paracelcus to see what was happening, anywhere on earth. He could wrap his cloak around himself and become invisible. Azoth was a one-legged dancer that danced on its own – or with the devil.

Nonsense, of course. To me, Paracelcus was the natural philosopher as hero. He was a revolution in walking boots. He was a one-man insurrection. He wandered Europe, subverting the comfortable, baffling the orthodox, infuriating the powerful. He cured the sick poor without charge and demanded big fees from the wealthy. He despised the wisdom of the ancients. Paracelcus believed only in what he could see, hear, touch and smell. He was a man of many slogans, but none more thrilling to me than his claim: 'I was there and saw it happen.'

But he was a troublesome companion. He was arrogant, quarrelsome, loud, bumptious, impatient and occasionally violent. He dressed like a Swabian princeling, but seldom changed his clothes. He was said to have stunk like a goat. He was never without Azoth, and when he was drunk (which was often) he would wave the sword around alarmingly. He could drink wine-pickled peasants under the table and still have the wit to dictate his notes. I watched him go on rampages that it took a dozen town guards to subdue. I drank, argued, brawled and whored (itself an exciting thought) my way across Europe with him.

Like Martin Luther, my master disdained to use Latin. He taught and wrote only in his native Swiss German. He refused to be browbeaten or intimidated. Together, Paracelcus and I supported the peasants against their masters and were gaoled in Salzburg for our pains. We loathed the Romish Church. 'No one from the priestly crew is fit for medicine,' Paracelcus announced. 'For medicine needs its own man.' We were hounded around Europe by an alliance of the Church, apothecaries, surgeons and wealthy merchants. I saw the hand of the Fuggers in all our tribulations and persecutions.

I wandered with him from university to university: Basle to Tübingen, Vienna to Wittenberg, Leipzig to Heidelberg, Cologne to Ferrara. I heard him voice his contempt for Latin teaching, scientific orthodoxy and the Wisdom of the Ages. I listened to him wonder aloud why 'the High Colleges of Europe contrive to produce so many High Asses'? And I heard him exhort his students to sit at the feet of 'old wives, gypsies, sorcerers, wandering tribes, old robbers and other such outlaws. A doctor must be a *traveller*. Knowledge is experience.'

I took part in the Peregrinations of Paracelcus. It was an epic wandering that led us to Florence, Rome, Naples, Sicily, Marseilles, Barcelona and across to Africa with the Spanish army. I wandered with him up through France and into England, Ireland and Scotland and then back to Germany.

Together we campaigned deep into Finland and Russia, were captured by Tartars, escaped into Latvia, fled into Hungary and became military surgeons in the service of the Republic of Venice.

With me, Victor Frankenstein, at his side, Paracelcus made his way through the heat, stench and flies of Egypt and the Levant, across to Cyprus and Greece and into Constantinople. I heard him tell the Arab physicians that while their medicine was once the glory of the world it was now outdated. And that their great mentor Ibn Sina – known to Europe as Avicenna – no longer deserved the title 'Prince of Physicians'.

I returned with him in triumph to Europe. I was there in Berne in June 1527 when he scandalised the High Asses by nailing his programme of lectures to the university door inviting anyone, educated or not, to attend. I cheered with the other students when Paracelcus made a bonfire of the books of Avicenna and the Greek physician Galen.

I heard him applauded when he railed against the *nostra* of the apothecaries: the salves, the infusions, the fumigants and the drenches which killed and maimed more people than they ever cured. 'You poison the people and ruin their health,' he told the physicians. 'Your schools teach nothing worth knowing. You belong to the tribe of snakes, and I expect nothing but venom from you.'

I sat with him in Nuremberg when he laboured deep into the night to produce his 'Eight Books on the French Disease', in which he proved that the orthodox treatment for syphilis – a fumigation of guaiac wood and mercury – was worse than useless. Although I had no idea what syphilis was, I raged with him when the Nuremberg city council prevented the publication of his work in case it brought down the wrath of the Fuggers in Augsburg. The Fuggers, he was told, had a monopoly on the import of guaiac wood into Europe. That must not be challenged.

Paracelcus told me time after time that the macrocosm of the physical universe was a huge, an unimaginably vast, chemical crucible. Everything in it, ourselves included, was part of a subtle and endlessly complicated chemical process. And that the only way to treat the body's ailments was to understand the elements with which it was made and the processes by which they were assembled. 'Man is a sun and a moon and a heaven filled with stars,' he used to say. For this he was denounced as 'alchemist' and 'warlock' by the Romish Church and the High Asses of Europe.

And I bled with him when he was battered almost to death by assassins in Salzburg, and watched him as he died on a camp-bed in the White Horse Inn in the Keygasse. Some say he had fallen foul of his patron, Duke Ernst of Bavaria. Others blamed the Catholic Church. Many hinted at a conspiracy among the physicians and the apothecaries. But I knew in my twelve-year-old bones that the cudgels which killed Paracelcus had been bought by the Fuggers of Augsburg.

At which point I was wrenched back into the year 1792 by Alphonse Frankenstein. My father snatched the book from my hand and scanned the title-page. 'What in God's name is this? *A Life of Theophrastus Bombastus von Hohenheim otherwise known as Paracelcus,*' he sneered loudly. 'It really is time, Victor, that you stopped wasting your energy on this . . . this sad trash. Because that's what it is. Sad medieval trash. Alchemy and witchery. Discredited notions. Exploded theories. Empty words from a time which knew nothing.'

He threw the book to the floor and left the room with a snort. I retrieved it, smoothed the pages and muttered an apology to the portrait of Paracelcus on the frontispiece. It was dated 1540, the year before he was murdered. The great round face in the engraving is haggard but the eyes are resolute. It was the face of a man who had looked heaven in the eye and been cursed for his pains. His meaty hand rested on the cross guard of his sword and companion Azoth, the one-legged dancer. I returned to the sixteenth century.

One Paracelsian myth was unfathomable. It lodged in my mind like a bone in the throat. After he was attacked, when Paracelcus knew he was dying, he sent for his friend, the surgeon Andrée Wendl. He made Wendl promise to chop his corpse into gobbets and place them in a large box. Then, after *exactly* three days Wendl was to return and open the chest. Paracelcus assured the mystified surgeon that instead of a mass of putrefaction he would find a living Paracelcus, no more than twenty years old, who would open his eyes, climb out of the box, stretch his limbs and shake Wendl by the hand. It would be a miracle of alchemical reconstruction. Life out of death.

Reluctantly, Wendl agreed. When Paracelcus finally died he was quickly dismembered and packed away in the great box. But then Wendl became fretful and impatient. Instead of waiting the agreed three days, he opened the box half a day too early and found a creature almost, but not quite, formed. The daylight had prevented the alchemical miracle. The process was halted too soon. Wendl's curiosity had transmuted the great Paracelcus into a pathetic, half-formed monster that went on to roam the earth in misery.

THE REPUBLIC OF GENEVA: 1793

I had never heard of the electrified locksmith of Geneva until one hot afternoon in August. I was sitting on a bench under the trees at the Puits Saint-Pierre dismantling a couple of old locks. One was a common spring lock made of iron, and the other a tumbler device of brass. In trying to fathom the difference between the two mechanisms, I had stripped them down, laid out the components on the bench beside me, and was now hopelessly confused. How could I, Victor Franken-stein, be baffled by such workaday devices? As I sat staring at the array of bolts, springs, screws, tumblers and keys, Uncle Ben came huffing up the steps from the Rue du Perron.

'Aha, Victor,' he shouted. 'Make way there for some much older bones.'

As he sat down beside me he was breathless. 'The same bones that used to climb the highest mountains of Savoy can now hardly get me from the Lower Streets up to here,' he panted. 'How have the mighty fallen, eh?' Then he stared down at the bits of metal lying on the bench. 'What's this?'

he asked. 'Been dismantling the Frankenstein household again?'

'Just trying to understand how these locks work,' I said.

'And do you?'

'Not too well.'

'Tricky things, locks,' he said. 'And philosophically, very interesting. They protect your house against bad weather or wicked men. They also keep good men locked away in misery. But do the locksmiths who make them care what they're used for? Of course they don't. Not so long as they get paid.'

Uncle Ben never missed a chance to conjure up a parable or a moral. It was probably his most irritating characteristic.

He picked up one of the lock cases, took out his spectacles and began to scrutinise the markings. 'Aha,' he said. 'That's interesting.'

'What is?'

'See here. This mark. It belongs to old Jacques Chaumier. The electrified locksmith of Geneva. A man renowned in medical history.'

'Why is he renowned?'

'Not for his locks, that's for sure,' Uncle Ben said frowning at the iron case. 'Just look at that workmanship. I could have done better myself. No, he was one of the first men in Europe cured by electricity. Or at least he was one of the first men that we know about.'

'Cured?' I said. 'Cured of what?'

'He'd hit himself with a heavy hammer, and was paralysed all down his right side,' Uncle Ben told me. 'For years he couldn't move an arm or a leg. Could barely speak. His right eye was practically closed. Poor old Chaumier. I remember him dragging himself around Geneva, his right leg trailing and his right arm useless. It seems he'd tried everything – doctors, surgeons, pastors, the mineral baths at

Aix-en-Savoye. But nothing did any good. His lock-making days were over. He had to hand everything over to his apprentices. Which, when I think about it, may account for this kind of workmanship.'

'But he was cured?'

'Somebody told him to go and see Jean Jallabert who was then the Professor of Experimental Philosophy at the university. Jallabert's son came up Mont Blanc with me. Strong as an ox. Anyway, the old man, his father, was dabbling in electricity. Playing about with Leyden jars. These were early days, of course. But Jallabert was quite a serious electrician.'

'Here in Geneva?'

'Yes. Here in Geneva. So when Chaumier came along with his frozen arm, Jallabert took on his case. Jallabert and a surgeon called Daniel Guyot. I knew Guyot quite well. Dead now, of course, but I talked to him about the case just before he died. It seems that poor old Chaumier's right arm was completely paralysed. The thumb and three of the fingers were badly swollen and locked solidly into the palm of the hand. The arm itself was emaciated, almost withered. The poor man hadn't *felt* anything for years. But then – something of a miracle . . .'

'A miracle?'

'Well, maybe not a miracle. But something. When Jallabert electrified Chaumier's arm from the Leyden jar, the locksmith felt a huge blow on the shoulder and what he described as a tingling all down his right side.'

'The electricity?' I said.

Uncle Ben nodded. 'The electricity. Most important of all, Jallabert noticed that the *muscles* in the chest, arm and hand were convulsed. Set moving. And that the locked fingers of the hand had started to twitch. That was important, Victor. It showed that electricity could, somehow, agitate muscles.'

'And was Monsieur Chaumier cured?' I asked.

'Not just like that,' he said. 'It took time. Professor Jallabert worked on Chaumier for almost two hours, every day, for more than two months. The more that Jallabert worked on him, the better he became. After a few weeks he could pick up a full glass of water. Then he could throw a ball. By the time Jallabert was finished with him old Chaumier had the full use of his right arm back.'

'And did it last?' I said. 'The electrical cure?'

'Seems to have done. The only effect was the flux. After a stiff jolt from the Leyden jar he'd spend the rest of the day soiling himself. God knows why. But I'm sure Chaumier was happy enough to trade a few pairs of dirty breeches for the use of his good right arm. I know I would be. So. The locksmith *redivivus*.'

'But how does it *work*, Uncle Ben?' I asked. 'I mean, what *happens*?'

He shrugged. 'There's something about electricity that suffuses dead tissue – or apparently dead tissue – with new life. Maybe it's the spark of life, Victor. Bottled up in a jar. Life in a jar. There's a thought, eh?'

Then he turned to the dismantled locks. 'Anyway, anyway. Let's see if we can put these devices together again. Never let it be said that a few rusty springs and tumblers can baffle the natural philosophers of Geneva. To work.'

Within five minutes both locks were reassembled.

THE REPUBLIC OF GENEVA: 1794

The year 1794 was the year that Clerval declared himself a revolutionary. For months the fat fool had been reading accounts of the beheadings, disembowellings and mutilations that had been going on in France, and had scared himself witless. The only way to escape the vengeance of the *égaliseurs*, he told me, was to join their cause. But having no idea *how* to throw his hand in with the 'suppressed humanity of Geneva' he made do with dyeing one of his grandfather's nightcaps red (he managed a kind of muddy brown) and honed the edge of an old kitchen knife sharp enough to cut his thumb.

He also wrote a long poem in which he compared the boatmen, fishwives and drunks of the Ile du Rhône with the Roman slaves who had 'fought and died with noble pride at the side of their hero, Spartacus'. He sent the poem to one of Geneva's literary magazines, who disdained to print it. Clerval regarded this as definitive proof of the reign of the Tyrants and the urgent need for revolution.

His imagination was as lurid as his sentiments. He saw

himself leading the *sans culottes* of Geneva up the Grand Rue to storm the Arsenal and topple the regime of The Two Hundred. He pledged himself to do what he could to protect me, Jean-Pierre and Elisabeth (especially Elisabeth) from the vengeance of the dispossessed. Then he stalked the streets of Geneva looking for the best place to erect the instrument of revolutionary justice. My suggestion that it should be built in the Cour Saint-Pierre was dismissed on the grounds it was too close to the Clerval house on the Rue de l'Evèche and would upset his mother. And anyway, the trees would block the view.

Jean-Pierre favoured the Place du Bel Air where there was a long tradition of hangings, floggings, flayings and beheadings, and from which corpses could be disposed of in the Rhône. Eventually, however, we settled on a site down in the old market-place of the Bourg-de-Four. Clerval surveyed it carefully and nodded. An ideal location for the guillotine he decided. Large enough to hold a good crowd, he said, and far enough away from the better class of houses.

Clerval was nothing if not assiduous. He was a one-man Committee of Public Safety. From the newsheets circulating in Geneva, he compiled a list of the Paris guillotine's more notable victims; King Louis XVI; Marie Antoinette; the Duc d'Orléans; Jacques-Pierre Brissot, Pierre Vergniaud and the other Girondin leaders; Madame Jeanne Manon Roland; Jean-Sylvain Bailly; Antoine Barnave; the followers of George Danton; Jacques-Réné Hébert, his wife and the other *Hébertistes*. Clerval's list, that winter of 1793 to 1794, was long.

He then went on to compile his own list of notable Genevans who deserved to follow them. It included almost the entire political and financial establishment: syndics, the Grand Council, the committees, every member of the

34

Venerable Company of Pastors, the Professors at the university, bankers, lawyers, the upper-class, English families at Cologny ('a nest of dangerous serpents' he decided) the officers of the City Guard and the masters at the Academy (or at least the ones he did not like).

It was a gory enthusiasm, even for Clerval, and it was brought to an end by Elisabeth. We were lounging around the Clervals' modest drawing room one rainy afternoon when she snatched the list out of his hand, and scrutinised it.

'Why are Mama and Papa Clerval not here?' she demanded to know. 'Or Mama and Papa Frankenstein? Or Jean-Pierre's parents? I thought revolutionaries were supposed to kill aristos? And aren't our families aristos? Surely you'd want to kill *them*?'

Clerval flushed, muttered something about the list being 'far from complete', grabbed it back and stuffed it in his pocket. We never saw it again. He did, however, write another long poem dedicated to the 'crystal-clear purpose' of the great Robespierre. A short while later Robespierre was arrested, tried and himself sent to the guillotine. After that Clerval gave up revolutionary politics.

But others did not. There were some revolutionaries in Geneva in the year of 1794, men and women who would have been happy to see the people on Clerval's list butchered in the Bourg-de-Four or the Place du Bel-Air. And they scared more than just Clerval. My father fumed in the drawing rooms and supper parlours of the *haute ville* about the need to take 'stern measures' against the *natifs* and their allies in the intelligentsia.

'Hang the ringleaders,' he growled over the dinner table. 'Hunt them down like the water-rats they are. Then chase the rest of them out of Geneva,' he growled. 'Let them disappear off to France if they want. Let them live with their glorious Revolution – if they can. And leave decent people alone.'

Uncle Ben shared my father's fears but dissented from his solutions. 'Reform, Alphonse,' he admonished. 'Reform. The people have a grievance. The Two Hundred have monopolised all the power and most of the money for centuries. We've got to learn to share. If we don't – then they'll take it away from us. And who's to blame them? Reform! A new constitution. Sharing power. That's the way to avoid what's happened in France.'

'Reform, rubbish,' my father replied, his mouth full of buttered trout. 'I know these people. I deal with them every day. They'll see reform as a sign of weakness and want more. Before we know where we are we'll all be out on the street with nothing but the clothes on our backs. If we're lucky. And the scum will be in here with their dirty feet on the furniture. After they've pissed all over the carpets. You call it reform. I call it the road to ruin.'

I followed this brisk exchange with interest. If Alphonse Frankenstein was for repression than I was for reform. If he wanted to hang the revolutionaries, then I wanted them spared. If he wanted to deny the *natifs* political power, then I was all for giving it to them.

The Frankensteins left for Bellerive early that year. My mother, for all her radical enthusiasms, wanted all of us out of harm's way. We did not flee into Switzerland (as many of The Two Hundred did) but my father boarded up the house on the Cour Saint-Pierre and moved into a set of rooms in the Taconnerie to sit out the crisis. As he was seeing us into the carriages he startled me by ruffling my hair, planting a kiss on my forehead and telling me to take care of my mother and sister. Guilt, I supposed.

We were only a few miles from the city but we were untouched by the upheaval that racked Geneva that summer of 1794. When the city fell into the hands of the mob in July, we heard about it second-hand from Josse, one of my father's barque skippers. He had put into the jetty at Bellerive to let us know that my father was safe. We crowded round him in the kitchen to listen to his account of the events in the city.

'Bastards!' he swore. 'Thousands of them. They just went on a rampage. Most of them were drunk for days. They broke into houses, wrecked furniture, paintings, tapestries, stole silver, china, linen. A lot of it ended floating down the Rhône, of course. If they can't eat it or drink it it's useless to them. Then they hauled off hundreds of people – folk like yourselves – and locked them up in that old barn in Les Granges.'

'Dear God,' my mother said, blinking back tears. 'Were people injured?'

Josse nodded. 'Yes ma'am. They organised something they called a revolutionary tribunal. A tribunal! Bunch of drunken day-labourers trying to lord it over their betters. Led by a swine of a locksmith called Le Clair. Rags on their backs, pipes in their mouths and pistols in their belt. They hardly had enough wit to string three words together. But the wretches had dared to sentence thirty-seven people – thirty-seven people – to be shot.'

The faces around Josse drained of colour, and sobbing came from one of the kitchen maids.

Josse hastened to soften the blow. 'It's not as bad as it sounds,' he said. 'Twenty-eight of them were long gone. They'd got away before the rabble took over. Another two were "reprieved". But they dragged seven men out onto the Bastions and shot them. In cold blood.'

'Was ... was Monsieur de Saussure among them?' my mother asked, her face drawn, her eyes shadowed. 'Or any of his family?'

Josse shook his head. 'No ma'am. None of the Saussures.'

'Thank the good Lord,' she said. 'One blessing at least.'

'How about the Clervals?' I asked.

'Safe,' Josse told me. 'At least as far as I know.'

My mother's fears for Uncle Ben's safety were real enough. He was an obvious target. She fretted about her old friend's plight until a servant arrived with a letter from Uncle Ben to say that the de Saussures and their handsome house in the Rue de la Cité had come through the 'Little Terror' unscathed. And that he was more determined than ever that the constitution of the Republic should be reformed.

I learned later that Clerval had missed it all. The Revolution passed him by. He had spent the whole summer in his bedroom with an infected throat, dosed with laudanum. The mobs rampaging through Geneva had passed by the Clerval household and none of his family had been hauled off to the old barn in Les Granges. He had slept through the musket fire. He had heard some shouting and the sound of breaking glass, but that was all. It was not much of a revolution for a dedicated enemy of power and privilege.

It was a dismal summer, but not entirely wasted. Burrowing through the stock of books at Bellerive I came across an old copy of Offray de La Mettrie's *L'Homme-machine*. My mother told me that the book had shaken France in the late 1740s and had led to the author being hounded all over Europe.

'Nowadays, it's hard to see what all the fuss was about,' she told me. 'But I think the book is still banned in certain parts of Europe. The more, ah, benighted parts. It's an interesting piece of philosophy. Some of it is quite funny, if a bit, ah, anatomical. It might amuse you on a wet afternoon.'

I was more than amused. I was gripped. I was fascinated

by de La Mettrie's idea that the human body was 'a machine that winds up its own springs ... a living image of the perpetual motion'. His notion of the human being as a complex, but ultimately fathomable, automaton of flesh, blood, bone and muscle struck at the root of religion. Or so it seemed to me.

But I blushed to think that my mother may have read his suggestion that this accounted for the propensity of the male penis to spring to life at the slightest encouragement. This was a phenomenon with which I was becoming increasingly familiar. 'Why does the sight, nay the very thinking, of a fine woman raise in us particular notions and desires?' Mettrie asked. 'Does what happens at this juncture in certain organs proceed from the nature of the organs themselves?'

When I wrote to Uncle Ben to enthuse about *L'Homme-machine* he wrote back advising me that while the book was 'certainly engaging' and contained a few interesting ideas, it was 'more of a description than an explanation'. He added that de La Mettrie's own machine had run away from him: he had died in 1751 after overeating huge quantities of pate and truffles – to the delight of his many enemies.

When I relayed this piece of information to my mother she smiled. 'Ah, the demons of appetite,' she said. 'We all must grapple with them, Victor. Just beware of the appetites of which the world approves. Those are the most dangerous demons of them all.'

THE REPUBLIC OF GENEVA: 1796

If ever I needed evidence of the automaton described by Offray de La Mettrie, I got it the evening that Uncle Ben introduced me to Germaine de Stael-Holstein. As soon as I clapped eyes on her my stomach lurched and my sixteen-year-old penis leapt to attention. By the time I had kissed her hand, the thing was stiff as a flag-pole. The fact that I was wearing my finest – and therefore tightest – silk breeches did not help. There I stood, in the middle of Uncle Ben's brightly lit *salon*, red-faced and speechless while my unruly member threatened to burst out and join the company. I was sure I could hear the ladies giggling. And I knew that my cousin Elisabeth was smirking behind her fan.

But de La Mettrie was vindicated. *L'Homme-machine* prevailed. The automaton had taken over. There was nothing I could do about it. No matter how much I willed it, the disreputable length of flesh refused to subside. I was smitten, hip and crotch by this stocky, dark-haired woman with the plentiful bosom and plump arms, not much younger than my mother. She smiled amiably, said a few polite words and moved away, leaving me awash with embarrassment. Had she noticed the uproar in my breeches? If so, would she ever speak to me again? I groaned quietly to myself and moved behind a high-backed chair.

I spent the rest of the evening trailing her with my eyes and picking up snippets of information. My mother told me that Madame de Stael was the wife of the Swedish Ambassador to Paris, and she had had leave the city after criticising the newly elected Directoire. From Uncle Ben I learnt that she had just returned to Geneva to live with her father, the financier Baron Jacques Necker, who had made a fortune in France and had been Louis XVI's finance minister.

Elisabeth told me that Germaine de Stael's marriage to the Swedish Ambassador was a diplomatic sham and that she was pregnant by her lover, Benjamin Constant, a poet. She also told me sniffily that the Neckers lived rather ostentatiously, shuttling between a walled mansion in the Rue des Chanoines and a grand estate at Coppet on the west side of Lac Leman. And that absolutely everyone in Geneva was trying to negotiate invitations to Germaine's *salon* at Coppet.

'She's certainly Queen of the Ball,' Elisabeth said, smiling at me. 'At least for the moment. But rather old and rather fat for you isn't she Victor?'

I ignored her and stared at Germaine until I was pop-eyed, and looked away, blushing, whenever she caught my eye. I found myself wondering why. She was certainly no beauty. A fringe of coarse dark curls escaped from under an ungainly turban which sat askew on her head. She had a round face, a heavy jaw, a double chin, a fleshy nose, a wide, full-lipped mouth, and protruding teeth. She affectedly carried a spray of greenery. She was almost twice my age and swelled by pregnancy.

But there was a directness about her that attracted me. I watched her as she moved from group to group. She

41

laughed easily but without coquettishness. She never flirted, never played little games with her fan, never feigned admiration. She was clearly an intelligent woman, happiest in the company of able people. When I finally left the gathering she was deep in conversation with my mother and Uncle Ben, while my father hovered in the background.

That winter Germaine de Stael became my mother's close friend and a regular visitor to the Frankenstein house. She was, as Elisabeth said, 'Queen of the Ball'. She talked politics, science, religion, literature and philosophy with great enthusiasm. My father seemed simultaneously attracted to and nervous of her. Even Uncle Ben was impressed; the only time I ever saw him blush was when Germaine told him that she had always wanted to meet him. She then went on to quiz him about his findings on the summit of Mont Blanc.

And she was remarkably considerate of the feelings of a love-struck sixteen year old. When she caught me hanging on to her words, she would try to coax me into the conversation.

'Your mother tells me you have been reading Offray de La Mettrie, Victor,' she said to me at one afternoon gathering.

I nodded.

'A terribly controversial piece of work in its time, as I imagine you know. It had all Europe in an uproar. I'd be interested to hear what you made of it.'

I was in disarray. My confusion was total. All I wanted to do was gape at her swelling white bosom, and listen to the sound of her voice. But I racked my brain for something to say, and came up only with Uncle Ben's view that *L'Homme-machine* was more of a description than an explanation.

With a laugh she disagreed. 'More than that, surely, Victor? I'm surprised you're not more impressed. At least by his theory of proportion.'

'Proportion . . . ?'

'That intelligence is determined by the size of the brain in *proportion* to the size of the body. And by the windings of the brain inside the skull.'

'Ah, yes, *that*,' I said.

'Surely that must be of interest', she said with a smile, 'to a man of science like yourself?'

I was devastated. She had found me out. She knew me for the hollow sham I was. I was unworthy of her interest. She would never speak to me again. I had to say something to save the situation. But all I could do was stammeringly quote de La Mettrie's notion that we should 'follow the direction of experience and not trouble our heads with the vain history of philosophers'.

'Such as Offray de La Mettrie,' she said, and then laughed at my confusion.

But she was a kind woman. She found a way to salvage my pride by reminding me that the recently executed revolutionary Jean Paul Marat had been a student of medical electricity and indeed had written a couple of 'reasonably accomplished' papers on the subject. Which, of course, gave me an opportunity to parade my knowledge of Priestley, the Abbé Nollet and Jallabert, all of whom, she claimed, were 'a complete revelation' to her.

Germaine made no secret of the fact that she missed Paris and her *salon* on the Rue du Bac. She regarded the French capital as the centre of the world and found the Republic of Geneva provincial. But there was no malice in her complaints. She regaled my mother's circle with descriptions of the firework extravaganzas at the Tivoli, the thronged restaurants, the theatres, the dance halls, the gambling emporia and the vivid *tableaux vivants* in the Jardins d'Italie. These tales from a wider, more dangerous world seemed to unsettle many of her admirers, but not me.

She was as interested in science as she was in politics. She regarded the execution of the French chemist Lavoisier as one of the worst crimes of the Revolution. 'It took these brigands only a second to remove his head,' she told me, 'but it will be another hundred years, maybe more, before we see another like it.'

Germaine had little enthusiasm for the ideas of the French Revolution. In fact, there were times she sounded almost as reactionary as my father. Her experiences in Paris had soured her passion for revolutionary politics, and she was wary of Napoleon Bonaparte, the young artillery officer who had saved France from the Royalists with a brace of eight-pound artillery pieces packed with grapeshot. It was the first time I had heard Bonaparte's name.

One wet Saturday at the beginning of 1796 the Franken-stein family, together with the Saussures, made the pilgrimage to the Necker estate at Coppet on the west bank of Lac Leman. The drive through the rain along the shores of the lake was long and tedious, exacerbated by my father's mood. My parents drove in one coach with me, while Elisabeth, Ernest, William and one of the maids followed in another. Uncle Ben and his wife were half a mile behind.

As we trundled in the rain down the tree-lined avenue to the château I was in a state of some agitation. Uncle Ben and I had prepared a little scientific 'entertainment' for the company (the equipment for which was now perched in two trunks on the top of the Saussure coach). With Uncle Ben's help I would dazzle Germaine with my brilliance. I would be revealed not as some callow sixteen year old, but as a scientist of great potential. Coppet would be graced with a coming man, whose familiarity with the mysteries of the universe would dazzle her.

While I shifted from buttock to buttock with anticipation, my father stared gloomily out of the window. He was

envious. The Château Coppet certainly made the Frankenstein *campagne* at Bellerive look modest indeed.

'Look at this place,' my father muttered shaking his head.
'I've done it all wrong. I should have gone to grovel to the
King of France – the *Catholic* King of France – instead of
remaining an honest Geneva merchant. There's a lesson
there, Victor. There's a lesson there.'

What that lesson was he never did say. But he was still
muttering to himself as we clattered through the gates of
Coppet and into the courtyard in front of the house. A
gaggle of liveried servants ushered us up the steps and into
the long, book-lined *galerie* where Germaine, her father,
Benjamin Constant and a little crowd of guests were waiting.

As usual, as soon as I clapped eyes on her I felt my face
burn, my tongue knot, my hands tremble. It was the effect
she always had on me. I tried to find a niche from where I
could admire Germaine undisturbed, but she insisted on
drawing me into the conversation. Germaine de Stael's *salon*
at Coppet was no place for shrinking into corners.

After coffee and cakes had been served the Coppet *salon*
went into full swing. The proceedings opened with Constant
reading from one of his poems – a long, vapid business full
of Greek gods and goddesses and their mortal playthings,
one of whom seemed to be the poet Benjamin Constant.
Necker himself read a long paper on French/Genevan
currency exchange, which prompted two awkward questions and no discussion at all. Then Germaine and one of her
maids acted out a playlet written by Germaine about a lady
and one of her maids. I thought it elegantly written and
handsomely acted, but Elisabeth dismissed it in a loud
whisper as 'paltry nonsense!'.

Then it was my turn with Uncle Ben. We were well
prepared. Together we had plundered Joseph Priestley's
book for unusual and entertaining experiments which we

had strung together as 'Saussure's Electrical Circus'. Uncle Ben was the ringmaster and I was his apprentice. As the servants trundled our collection of Leyden jars and generators into the drawing room Uncle Ben announced in a mock ringmaster's voice that the distinguished company of Coppet was about to be entertained in ways they had never previously been. They were about to glimpse one of the deepest mysteries of the universe – electricity.

We began by introducing them to The Power. When a moderately sized Leyden jar was charged and in place we invited the Neckers and their guests to stand up and link hands in a circle. We each held wires from one of the Leyden jars. Then, when I closed the circle by taking Elisabeth's hand, a circuit was completed and a charge of electricity ran through the guests. It was only a very modest bolt, but it was enough to elicit gasps of surprise, nervous laughter and shrieks from the company.

'It tingles,' Elisabeth simpered.

Uncle Ben held up the Leyden jar for them to examine. 'What you have just experienced', he said, 'is the power of one, small, electrically charged Leyden phial. Imagine, if you will, the power that can be produced by a battery of such jars.'

'Enough to kill a man,' my father growled, rubbing at his wrist.

'As you say, sir, enough to kill a man,' Uncle Ben replied. 'But killing men is not the object of the electrical philosopher. And it is certainly not the object of "Saussure's Electrical Circus", whose only purpose is to inform and entertain. To which end, my distinguished assistant Victor Frankenstein and I will demonstrate to you a few – a very few – of the things that the wondrous power of electricity can do.'

The shutters were drawn across the windows and for fifteen minutes we entertained Germaine's *salon* with some of Joseph Priestley's more engaging drawing-room experiments. We attached the head of a china doll to wire and heard the audience laugh as the silken hair separated and stood on end. We dangled a set of three small bells from a conductor, two on metal chains and one on a silk thread, and listened as they rang and sparked without being touched. We created two kinds of electrical light using a jar in which a vacuum had been created. And there were shouts of wonder at the 'Electric Jack', a wooden wheel ringed with metal thimbles which spun round as the metal was repelled and then attracted by Leyden jars placed at either side.

The show culminated in what Uncle Ben described as a demonstration of the famous electrified apprentice. A smooth wooden board was placed on the carpet, on top of which was set a heavily insulated stool. I climbed onto the stool and in one hand took a wire from one of the largest of the charged Leyden jars. To my gratification Uncle Ben selected Germaine from the audience and brought her to stand in front of me. He then invited her to touch the body of the electrified Victor Frankenstein.

She smiled up at me and tentatively touched my hand. There was crackle and a bright blue spark shot out of my hand. Germaine jumped back with a cry of alarm. The rest of the guests laughed a little nervously.

'Never fear madam,' Uncle Ben assured her with mock gravity. 'The electrified apprentice is a harmless creature. He cannot harm you. It is not in his nature. Touch him again, and you will see what I mean.'

She did, and another blue spark leapt out of me. Then another. Then another. Germaine's curiosity was now thoroughly roused, and she began to walk slowly around me raising sparks as she touched me on the arm, the shoulder, the jaw, the calf, the ankle, the nape of the neck. In the flickering light of the sparks her expression was grave, interested. Then her touches were replaced by little stroking motions which seemed to produce even bigger sparks.

It was a disturbing and intimate experience. The room was in darkness. The guests were totally silent. Germaine and I were alone in a circle of light and energy. As she moved around me, her fingertips playing across my body, I felt the familiar stirring in my breeches. I was thoroughly aroused. I blessed the darkness. If she had once touched me between the legs I think I would have blown apart in a blizzard of sparks like the old oak tree at Bellerive.

'Saussure's Electrical Circus' was judged a great success, and met with resounding applause. Even my father seemed amused. Later we dined in the small 'summer' dining room whose windows overlooked the rain-swept park and skeletal trees. It was an amiable and noisy affair during which Uncle Ben, my mother and Germaine argued politics, my father and Necker talked banking and Elisabeth feigned interest in Constant's dramatic verse. The poet seemed much taken by Elisabeth's coy ways, and clearly enjoyed the little touches of her fan. I contented myself with hanging on to Germaine's every word.

After the meal I lingered in the dining room to scrutinise a set of Chinese engravings hanging on the walls. They had been given to Necker by the King of France, no doubt as a reward for some financial sleight-of-hand. Originally painted by French Jesuit missionaries in China and then redrawn by skilled artists, they depicted the famous victory of the Emperor Kien Long over his Mongol enemies.

I stared at the pictures, fascinated. In their spare lines I glimpsed real war. This was not some blundering skirmish in the *haute ville* of Geneva, such as we had seen in 1794. Nor was it a raid by a few score Savoyards and Spaniards on the ramparts of Geneva, as had occurred in 1602. Here were armies of spear carriers, legions of archers, uncountable numbers of swordsmen, many hundreds of horsemen, countless corpses. Here was unimaginable slaughter. Death in all its variety. And on the grandest scale.

I travelled back from Coppet in Uncle Ben's coach. I was still in a state of excitement over the success of 'Saussure's Electrical Circus'. As we jolted our way back to Geneva, I enthused about the joys and excitements of natural philosophy in general and electricity in particular. Above everything I wanted to follow in his footsteps. I wanted to be a man of science. That, to me, was everything. There was nothing else to be.

Uncle Ben looked at me strangely. 'In that case, Victor,' he said in a cold voice, 'I suggest that you read – and read carefully – the last few paragraphs of the preface to Joseph Priestley's work on electricity. The very work that you and I used to give so much pleasure and interest today.'

I was puzzled and faintly hurt by his tone and we spent the rest of the journey in silence. Back at the Cour Saint-Pierre I took my volume of Priestley down from the shelf and read the passage carefully. The sentiments were not Priestley's own but those of an English philosopher called Hartley. 'Nothing can easily exceed', he wrote, 'the vainglory, self-conceit, arrogance, emulation and envy that are found in the eminent professors of the sciences . . .' Science without moderation, he warned, 'will get possession of our hearts, engross them wholly, and by taking deeper root than the pursuit of vain amusements, become in the end a much more dangerous and obstinate evil'.

THE REPUBLIC OF GENEVA: 1796

Although relations between my parents were always stormy, they usually contrived to settle their differences well enough. But they clashed with remarkable bitterness over where I should be educated. I wanted to go to university in Paris, to me not only the centre of the intellectual universe but also close to Germaine. Or failing that, Leyden in Holland. My mother favoured the University of Geneva. It would keep me at home and the teaching was soundly Calvinist. But my father had other ideas. He declared that it was important that I should see a bit more of the world and had decided that I should attend the University of Ingolstadt in Bavaria.

'I've heard many excellent things about it,' he told us brusquely. 'It's an old university. I'm told the teaching is first rate. There's a medical school attached to it, if he's inclined in that direction, although God knows why he should be. It will do the boy no harm to perfect his German. He'll make introductions that will serve him well. For when he returns to take over our business interest.'

My mother was horrified. Bavaria was the dark heart of

the Counter-reformation. It was a nest of Jesuits. It was no place for a gently raised young Calvinist from the Republic of Geneva. The idea was out of the question. All my fine, expensive, Geneva education would count for nothing. It would be obliterated by the obscurantism of Rome. Wiped out in a few years of Catholic indoctrination.

I shared my mother's tears. I imagined a dark, cloistered place staffed by cowled, chanting monks. I saw myself scuttling between ranks of hooded penitents. I would be forced to flagellate myself. I would have to spend hours prostrate before a crucifix, to genuflect to painted statues of the Virgin or the bones of saints. They would take my Bible away. I would never open a book of science. The mysteries of the universe would be closed to me. I would be condemned to learn nothing beyond the mouthings of the saints.

'You cannot do this, Alphonse,' my mother said, whey-faced with anxiety. 'Please. The boy cannot go to a place like that. Not Bavaria, I beg of you.'

'Don't be so damned superstitious madam,' my father snapped. 'There's more to life than religion. Catholics are not necessarily monsters. And the Germans – even the Bavarians – are highly learned. The world seems to forget that in its obsession with everything French.'

'No, Alphonse,' she persisted. 'This is not right. Not for Victor. He needs to stay here, in Geneva.'

'At home with his ever-affectionate mother, you mean,' my father said with an unpleasant smile. 'And, of course, his *Uncle* Ben.'

She flushed and bit her lip. 'Naturally I would prefer my son to be at home,' she said with some dignity. 'Any mother would.'

'Well this *father* wouldn't,' he said. 'It's time the boy got out of Geneva. Which, I might remind you, is not exactly the safest place for a family of means. As we've seen over the last few years.'

'But safer than Bavaria, I would suggest,' she countered.

'Then you would suggest wrongly,' he said. 'At least there are no revolutionaries in Bavaria.'

'But Victor is a scholar,' she reminded him. 'A scientist. Ben says . . .'

'Much as we all value Ben's opinion,' he said caustically 'the decision is mine. Victor is my son and not Ben's. Or at least so I've been led to believe. *I'll* decide how, and where, he is to be educated. I would have you understand that Madam. The decision belongs to me, and not to Horace-Benédict de Saussure.'

She winced but persisted. 'But Bavaria, Alphonse. *Bavaria*! What can the boy possibly learn in Bavaria that he could not learn here in Geneva?'

'Oh for God's sake woman,' he said impatiently. 'He'll learn to sharpen his wits. To deal with the world. To meet other, different, people. Can you not appreciate that? Or is your bigotry too strong? Are you so fearful of the Catholics – your fellow Christians I would remind you – that you have forgotten all your liberal sentiments?'

'I am not a bigot, sir,' she said. 'I am a mother concerned for the future of her son.'

'And I am a father with precisely the same concern,' he retorted. 'But with rather more experience of this world and its ways. And that experience tells me that the boy would do well to get out of Geneva. Away from . . . all this . . .'

'You mean away from me, his mother?'

'I did not say that, madam. But perhaps you are right. Maybe that would be for the best.'

'But why?' she asked. 'Why, for God's sake?'

He shrugged. 'A boy has to grow up. To get away from his, ah, family. Learn to be a man. Before he's smothered.'

'Smothered . . .' she said. 'But Alphonse . . .'

He held up his hand to silence her. 'No madam, I'll not be persuaded. My decision is made. Ingolstadt it is. Arrangements have been made. Victor's tuition has been paid for. Lodgings have been organised. A banking account has been opened in his name. He will not have a fortune, but enough for him to live in comfort. He will go to Ingolstadt in the autumn. And there's an end to it.'

That evening, after breaking the fearful news to Jean-Pierre and Fat Clerval, I wandered disconsolately down to the Rue de la Cité to unburden myself to Uncle Ben. I had a vague idea that, somehow, he could intervene and save me from the Roman Catholic darkness. I found him, as usual, in his laboratory. But he was surprisingly unsympathetic.

'Your father is right,' he said firmly. 'It'll do you nothing but good to spend a few years out of Geneva. This republic is a small place, and a man needs to see worlds. Larger worlds.'

'But *Ingolstadt* . . .' I protested. 'In Bavaria . . .'

'I know what worries you,' he said with a smile. 'But your fears are groundless. Well, almost groundless. There's not much wrong with Bavaria that a few more good Protestants like yourself couldn't put right. It's not Africa, you know. Ingolstadt is a fine university, with a decent medical school. There are some good people there.'

And he smiled and shook his head at my suggestion that Bavaria was the epicentre of European reaction. 'You are Caroline Beaufort's son,' he said. 'Huguenot to the bone. Even after all these generations.'

'But if you . . .'

He held up a hand to silence my arguments. 'No, Victor. It's not for me to intervene. Go to Ingolstadt. Learn what you can. Meet new people. See new places. Take what it has to offer. Enjoy yourself. Make the most of the opportunity.'

Vaguely heartened, but as yet unconvinced, I returned home to find my mother still pleading with my father. She was distraught, he was determined. She pleaded, she sobbed, she begged, she cajoled, to no effect. Nothing penetrated Alphonse Frankenstein's armour when it was in place. Everything had been decided. I would go to the University of Ingolstadt. And nothing she could say would affect his decision.

I thought then – and I still think – that he was working out some elaborate revenge on her. I was his weapon. But, as events transpired, he need not have troubled himself.

THE REPUBLIC OF GENEVA: 1796

I suppose that my notebook was my most precious possession. It was certainly one of them. A present from my
mother, it was a handsome, leather-bound affair, large
enough to be useful but small enough to be carried in my
coat pocket. Everywhere I went, the notebook went with me.
It was my faithful companion. There was a canvas wallet
attached to the marbled end board. In this little pocket I kept
the detritus of my curiosity: scraps of paper, dried leaves,
feathers, flakes of mica, sycamore seeds, small bones, flower
petals, the occasional dead insect.

And unless I forgot – which did not happen often – I wrote
up a diary every evening. I made rough notes in pencil
during the day, and then copied them out in ink. The dates,
times, locations of all my observations were faithfully
recorded. My handwriting was tiny, spiky and almost
illegible. I husbanded the space with care. Nothing was
wasted. Every margin contained notes, sketches, calcula-
tions. I wrote between the lines as well as on them.

The notebook was packed with information, most of it

useless, some of it interesting. The destruction of the Bellerive oak, for example, took up three whole pages. The book contained the record of my forays into the Salève along with Clerval and Jean-Pierre. There were notes on the rocks, flowers, mosses and lichens we had seen. Our experiments with the longevity of insects were there. So were my observations on the fish and water-weeds off the jetties of Geneva, sketches of peculiar cloud formations over the Jura, the form and frequency of the waves on Lac Leman, a carefully rendered drawing of the skeleton of a huge carp I had found on the beach at Bellerive.

Of course Uncle Ben loomed large. I recorded almost everything he told me. His account of the death by lightning of Professor Richmann of St Petersburg was faithfully entered, as well as his remark to my father that 'philosophy has its martyrs'. Uncle Ben's opinions on Paracelsus, Offray de La Mettrie and Priestley all went into the Frankenstein record. Everything I could remember about Jean Jallabert and the electrified locksmith of Geneva was written into the notebook. All the experiments that made up the triumph of 'Saussure's Electrical Circus' were written up in great detail. I only made one totally unscientific concession to my passion for Germaine de Stael-Holstein. I sliced a lock of hair from my little brother's head and inserted it into the wallet, pretending to myself that it was one of Germaine's dark curls.

But by far the most significant event I recorded in my notebook was the death of my mother. I wrote up every stage of Caroline Beaufort Frankenstein's decline. Every sympton she developed was entered in the book. I made no judgements. I expressed no outrage. I never railed against God, the heavens or the fates. I simply wrote down the events as and when they happened.

And what did happen was this: Elisabeth had gone down

with an attack of scarlet fever, all through which she had whimpered, fretted and sulked. She was demanding, petulant, bad-tempered. My father hired the best nurses in Geneva, but this was not sufficient for Elisabeth. She whined for the attentions of my mother who, ignoring my father's protests, insisted on taking over the nursing. Then, as Elisabeth rapidly recovered, my mother took to her bed complaining of a fever and a painful throat.

I haunted her sick-room. Time after time the nurses and my father chased me away, but I always returned. Her illness was dramatic. Her temperature rose, her pulse increased and she was racked by vomiting and headaches. A rosy-red rash appeared on her arms and chest, and soon covered her whole body. It also covered her face, except for the skin of her nose and mouth which became deathly white. I observed that the rash was made up of thousands of tiny red pustules.

She found it at first difficult and then impossible to speak. Her throat constricted and her tongue swelled and became covered in a thick, yellowish-white fur. Then it became raw, pitted and red, like some monstrous strawberry. As the rash faded, the skin on her face and neck began to peel away in strips. Her thin face became a patchwork of colours and textures, often stained with tears.

The physicians came and talked quietly to my father. They shook their heads and he stared blankly at them before retreating to the library. The nurses did their best to maintain my mother's strength by feeding her milky pap, but without much success. She begged to be moved from the Cour Saint-Pierre to Bellerive but the doctors forbade it. They warned my father that the six-mile journey might kill her.

At one point she seemed to be recovering and the gloom in the house lifted. Then her illness returned. I could sense some catastrophe deep inside her. She began to vomit profusely and complain of pains in her loins and the small of her back. Her face and neck swelled, her eyelids puffed and her bright grey eyes were reduced to slits. Her ankles and wrists swelled, and her body began to bloat. The tiny quantities of her piss that the nurses carried from her room were the colour of dark blood. Her pillows were stained by a yellow discharge from her ears.

She grew weaker by the day, and began to slip in and out of consciousness. In her delirium she was often profane, foulmouthed and cruel. She rambled and muttered and drooled. When we gathered round her bed she would sense we were there, try to smile, then collapse into unconsciousness. Once she clutched Elisabeth's hand, uttered a harsh little laugh and cried out 'The bitch, the bitch, the little bitch'.

By the evening of the twelfth day it was over. I was alone in the room with her when she died. I stood beside her bed, my notebook in my hand, and watched her groan and thrash and finally lie still, blood trickling from her nostrils and mouth into her tangled hair. Her lips were curled back from her teeth, and her eyes were half open, her face a mask of ferocity and resentment. I noted that she died at precisely six forty-one in the evening.

When my father burst into the room, followed by the nurses, he looked at the figure in the bed and gave a howl of pain. He was beside himself with rage and grief. Then he turned to me and saw the notebook. He tore it from my hand, read it for a few seconds and then threw it into a corner of the room. Then, to the cries of the nurses, he felled me with a heavy blow to the side of the head.

'Get out of here!' he shouted. 'Go on! Get out! Get out, before I break your damned neck!'

I retrieved my notebook and fled to the safety of my room, my head still ringing with the blow on the head. But then I

58

began a terrible process. I began to fill the pages of my notebook with questions. What would happen to Caroline Beaufort now? I knew that she would decay, but how would it happen? In the wet dark of the grave, what part of her body would go first? Would it be her fine grey eyes? Or would it be her ever-active brain? Or would her entrails dissolve into some hideous broth leaving her shell deflated but intact?

Would she disintegrate from the inside out or from the outside in? Would the rot spread from the skin to the bowels, or would the entrails corrupt the skin? Would she collapse in on herself, or would she swell with gases and burst open in the coffin? How long would it be until the grave worms did their work? How many days, weeks or months would have to pass before there was nothing left of Caroline Beaufort Frankenstein but a litter of bones and a grinning skull?

Wrapped in misery I quit the shuttered and grieving house in the Cour Saint-Pierre and made my way down through the *haute ville*. I was astonished to find that it was business as usual in the Grand Rue and down in the Place du Bel Air. The ale houses and taverns were crowded and noisy and raucous singing came from one of them. Two drunks were scuffling in the street surrounded by a laughing crowd. Did the rest of Geneva not realise that Caroline Beaufort Frankenstein was dead? Or if they did know, did they not care?

I stood for an hour on the bridge to the Ile du Rhône, watching the grey-green water surge out of Lac Leman and into the river. I wondered what it would be like to pitch myself into that cold, smooth, powerful current and be swept down into France, away from Geneva, away from my dead mother and away from Alphonse Frankenstein.

And in the dark water it was as if I saw Death himself. His

smile was not some graveyard grin: it was subtle, knowing. He had the complacency of the eternal victor. And his was a round, sly, well-fed face, not without kindness. Death was a polished seducer. Into his arms leapt distraught maidens, ruined merchants, widowed mothers and disgraced clergymen. He was the last comfort of a pain-crippled invalid. He was a merciful release to a dying child. He spirited away the deserving with the same ease as he took the undeserving.

My imagination raced with the currents under my feet. Everything about him gleamed. His skin was as silk to the touch. His teeth shone. His eyes were reassuring. His voice was melodic, comforting. It hinted of warmth, forgetfulness, the reassurance of the dark. But there was also a voracity in his eyes that I loathed. I saw a hunger that could never be appeased. He would always want more. And now he had Caroline Beaufort Frankenstein to chew on, and then spit out as a few bones and a skull.

I took my notebook from my coat pocket, leafed through the pages, read the final entries and tossed it into the water. As I watched the book swirl around and then disappear, I cursed Death. And I pledged myself to become Death's implacable enemy.

STUDENT

INGOLSTADT, BAVARIA: 1796

I was both relieved and strangely disappointed to find that Roman Catholic Bavaria looked much like Protestant Geneva. The young priest that I met as I descended from the Geneva diligence outside the Moritzkirche in the centre of Ingolstadt did nothing more sinister than grin amiably and wish me 'Grüss Gott'. There was not a hooded penitent or scuttling nun in sight. The only chanting I could hear came from a group of blue-coated soldiers reeling their way along the Hieronymous-Strasse in the direction of their barracks. The louts spilling out of the nearest hostelry were the same kind of raucous beer swillers I had left behind in the Place du Bel-Air. A drunk is a drunk in any religion.

Befuddled, bone-weary and stiff-jointed after the long journey, I hired a couple of the youths hanging around the stage halt to transport myself and my luggage to my lodgings in the Hochschulestrasse. They gave no indication that they suspected I might be some kind of Calvinist demon. They just trotted along in front of me, 'yaw-yawing' in their rotund German, and seemed happy enough with the coppers I gave them when they delivered me to the door of my lodgings.

Frau Horst's boarding house for gentlemen was a narrow, four-storey house within yards of the university. And my landlady ushered me over the doorstep with as much welcome as she could muster. She was a burly little woman with bright little eyes in a red face, and set of much blackened teeth. I followed her ample backside up the timber staircase to the second floor and into a set of spotless rooms.

As they were to be my home for the next three years I examined them with some care. They were spotless: a low-ceilinged sitting room with a huge, blue-tiled stove in one corner and a scrubbed deal table in the other. The chairs were plain but they looked comfortable. The room was bright with two windows, and the ledges were lined with glass bottles and flasks, some of them oddly shaped, and one or two wrapped in leather and basketry. I was slightly startled by the small crucifix in dark wood fixed to the wall over the table.

The bedroom was furnished with a large four-poster bed, a wardrobe, a chest and small bookcase. Most of the furniture was brightly painted. And every panel in the room – in the doors, the bedhead, the drawer fronts, the wardrobe – was decorated with some kind of pastoral scene. Crudely painted shepherds, milkmaids, nymphs and cowherds cavorted across emerald-green grass. It was hardly the Frankenstein town-house in the Cour Saint-Pierre, but it was clean, decent and comfortable enough.

'Is everything to your satisfaction Herr Frankenstein,' Frau Horst asked anxiously.

'Eh, yes. Very pleasant,' I said. 'Thank you. Very nice indeed.'

She beamed happily. 'My room is upstairs at the top of the house,' she told me. 'If there is anything that you need there is a bell on the table. I cook at breakfast time and in the evening. My other gentlemen buy their own dinner during the day. There are plenty of inns and coffee houses in the town. Too many, some of us think.'

'And who are the other gentlemen?' I asked her.

'There are only three,' she told me. 'There is Herr Eybenschutz, who lives below. He's a very jolly gentleman, I think you'll find, from Bohemia.'

'Bohemia,' I said. 'That's interesting.'

'Then there is Herr Saracino who tells me he is from the city of Bologna. But a very pleasant gentleman, very nice. All my gentlemen are. And then, of course, there is Herr von Grafenberg. A fine Austrian country gentleman.' Her voice dropped to a whisper. 'From a very old family. Very old. He has a room above you. He could have lodged anywhere in Ingolstadt, of course. But he chose to live here. In my house.'

'I see. And they're all students at the university?'

'All my gentlemen are students,' Frau Horst told me with a trace of indignation. 'They have been, ever since my husband Herr Horst – God keep his soul – died eleven years ago. I insist on it. Students only. And of the better sort. The quieter sort. The more refined sort.'

I smiled. 'Well, in that case I shall do my best not to disappoint you Frau Horst.'

She smiled back, but her eye was flinty. 'I'm sure that you will not, Herr Frankenstein. But there is one other thing. I have a girl who comes in to help me to clean the house and wash the linen. Her name is Renate.' There was a pause. 'I would thank you to, ah, pay her no attentions. She's a good Catholic girl from an honest family. I don't want any of my gentlemen, well, chasing her away. She's a hard worker. And good girls are hard to find.'

'They are indeed,' I said with some feeling. 'But the young lady's honour will be safe with me. You have my word.'

Reassured, the dumpy little woman dropped a curtsy that would have become a sixteen year old, and left me to my unpacking.

She had no sooner gone than there was a banging on the door and a huge, burly, blond youth barged into the room, followed by two others. My neighbours, I presumed. The refined young gentlemen from Bohemia, Bologna and the Austrian countryside.

'David Eybenschutz of Prague,' the big tow-haired young man introduced himself in a curious German, his hand outstretched. 'Schutzi to my friends and to the whores of Ingolstadt. Herr Eybenschutz to my creditors, who are legion.'

I shook his huge paw. 'Victor Frankenstein,' I said. 'From Geneva.'

'Finkelstein?' said the Bohemian.

'No. Frankenstein.'

'Oh. Right. This is Giovanni Saracino, scion of the finest family of watchmakers in Bologna. He says. And the other is Lothar von Grafenberg, an Austrian from some wretched turnip infested backwater which his family – who stole it off the peasantry – now claims to own.'

I smiled and shook them both by the hand. The Italian was a freckled, carrot-haired youth of middling height with a quiet manner and watchful grey eyes. The Austrian was short, lean and dark to the point of swarthiness. The left side of his narrow face was marred with a duelling scar. But he had a friendly enough grin.

'Welcome to Bavaria, Victor Frankenstein of Geneva,' he said amiably. 'We don't get many of your sort in this town.'

'What sort is that?' I asked.

'Genevans,' he replied.

'Too Catholic for Genevans,' Schutzi said. 'Am I right Herr Frankenstein?'

I shrugged. 'I don't know.'

'Course I'm right,' Schutzi said. 'But I wouldn't let the Catholic thing bother you. For every pious Catholic in Ingolstadt, there are a hundred sinners. Like these two here. Already bound for hell, unless I'm very much mistaken. And the spit on which they'll roast is already turning.'

'Frau Horst warned me that you were a "jolly gentleman",' I said wryly.

He grinned. 'That's me. The jolly Jew. Always ready with a smile, a song and a quip from the Talmud. Steeped in the wit of the ancients. We learnt all our best jokes in the Egyptian desert, you know.'

I was intrigued. 'A Jew,' I said. 'I've never met a Jew before. At least I don't think so.'

'Well your luck's just run out Frankenstein,' von Grafenberg said drily.

'There speaks the envy of an inferior, unchosen race,' Schutzi said. 'You see before you, Frankenstein, not just any Jew, but a member of the legendary Eybenschutz family. The aristocracy of Prague Jewry. And a great nephew of the late Jonathan Eybenschutz of Prague, one-time Rabbi of the five cities, and Talmudic scholar extraordinary . . .'

'If you say so,' I said breaking in. 'I am pleased to meet you in any case.'

'If you're from Geneva,' von Grafenberg said, 'I suppose you're some kind of Protestant?'

'That's right,' I replied.

'What kind?' he asked.

'The half-hearted kind,' I told him.

He grinned broadly, his teeth white against his dark skin.

'Well, speaking as a half-hearted kind of Catholic, I'm pleased to hear it. Has old mother Horst given you her hands off Renate lecture yet?'

'She has.'

'This you will find very easy to do,' Schutzi said. 'Renate has the sexual attraction of Gustav's Horse.'

'What's Gustav's Horse?'

'You'll find out. What are you planning to study?'

I shrugged. 'Natural philosophy. Chemistry. Physics. Some mathematics. Biology. That kind of thing.'

They exchanged grins. 'Same kind of thing as us,' von Grafenberg said. 'That's good.'

'But why Ingolstadt?' Schutzi wanted to know. 'I mean, what's wrong with Geneva? Or Paris? Or Leyden? Or just about anywhere else in Europe for that matter?'

I shrugged again. 'My father's idea,' I told him. 'He wanted me to get out of the Republic. Meet some useful people. To see a bit of the world.'

He laughed. 'I wonder who told him that Ingolstadt was in the world? Or that you'd meet anybody useful in Bavaria. That's what I'd call a contradiction in terms.'

'Nothing wrong with Bavaria', Saracino said, 'that some tankards of beer won't cure. So we're off to sink a few at the Brown Bear. Will you join us, Frankenstein?'

I shook my head. 'Too tired. It's been a long journey. I thought that my head would leave my shoulders the way the coach was lurching. I'm as stiff as plank and could sleep for a month. But try me again tomorrow.'

'Right you are then, Victor Frankenstein of Geneva,' Schutzi boomed, heading for the door. 'Sleep well! Dream of home. We'll try not to wake you on our way back in.'

'Thanks,' I said.

'But I'm making no promises,' he said. 'Last man to the Bear buys the first two rounds ...'

They thundered down the stairs, shouting and cursing, and spilled out into the street. I heard Frau Horst call something after them, her refined young gentlemen of the better sort. Then I finished unpacking, undressed quickly,

climbed into my brightly painted four-poster and slept the
sleep of the dead.

INGOLSTADT, BAVARIA: 1796

The next day, at eight o clock in the morning, I made the short journey to the university to present my letters of introduction. I had expected it to be profoundly Catholic, Gothic, hushed and cloistered. Instead, I found a squat, utilitarian structure set down in a tangle of busy streets and narrow lanes. The university was large, plain and rather ugly, with a steeply pitched roof at the north end of which stood a small bell-tower. The University of Ingolstadt was no beauty, but its businesslike appearance cheered me as I entered.

My mood did not last. A cadaverous college servant directed me to the rooms of Professor August Krempe, who kept me waiting for twenty minutes before reading my letters. Krempe was an unprepossessing creature. He was short and broad with a massive head, a pock-marked face and a curious frog-like mouth. I noticed that his hands trembled slightly. His linen was stained and his clothes were grubby. He was gravel-voiced and slow-spoken and had an accent that I could not identify but that I later learnt was Saxon.

'Why natural philosophy, Herr Frankenstein?' he growled, tossing my letter down on his work table. 'Why not divinity? Or the law? Or astronomy?'

It was a fair question, but I took exception to the way it was asked. 'Because I want to understand the world in which I live, sir.'

'And you think that natural philosophy will enable you to do that?' he asked.

'If it cannot, then what can?' I retorted.

There was a short silence, then he said: 'And in your studies at, where is it, Geneva, did you read much natural philosophy? Is such a thing taught there?'

'It is,' I said. 'And I read some. But not systematically.'

'Ah. So you are a young man of science without system?'

'Which is why I'm in Ingolstadt,' I replied. 'To learn.'

I was now determined not to lose my temper.

He shook his head slightly. 'And how is your Latin, Herr Frankenstein? I presume they teach Latin too in your, ah, Geneva?'

'They do, sir. Very well. And my Latin is good.'

'We will see. And your German?'

'Adequate. And improving. I also speak English. And of course my native French.'

'And authors, Herr Frankenstein? What authors? Who have you been reading?'

I told him what little I knew of Lavoisier, von Humboldt, Newton, Berthollet and of course Aristotle and Galen. He frowned at the name of the Baron d'Holbach, and looked faintly amused when I mentioned Offray de La Mettrie. He recognised the name of Benjamin Franklin, but appeared to be ignorant of Joseph Priestley, the Abbé Nollet or Jean Jallabert of Geneva. Then I mentioned my interest in

71

Albertus Magnus and Paracelcus, which proved to be a mistake.

'Good God,' he said staring at me as if I had crept out from under a wet rock. 'Have you really spent – I should say wasted – your time studying such arrant *nonsense*? Is your Geneva such a benighted place?'

I was taken aback by this sudden attack on my one-time heroes and on my home town. I felt my face redden with anger and embarrassment. But I mustered enough spirit to reply. 'I cannot agree that it is nonsense, Herr Professor Krempe.'

'Oh you cannot agree, can you not?'

'No sir,' I argued. 'Paracelcus was an important figure. A radical thinker. A great observer. A true scholar. A man with a following across Europe. In his day.'

But Krempe would have none of it. He pressed on, his voice heavy with disdain. 'But that day, Herr Frankenstein, is gone. And every minute that you have wasted on these books is utterly and entirely lost. You have burdened your memory with *exploded* systems. Useless names! Discredited ideas!'

Every word he spoke remind me of Noble Alphonse Frankenstein, senator and merchant of Geneva. I could hear my father in every syllable. Perhaps this toad of a man was why he had insisted I study in Ingolstadt.

I decided not to argue. If he knew nothing of Paracelcus it was his loss. The man was plainly a blinkered fool. This was one of that species of witless pedagogues that Paracelcus himself had labelled the 'High Asses of Europe'. Krempe was a prime specimen. A fool with the face of a toad and the ears of a donkey. The High Ass of Ingolstadt.

'I little expected', The Creature droned on, 'in this enlightened and scientific age to find a disciple of Albertus Magnus and Paracelcus. My dear Herr Frankenstein, you must begin your studies entirely anew. You must clear your head of this, this *lumber* from the past. Before it blocks out the light entirely. There is no other way.'

He then scribbled out a list of books which he instructed me to buy, told me that his course of lectures began in three days' time and dismissed me with a wave of his hand. I left the university building in a foul mood and spent the rest of the day trudging around the bookshops of Ingolstadt in search of the books on Krempe's list. By the time I got back to my rooms I was ready to pack my trunks and return to Geneva.

But when I poured out my tale to Schutzi, he surprised me.

'Old Krempe's not so bad,' he said. 'A cantankerous old bastard, certainly. A bit cranky. But decent enough. He's been here for decades and got nowhere, probably because he's a Saxon. Von Grafenberg says that the poor old thing has been passed over so often that he's just gone sour. Curdled like cream in the sun. Or, if you prefer, left to wither on the branch. From plum to prune.'

'Well I just hope to God that the rest of them are not like Krempe,' I told him, unconvinced by his defence of the curmudgeonly old Saxon. 'Or I'm off.'

But my irritation at Krempe was forgotten when, later that day, I received a letter from Geneva. It was from Elisabeth, and it was to tell me that Uncle Ben had been felled by a brain storm. It had been catastrophic, and he was now virtually helpless. Elisabeth spared me none of the details.

'It is such a sad, sad sight to see,' she wrote. 'Your poor friend is as much at the mercy of others as a baby. His face is all twisted, his left eye is almost closed, and he cannot speak. All he can do is make strange, animal-like noises. He dribbles all the time and a servant is constantly in attention to wipe his face. He has to be fed by others, and as a result spills much of the food on his clothes. It is a *most* distressing sight, poor man.'

My eyes filled with tears as I imagined the sharp, brisk, wiry, bright-eyed man, who had tamed Mont Blanc, reduced to such a plight. He seemed to have been transformed at a stroke into some kind of mute, dribbling, leaking, semi-corpse. Poised in misery, halfway between life and death.

'Father and I called on him yesterday,' Elisabeth continued, 'and I did try to explain to him that you were now studying in Bavaria. But I do not think he heard me. Or if he did, I don't think he understood, or would have known where Bavaria was. The poor dear man. And to think that he was once so clever and witty and engaging. So much sought after. It is such a tragedy.'

Bitch!, I thought. I almost admired her ability to dress malice in the clothes of sympathy. It was one of the black arts she practised. Every detail of Uncle Ben's condition was a laceration on my hide. She knew it and loved it. I read on.

'But most painful of all, Victor, it seems that he has no control over his body (if you understand me) and smells most awfully. He is, therefore, not fit for polite company and is seldom seen in Geneva. His poor wife and family are being very brave. Madame de Saussure is much admired in Geneva. She is being a tower of strength. Our father says it would have been better if Uncle Ben had died, but I disagree. One cannot know how precious life is. Even to someone in such a degraded condition as Monsieur de Saussure now finds himself.

'Anyway, Victor, I am sorry to burden you with such sad news. Especially coming as it does so soon after the death of our dear mother. I know how much your Uncle Ben meant to you. But you will be pleased to know that Father is very well. Your loving cousin, Elisabeth Lavenza.'

I stared at the letter for another ten minutes. I could see the

74

smile on Elisabeth's pretty mouth as she wrote it. Then I threw it into the stove and went to find the others. We started drinking in the Paradenplatz and then worked our way back along the Hieronymous-Strasse. By the time we got to the Moritzkirche I could hardly stand. I am told that von Grafenberg and Saracino carted me back to Frau Horst's (who was shocked to see me in such an unrefined state), stripped me to my drawers and dumped me on my bed.

That night I had a fearful dream about my mother, and then was sick all over the floor. After which von Grafenberg had to use all his aristocratic charm to persuade Frau Horst to let me stay.

INGOLSTADT, BAVARIA: 1796

I spent the next few days making my acquaintance with Ingolstadt. Like Geneva it was a hedgehog of a town, ever ready to curl up and show the world its spines. Having grown astride one of Europe's much frequented military routes, Ingolstadt had made a priority of defending itself against marauding armies. The walls seemed to my untrained eye a masterpiece of the fortress builder's art. They formed an elaborate tracery of bastions and ramparts, casements and firing platforms, ditches and moats which zig-zagged their way around the little city.

The city's two bridges over the Danube were guarded on the south bank by a heavily built hornwork. And out in the surrounding fields and oak woods lay no fewer than ten huge, free-standing bulwarks facing all points of the compass. Ingolstadt must surely be one of the most strongly defended towns in Europe. From the Danube countryside it had the appearance of a set of bared teeth.

It was also a garrison town. A thousand or so blue-coated soldiers of the Elector of Bavaria's army were barracked in the Neuschloss at the west end of the town. Daily they trooped across the drawbridge and strutted noisily around the Paradenplatz in front of the schloss, to the delight of the ladies. At first sight they looked impressive in their blue coats, white breeches, black gaiters and leather helmets with horsehair crests. But I could see that many of them handled their muskets clumsily. And most looked like slow-moving country lads, and not very warlike.

Schutzi, who seemed to know everything about Ingolstadt after three weeks' residence, told me that the army had just been turned upside down and inside out by an émigré American royalist called Benjamin Thomson who had recently been rewarded by the Elector with the title of Graf von Rumford. Their officers, according to Schutzi, 'were now spoiling for trouble, the fools. They'll probably get it, the way that the French are behaving. Although God only knows whose side they'll be on if anything starts.'

But inside this military carapace, Ingolstadt was an agreeable enough place of wide streets, decent inns and useful shops. The houses were ornate, handsome with steeply pitched, red-tiled roofs and crow-stepped gables. The old quarter around the Moritzkirche was a labyrinth of crowded and narrow alleyways squeezed between the Danube and the Ludwigstrasse. The town centre was dominated by the white spire and onion-shaped dome of the Moritzkirche. The east end of the town was dominated by the huge squat bulk of the cathedral. Apart from the fact that every second gable end and corner sprouted a statue of the Virgin or one of the saints, the town differed little from my own Geneva.

And Ingolstadt was not without its pleasures. The narrow lanes of the old town were well stocked with beer cellars and pothouses of every description. Some of them were the exclusive reserve of troopers from the Neuschloss. Others were the haunts of students, schoolteachers and clerks. The Old Black Goat seemed to serve only carters, farm labourers and cowherds. There was also a discreet hostelry hard by the Kreuze-Tor which, it was rumoured, was dedicated to the tippling (and other) habits of Jesuits.

But the attractions of ale houses and wine cellars in Ingolstadt paled beside the whorehouse on the Paradenplatz. Schutzi, von Grafenberg and Saracino lost no time in introducing me to this remarkable establishment. It was there that a wiry, red-headed country girl with freckled breasts relieved me of my virginity and with an exuberance that left me startled but enthusiastic. Schutzi claimed that fornication was not so much a pleasure as a religion. If that was so, then I was a convert. Thereafter I became a most regular customer.

It was von Grafenberg who had wheedled our way into these delights. Strictly speaking the place was for officers only, serving the Neuschloss garrison. It was run by a shrewd old harridan who called herself Madame Hortense, who had never been further west than the Kreuze-Tor, the western gate. With his military connections and aristocratic ways, von Grafenberg had persuaded her to allow a few gentlemen from the university to avail themselves of her establishment. She accepted students reluctantly on condition that there must be *no* duelling. This was a serious warning. The students of Bavaria were notorious duellists. Many of them spent more time practising with sabres than the soldiers did.

We all agreed that Madame Hortense ran the finest whorehouse we had ever patronised. I omitted to tell the others that she ran the only whorehouse I had ever patronised. Her girls were young, clean, good natured and energetic. A few were even pretty. She inspected them

78

regularly for traces of the pox. The beds were free from bugs, the linen was changed regularly and the bedrooms were aired frequently. The wine was respectable and not too expensive, and there was food to be had after we had copulated ourselves to a standstill.

And, in a witty parody of the decoration typical of Upper Bavaria, every door-panel, bedhead and wardrobe in the house was decorated with nymphs and goatherds, shepherds and milkmaids – all fornicating enthusiastically in forest glades and Alpine meadows. Every sexual ploy known to the human race was recorded. The rural gallants had members that a stallion would have been proud of. The milkmaids and shepherdesses flaunted their rumps with mesmerising athleticism. In their brightly painted universe they prodded and licked, poked and groped with abandon. It was a riot of carnality. The artist had plainly enjoyed his work.

'Finest art collection north of Florence,' was Saracino's opinion. And I do not believe he was jesting.

It was on our return from my first visit to Madame Hortense's that Schutzi introduced me to Gustav's Horse.

'Now that you have met the mares of Ingolstadt,' he said, 'you might as well meet the stallion!'

We marched into the old Rathaus past an indifferent town servant, up some stairs and into a dusty, lumber-cluttered room that served as a kind of chaotic museum. Standing in one corner was a small stuffed horse.

'Victor Frankenstein,' Schutzi said loudly. 'Meet Gustav's Horse. Dead this one hundred and sixty-three years.'

'What the hell is it?' I asked, staring at the woebegone object. It was a dingy, dappled grey colour, there was little left of its tail, its ears were badly moth-eaten and straw leaked from every seam. There was even a bleariness about its glass eyes. It had the look of a neglected toy.

'This, my dear Frankenstein, is Ingolstadt's greatest trophy,' Schutzi pronounced. 'This represents the triumph of Catholicism over Protestantism. Of faith over heresy. Of light over darkness.'

'What's he talking about?' I asked von Grafenberg.

'What the fat He-Brew is trying to tell you,' he replied, 'is that this was once the mount of Gustavus Adolphus.'

'What?' I laughed. '*The* Gustavus.'

'It's true,' Schutzi said. 'This is what is left of the Protestant demon-king's horse. The Swedish Antichrist's very own charger.'

'It's been here since 1632,' said von Grafenberg. 'When Gustav was besieging Ingolstadt. He had his horse shot from under him. And this is it.'

Schutzi took up the tale. 'When Gustav decided – very sensibly in my opinion – that Ingolstadt was too boring to capture, he packed up and left. The heroes of Ingolstadt waited until he was at least fifty miles away and then crept out – in the dead of night – to make a prisoner of his horse. The fact that it was dead helped. Otherwise they wouldn't have risked it. It was possibly Bavaria's only military success.'

Von Grafenberg bridled. 'Unlike the He-Brews,' he sneered, 'who are renowned for their military prowess. I mean, they don't really get chased from ghetto to ghetto. They make tactical retreats and strategic withdrawals. Until one day they'll fall off the edge of the world.'

Schutzi ignored him. 'And so, they brought him back to Ingolstadt in triumph. Then they had him stuffed and mounted on a wheeled trolley, for all to see and to worship. Gustav's Horse is now regarded as clear proof that God favours the Roman cause.'

Saracino stopped the banter with a question: 'What's its name?'

'I've no idea,' said Schutzi.

'I just asked,' Saracino said. 'Still, I wonder what we'll look like in a hundred and sixty years time? Not as good as old dobbin here, I don't suppose.'

'Oh, I don't know,' Schutzi said, scratching his coarse, straw-coloured thatch. 'Bleached bones have a certain austere charm. Personally, I think this nag looks even older than its years.'

'Past reviving I'd say,' I told him. 'Long gone. Just about the deadest thing I've ever seen.'

INGOLSTADT, BAVARIA: 1796

My impressions of the University of Ingolstadt improved three days later when I wandered into the lecture room of Professor Felix Waldman. Physically, Waldman was even less impressive than Krempe: a short, bald, mild-looking man with a thin, high-pitched voice. His language was stilted, cumbersome, but he talked on his subject with an odd passion. He began with a recapitulation of the progress of science and the role of the men he called 'the great practitioners of the great art'. In an hour of inspired teaching he conjured up, and put to work, the shades of Aristotle and Galen, Galileo and Boyle, Newton and Fallopius and the recently executed Lavoisier.

It ended in a tribute to the men of science. 'These philosophers,' he said, 'whose hands seem made only to dabble in dirt, their eyes to pore over the microscope or crucible, have performed miracles. They penetrate into the recesses of nature and show how she works. They ascend into the heavens. They have discovered how the blood circulates and the nature of the air we breathe. They have acquired new and almost unlimited powers. They can command the thunder of heaven, mimic the earthquake and even mock the invisible world with its own shadows.'

It was not so much Waldman's sentiments that excited me as his enthusiasm. He said nothing of substance. He delivered no great insights. Most of what he said was rhetoric. All he did was to offer up a paean of praise to the modern world and its natural philosophers. But his conviction inspired me. There was a note in his voice that stirred something within me. His audience, myself among them, were enthralled. I suspected that he was a better teacher than a scientist.

Once again, the very idea of science shook me to the core. My mind began to fill with one thought. So much has been done. So much more is still to be achieved. And I was one of the men to do it. I would blaze new trails. I would scale new heights. I would plumb new depths. I would describe hitherto unknown powers. I would unfold to the whole world the deepest mysteries of its own creation.

After a restless night mulling over Waldman's words, I took my courage in my hands, dressed carefully, wheedled his address from Frau Horst and set out to visit him at his house on the Ludwigstrasse. It was a large, pink-washed establishment on six floors. It had thirty-two windows and a stately entrance which opened onto the street. I learnt later that Waldman's wife had been the daughter of a wealthy Munich banker. She had died young, leaving Waldman more money than he would ever need. So the little professor lived in splendour on the Ludwigstrasse with a houseful of liveried servants and his one and only child. She was eighteen, and according to von Grafenberg was 'definitely one to look out for'.

Waldman met me in the hallway, ushered me into his book-lined study on the ground floor, insisted that I take the most comfortable seat and ordered coffee and chocolate cakes, for which he confessed an unseemly and foolish appetite. He quickly identified my accent and we spent some time discussing Geneva and the cities of Switzerland. He asked me why I was starting my studies three weeks late, expressed his condolences at the death of my mother and generally did his best to make me feel at ease.

But when the conversation turned to my studies I grew wary. And when he quizzed me about my reading I deliberately threw in the names of Cornelius Agrippa, Albertus Magnus and Paracelcus to see how he would react. For all I knew he could have been yet another High Ass. But he was not.

'These were men to whose zeal modern philosophers are indebted,' he said after a thoughtful silence. 'Indebted for most of the foundations of their knowledge. And the labours of men of genius, Herr Frankenstein, however erroneously directed, scarcely ever fail in ultimately turning to the advantage of mankind.'

Which was nicely, if not neatly, put.

'I know precious little about Albertus Magnus and Cornelius Agrippa,' he went on. 'Except that Albert taught Aquinas, and that Agrippa preached that the Good Lord created three worlds – an idea which labelled him heretic. But every natural philosopher worthy of the name knows something of Paracelcus. The Martin Luther of medicine. A Swiss, wasn't he?'

'Then you wouldn't dismiss him as a mere necromancer?' I ventured. 'As I heard him recently described.'

He smiled and shook his head. 'I wonder who that was?' he said. 'No I would not describe Paracelcus as a necromancer. Although I've heard the term used. That and worse.'

'Worse?'

84

'Much worse. Wizard. Warlock. Satanist. Devil worshipper. Antichrist. Dabbler in the Black Arts. All nonsense of course.'

I nodded solemnly. 'I agree.'

'Good!' he said, with a laugh. 'And as you appear to be interested in the man, perhaps you would prepare a paper for me on his work?'

'A paper? On Paracelcus?'

'Certainly. Shall we say, ah, six pages. The subject, oh, which Paracelsian researches – and theories – are still of interest to modern science. And I would like to have it on my desk by the end of lectures on the day after tomorrow. That gives you two evenings to work on it.'

It was a tall order but I was happy at the prospect. It seemed to vindicate all the hours I had spent poring over the life and times of that outrageous, drunken, wandering genius. It was also, to me at least, a snub to the Noble Alphonse Frankenstein who had dismissed Paracelcus as so much rubbish. In a rush of enthusiasm I told Waldman that I intended to study chemistry and natural philosophy at his feet. He did not seem unduly flattered.

'Happy as I am to gain a disciple,' he said drily 'a man needs many mentors and not just one. But if your application is equal to your enthusiasm, Herr Frankenstein, you'll do well enough. And you will need more than just chemistry.'

'More, Herr Professor?'

'Much more. A man would make a very sorry chemist if he attended to that department of human knowledge alone. If your wish is to become a true man of science – and not merely a petty experimentalist – I should advise you to apply yourself to every branch of natural philosophy. Including mathematics.'

'I understand sir,' I said.

Waldman then asked me if I would care to look around his

modest laboratory. I said that I would and followed him up the wide staircase to the top of the house. When he threw open the doors I was stunned. It was like nothing I had ever seen before. It made Uncle Ben's laboratory on the Rue de la Cité look like the back-shop of a village watchmaker's. Waldman had created a wonderland high above the Ludwigstrasse. The sun flooded in through high windows and the ranks of jars, bottles, retorts and instruments gleamed and sparkled in the light.

There was flask after flask of chemicals. He seemed to have acquired every chemical under the sun: alumina, magnesia, carbon, sulphur, iron, soda, white arsenic, borax, potassium, nitre, corrosive sublimate. There were huge flasks of distilled water, bottles of every size. Each workbench was lined with beakers, gas jars, flasks, specimen jars and racks of test-tubes. There were lamps, burners, balances, scales, measuring rods, shelves full of scientific texts, notebooks, laboratory records.

The huge room contained everything that a scientist could possibly need. As he walked me around the room I could only gape. Three of the walls were lined with shelves, and every shelf was crammed with equipment. All of it was meticulously labelled in fine, neat handwriting. One of the walls was covered with charts and diagrams, tables and maps. A man could lock himself away in here and never come out.

'Well then, Herr Frankenstein,' Waldman said, beaming at me behind his thick spectacles. 'What do you think of my modest little laboratory?'

I could only shake my head, open-mouthed with wonder.

He laughed at my reaction. 'Interesting, isn't it?'

We then progressed through a set of double doors into another large room. Every electrical engine I had seen illustrated in Priestley's *History of Electrity* was there. Leyden jars of varying sizes sat side by side with Cruikshank generators, clockwork contact breakers, machines by Nairn and Ingen-Hausz, a horizontally fixed plate device with an electrometer attached. I noticed a boxed 'travelling' cylindrical machine which boasted (in English) that it could mimic a 'thunder house', 'sett of bells' and a 'magic picture'.

There was also one huge piece of apparatus built, according to the label, by one John Cuthbertson of London. It was gigantic. It consisted of a highly polished, thick glass disc, at least six feet in diameter, mounted into a heavy timber and brass frame. The glass plate was cranked by an elaborately geared handle. I wondered how much the plate weighed, and what kind and size of electrical spark it generated.

'I call this one my pride and joy,' Waldman said, giving the huge glass disc a little spin which made it give off a low whine. 'I'm told there's another just like it in Herr Teyler's Foundation at Haarlem in the Low Countries.'

'You're an electrician?' I asked.

He looked at me in surprise. 'You know the term?'

I nodded. 'Yes I do. But I've never seen such machines.'

'Then what do you know of electricians?'

'A little. I've read some Priestley. And some Franklin. And my Uncle Ben told me about Jean Jallabert . . .'

'The famous electrified locksmith of Geneva. How interesting. And who is your Uncle Ben?'

'Horace-Benédict de Saussure,' I said.

'Saussure! You're Saussure's nephew?'

'Not his real nephew. He's an old friend of the Frankenstein family. A Huguenot, like my mother.'

'How extraordinary,' Waldman said. 'How very extraordinary. I've been corresponding with your distinguished, ah, Uncle Ben, for many years. Saussure's electrical observations on his expedition to, where was it . . .?'

'Mont Blanc.'

'Yes. Mont Blanc. They were most useful. Most useful.' He shook me by the hand again. 'Well, Herr Frankenstein, it is a genuine pleasure to meet a friend – a relative almost – of the eminent Horace-Benédict de Saussure.'

'Thank you, sir.'

He seemed genuinely impressed with my acquaintance with Uncle Ben. And then genuinely distressed when I told him that my old friend, and his old correspondent, had just been laid low by a second, calamitous apoplexy.

'Ah me,' he said, shaking his head. 'A grievous tragedy. Such a fine brain. One of the best in Europe, I think I can say. Exploding, as it were, in on itself in such a terrible way.' There was a thoughtful silence, then he said: 'And you, I take it, are keen to follow in Saussure's footsteps?'

'I am sir,' I said. 'If I can.'

'Then I must do what I can to help you on your way.'

'Thank you.'

'Short, that is, of favouritism. I cannot abide favouritism. Or carelessness. I never overlook carelessness. Sloppy work can never be countenanced. It's my first rule.'

'I understand, sir.'

'But if . . .' and he looked at me gravely. 'But if you prove yourself to me. And to the other professors. Then it may be possible, *may* I say, for you to come and work here. With me. Occasionally.' He smiled. 'I take it you would like that?'

I looked around at the glittering array of machinery and instruments and knew that I was looking at the finest that money could buy. This was one of the best electrical laboratories in Europe. There was nothing, absolutely nothing, that I would like better than to work here.

'Yes, sir,' I said. 'I would like that.'

Felix Waldman was as good as his word. When he saw that my enthusiasm for electricity was genuine and that I was not particularly ham-handed he allowed me to work with the electrical machines in his laboratory in the Ludwig-strasse. After a few weeks of conscientious labouring alongside him I persuaded him to extend the privilege to Saracino. (Schutzi preferred to take his natural philosophy from books and von Grafenberg had other things on his mind.)

Saracino was even more impressed than I had been with Waldman's panoply of electrical machines. It was plain that the professor had spent much of his late wife's money on some of the best instrument-makers in Europe. Saracino recognised one small vertically held plate-glass generator which had been made by his own family in Bologna. And when he saw the huge machine Waldman called his pride and joy, he walked round it open-mouthed for the best part of ten minutes.

Every now and again Waldman's daughter Erika would make a foray into this philosophical wonderland. She would wander around the benches, poking at the machines and pestering her father with questions. He tried to discourage her, but she was not easily discouraged. Nor was she offended by our messy electrical experiments with live frogs, mice and rats. She watched with fascination as the tiny limbs thrashed and jerked. Waldman would put up with her for ten minutes or so, then order her back to her own books and tutors.

'Christ I wouldn't mind a slice of that,' Saracino muttered under his breath during one of her visits. 'That must be the finest backside north of the Alps. She can come and play with my generator *any* time she wants.'

I looked at the shapely Erika and at the gleaming equipment in her father's lavishly equipped laboratory and agreed with Saracino. Erika Waldman – and all that went with her – was indeed a prize worth acquiring.

INGOLSTADT, BAVARIA: 1797

The Ingolstadt Society of Golemites was born one night in
Madame Hortense's whorehouse when Schutzi Eybenschutz
staggered to his feet and announced that 'electricity is but
the name of God'. The big Jew made a ludicrous sight,
swaying in the centre of the room, clutching a bottle of red
wine, his breeches at his ankles, while two giggling whores
tugged at his drawers. But when von Grafenberg demanded
to know 'what the lard-bellied He-Brew' was talking about,
Schutzi drew himself up to his full dignity.

'Just as there is no end to the erudition of David
Eybenschutz of Prague,' he declared, 'so there are no depths
to the ignorance of the Goyim. Particularly the Austrian
Goyim, from whom Jehovah protect us all.' He took a swig
of wine. 'I do not suppose for a moment that any of you
ignorant lumps of cowdung – ladies always excepted – have
ever heard of the Golem? I thought not.'

The Golem, he rambled on, are mannikins of Jewish
legend, creatures of mud and clay which can only be
animated when a Rabbi inscribes the name of God on their

foreheads. 'Mostly they are harmless and useful beings,' he said. 'Rather like the ladies now hovering in the region of my artfully circumcised member. But many years ago, in the wondrous city of Prague, a certain Rabbi Loew created a huge and fearsome Golem to protect decent Jews from the depredations of the Christians . . .'

'Waste of time,' von Grafenberg muttered. 'We'll get you in the end.'

Schutzi ignored him. 'Gentlemen,' he went on. 'I regret to say that the good Rabbi Loew made a mistake. The creature ran amok. It turned on its creators. Instead of confining itself to biting off the heads of Christians – a blameless activity – it started munching on Jews as well. It could not be killed. It destroyed the pleasant homes of the Jews as well as the hovels of the Christians. It wrecked much of Prague. People were not pleased. Something had to be done.'

It seems that the Golem's rampage around Prague was finally halted when its creator, the Rabbi Loew, tricked it into kneeling in front of him, whereupon he removed the sacred name of God from its forehead and the Golem reverted to a pile of mud. 'That mud dried into dust,' Schutzi said, 'and was blown by a north wind into Austria where it congealed, in the most horrible fashion, into the von Grafenberg family . . .'

At this von Grafenberg jumped up and emptied a jug of red wine over Schutzi's head. The roaring Jew was obliged to remove his undershirt, exposing his ample belly and his formidable, but still dangling, circumcised member.

Thereafter the evening took its course. Our attention turned to the whores. I recall Saracino's ginger head buried between the thighs of one of Madame Hortense's finest, and Schutzi's huge pale buttocks bobbing in a corner. I remember nothing of my own efforts, except that the girl did all the work. In the early hours of the morning we returned to our rooms, exhausted, drunk and penniless. The evening had been a fine one.

In the morning Saracino, von Grafenberg and I were faintly ashamed of our excesses but Schutzi was his usual sunny self. And while the rest of us did our best to forget, Schutzi wanted to compare the prowess of our respective whores. 'Mine fucked me as dry as a sheep turd in high summer,' he declared. 'My member's as dead as Gustav's Horse.'

When von Grafenberg and I snarled at him, he just beamed. 'Save me from the conscience of Catholics and Calvinists,' he said. 'Two breeds divided by their similarities. Neither able to accept God's gifts with good grace. Gentlemen, let me recommend to you the ancient faith of Judaism.'

Schutzi's early morning cheerfulness never failed to irritate von Grafenberg. 'Damned fat snipcock,' the Austrian grumbled. 'So much lard in his breeches there's not enough wine in Bavaria to give him a sore head.' Then von Grafenberg's face cracked into a wicked grin. 'Maybe we should hand old Schutzi over to Waldman for one of his electrical experiments. Maybe he could stick a rod of brass up Schutzi's fat backside and attach it to one of his machines. Maybe he'll want us to write a dissertation on how long it takes to fry a He-Brew.'

'A lot longer than it would take to cook a bladder full of Austrian cowdung,' Schutzi retorted noisily. 'You'd evaporate in seconds. Gone in a cloud of steam and stink. Although I admit the incredibly high proportion of bone to brain in the skull might slow things down a bit.'

Honour satisfied, both men attacked the breakfast which Frau Horst had set in front of us. I never understood the satisfaction that Schutzi and von Grafenberg got from baiting one another. In the year I had spent in Ingolstadt I had seen sabre duels fought and men scarred for life over the

92

kind of insults which they traded daily. But I had also seen the big Jew and the little Austrian fight side by side in liquor-shop brawls.

'Schutzi,' I said. 'You were ranting on last night about something called, the goyem is it . . .?'

'The Golem. What about it?' he asked.

'Something about electricity being the name of God,' Saracino chipped in. 'At least I think that's what you said.'

'Did I say that?' Schutzi said. 'That's not bad.'

'So what *were* you talking about?' von Grafenberg demanded. 'Some dumb He-Brew folk story, I suppose.'

'A bit more than that,' Schutzi told him. 'But not much. The Golem is a creature from the Talmud. Mud and clay and lifeless until the word *emet* – that's Hebrew for God – is traced on his forehead. Then he comes to life.'

'So . . .' I said. 'We're animated by electricity as the Golem is animated by the name of God. Is that what you meant?'

'I think that's what I meant,' Schutzi said.

'So that makes us Golemites,' the Italian said thoughtfully. 'The men who study the power that animates.'

'The Golemite Brotherhood,' I suggested.

'The Society of Golemites,' von Grafenberg countered.

'The Society of Ingolstadt Golemites,' Schutzi pronounced. He raised his coffee cup. 'Gentlemen. Here's to the Society of Ingolstadt Golemites. Long may it shock.'

More than two dozen flocked to the Golemite banner. Soon it was surrounded by a group of lively, disputatious young men, all dedicated to the study of electricity. The fact that the university authorities disapproved of the Golemites added spice to our meetings. We came to see ourselves as something dangerous, a new arm of the illuminati. We were a freemasonry of science which the High Asses and their masters would never comprehend.

Naturally, electricity became enmeshed in our minds with

revolutionary politics. It was the force that would transform Europe. In our innocence we saw the Society of Ingolstadt Golemites as a centre of change. Our ideas would transform the world. It was also, it has to be said, one of the most dedicated and energetic drinking and whoring clubs in Ingolstadt.

By the end of my first year at Ingolstadt I was thoroughly enjoying myself. I liked Ingolstadt. The company was good, the teaching was reasonable and Catholicism held no more terrors for me. The Roman Catholics of Ingolstadt seemed as schismatic as Calvinists. Some were blinkered in their piety; most were casually orthodox; a few were just this side of atheism. We argued religion and politics, philosophy and science, military and sexual strategies, noisily and happily deep into the night.

My stock with the Golemites soared when I received a letter from Paris from Germaine de Stael. Even Schutzi, never a man to be impressed, was awestruck. I lied casually that Madame de Stael was an old friend of the Frankenstein family. With the letter she enclosed a copy of a political cartoon which she thought 'might amuse, given your enthusiasm for politics and things electrical'. Most of the Golemites thought it was a masterpiece.

The cartoon depicted a blue-coated French revolutionary cranking the handle of a generator on which was inscribed the words 'Declaration of the Rights of Man'. Along the wire which stretched from the generator ran the words 'Liberty, Equality, Fraternity, Unity, Indivisibility of the Republic'. The wire ran under the thrones of Europe, toppling their occupants. Among the electrical revolutionary's victims were the Emperor Joseph, the Pope, the Despot of Spain, the Tyrant of Prussia and King George of England. 'Republican Electricity', said the slogan 'gives the Despots the shock which overturns their thrones.'

The French cartoon thrilled us. And it summed up the philosophy of the Society of Ingolstadt Golemites. The cartoon became our icon and I became its keeper. Crude copies of it were made and distributed. Eventually Saracino hit on the notion of hiring an Ingolstadt painter to reproduce it on the ceiling of one of his rooms (in place of a cow and a milkmaid in an Alpine meadow). Frau Horst was prepared to give her permission just so long as Saracino paid for it and the painting contained no uncovered human parts that might embarrass the squint-eyed Renate.

Our preoccupations took some engaging twists. The curiosity of the Golemites knew no bounds. An evening at Madame Hortense's declined into a seminar on tumescence. It began with a befuddled von Grafenberg sitting staring at his erect member with which his favourite whore, an ample Swabian called Rutte, was toying idly.

'What makes it do that?' he demanded to know. 'Stand up like that?'

'So you can get the poor little thing into Rutte,' Schutzi explained with elaborate patience.

'Suffusion of blood,' I said. 'The question is, what causes the blood to suffuse von Grafenberg's member?'

It says something for the Golemites that they stopped whatever they were doing (they were at the early stages) to join the discussion.

'So!' Schutzi said. 'What we want to know is just how the sight and feel of this lady's moister parts cause my superb Jewish weapon to go rigid? What little carrier pigeon flies from my brain to my privy parts?'

'Electrical impulse,' I suggested. 'From the eye, to the brain, to the blood vessels in the penis. In an instant.'

'Electric lust,' Schutzi ruminated. 'Libidinous lightning. The very spark of devilment. But then, why do women take so much longer to rouse? Especially as their brains are that

95

bit nearer their backsides. What happens to their signals? Do they go the long way round? Or what?'

But as nobody could supply Schutzi with any kind of answer, and the Paradenplatz whores were growing restless, we got back to the business at hand. As one of the women pointed out with some irritation, time was money.

INGOLSTADT, BAVARIA: 1798

To my Calvinist eye the Maria-Viktoria-Kirche in the Neu-baurstrasse looked like a whorehouse for angels. The sumptuousness of the place was sensual to the point of eroticism. The images were the usual saints, angels, sera-phim, virgins etc. – but they were of a peculiar plump and glistening variety. To me they spoke of a fleshly not a spiritual universe.

The huge white and gold space was dominated by a painted ceiling depicting the races, nations and beasts of the earth, all gazing upwards, with slave's eyes, at a trinity of God, Jesus and the Virgin Mary. Schutzi assured me that the ceiling painting – by an artist called Asam – was a masterpiece of its kind. I thought it was Roman Catholicism at its worst. The pastel-coloured dregs of the Counter-reformation.

But I was not in the Maria-Viktoria-Kirche to admire the ecclesiastical scenery. I was lying in wait. Every afternoon Erika Waldman made a pilgrimage from her father's house on the Ludwigstrasse to pray in the Maria-Viktoria-Kirche.

Schutzi assured me that she was pious to the point of lunacy. Every likely lad at the university had taken a run at her maidenhead and got nowhere. Her religion pinned her legs together as firmly as if they had been bolted at the ankles.

So there was no way into her drawers without either overcoming or circumventing her Catholicism. Which meant that I could either wheedle my way into her affections and then subvert her resolve from within. Or I could try to breach the Catholic walls with the battering-ram of reason. The latter seemed the more manly course, although I was quite prepared to try the former.

When I had discussed my stratagem with Schutzi he was liberal with his advice.

'Get her attention,' he said. 'What's she interested in? God, that's what she's interested in. So bone up on God. And Jesus. And the Christian saints. So that when you just happen to run into her in some church or other you can discourse on the martyrs. Maybe you can bore the drawers off her. God knows you've bored the drawers off the rest of us.'

'But what would I be doing in a Catholic church in the first place?' I wondered.

'How should I know?' he said. 'Use your imagination.'

'I suppose I could be utterly fascinated by Catholic art and architecture,' I suggested.

'Not bad,' he said. 'Not bad at all. Take your notebook. Make it look authentic.'

Erika's piety made her predictable. Every afternoon she slipped away from her tutors to pray. The venue for her morning praying sessions varied, but every afternoon, without fail, she returned to the sugar-plum interior of the Maria-Viktoria-Kirche. She was plainly startled to find me sitting in one of the pews, gazing with apparent interest at the gilt-bedecked high altar. I had my notebook with me and had scribbled a few notes and a sketch or two to impress her.

'Herr Frankenstein,' she said in a whisper. 'I'm surprised to find you here.'

I feigned surprise. 'Ah! Fraulein Waldman. Good afternoon.'

'But, you are not a Catholic?'

'No,' I agreed.

'Then what . . .?'

'Your religious art and decoration interest me,' I explained. 'They are so unlike anything I'm used to.' That much at least was true.

I saw a glimmer in her grey eyes. 'Indeed. And what are you used to?'

I shook my head. 'Something much simpler,' I said. 'Plainer. More severe. As I'm sure you must know.'

'I fear I've never had cause to enter a Protestant church,' she said hesitantly.

'Well when you do, you'll find it very different.'

She looked startled at the very idea of setting foot in such a place. I'm sure that only politeness stopped her crossing herself. Then she looked around her with pleasure and some pride. 'But this is a beautiful place, isn't it?'

'So people tell me,' I said.

She looked surprised. 'You don't think so?'

I shook my head. 'No I don't.'

'Not even the Asam ceiling?'

'Especially not the Asam ceiling.' I pointed up to the representation of Africa and laughed. 'The man who painted that had never seen a crocodile in his life. It's like some kind of sea serpent out of a children's book.'

She bridled slightly. 'I cannot think that the anatomical details of a crocodile are important,' she said.

'Then what is?' I asked her. 'And what's Pegasus the

winged horse, who is a creature straight out of pagan Greek myth, doing in a Christian version of heaven and earth? I know little enough of Catholic art, but the whole thing seems preposterous to me.'

'It is *not* preposterous,' she said with some heat. 'It shows God's dominion over all creatures, the mythological as well as the natural. It shows how our holy faith embraces and understands all things. All thoughts. Even the myths of the pagan Greeks.'

'Well perhaps you can explain it to me?' I suggested. 'Tell me what it all means? I may not like it, but it does intrigue me.'

Which was true enough. Herr Asam's ceiling was an odd piece of work. In the centre of the ceiling was a white-bearded God from whose chest a great beam of yellow light issued like a bolt of lightning. It shot diagonally across the room, struck the chest of Jesus, from which it proceeded to the breast of Mary. On striking the Virgin the bolt fragmented into slender rods of pale light which reached into every corner of the painted universe. A world of faith animated by heavenly electricity.

'God's love proceeding through Christ, to his Holy Mother to all the peoples of the earth,' Erika explained without much hesitation.

Then she excused herself and went off to attend to her devotions. I sat watching her at her prayers. She was, without doubt, a handsome creature. She had a small, round head poised on a long slender neck. There was a cast to her high cheeks and a slight slant to her eyes. She had a biggish nose and a fleshy mouth. I liked the set of her square shoulders, the long tapering back, the strong legs. As I relished the sight of her I felt the familiar stirring in my groin.

On the way out of the church she stopped to point out the

100

Lepanto Monstrance, an elaborately crafted vessel in which the consecrated wafer is displayed. It was a bizarre and beautiful object, dedicated to Don John of Austria's naval victory over the Turks in 1571.

Erika showed it to me with pride. 'Even you, Herr Frankenstein, must agree that this is a beautiful thing.'

'A beautiful tribute to a terrible slaughter,' I told her, and watched her smile fade. 'More than thirty thousand men died at Lepanto. And they weren't all Turks.'

She left me on the Neuebaustrasse with a strained smile. My comments had pained and perhaps even disturbed her. She would probably fret about the condition of my Calvinist soul. She might even confess to her priest that I had provoked in her the sin of anger. But I had her attention. I felt I had done a good hour's work.

So for the next few weeks I stalked Erika Waldman around Ingolstadt, accidentally confronting her in the city's churches. I took Schutzi's advice and read up on the various saints to whom the Ingolstadt churches were dedicated. In the Moritzkirche we discussed the significance of St Moritz, the fourth-century Roman legionary who was butchered for refusing to take part in a pagan (i.e. Roman) ceremony. She saw him as a Christian hero; I described him as 'rather foolish'.

We climbed the Moritzkirche bell-tower – the highest point in Ingolstadt – and admired the views over the Danube. I walked behind her up the narrow staircase and revelled in the rythmic swing of her backside. When we got to the top her face was red with exertion and she licked the sweat from her upper lip. I had some trouble hiding the bulge in my breeches.

In the Franziskanerkirche in the Herderstrasse we disputed the failure of the Roman Church to adopt the poverty, chastity and obedience preached by St Francis. She flushed when I derided the way Francis had confronted the demon of his lust by throwing himself into a thorn bush. 'An odd antidote to lust,' I suggested, and poured scorn on the notion that red roses sprouted in the snow where his drops of blood fell.

She was no fool. My disguise as an art historian was only good for the first few encounters. But as a pious Catholic she could hardly discourage me from browsing around the churches. There was always the hope that my soul might be saved from scepticism and heresy. And although I irritated and sometimes confused her, she was strong-minded enough to take some pleasure from tussling with a creature from the Protestant darkness.

It was in the huge, squat Liebfrauenmünster that our debate reached a crisis. When I walked through the door I was in a sour mood. I had been circling her for weeks, getting nowhere. I had made a few dents in the chastity belt of her piety, but nothing pronounced enough to spring the lock. As I prowled the scented gloom of the cathedral looking for her, I was angry, frustrated. The Last Paracelsian reduced to this.

I found her behind the high altar, gazing at one of the paintings on the altar. It was one of Ingolstadt's more renowned images, a triptych of St Catherine of Alexandria, the patron saint of pedants and bores, who was seated in the usual blaze of light, lecturing to dozens of learned old men in fifteenth-century costume. Most of them, I had been told, were teachers and professors from the University of Ingolstadt. St Catherine herself was represented by a plump, dim-looking sixteen year old.

'My master Paracelcus had a name for men like that,' I told Erika, satisfied that I had startled her. 'He called them the High Asses. He was always amazed that the high colleges of Europe produced so many High Asses.'

She turned with a cold stare. 'Your master?' she said angrily. 'We have only one master, whether we are Protestant or whether we are Catholic. Our Lord Jesus Christ.'

I shook my head. 'Not me,' I said. 'I have another master. The great Theophrastus Bombastus von Hohenheim. A Swiss. The one and only saint of the retorts and vats. The prophet of the chemical universe.'

She stared at me in incomprehension, looking for some sign that I was teasing her. But she could see I was not joking. 'And what does he teach, this master of yours?' she asked slowly and with fine contempt.

'To believe in what I can see, what I can hear, what I can touch and what I can smell,' I informed her. 'To question everything. To accept nothing. Not to believe what I'm told simply because it has been told for two thousand years.'

'You mean the holy scriptures?' she asked.

I shrugged. 'Call them what you will.'

'Then your master is the devil himself,' she said.

'No,' I replied. 'He was a great natural philosopher who was martyred by the powerful.'

'A mere wizard.'

'A man of science.'

'And you believe this "man of science"?'

'More than you believe this ridiculous fable,' I said, pointing to St Catherine and her scholarly audience.

'You've no right to say that. You've no idea what I do and do not believe.'

'You're an intelligent woman,' I told her. 'Do you really believe that this half-educated Egyptian virgin converted fifty philosophers to Christianity? Then that the wheel on which she was about to be tortured was mysteriously shattered by a bolt of lightning. And when they finally did cut her head off, a band of angels swooped down and spirited her corpse away to the top of Mount Sinai. Where

103

her bones were found four hundred years later. Do you *really* believe all that?'

When she responded there were tears in her eyes. 'I try to be a good Catholic, Herr Frankenstein,' she said, 'and I hope a good Christian. It's not given to us to know everything. Maybe there are things that I find difficult. But that does not mean . . .'

She broke off suddenly, turned away and walked quickly out of the Liebfrauenmünster. Feeling slightly ashamed of myself, I followed her and caught up with her in the Theriesenstrasse. When I tried to take her elbow she pulled away. But I persisted, persuaded her to accept my apology and coaxed her into walking with me among the willows beside the Danube. She said little and I noticed that her hands were trembling.

Then under a ruined oak she surprised me by accepting my kiss. Her mouth opened and her tongue fluttered against my teeth before she pulled away. I walked her back to her father's house on the Ludwigstrasse into which she disappeared without a glance.

That night I celebrated my small conquest with a long roister in Madame Hortense's whorehouse. I went alone and treated myself to one of Madame Hortense's most expensive harlots. Then I reeled back to my rooms in the Hochschulestrasse where my sleep was racked by a terrible dream. The image of Erika on the streets of Ingolstadt melted into that of my mother. But when I tried to embrace her my kiss turned her livid, corpselike, dressed in her shroud, and the grave worms crawled in the folds of the flannel.

I woke up shouting and sweating.

THE REPUBLIC OF GENEVA: 1799

Alphonse Frankenstein and I were happy to keep one another at arm's length. Any communication with my father was normally through his lawyers. In fact, in the four years I spent studying at Ingolstadt I only ever received two letters bearing the elaborate Frankenstein seal. One was a curt note, dated 2 February 1799, to inform me that Horace-Benédict de Saussure – my Uncle Ben – was dead. 'He was laid low by a final apoplexy', my father wrote 'from which he died within a few days. My condolences.'

His second letter arrived in the middle of May. It was to tell me that my six-year-old brother William had been murdered by one of the servants – a girl named Justine Moritz – and that it would be 'fitting' if I returned to Geneva to attend her trial.

It seems that one warm evening at the beginning of May my father, Elisabeth and my two brothers Ernest and William went for a walk in the Plainpalais. William and Ernest went on ahead while my father and Elisabeth sat on a bench to rest and enjoy the evening. No doubt she sat patting his hand and making cooing noises as he described the toils and hardships of being a Geneva merchant. Some time later Ernest came back looking pale and frightened asking if they had seen William. They had not.

According to Ernest, his little brother had run away from him to hide in the bushes and then had just vanished. Ernest had wandered around calling for him but got no answer. After spending an hour or two scouring the Plainpalais in the dark they returned to the house in the Cour Saint-Pierre hoping that William had made his own way home. He had not. So the servants were rounded up, everyone was issued with torches and a full-scale search was set under way. Just before dawn my father found William's body, half-concealed in long grass. He had been strangled and a miniature that William had been wearing had been stolen.

The miniature had been the undoing of the culprit. Justine Moritz – an unpopular Catholic girl from the South of France – had taken to her bed with a fever shortly after William's body had been found. One of the servants had been helping her undress when the jewelled miniature fell out of Justine's pocket. The city officials were called, and in her fevered state Justine made what everyone agreed was a confession. Enough of a confession, anyway, for Justine to stand trial for the murder of William Frankenstein. She was now lying in the city gaol waiting her assize.

'It would be fitting, Victor,' my father wrote, 'that you be present in the court with the rest of the Frankenstein family to hear the fate of this wretched woman. We do not seek revenge, of course. Only justice for poor, dear William.'

Poor dear William had been lying beside his mother in the Frankenstein tomb for three weeks before I stepped off the last of the string of coaches which had made up the bone-jarring journey from Ingolstadt to Geneva. My young brother Ernest met me off the coach. I was surprised by the strapping, level-eyed young man of sixteen who took my hand when I stepped down from the diligence

'Thank God you've come, Victor,' he said as we trudged up the Rue de la Cité. 'This business has hit the old man hard. Worse than the death of our mother. He hasn't come out of his library for days. Has all his meals sent in and then doesn't eat anything. I think he is going mad. D'you think he could go mad?'

I shrugged. 'I doubt it,' I said. 'If he does it will not be for long. Madmen don't make money. How's Elisabeth?'

It was his turn to shrug. Ernest was no more fond of Elisabeth than I was. 'How d'you think?' he said.

'Making the most of it, is she?'

'I suppose so.'

I found the Frankenstein town-house shuttered and the rooms draped in black. I had left it in mourning for my mother and returned to find it in mourning for my brother. My father brooded among his books, while Elisabeth had the vapours in her room. The servants flitted about, sniffing loudly. I had no reason to doubt their sorrow. William was always a cheerful and good-natured child. Most of them had known him since the day he was born.

Ernest and I were chewing on a dismal cold supper in the breakfast room when Fat Clerval came wheezing in to offer me his condolences and his support 'as your oldest, dearest friend'. In the few years since I had seen him Clerval had become fatter than ever. He was now almost as wide as he was high and bursting out of his breeches. His round face was flushed and beads of sweat stood out on his upper lip. One of his doting grandparents had settled a handsome sum on him, so the fat fool had no need to work. He spent his day writing poems and plays which no one in Geneva (or anywhere else) wanted to publish or produce.

Later, Ernest told me that Clerval had set his cap at

Elisabeth and she was playing him cruelly on the end of her line. She had him thrashing about like one of the plump carp that he, Jean-Pierre and I used to fish out of Lac Leman from the Bellerive pier.

'I've composed a poem in William's memory,' Clerval said solemnly, producing a sheet of paper from his waistcoat pocket. 'Shall I read it to you?'

'Not now, Henri,' I said. 'I'm just off the coach. I'm a bit too tired to do justice to your literary efforts. Some other time, perhaps.'

'It's not long,' he persisted. 'A few lines.'

'You heard Victor,' Ernest said sharply. 'He's exhausted. I'm tired. We both have a lot to talk about.'

'Ah, yes, well,' said Clerval, settling into a chair.

'Family matters,' Ernest said abruptly. 'If you don't mind.'

The fat fool looked bewildered and then finally understood. 'Yes. Yes of course,' he said getting to his feet. 'I'm, ah . . .' and he left the room.

I was taken aback by the way Ernest had dismissed Clerval. I studied my young brother. He was growing up fast. He had the fair, light-boned looks of our mother, but he had a way of drawing down his brows and setting his mouth in a line that was all Alphonse Frankenstein. I could see that when the time came Ernest would step into my father's shoes.

The trial of Justine Moritz was a foregone conclusion. The court-room was crowded, with all the Frankensteins in attendance. Outrage had been committed on one of Geneva's élite families. Someone had to pay. The girl's confession was all the evidence that the High Asses of the Geneva Bench required. She was a Roman Catholic accused of a foul murder in the very heart of Calvinism. Even her looks weighed against her: she was small and lean, black-haired and dark-complexioned. Her French was strangely accented,

Mediterranean. She could have been the descendant of one of the Spanish soldiers who tried to scale the walls of Geneva in 1602.

But the young woman stood her ground. She was calm enough in the face of the barracking from the advocates. She agreed that she had been near the place where William's body was found but said that she had spent the previous day at the home of her aunt in Chene, a few miles from Geneva. When she tried to enter the city that evening she found the gates closed and so she was forced to spend the night in a barn not far from the city walls.

As to the miniature, she claimed to have found it lying on the floor in the house and slipped it into her pocket meaning to return it to William. At one point she held up her hands and asked the judges if they thought there was enough power in these slender fingers to crush the throat of a robust, healthy, six-year-old boy. I saw flickerings of doubt cross the faces on the bench. Justine had made a good point.

But not good enough. The verdict was announced next morning. Justine Moritz was guilty of the murder of William Frankenstein. The sentence was death. To be carried out the following day. It was the highest of high drama and it entranced Elisabeth. When she insisted on visiting the wretched girl in the city gaol ('I wanted us to pray together') Justine spat in her face.

Although I had the right to a place near the gallows, I did not attend the execution. Instead, I wandered out of the city and along the south bank of Lac Leman, almost as far as Bellerive before turning back. On the way back I stood on a rock and watched a big carp move sluggishly in the shallow water. Its back was covered in some kind of whitish mould or fungus. It looked as if it were dying.

I returned to the Cour Saint-Pierre a few hours after Justine met her end. I found my father brooding in his library and reeking of brandy. He barely acknowledged me as I settled into a chair opposite him.

'Your mother never wanted that girl, you know,' he said suddenly. 'She did not trust her. The girl was a papist and your mother never trusted a papist. Especially a French papist. She thought that the little papist would teach William her papist ways. That's what your mother thought. By God, I wish I had listened.'

Then he lapsed into a morose silence. 'But I wouldn't listen,' he said after a while. 'Not me. Not Alphonse Frankenstein. I laughed at her. And I insisted – insisted, mind you – on taking that papist bitch into this house. And do you know why I did that? Because your mother didn't want her. That's why. That's why my son William is dead. Because I wanted to annoy your mother. What do you think of that, Victor Frankenstein?'

INGOLSTADT, BAVARIA: 1800

I courted Erika Waldman for another year. Three weeks before the Golemites graduated I finally seduced her. It was a miserable business, carried out in an oak wood near the village of Finkel. Frankly I was not up to it. The flesh was weak and the spirit was not nearly willing enough. Even the handsome body that I had spent three years longing for could not fill me with ardour. Long months of cramming and overwork had left me drained and mentally exhausted. I found that I could not pretend a passion I did not feel.

After a few minutes of half-hearted pushing and shoving we broke apart. As we separated I glimpsed blood on her thighs. My erection collapsed and she pulled her skirts down and then lay staring up into the branches of a big oak. Then she closed her eyes, clasped her hands together and muttered a prayer. I could see that she felt insulted, misused. Her precious gift had been grubbily handled. I shared her wretchedness.

But to this day I am not sure which of us was manipulating the other. Was I the user or the used? To Erika our few minutes of fornication under the oak trees of Finkel were decisive. From the moment I entered her she and I were betrothed. My pleasure was my commitment. There was no going back. Marriage was only a matter of time.

My conquest of Erika was a trap of my own making. I had used her affections to insinuate my way into her father's confidence, house and workshops and there was now no way out. If she accused me of debauching her I would never set foot in the Waldman house again. Her father had enough power to have me run out of Ingolstadt. And with some well-placed letters he could ruin my reputation as a scientist. I had to marry Erika. I had no alternative.

But when, shortly before I was due to graduate, I did what I thought was the right thing and asked Waldman's permission to marry his daughter, he was far from pleased. In fact he was positively grudging.

'Are you the man to make her happy, Victor?' he asked me. 'Have you asked yourself that? We both know that she does not have a tenth of your mind. Nor does she share your interest in this world of ours. Will you be able to accept her, ah, religious enthusiasms when she is a middle-aged lady? With a string of children – my grandchildren – at her knee?'

His questions took me aback. I had no idea how to answer or what he wanted to hear. 'All I can say is that I'll do my best, sir. I'm not sure any man can say more.'

He shook his head. 'I like you, Victor. You know that. You're an able young man and have the makings of a good scientist. Maybe even a great one. But I cannot deny that I have my misgivings about you.'

'Sir?' I was puzzled.

'Erika is my daughter,' he said. 'I love her in ways you'll never understand unless you have a daughter of your own. She's a motherless girl without a woman to talk to. I fear for her happiness when I'm dead. She'll have this house, money and little else. She needs a husband, yes. But she needs the right husband.'

'Then you are refusing us permission to marry?' I challenged.

He looked at me and sighed. 'No. Not that. That would break her heart. I can see how she feels about you. But I must insist on a decent period of betrothal. To give her – and you – time to consider her future. I will insist on that.'

I agreed. A period of betrothal – the longer the better – suited me as much as it suited Waldman. But later that evening when I told Schutzi that I was to be Waldman's son-in-law he looked at me oddly and said 'Poor girl'. He refused to tell me what he meant and declined to offer his congratulations.

The Ingolstadt Golemites graduated one bright day in June in the year 1800. We were the last graduates Ingolstadt would see. The Bavarian authorities had decided that the university was to be closed and its inhabitants, books and apparatus moved forty miles east where they would be swallowed up by the University of Landshut. Waldman decided that he was too old and comfortable to move, and decided to retire. Krempe opted to go back to Saxony.

That night Schutzi, Saracino, von Grafenberg and myself caroused with our favourite whores and drank quantities of the best wine that Madame Hortense had to offer. The revelry was slightly marred when a drunken young officer from the garrison declared that Ingolstadt was 'well rid of the college scum' which earned him a bloody nose and a swollen lip from Von Grafenberg's fist. Only Schutzi's good-natured diplomacy and a couple of bottles of good French wine prevented a potentially fatal duel.

A few days later we went our separate ways, swearing to keep in touch with one another and doubting we ever would. I was staying on in Ingolstadt to work with

Waldman. Saracino was going south to Bologna to study with his uncle, the renowned Giovanni Aldini. Von Grafenberg was bound for Vienna and a commission in the army of the Emperor Joseph. Last to leave was Schutzi, who was making his way northeast, back to commerce among the Jews of Prague.

Just before he mounted the coach, the big Jew took my hand and fixed me with his level gaze. 'Let me tell you something that you already know, Franko,' he said. 'You were always the best of us. Now let me tell you something you don't know. You scare me, you really do. You always have done. But it's been good knowing you.'

I was startled. It was not the farewell I had expected. But before I could say anything Schutzi was inside the coach and it was pulling away across the cobbles. Then he stuck his head out of the window and yelled back to me. 'Franko! Remember the Golem. Remember the Golem . . .'

APPRENTICE

INGOLSTADT, BAVARIA: 1800

My apprenticeship as an electrician began when I persuaded Waldman to open Ingolstadt's first electrical clinic. He took much persuading. The idea of using his electrical instruments for the benefit of the Citizens of Ingolstadt had never occurred to him. He knew that electrical clinics thrived elsewhere in Europe but it never seemed to have entered his head that Ingolstadt should have one. His nursery of toys were for his pleasure alone. And for the occasional bright student, like myself, to whom he took a fancy.

But I judged the time to be right. With the removal of the university, the younger men had moved too, and the professors of the old regime were scattered to various corners of Bavaria and Franconia. Waldman was now a fish out of water. He badly needed something to do. Writing letters to his circle of correspondents would not be enough. An electrical clinic was an obvious enterprise. Or so it seemed to me.

I used Erika's piety to advance my argument. It was an obvious strategy. Such a clinic was God's will, I told her. He had been generous with His gifts to Waldman and myself. It was our responsibility to see that they were not squandered. They must be used in the service of His faithful people. Especially the poor, the lame and the halt.

My apparent concern for the humble Catholics of Ingolstadt delighted her. It was one of the many things for which she had prayed. She saw it as a first stage in my gradual conversion to the true faith. Part of the slow retreat from the malign wizardry of Jean Calvin. She lived in the pious hope that I would one day join her in the confessional of the Moritzkirche.

And she loved the idea of using her father's mysterious, dangerous-looking devices to relieve misery. There was even, I hinted, the possibility of 'miracles'. She was beguiled. Here was piety in action. This was Christ's work in the whirring of the machines. It would be a kind of scientific laying on of hands. We would be a little order of scientific friars, and she would be our handmaiden. Her daily prayers to Maria Viktoria at the Asamkirche would be our connection to heaven. To her the logic was irresistible.

'Victor is so right, father,' she told Waldman over the dinner table. 'You must see that. You've spent all these years gathering such great knowledge. No one has more. Now the time has come to use that store of knowledge for the good of God's people. And it is a task that only you – and Victor – can do. Please father, tell me you will consider it?'

'I'd always thought I was of some use where I was,' he said drily. 'That some good came of all these years at the University of Ingolstadt.'

'Of course it did father,' she said. 'Every student you have ever taught remembers you with affection. Well, most of them anyway. But those days are over. The University of Ingolstadt is no more. You must accept that. And move on to other things.'

'As you say, those days are over. But I'm not sure I want to move on to what you call "other things",' Waldman told her. 'Perhaps I'm too old for the other things you have in mind.'

'That's nonsense, father,' she replied. 'You're not yet sixty. You have years of useful work ahead of you. And working with Victor will keep you young.'

He looked at me with an odd expression. 'I'm not so sure about that,' he said. 'Sometimes I suspect that your Victor is older than I will ever be.'

'What a curious thing to say, father,' Erika said, vaguely hurt. 'About poor Victor.'

I smiled bravely, unoffended.

'It's the wine,' he said, patting her hand. 'Ignore me. I'm beginning to ramble.' He turned to me. 'Would it work, Victor? Truthfully?'

'Yes, sir,' I said sincerely. 'I honestly think it would work.'

'How?' he asked.

I launched into my plan. 'We charge decent fees from those who can afford it, which is most people, but we charge the poor nothing. Or next to nothing. The affluent help pay for the needy. The rich feel good and the poor get treated.'

'I see,' he said.

'We do house calls using the smaller machines,' I went on. 'But at a price. Let us say twice what we charge for treatment on the premises. If we become fashionable – and I'm sure we will – there will be a big demand for our skills. We might have to train an assistant or two.'

'I'm not sure I wish to be fashionable,' he said sourly.

'Popular, then,' I replied with a slight trace of impatience. 'Useful. Indispensable. Important. Whatever word you prefer.'

'You've thought it through, haven't you?' he asked.

'Of course,' I said. 'Or I wouldn't have suggested it in the first place.'

'Do we have the equipment?'

'Yes we do. Or at least you do. There's far more equipment in your laboratory than we'd ever need in a clinic. One or two of the machines would be sufficient.'

'One or two?' he said dubiously. 'Are you sure about that?'

'Well, maybe three or four. But no more. Then all we have to do is rent a set of rooms somewhere in the town. Preferably in the centre. And fix our plate to the wall.'

'Waldman & Frankenstein,' he said sardonically. 'Medical Electricians to the Quality of Bavaria.'

But I had a sly thought. 'Why not the St Moritz Clinic?' I suggested. 'After Ingolstadt's own saint. And in the shadow of his own church.'

Erika could of course hardly resist this. 'Oh yes,' she said, her eyes gleaming with satisfaction. 'Oh yes. Father, that would be wonderful . . .'

Waldman gave me a bleak smile. 'Nicely done, Victor,' he said. 'Nicely done.'

'Yes Victor,' Erika agreed. 'It's a wonderful name.'

'And what we learn,' I said, baiting another hook, 'we pass on to your correspondents around Europe. They know you for a scholar. Now let them see you as a practical man of science.'

'You're a persuasive young man, Victor,' he said. 'But I've never seen myself as a practical man of science.'

'Then you should, sir,' I said bluntly. 'What use is learning if it cannot be applied? And think of what we would learn. There would be ailments of every kind, queuing up at our door, waiting to be treated, explored. People that the physicians and surgeons have failed . . .'

'All flocking to the St Moritz Clinic to be relieved of their suffering,' said Erika, taking up the refrain. 'They'd come from all over Bavaria. Oh father, we must do it. We must!'

So we did. Within two days of our dinner-table conversation Waldman's lawyers had located, and rented, four handsome rooms in the Hieronymous-Strasse. They were perfect. And to Erika's delight they were within a hundred yards of the Moritzkirche, in which she spent hours every day praying for the saint himself to intercede on behalf of our venture. She prayed until her knees were so stiff she could hardly walk.

Within two weeks the rooms on the Hieronymous-Strasse had been cleaned, scrubbed, repainted and rendered as spotless as the Holy Virgin. Within four weeks some of the best of Waldman's electrical machines had been transported (very gingerly) across the Ludwigstrasse and installed in the new premises. And within five weeks the St Moritz Clinic was treating its first patient.

Her name was Kirsten, the twelve-year-old daughter of a prosperous farmer from the village of Dunzlau. She had fallen awkwardly from a hay-wagon and lost the power of her legs. She had been poked, prodded, bled, cupped, leeched and manipulated until she was exhausted. Every physician in Ingolstadt had examined her and none had anything to offer other than advice on invalid-chairs. Waldman and I examined her carefully, could see no damage to the legs, and concluded (or at least guessed) that Kirsten's problem lay somewhere in her spine.

We lay her face down on a table and while her mother bared the child's back I charged one of our larger Leyden jars. When I completed the arc between the bottom of her spine and the back of her right knee the girl's body jerked violently in a series of spasms. She whimpered loudly and complained of a blow like a hammer to her right leg, followed by severe tingling and a sensation of heat. Encouraged, we repeated the process with the left leg, with the same results. Then we sent her home, and told her to come back the next day for more.

Kirsten was a stroke of luck. She was a robust child and her treatment was a success. After five days of shocks to the spine and legs she was able to stand without support. After eight days she could walk gingerly around the room. And after three weeks of daily bolts (bravely borne, but decreasing steadily in power) she seemed to be almost fully recovered. She did, however, walk with a slight limp in her right leg. When we finally dismissed Kirsten her father's eyes were brimming with tears and her mother covered my hands in kisses.

I thought then, and I still think, that Kirsten's treatment was one part skill and nine parts luck. By sheer good fortune I had applied the right amount of electricity to the right part of the child's spine. Whatever spinal twist or blockage had locked Kirsten's legs, it had been a minor one and easily cleared by the electrical current. But so far as Kirsten and her family were concerned, we had succeeded when all else had failed. It had been a miracle. Erika, of course, put it down to the intercession of Moritz and redoubled her prayers.

Whoever did it – Erika's god, me or Kirsten herself – the name of the St Moritz Clinic was made. The waiting room began to fill with sick and injured people, many of whom medical men of Ingolstadt had given up on. We were presented with a huge variety of ailments and complaints. We made no promises. We made it plain to all our patients that the treatment might not work. That had to be understood. What worked for some might not work for others. We were medical electricians, not miracle workers.

The St Moritz Clinic was doing very well when the world broke in on us. The century was less than a year old when a

French army swept into Bavaria to settle accounts with the Austrians. And as the Elector of Bavaria was an ally of the Emperor of Austria, Bavaria was at war. The Bavarian army, which had undone most of von Rumford's sensible reforms, was about to be pitted against the revolutionary zeal of the French.

I learnt the news from one of my patients. He was a young grenadier from the Neuschloss garrison who had been almost deafened by an accidental blast from a carbine. We were trying to restore his hearing. He had to cut short his treatment and pay his bill. The troops of the Ingolstadt garrison were moving out the next day. They were marching east to join the Austrians to destroy once and for all the French invaders.

I watched Ingolstadt's two fusilier battalions march out of the town through the Danube Tor with banners snapping, drums beating and trumpets blaring. They made an impressive sight in their cornflower-blue coats, gleaming brass buttons and high leather 'Raupenhelms'. From a distance, the marching fusiliers looked like story-book giants. Rank after rank of shiny monsters, towering over the excited crowds. They certainly impressed their compatriots. But would they impress the French?

What concerned me most was their helmets. They were a triumph of pomp over sense. The light, practical 'Rumford Kasket' with its horse-hair tail had been scrapped as unmilitary. In its place, a heavy, high affair topped with a thick crest of lambskin was hung about with brass crests, chinstraps, bands and hinges. The thing was ludicrous. There was enough room inside the average Raupenhelm to carry a week's rations. Officers topped theirs with a huge cockade of feathers.

Most of the helmets wobbled as their wearers tramped through the streets. The Raupenhelm's centre of gravity was so high that it was a miracle that it stayed on at all. If it was this clumsy to march in, what would the Raupenhelm be like to fight under? And just how good were the farm boys, counting-house clerks, brick-layers, carpenters and goat-herds who marched beneath them?

Not very good, it seemed. A few weeks later the pride of Ingolstadt came straggling back into the town having been routed by the French near the village of Hohenlinden near Munich. The battle took place in driving snow. General Jean-Victor Moreau's ragged Frenchmen out-thought and out-manoeuvred the Imperial troops, then ground them to pieces. The butcher's bill was considerable. The Archduke John of Austria lost more than 20,000 men, 12,000 of them as prisoners. It was a miserable day for the Empire.

The Bavarian army was in shock. The blow to its pride was fearsome. Grief hung over the Paradenplatz like a cloud. The strut went out of the Neuschloss bluecoats. Young officers confined themselves to their barracks. The contempt of civilians galled them and their sympathy was even worse. Business slumped at Madame Hortense's whorehouse. The most popular whores were always available. The injured and maimed made their way back to the farmyards and village workshops from where they had come.

The casualties of Hohenlinden seemed to be everywhere. More and more beggars appeared on the streets. There were empty sleeves and empty trouser-legs at every street corner. The poor-boxes of the town's churches were stretched to their limits. Crippled young men hung about doorways. Some were missing eyes, hands and feet. Others had faces that were a mass of scar tissue. One handsome young man trundled back and forth along the Ludwigstrasse on a wooden trolley, having lost both legs at the hip. A few

124

wandered the streets muttering to themselves, unharmed but unhinged

And amputees began to appear in the St Moritz Clinic. Most were seeking relief from pain and misery in arms and legs that were no longer there. It was an extraordinary and baffling phenomenon: real agony from phantom limbs. All the trouble of an ailing leg or arm without any of the advantages. Endless grief from body parts that had been left in the fields of Hohenlinden.

Meanwhile the Elector Maximilian Joseph (whose 'MJ' adorned the bizarre Raupenhelm) decided to throw his hand in with the French. Having been mauled at Hohenlinden, Maximilian Joseph had no wish to repeat the experience. From now on the enemies of France were the enemies of Bavaria. And vice versa.

INGOLSTADT, BAVARIA: 1801

In the same year that ended with Jean-Victor Moreau chasing the Bavarians and Austrians around the woods of Hohenlinden, Alessandro Volta published the results of experiments that were to become famous. At one stroke the practice of the electrical arts was pitched into the new century. And all our beautiful instruments, with their hardwood frames, intricate winding-gear, glass globes and carefully ground glass discs were suddenly and hopelessly out of date. They were fit only for the old Rathaus, along with Gustav's Horse.

'This really does change everything,' Waldman told me after muttering his way through a long letter he had received from one of his correspondents in England.

He handed me the letter to read. Alessandro Volta had transformed the trade. The electricians of Europe had been given a new tool. The Voltaic pile. They now had the means to provide themselves with a continuous supply of electricity. To be tapped, like Bordeaux wine from an oak barrel.

Volta had experimented with alternative metals and

126

different ways of using them to produce electricity. And what he came up with was a 'pile' of metal discs, placed one on top of the other, each pair separated by a disc of moistened paper or card. When an arc was completed between the top and bottom of the pile, electricity was the result. The bigger the pile, the more electricity.

And, what was most important, the current of electricity from the pile was continuous. Volta's pile provided a steady supply of electricity. It did not, as the Leyden jar did, discharge everything in one bolt of power, and then have to be recharged. The pile recharged itself. It could be used repeatedly.

Waldman and I went into a frenzy of experimentation. Within two weeks we had put together our first Voltaic piles of different sizes. They were straightforward copies of the device described by Volta. And they worked, exactly as Volta said they would. We experimented with different combinations of metal – lead, iron, tin, copper, graphite, even gold – but found that zinc and silver gave the best results.

As Volta had described, the greater the number of pairs, the more electricity. It was simple. A pile of sixty discs appeared to give twice as much electricity as a pile of thirty discs. I had no idea what the limits were. But I found that a hundred pieces of silver and zinc, each three inches in diameter, divided by acid-soaked card and arranged in a column, could deliver a prodigious bolt of electricity. And could do so time after time after time.

So the St Moritz Clinic's collection of electrical machines and Leyden jars fell into disuse. Most of them were removed to Waldman's laboratory in the Ludwigstrasse where they gathered dust. They were replaced by an array of Voltaic piles of varying sizes and power. Anything under twenty pairs we judged to be virtually useless; anything over 120 pairs appeared downright dangerous.

These silent columns of electrical power seemed to alarm our patients more than the noisiest of our old machines. Maybe it was because the power seemed to come from nowhere. Most of our pious Bavarians clients crossed themselves before they were plugged into the pile. 'St Moritz's fire' as Erika described the process one awestruck moment.

Alessandro Volta became the man of the moment, fêted wherever he went. In 1801 he set out on a triumphal tour of Europe that took in Geneva where he demonstrated his experiments at the home of my Uncle Ben's friend Senebier. Volta's progress culminated in three lectures delivered to the *Institut* in Paris. Napoleon Bonaparte himself attended all of them. Clearly, it seemed to me, the First Consul could see that electricity was the way into the future. It was another revolution, as radical as the one that had shaken France. Great electricians like Volta were its tribunes. Their skills would transform Europe. I imagined that the Corsican artilleryman, whose instinct for power was profound, could see that, that he wished to have the electricians' skills and place them at the disposal of revolutionary France.

INGOLSTADT, BAVARIA: 1802

My old student friend Giovanni Saracino arrived in Ingolstadt one wet November night with an extraordinary tale to
tell. 'The most extraordinary *thing* I've ever seen,' he told me,
his freckled face flushed with wine and excitement. 'Amaz-
ing, it was. I mean, the man had been dead for more than an
hour, for God's sake. Decapitated. His head axed off his
shoulders. Neat as you like. He was as dead as you can be!'

'Dead as Gustav's Horse?' I asked, reviving the ancient
joke.

'Deader,' he said with a grin. 'And yet there it was, his
head I mean, not Gustav's Horse. Sitting on the table, its eyes
opening and shutting, pulling faces, like some kind of clown.
The tongue going in and out like an idiot's. The mouth and
lips twisting and moving. As if the poor chap was trying to
say something.'

'Wonder what he was trying to say?' I mused.

'Help! probably. But it was the action of the eyes that was
the strangest thing. The eyelids were blinking rapidly.
What's the word – fluttering. Then Aldini yanked out the

tongue and made an arc between it and the left ear. A bucketful of saliva dribbled down into the beard. The thing was slobbering. Dead but dribbling.'

'And how did the audience take all this?' I asked.

'Just how you'd expect. Most were crossing themselves like maniacs, and calling down Christ and all his saints and angels. One fool vomited down the back of the man in front of him, which started a fist fight. And some of the rest were shouting "blasphemy", or were running out of the door. Utter chaos.'

I had never seen Saracino quite so agitated. Normally he was the most placid of men. But as he sat in my rooms recounting what he had seen in Bologna that January he grew increasingly more excited. This had happened eight months ago but his recollection of it was vivid. What he had seen was a series of experiments performed by his mentor Giovanni Aldini on the headless bodies of two criminals brought directly from the Bologna scaffold.

Saracino had banged on the door of the St Moritz Clinic demanding to see the 'so-called Dr Frankenstein'. I was delighted to see him. After giving him a quick tour of the clinic, which seemed to impress him, I took him back to my rooms where we ate copiously and then attacked my supply of Bavarian wine. The more he drank, the more vivid his account of the Aldini experiments became.

'Know what Aldini did then?' he said. 'He took both the severed heads, and put them on the table, about two or three feet apart. But they were linked by a big puddle of body fluids – blood, spinal fluid, mucus, saliva. Then he made an arc from the right ear of one head to the left ear of the other.'

'What kind of machine did he use?' I asked.

'No machine,' he said. 'It was a pile of silver in a tall glass jar.'

'What size?'

130

'I don't remember. I have it in my notes somewhere. I think it was a hundred pieces. Something like that. Oh, and the ears on the heads were moistened with salt water. That seems to make a difference.'

'Then what?'

'Jesus, Franko, you should have seen it. The faces that these poor buggers pulled. The eyes shot open, the mouths twisted, the tongues slobbered, the eyebrows went up through the hairline, the cheeks twitched. Some of the expressions they pulled were incredible.'

'Both of them?'

'Both of them,' he replied.

'It was like some kind of face-pulling competition for severed heads. One bright spark in the audience started laughing hysterically. And then he fainted. Aldini tried to explain what was going on, but I suspect few of them took it in. They were all too startled.'

'I'm not surprised,' I said. 'I'd have been rather taken aback myself. So, what happened after he'd finished terrorising the burghers of Bologna?'

'He took one of the heads, the younger one, sliced the top off the cranium, cut through the arachnoid membrane and the *dura mater* to the ... what's it called?'

'The *pia mater*?' I suggested.

'That's it. The *pia mater*. Then he created an arc from the ear into the brain.'

'And?'

'Same thing. The head pulled more faces than a clown at the *commedia*. This time the tongue came out and stayed out. The eyes opened and stayed open. I remember that its ears waggled.'

'And after that?'

'After that', Saracino said 'he went to work on the trunks. Which, I must remind you, hadn't a head between them.'

Saracino went on to describe the rest of Aldini's labours on the decapitated corpses of Bologna. It seemed that every time he created an arc between one part of the dead body and another something happened. When he made the connection between the muscles of the arm and the exposed spine, the forearm lifted. When he connected the spine to the fingers of the left hand, the hand rose and the fingers clutched at air. When he completed the arc from the bicep of the arm to the spine, the hand extended and the arm rose some seven-and-a-half inches. Under the influence of the current the headless man was even able to lift things, first a coin and then a pair of heavy iron pincers.

'But Aldini couldn't do anything with the heart though,' Saracino said. 'He tried hard. He opened the thorax on one of the bodies to expose it, and made an arc on the pericardium. Nothing happened. Tried about six times, but there was nothing.'

'How long had they been dead?'

'By then – oh, about one-and-a-half, maybe two hours.'

'And there was nothing at all?'

'Not a flicker,' Saracino said. 'Although he thought it was just possible that something was going on deep inside the heart. Maybe there was. But there was nothing that he could see.'

'But it's a thought, isn't it?' I said. 'Starting a heart that's been stopped.'

'Yes it is,' he said.

'Was Aldini pleased with the results?'

'I suppose so,' Saracino said. 'Although he seemed rather melancholy later. He's rather soft-hearted. At the end of the performance he announced to the audience – or what remained of it – that it was "grievously painful" to a philosopher like himself that his work depended on healthy men falling under the sword of justice.'

132

'So why doesn't he use corpses that have died through illness?' I asked.

'He's tried that,' Saracino said. 'He's been in and out of the hospital in Bologna, trying his box of tricks on all kinds of cadavers. Folk who've died of putrid fevers, pleurisy, typhoid, even scurvy. But he swears that they're useless. He says the illness that killed them also killed their "animal electricity" – or whatever it is that responds to the power of the pile.'

'The power of the pile,' I said. 'I like that.'

'That's what he calls it. He suspects that the power will only work on healthy corpses.'

'Healthy corpses?' I laughed.

'That's right. Healthy corpses. And the younger the better.'

'I suppose that makes sense,' I said. 'So he haunts the scaffolds?'

Saracino agreed. 'He sits beneath them catching the heads as they roll. He knows every executioner south of the Alps. But, Franko, the word is beginning to get around. People are interested in the work. They're beginning to see the possibilities. Now he's been invited to show the English, of all people, how it's done.'

'To introduce them to the power of the pile.'

'He's on his way to London,' Saracino said, 'where I'm supposed to meet up with him. Everything's been arranged for the beginning of January.'

'Good for you,' I said.

'So, Franko. Will you come? To lend a hand and to see if the electrified corpses of England dance as high as the corpses of Bologna?'

I hardly hesitated. It was too good an opportunity to miss. Waldman could look after the clinic on the Hieronymous-Strasse for a few weeks. Erika could do without me for a while. It would give her a chance to do some serious praying. The opportunity to observe Aldini's experiments and to see something of medical London was too good to miss.

'Try keeping me away,' I told Saracino.

'Good man,' he said, and raised his glass. 'So here's to a successful jaunt to England.'

'And to the corpses of London,' I added. 'May they learn to appreciate the power of the pile.'

LONDON, ENGLAND: DECEMBER 1802

To say that London took me aback would be a serious understatement. London stunned me. London was vast. Beside London, Geneva was a lakeside village and Munich was a country market-place. All the little French towns we had passed through on the way were nothing but hamlets. Compared to London the port of Rotterdam was a collection of fishermens' hovels and a couple of harbour walls. London was a world of its own. It was an urban labyrinth, punctuated by church spires and reeking chimneys. A universe of brick, smoke, iron.

By the time our coach reached the approaches to London Bridge, the street was jammed with humanity and every kind of vehicle imaginable. We picked our way through them: manure carts, stage-coaches, fishmongers barrows, three-horsed wagons, timber vans, gilt-painted open carriages, old-fashioned sedan chairs, a few ancient wains creaking under mounds of hay.

One horse had foundered in its shafts and was refusing to rise. Its driver was being cursed noisily by the drivers behind him. A raddled old woman in silver finery stepped out of a sedan chair and started picking her way across the mud, aided by a black boy in a silver turban. A company of shabby, red-coated infantrymen led by a fat young officer on horseback plodded its way south. They were being jeered by a knot of ragged women.

A light, chill drizzle was washing across the city. It was the middle of the afternoon and already dark. The road was a quagmire; there were puddles everywhere and foul-smelling steam drifted across the street. There was smoke.

'Jesus Christ, Franko,' Saracino said, his face livid against the darkness. 'Have you ever seen anything like this? What a place. Do they ever see the sun? This is Babylon itself. With rain. And smoke.'

'And that, I suppose, is the ziggurat,' I said, pointing to a huge church in pale stone topped by a green-coloured dome.

'Maybe not,' he replied with a laugh, 'but it's damn near as big as Saint Peter's itself. That must be St Paul's. That'll be worth having a look inside.'

'If you say so,' I said. 'All I want to see is the inside of a decent tavern. Which, by the look of the ragged bastards around here, might be pretty hard to find.'

But I was wrong. Our coachman directed us to a narrow street just off the City Road where we found a quiet hostelry called the Eagle and Lamb. We were welcomed by an amiable, lard-barrel of a woman who introduced herself as Mrs Flaskett, and who promptly served up a hot meal, decent wine, warm rooms and clean beds. Fed and watered, I went to sleep thinking that England was not quite the damp and smoky hell it had seemed from London Bridge.

Next morning, after breakfasting on mutton, bread, beer and coffee, Saracino and I went our separate ways. We agreed to meet back at the Eagle and Lamb for supper. He set out for a hospital called St Thomas's where he had

136

arranged to meet Aldini. I set out to try to locate the various electrical dispensaries with which one of Waldman's correspondents claimed London was peppered. One of the best of them, he wrote, was the establishment run by one Francis Lowndes, of St Paul's Churchyard.

I had no trouble finding the dispensary, or Lowndes himself. He proved to be a small, cheerful, middle-aged man with a merry blue eye. Lowndes was only too happy to show a fellow electrician around his clinic. I liked it. The place was spotless, the servants looked cheerful and clean and his machinery was well built and well tended.

And Lowndes had an encyclopaedic knowledge of the medical electricians of Britain. 'Electricians!' he said. 'I tell you Mr Frankenstein, there's electricians in every corner of the land. The infirmary at Edinburgh's been driving electric machines for the last fifty years. Now you'll find 'em in Leeds, Middlesex, and at Bartholemew's and Thomas's here in London. These days a man can hardly spit in the street without hitting an electrician.'

When I asked him to recommend another London clinic to visit he smiled. 'If you're a serious man,' he said to me, 'then I suppose you'd better talk to Bemrose at the London Electrical Dispensary. It's in the City Road, and it's easy to find. I wish you well of him. He's a withered stick, is Henry Bemrose. But he seems to know his job.'

Lowndes's description of Henry Bemrose was apt. The resident electrician at the London Electrical Dispensary was indeed a withered stick. He was a long individual with a thin voice that seemed to issue from his long nose. Apart from his linen he was dressed entirely in black which, he assured me, was the only apparel for a man of medicine. He agreed, with great reluctance, to show me around his clinic only because I had come to pay tribute to the superiority of England over the rest of Europe.

137

As we made our way slowly around the rooms and corridors, Bemrose gave me some facts. In the five years in which it had been open the dispensary had treated 3,274 patients of whom 1,491 were adjudged cured, and 1,232 relieved. The dispensary cost more than £150 a year to run, and was operated as a Christian charity under a strict set of rules.

'And what kind of ailments do you find that you are asked to treat most often?' I asked.

'Almost everything with which the human frame is afflicted,' he said sonorously. 'Violent headaches. Stomach cramps. Encroaching blindness. Inflammation of the liver. Jaundice. Irritation of the bladder . . .'

'Very impressive,' I said, trying to cut him short.

'Melancholia. Flatulence. Paralysis,' he continued relentlessly. 'Loss of memory. Obstruction of the gall ducts. Diarrhoea. Even dreams and nightmares. We have had some notable successes, Mr . . ., eh, ah, yes. Some notable successes.'

The truth of which I doubted when he revealed the dispensary's equipment. There was nothing that Waldman and I did not have at the Saint Moritz Clinic. Much of Bemrose's machinery was old-fashioned, and some of it looked badly maintained. There was not a pile amongst it. And the library, which he assured me was one of the finest in Europe, was about one tenth of the size of Felix Waldman's.

When I told him that I had come to London to witness Aldini's experiments and was interested in the life-saving properties of electricity, he held up his hand and told me that he had the very papers for me. He rummaged along a high shelf and handed me a grubby pamphlet. It was entitled *An Essay on the Recovery of the Apparently Dead* by a physician called Charles Kite.

138

'I'm surprised you haven't heard of Dr Kite's work Mr eh . . .'

'Frankenstein.'

'Mr Frankenstein. It's very well known. In England anyway. But then England is, well, England. In fact, if I recall, and my memory is very good, it won the Royal Humane Society's silver medal. For the year 1789.'

'1788,' I said, glancing at the cover.

'Ah yes. 1788. I stand corrected.'

'May I borrow it?' I asked.

'No,' he said firmly. 'But you may *buy* it. For five shillings. The Dispensary has another copy'

I fished in my coat pocket, located some coins and handed him the five shillings. 'Is this Dr Kite still alive?' I asked.

He looked at me with some surprise. 'Well if he *is* alive, I'm sure that you will find him in the town of Gravesend, in the county of Kent. It's quite near to London. You can take a ferry.'

I shook his hand, told him that my name was Frankenstein, spelled it out, and thanked him for the favour he had done me by showing me round the London Electrical Dispensary. I also expressed my abiding gratitude for the Kite pamphlet and left him puzzled and no doubt disdainful of the ignorance of foreigners. As I walked back down through the chaos of the City Road in the direction of the Eagle and Lamb I noticed that the original price of the pamphlet was two shillings and sixpence.

But Bemrose had done me a favour. As I sat at a table in the Eagle with a bottle of Mrs Flaskett's wine at my elbow, I read the pamphlet with mounting excitement. Kite deserved his silver medal. Here was a brilliant account of his work as a surgeon in the riverside town of Gravesend (Grave's End . . .?) and concentrated on his efforts to revive unfortunates who had apparently died of drowning, strangulation and lightning strike.

So far as Kite was concerned, nothing was more efficacious in resurrecting the dead than electricity. Why not, he wrote, 'have recourse to the most potent stimulus in nature, which can instantly pervade the inmost recesses of the animal frame? Why not immediately apply electrical shocks to the brain and heart, the grand sources of motion and sensation, the *primus vivens* and *ultimum moriens* of the animal machine?'

By the time Saracino returned to the Eagle and Lamb I had made up my mind to search out Charles Kite, surgeon of Gravesend. The fact that Aldini's experiments had been postponed until a suitably young and healthy criminal was due for execution was a help. Kite's pamphlet had pitched me into a state of some excitement.

GRAVESEND, ENGLAND: 1802

Surgeon Charles Kite of Gravesend, winner of the Royal Humane Society's silver medal for the year 1788 and author of the renowned work *On the Recovery of the Apparently Dead*, proved to be something of a surprise. I located him in the grounds of the New Tavern fort in Gravesend, tricked out in the uniform of a major of the Gravesend Company of Volunteer Artillery. He was sitting on a weary-looking old horse, watching his part-time gunners drill to the music of a little band of trumpeters and drummers. I waited until the display of martial prowess was over, and then introduced myself.

'Frankenstein,' he said quizzically, staring down at me from his nag. 'From Geneva, eh? I've never met a man from Geneva before. French and Germans aplenty. Dutchmen too, of course. Even the odd Russian and Swede. But never a man from Geneva. Well, well. And what can I do for a man from Geneva?'

Medical matters, I told him. I explained that I helped to run an electrical clinic in Bavaria, and that I was in London to visit English electrical establishments. I had been given a copy of his 1788 pamphlet which had impressed me and I wanted to discuss the contents with him. He listened to me with surprise stamped on his broad face. He was flattered by my attentions, but dubious.

'I think you've had a wasted journey Mr Frankenstein,' he said bluntly. 'I wrote that paper nigh on fifteen years ago. I'm not sure I can even remember what's in it.' He waved a hand around him. 'And as you can see, I've had other things on my mind since then. Mainly the damned French.'

'But you're still a working surgeon?' I said, anxiously.

'Oh, aye,' he laughed. 'Still sawing bits off the good folk of Kent, and being paid for *their* pains. And still trying to breathe the spark of life into some of the bodies that come floating down the Thames. Which, I reckon, is what you want to talk to me about. Am I right? You'd like to know when is a dead 'un not a dead 'un?'

'Yes,' I said. 'That's right.'

'And how can a dead 'un be turned back into a live 'un?' I nodded.

'Well, they're questions I'm always happy to discuss Mr Frankenstein,' he said cheerfully. 'So why don't you and I take a walk back to the Kite household and discuss 'em over a leg of mutton and a glass or two of wine?'

'You're very kind,' I said. 'Thank you.'

'But first', he said 'let me show a man from Geneva just how the men of Kent plan to beat off the Frenchies. Not some kind of spy are you? We're not at war with Geneva are we?'

I told him that I did not think so, but who could tell these days.

'Oh well, if you are we can always shoot you. If I can ever get one of those bone-headed lightermen to load a musket properly. Which I doubt.'

142

Kite then took me on a tour of the ramparts, ditches, blockhouses and magazines of the New Tavern fort. It was nothing much compared to Geneva and Ingolstadt, but he assured me it was a key to the defence of London. Even my unskilled eye could see that it was not built to withstand a siege army, but to fend off marauding warships.

The fort's fifteen cannon were trained north and east, out across the river, and had overlapping fields of fire with the guns of the Tilbury fort on the north bank. Kite told me that the warship was not built that could run the gauntlet of fire which the two forts could lay down. Especially from the white-hot cannonball heated in the forts' shot furnaces.

'Not that we've ever been used in anger,' Kite told me as we watched the lights from the river-craft swarm over the water like fireflies. 'The only thing we've ever done is help put down a mutiny on a Dutch East India prize ship, and that was five years ago. Nasty business. Organised by a damned Scotsman called Wallace. Can't stand the Scotch, myself. Treacherous dogs, every one of them. My lads were called out to man their guns. Just in case some grapeshot was needed.'

'And was it?' I asked.

He shook his head. 'No. The business was put down by the militia. A few musketballs and it was all over. But the wretched Wallace shot himself in the head rather than take his punishment like a man. So we gave him a traitor's reward. What was left of him was hauled on a sledge through the streets and then buried without a coffin. With his head to the east and a wooden stake driven between his thighs. If it had been left to me, I'd have thrown him in the river and let the crabs and eels have him. The Scotch dog.'

Kite's distaste for the Scotch seemed as strong as his dislike of the French. But his mood lifted as we made our way through the streets of Gravesend to his modest

143

establishment, and he began to regale me with the medical opportunities of a riverside practice.

It was Gravesend that made me realise how much the ocean meant to the English. Compared to the traffic on the River Thames the Lac Leman barques on which I had spent my summers as a boy were lake-top playthings. Huge, ocean-going transports and warships stood like wooden cliffs off Gravesend, either waiting for the tide or to pick up passengers or pilots. Every ship was surrounded by a pack of what Kite described as 'bumboats', small craft that ran supplies out to the ocean-bound ships, and removed refuse.

Lumbering among the ships were barges loaded with timber, coal, grain, clay or building stone. Excise cutters flitted from ship to ship, checking cargo manifests and sniffing out contraband. Dozens of skiffs, bank-to-bank ferryboats and fishing boats dodged around the shipping, like terriers among carthorses. A brace of longboats stuffed with red-coated soldiers made their way across to the fort at Tilbury. Gravesend was home to more vessels than I ever knew existed.

The whole maritime swarm reeked of money. This was trading on a scale worthy of the name: nation to nation, colony to mother country, continent to continent. It was a huge commercial engine, lubricated with rivers of cash. It was a sight that Alphonse Frankenstein of Geneva, trading man to the bone, would have relished. And I felt an odd pang of sadness that he had never seen what I was seeing now.

'Never any shortage of dead 'uns in Gravesend,' Kite told me as we made our way through the town. 'Half the lightermen, bargees and fishermen on the river put out from the quay as drunk as lords. They're forever running into one another or falling overboard. Then there are the self-

murderers. Bankrupt merchants and lovestruck girls, usually. Drowning their sorrows along with themselves. There's
always somebody for a Gravesend surgeon to practise his
arts on.'

Kite lived in a clapboard house at the top of the High
Street in which his wife laid out a hot and generous dinner.
By the time Kite turned to the business of reviving the dead
he was more than a little drunk. He rose to his feet,
staggering slightly, left the room and returned carrying a
large mahogany box on top of which lay an odd-looking
device. It consisted of a flexible leather tube, about twelve
inches long, at the end of which was an ivory mouthpiece. At
the other end was a narrow tube, also made of ivory.

'Kite's Resurrector I call this,' he said, handing it to me to
examine. 'Saved a few souls with it in my time, even if I do
say so myself. Devised it myself, too, and had it specially
made. By a man who's now a battery sergeant in the
Gravesend Volunteer Artillery. He's a cobbler by trade, but a
wizard with his fingers. He can make anything.'

'How does it work?' I asked.

'Simple,' he told me. 'When a dead 'un is hauled out of the
water I fish the muck out of his nose and mouth and stick the
narrow tube up one of his nostrils. Then I pinch the other
one, and blow like a mad trumpeter down through the
mouthpiece. The idea – or at least the hope – is to inflate the
lungs, and get them moving again. Blow them up like a
child's balloon. Sometimes it works. Sometimes it doesn't.'

'Sounds like exhausting work,' I said.

'It is,' Kite agreed. 'And if there are two or three of you in
attendance, as we doctors say, it's best to take turns. One
man's breath is as good as another's. At least it is to a
drowned man. But look closely at the mouthpiece. See how it
narrows?'

I studied the device closely and nodded.

'Well that's to accommodate the nozzle of an ordinary fireside bellows. Which, I've found, can do the trick just as well. I've spent many an hour kneeling in the mud, pumping away like a kitchenmaid with the end of this stuck up some poor chap's nose.'

Then he slowly opened the mahogany box. 'And this', he said with some pride, 'is Kite's Electrical Resurrector. I charge it up every morning with a little Cruikshank machine I have in my study. Just in case I need it sometime during the day. Handsome, isn't it?'

Kite's Electrical Resurrector was a Leyden jar, about eight inches high and four inches in diameter, from which led two metal wires. The wires were attached to a pair of brass rods with spherical ends. Both the brass rods were sealed into hardwood carrying handles.

'Explains itself, doesn't it,' he said. 'Open the dead 'un's shirt and stick the rods on him. Give a him jolt of Kite's home-made lightning and watch him jump. They always *do* jump, you know. And with a bit of luck – or at least with a lot of luck – his old heart and lungs will start their pumping and thumping.'

'Either side of the chest?' I asked.

He frowned and shook his head. 'No. I've found it better to put one rod on the left side of the chest and the other on the diaphragm. Don't know why. Seems to be the part most readily excited. Nearest the heart I suppose. Something like that.'

'Could be,' I agreed.

'Trouble with it is', he said, 'you can only invoke the lightning once. And the Cruikshank generator is too heavy and awkward to haul around the mud. I'd need a horse and cart to take it with me. And anyway the wetness of everything seems to get in the way. The jar never charges properly out on the river.'

146

'Have you tried using a pile?' I asked him.

He looked at me blankly. 'I can see I'm out of touch. It's this damned war and the damned French. What's a pile?'

I gave him a swift, lesson in the principles of the Voltaic pile and sketched on a piece of paper the kind of tall glass container normally used to contain it. I suggested he try the classic pile of silver and zinc separated with cardboard discs soaked in salt water.

'And it works?' he asked, dubiously.

'It works,' I said. 'The charge is not as powerful as the one you'd get from a big Leyden jar. But, as I said, it's a steady source. You could give shock after shock to one of your, ah, dead 'uns, and still have electricity left in your bottle. If the first one doesn't work, give him another. Then another. And so on.'

Kite looked at me thoughtfully, and then at the gleaming mahogany and brass of Kite's Electrical Resurrector. 'Well, my knowledgeable young friend from Geneva,' he said slowly. 'If what you say is true – and I do not doubt you for one second – then the Leyden jar and the electrical machine will shortly be things of the past. Nothing but pieces fit for a museum.'

'Probably,' I agreed.

'Just like me,' he said wryly, recharging both our glasses and raising his in a toast. 'In that case. Here's to Signor, what was his name . . .?'

'Volta.'

'Here's to Signor Volta and his electrical piles. May their lightning never go out and their thunder always crackle. May they lighten our darkness, lengthen our lives and cause ruin and havoc to our enemies. Especially the French, may the Good Lord damn their eyes.'

After which the evening grew steadily more bibulous and philosophical. The room was warm and the wine was good.

By the time we were three-quarters of the way down our sixth bottle of Bordeaux we were very drunk indeed. Kite was face down on the table and trying to talk out of the side of his mouth. Then he suddenly sat up straight, almost toppled out of his seat and regained his position with what little dignity he could muster.

'I've had a thought,' he said slowly. 'At least I think I've had a thought.'

'That's good,' I said.

'Want to know what the thought I think I've had, is, Dr Frankenstein?'

'Tell me your thought, Surgeon Kite,' I managed to reply.

'There's ... somebody ... else ... inside ... us,' he said with great deliberation. 'That's my thought. There's a creature in here', and he banged his chest, 'that lives on lightning. And if we want to keep him alive, we've got to feed him lightning. From machines. Or Leyden jars. Or Signor Volta's piles.'

Kite was rambling, I knew that. He was spouting what Schutzi used to call the 'Wisdom of the bottle too many'. But his thought had placed a thought in my head. As I half listened to the drunken Englishman, an image slowly formed in my mind's eye. I saw a strange, shimmering, irridescent creature. He was a being so beautiful that the idea of him almost stopped my heart. A complete man – but made entirely of light.

The Man of Light took shape in the drunk, middle-aged man in front of me. He hovered somewhere between skin and bone. He was made up of an infinite number of webs which intermeshed with a complexity that my mind couldn't grasp. The Man of Light flickered and danced in the chambers of the heart and the tissues of the liver. He lit up the reeking caverns of the stomach and the windswept reaches of the lungs. He was at his most dazzling in the

148

convolutions of the brain. There wasn't a crack or cranny of the body that The Man of Light did not illuminate. He was everywhere.

And I knew that he was life itself. He was the substance of lightning. He was the stuff of the stars. He was the spark of life. And he could only be touched and healed by electricity. Kite's drunken insight was essentially correct. The Man of Light fed on lightning.

LONDON, ENGLAND: 1803

'Damned wolves,' Saracino muttered as we shoved and elbowed our way through the huge mob crowded around the gallows outside Newgate Gaol. 'Look at them! Listen to them! Wolves, that's all they are. Makes you despair. There's nothing they enjoy more than seeing some wretch meeting his end. At the end of a rope. Under an axe. It's all the same. It's the same everywhere you go in this miserable world.'

For my part, I just felt excited. The prospect of seeing what lessons the great Aldini could tease out of the body of a recently killed man filled me with anticipation. Nor did I share Saracino's contempt for the crowd around the gallows. Death was an all-absorbing subject. Everyone viewed it with awe. And the mob had only one question in its collective mind: what will it be like when my turn comes?

By the time we had battered our way through the mob to reach the gates of the gaol my friend was in a foul mood. Which was not abated by the reluctance of the gatekeeper to let us through, despite our written permissions. After ten minutes of wheedling, noisy argument and threats of higher authority, the turnkey accepted our documents and directed us to the Governor's quarters where Aldini and the medical élites of London were gathering.

The great man was not as I had expected. Rather than a dust-dry old party with the vivacity of Gustav's Horse, the man who detached himself from the circle of physicians and came towards us with a broad grin on his face looked more like a Corsican brigand than a medical man. He was a raffish-looking figure of no more than forty, dressed in an elegant bottle-green coat and breeches. Thick black curls framed his sallow face and spilled over his collar. Shrewd, dark eyes looked out from under heavy brows. When Saracino introduced me Aldini stuck out his hand, and greeted me in excellent English.

'Happy to make your acquaintance Signor Frankenstein,' he said. 'The ginger rascal here has told me something about you. And about your so-called studies at Ingolstadt. Sounds really disgusting. I wish I'd been there.'

'How do you do, sir,' I said politely.

'You're something of an electrician I believe? Well, I think we can promise you some entertainment here today. I hope so anyway. But before we electricians and philosophers can get down to business, the magistrates have still to finish what they have begun.'

'And throw the meat to the wolves at the gate,' Saracino muttered.

Aldini gave him a friendly slap on the shoulder. 'Cheer up, ginger,' he said briskly. 'Truth is everything. We're here to observe and record. A tender conscience is a fine thing but it's a serious flaw in a man of science. Is that not so Signor Frankenstein?'

'So I have been told,' I replied.

'Well you have been told correctly,' Aldini said, his exuberance undiminished. 'Anyway. I've been down to the condemned cell and run an eye over today's specimen. His name's Foster, he's about twenty-six years old and he's a big, healthy brute, about six feet high. I'd say he weighs about 160 pounds, or thereabouts.'

'So what will we need?' Saracino asked.

'A fair-sized pile,' Aldini replied. 'Let's say zinc and copper. And let's start with forty plates of each. That should do what we want it to do. If it doesn't, well we can step it up to sixty.'

There was a loud, baying sound from the crowd outside the gate, at which Saracino visibly paled. The wolf pack were in full throat. They were closing on the gallows. And they were about to be shown red meat. Aldini looked at his watch.

'Sounds as if the proceedings are about to start,' he said. 'So we'd better make haste. I don't want any delays. We'll get more out of fresh beef than spoiled. Frankenstein, how would you like to contribute to the advancement of science by assisting my assistant? If you see what I mean?'

'I would be honoured,' I said.

'Good man. Right then. You'll find all the equipment in the prison infirmary.'

It took Saracino and me fifteen minutes to assemble the apparatus Aldini needed. My friend was plainly an expert and I watched him with admiration. Generations of Bologna clockmakers showed in his deft fingers. I carefully counted the pieces of metal and card and handed them to him while he inserted them into their glass containers. The sequence of zinc and copper was crucial. One disc in the wrong place and the pile would fail.

We made three separate piles: one of forty plates of zinc and copper, another of sixty plates of the same materials and a third of eighty pieces of zinc and silver. The last was my idea. Saracino and I worked in silence, while the crowd at the gate rumbled and howled, sang psalms and yelled abuse as a succession of felons met Death at the end of the hangman's rope. It was a noisy business, but there were always a few minutes of silence just before someone was turned off. No doubt it was to give the wretch a chance to say a few last words.

When the roaring came to an end, the infirmary began to fill up with Aldini's audience. Ten minutes later the naked body of the late Foster was carted into the room on a litter, and laid out on the table beside the electrical apparatus. He was, indeed, a big healthy looking brute. At least, six foot with wide shoulders and heavily muscled arms and legs and broad, powerful hands.

But the hangman had done his work well. The big head lolled like a puppet's and the tongue protruded from a darkened face. His eyes, bright blue, were half opened. Two minutes after Foster made his appearance Aldini came into the room wearing a long white apron.

Aldini was a showman, a ringmaster in charge of the clowns. As I watched him bow to the audience and launch into his preliminaries I was reminded of Saussure's Electrical Circus. And of that wet January afternoon so many years ago when Uncle Ben and I had enthralled the Neckers and their guests at the Château Coppet with our electrical tricks. I saw again Germaine's solemn face lit by the flickering sparks from my body.

Aldini's performance was impressive. After some hesitation he opted for the forty-plate, zinc-and-copper pile. Then he began by making an arc from Foster's mouth to his left ear. The effect was startling. The dead man's jaw started to quiver. Then it twitched. And the muscles of his face began to convulse furiously. After a few seconds the dead left eye popped open. As he stared sightlessly at the ceiling the audience gasped. Aldini looked pleased.

153

The Man of Light was beginning to respond to Aldini's ministrations. The Italian then made an arc between the two ears, at which the convulsions of the face were so strong that the head began to move on the table. It looked as if the hanged man was waking from a short sleep. Aldini's electrical pile was prodding him into some kind of life.

The third arc produced the most startling effect. One electrode was attached to Foster's ear and the other inserted into his rectum. When the arc was completed the corpse started to thrash. The muscles of the neck, torso and legs writhed and heaved. The body began to move on the table. Even the penis began to stiffen. Somewhere in Foster's dying tissues the Man of Light was still alive, still flickering.

The audience were enthralled. Some of them were open-mouthed. Aldini had them in the palm of his hand. 'As you can see gentlemen,' he said, 'the action of just this modest Galvanic pile can produce remarkable effects. Even on a man as thoroughly dead as our fine specimen here. This, I would contend, is due to the animal electricity in the body – as described by my uncle, the late Luigi Galvani.'

After which, the experiment became bloody. While Saracino and I held down the body, Aldini sawed through the sternum and opened the thorax with a loud crack to expose the dead heart. There was blood all over the floor. I saw the Governor of Newgate – who was sitting in the front row of the audience – staring with distaste.

The work on the heart proved to be an anticlimax. Aldini had plainly hoped to get it beating, even for a few seconds. But repeated arcing produced little result. The bigger, sixty-plate pile did persuade the right auricle to contract briefly, but that was all. The ventricles remained inert. The heart was as dead as the beef on a butcher's slab. The Man of Light had fled its interlocking chambers. He had faded, gone. The hangman's work was done, at last.

Aldini was disappointed. The dead Foster had let him down. But his audience were rapt. They had witnessed medical history in the making. They had been shown a hint of something beyond their comprehension. While the Newgate servants removed the ruined corpse of Joseph Foster to his unmarked grave, the medical men crowded round Aldini to shake his hand and bombard him with questions.

Why had one eye opened and not the other? Could the brain still see? When the mouth had moved why had no sound been uttered? Did the working of the fingers signify anything? Could the electricity work on the vocal cords? What were the prospects for restoring the circulation? Had electricity ever been successful in restarting the human heart? How effective was it on the lungs? Was there a time-limit beyond which revival was impossible?

One physician suggested that a combination of electricity and oxygen gas might be more effective than electricity on its own. Another asked Aldini if he had considered the morality of resurrecting a fellow of whom the Lord had disposed? His question sparked off a debate that rattled round the room for half an hour. Then the audience trooped out into the street, still arguing over the day's events.

That night, in my narrow bed at the Eagle and Lamb I dreamed again of my mother. She was lying, naked and dead, on the table of an anatomy room, somewhere in Geneva, somewhere in London, somewhere in Ingolstadt. Her body was young, firm-breasted, beautiful. There was an audience, but none of the faces were familiar. Giovanni Aldini, but someone who was not Aldini, was about to cut open her chest to reveal her heart. I stood beside him holding a box full of instruments.

When he drove the blade of his big cutting knife between her breasts her body arched violently, her grey eyes opened

155

and she screamed my name. But the voice that boomed out of her open mouth was that of my father, Alphonse Frankenstein.

INGOLSTADT, BAVARIA: 1804

Germaine's occasional letters gave me a glimpse of great events. They were tales from a changing world. They both exhilarated and depressed me. While I laboured assiduously among the Voltaic piles of the St Moritz Clinic, she waltzed around Paris. I assembled my little columns of metal, cardboard and acid to try to spark new life into the burghers of Ingolstadt while she debated with the finest minds in Europe. I tinkered in safety while she was in danger. I envied her, lived vicariously through her and despised myself for doing it.

And there was always a whiff of sensuality in her letters. Some hint of the bedroom. Whispers from the pillows of Paris. Echoes of sexual manoeuvrings and manipulations. Just enough of it to conjure up those fleshy arms, that plump bosom, those level, dark eyes.

At the end of 1803 Germaine fell foul of Bonaparte. 'In what passes as his wisdom,' she wrote 'the First Consul has banned me from Paris. I have been expelled. I am not to set foot within forty leagues of the city where I have my home. Can you believe such a thing?'

I shared her indignation, but was also relieved. Banishment to the Château Coppet did not sound so bad. Given the record of the French over the past fifteen years and the notorious touchiness of Napoleon, she had done well to escape. She might have spent years in gaol on some contrived treason charge, or have been separated from her clever head by Doctor Guillotine's clever machine.

But Coppet did not hold her for long. Her next letter was to inform me that she had decided to learn more of the countries of German-speaking Europe which, she assured me, were 'the lands of the future'. Along with her 'companion', Benjamin Constant, and her two sons (now aged three and five), she was off to Weimar and Berlin 'to see what there is to see and to meet whoever will deign to meet a poor widow from Geneva'.

Of course, literary Germany welcomed her with open arms. In Saxe-Weimar-Eisenach she met – and apparently dazzled – Schiller and Goethe. 'Schiller was most kind to me,' she wrote. 'And it seems that Goethe is working on his own version of the Faust legend and has been since the year 1775. An intriguing tale. About the scholar who sold his soul to Satan in exchange for worldly happiness and worldly knowledge? I presume you know the story, Victor?'

I know more than that, Germaine, I muttered as I read the letter. Georg Faust, the historical wandering scholar about whom the legend grew, once taught in Ingolstadt. And the Faust myth owes even more to the alchemical work of the great Paracelsus.

Germaine's noisy grand tour of Germany continued into 1804. Everywhere she went she added to her wake of admirers. She ploughed through German society like a ship of the line in full sail. Her opinionated talk and outrageous gossip left the élites of the German-speaking world breathless.

It was Jacques Necker who interrupted Germaine's progress by keeling over and dying one March afternoon in the Château Coppet. Germaine was distraught. For some reason she worshipped the old money-shuffler to the point of idolatry. She rushed home to Geneva from Vienna, entombed the old banker in some style and launched herself into writing, printing and publishing an elegy entitled *On the Character and Private Life of Monsieur Necker*. It was awful. Her grief had addled her judgement.

But she recovered. 'I'm off to Italy now,' she informed me at the end of 1804. 'Partly out of curiosity, and partly to forget the loss of my dear Papa. A group of us will be travelling together – von Humboldt, Schlegel, my faithful Bonstetten and, of course, Benjamin. As fine a party of minds as Europe has to offer, you must confess.'

And every one of them panting to get under your skirts, I thought sourly. Perhaps they had come to some reasonable accommodation: she would be available to Schlegel on Mondays, to Bonstetten on Wednesdays, to von Humboldt on Fridays leaving Sundays to Benjamin Constant. Which would be a fine end to her week, and leave her Tuesdays, Thursdays and Saturdays for any amount of sexual sightseeing.

The idea of the intelligentsia of Europe availing themselves of Germaine in the Italian sunshine while I laboured in Ingolstadt rankled. I became irritable and distracted with jealousy. There were days I could hardly work for the thought of Germaine whimpering with pleasure under some Prussian.

I needed to vent my jealousy and spite. This I did with the Paradenplatz whores, by demanding sexual refinements that startled them. Eventually Madame Hortense took me aside and warned me that the girls were complaining and that unless I moderated my appetites I would no longer be welcome. So I apologised profusely to Madame Hortense and showered the whorehouse with the best fruit, sweetmeats and pastries that Ingolstadt had to offer. The whores were charmed and my apology was accepted. But they remained nervous of me for some time.

INGOLSTADT, BAVARIA: 1804

St Moritz was an odd name for the clinic. The saint himself was an Egyptian from the city of Thebes, a fourth-century Roman soldier, a Christian convert and commander of the Theban Legion serving in what is now France. I imagined him as a slightly built, dark-skinned man with a thin beard and moustache and bright dark eyes. Moritz's troubles began when the Roman Emperor Maximian Herculeus ordered his troops to perform pagan rites. Moritz and his legion refused. They were Christians, faithful to the cult of the long dead, crucified Jew.

Maximian could not countenance such an affront. His legion commanders were instructed to make Moritz and his Thebans obey. The Egyptian was warned that unless his men bent the knee the Theban Legion would be decimated. Moritz refused and ten per cent of the men were duly butchered. But still the stubborn Egyptians disobeyed. So the irascible Emperor Maximian ordered that the entire legion be put to death.

For months I could never see the name-plate on the door

of the clinic in the Hieronymous-Strasse without imagining the killing. The Egyptians, disarmed, hands tied behind their backs, on their knees in some damp meadow in the middle of France. Behind them, pale-eyed German or British auxiliaries, their short swords sharpened for the day's work. Beyond them a ring of cavalry bristling with spears. One last chance was offered. Moritz shook his head. The killing went ahead.

The logistics of such a mass execution intrigued me. There would have been around 6,000 men in the Theban Legion. They would have been some of the best soldiers on earth: trained, battle-hardened fighters. What kind of force was needed to disarm, and then kill, that number of men? Another legion of 6,000? Two? And would it be done with stabbing swords, cavalry spears or arrows?

And did the Egyptians submit quietly to their fate? When the end came, did they struggle and thrash? Or did they kneel silently in the rain, dreaming of Thebes, the rocky, sun-baked city on the Nile. Was Moritz the first to go? Or was he the last? Last, I decided. He would have been forced to watch the butchery of his men before being butchered himself.

'Mere folk tale and fable,' according to Waldman. 'Over-heated medieval imaginings. Catholicism at its worst. Recreating, no, inventing, history to serve its own ends. I have investigated the story and there's not an iota of historical fact in the whole business. But don't tell Erika I said so.'

But the air of piety that the name gave to the clinic appealed to the Catholics of Ingolstadt. St Moritz laid his blessing on our work. And once the doctors of Ingolstadt got over their distaste for the idea of medical electricity – although some of them never did – they began referring cases to us. When conventional medicine failed, people were pointed in the direction of the St Moritz Clinic.

Erika compiled lists of the most deserving cases, and prayed for their health in the Moritzkirche. She told me she could usually get through about fifteen or twenty cases a day, which was a better work rate than Waldman and I managed. I am sure she felt that her supplications did as much good for the patients of the St Moritz Clinic as the Voltaic piles. And perhaps she was right.

But we did have our successes. I calculated that almost half the people we treated either found some relief or were partly or wholly cured. And the limitations of the treatment gradually became apparent. Tumours, ulcers, gangrene and open sores were immune to the stimulus of the Voltaic pile. But palsy, dyspnoea, some eyesight problems, paralysis, deafness, rheumatism and melancholia did seem to be susceptible to our electrical treatment. We failed often. But we succeeded enough to take encouragement from the work.

I kept careful notes of all our cases and I did my best for everybody, but some cases interested me more than others. One of the most intriguing was the blind boy from Eichstatt, a village a few miles northwest of Ingolstadt. He was a scrawny, eight year old called Jurgen, one of five children that a harassed young widow was rearing in poverty. According to his mother, Jurgen had developed a fever one Saturday evening and emerged from it on the Tuesday morning with his pupils hugely dilated and his eyesight gone. He was completely blind. And all the widow's prayers to the Blessed Virgin had done nothing to restore his sight.

Waldman and I were almost as much in the dark as poor Jurgen. We examined the boy with care and discussed him at length. The case seemed impossible. Jurgen's dilated pupils were merely black holes in his face; he was beset with a darkness so thick that no light could penetrate. Erika took the boy's grubby face in her hands, gazed at him for a long moment and then announced that she would say special (that is lengthy) prayers to the saint.

While Erika left for the Moritzkirche to pray, her father and I considered the way ahead. Neither of us knew much of the anatomy of the human eye. But we did know that the mechanism was delicate, and that a child's eye was almost certainly doubly delicate. Too much electricity, we reasoned, could blast its way through Jurgen's eyes like a charge of gunpowder and case-shot. Too little, and poor Jurgen would remain in the dark.

Recalling that Aldini had used a Voltaic pile of forty discs on the strapping, albeit dead, Foster I argued that we should try a twenty-five-disc pile on Jurgen.

'Not enough,' Waldman said. 'Let's make it thirty-five.'

'Too much,' I said. 'Too risky. Let's try thirty.'

He nodded. 'Thirty it is.'

We laid the whimpering boy on the table, fastened one electrode to his ankle and the other to his temple. When the arc was completed the boy's body arched violently and he screamed loudly. His mother broke down in tears. Ignoring their distress we repeated the treatment. By the end of the session Jurgen was sobbing piteously and as sightless as ever. His mother was trembling with distress. As neither of them were in any shape to make the journey back to Eichstatt, Waldman insisted that they stay overnight at his house in the Ludwigstrasse. The woman was awestruck. She had never experienced such luxury. She kissed his hand, and then mine.

Next morning Jurgen could see something. He thought it was the window. He told his mother it was dull grey and window shaped. When we examined his eyes we found a suggestion of light grey around the iris. After feeding Jurgen a formidable breakfast we made him spend the rest of the morning in bed, and then treated him once more in the afternoon. Again we gave him four shocks from a thirty-disc pile. Again he arched and squealed. Again he was packed off to bed.

And again his sight improved a little. The window was clearer, less grey. He thought he could see something white. He seemed to sense when I passed my hand between his eyes and the light of the sun. And the light grey of the iris seemed to be expanding. Once again Jurgen was led down to the Saint Moritz Clinic, given four shocks from the thirty-disc pile and sent back to bed.

On the fourth day we reduced the charge to a twenty-five-disc pile with much the same results. Jurgen's sight continued to improve. By the fifth day he could distinguish colours. By the sixth day he could make out faces, by the seventh identify his mother. By the eighth day his eyesight was restored to an extent. It was far from perfect, but it was good enough for him. He refused to take any more shocks. Nothing that we or his mother could do would induce Jurgen back onto the table. He had had enough of electricity.

When Erika heard of our success with Jurgen she was ecstatic. It was a miracle! St Moritz himself must have interceded on Jurgen's behalf. No Voltaic pile or electrical machine could have worked such a wonder. It was proof of the power of prayer. She would redouble her efforts. The Egyptian soldier-saint would be solicited, night and day, to cure the Bavarians of Ingolstadt. Serves him right, I thought as I walked past the Moritzkirche on the way to my rooms. He should have obeyed orders in the first place. Or remained a pyramid worshipper or whatever it was Egyptians worshipped in the days of the Roman empire.

But paradoxically, our successful treatment of the Eichstatt blind boy unnerved me. We had cured him but *how* had we done it? The truth was that we had no idea. Neither Waldman nor I had any intuition as to what was going on

165

inside the boy's head. All we had done was wire him to a Voltaic pile and hope for the best. We were as much in the dark about what we were doing as Erika was on her knees in the Moritzkirche.

That night I ransacked my notes of the other cases we had treated. They were all the same. All these people coming to us with their various symptoms. We had no idea what we were doing to them. All we knew was that if we applied considerable amounts of electrical current to what seemed to be the appropriate parts of the body, sometimes something happened.

As I ploughed through my papers, it occurred to me that we could be curing them in the short-term and killing them in the long. In our ignorance, we might be condemning them to a life of pain and misery a few years – or even months – into the future. There was a dangerous disjunction here between cause and effect. We were experimenting. The anxious, trusting Bavarians in our waiting room were no more than the ants in Jean-Pierre Huber's specimen jars. Experimental material.

And Waldman shared my misgivings.

'I think what we're doing is right,' he said as we were tidying up after a day's business. 'Or I wouldn't be doing it. And all the evidence is that we're doing *some* good at least. Certainly the people we've treated seem to think so. Most of them anyway. But . . .'

'But, what?'

'But at the back of my mind I have this fear – this dread if you like – that we're going to do someone some terrible injury. A child perhaps. Or a pregnant woman.'

'What do you mean,' I asked.

He shrugged. 'I don't know. Blind a man whose eyesight is on the point of healing itself. Or make some wretched woman's palsy worse than it is.'

166

'It could happen, I suppose' I said.

'And if it does happen it will happen as a result of our ignorance. But then a philosopher would argue that more destruction was wrought by ignorance than was ever wrought by wickedness.'

'We need to know more' I told him. 'More chemistry. More electricity. More anatomy. Above all, more anatomy. I have to understand – or at least try to understand – how the whole organism works.'

'I'm not sure that we'll *ever* know that, Victor,' he said.

'Well as much as I *can* know,' I insisted. 'Otherwise I'm wasting my time. What I learned at the anatomy school in this town was nothing short of pitiful.'

'Not the best of Ingolstadt's faculties, I agree,' he replied.

'Scratching around on the same mummified corpses week after week,' I went on. 'With never a fresh cadaver to work on.'

'And I don't imagine that things have been improved as a result of moving to Landshut.'

'I shouldn't think so,' I said.

'But there is an alternative, you know. If it's corpses you want.'

'What's that?' I asked.

'Join an army.'

'An army? What army?'

'Any army. Armies are never short of corpses.'

SOLDIER

DONAUWORTH, BAVARIA: OCTOBER 1805

Just about the only thing that Schutzi ever told me about the Bavarian town of Ulm was that the burghers did good business in edible snails. It was in his words 'The mollusc metropolis of central Europe'. The Romish Church had declared that the beasts were 'neither flesh nor fowl' and could therefore be devoured on a Friday by the pious, with no danger to their immortal souls. To a Jew like Schutzi and a Calvinist like myself, this seemed like a typical, if in this case harmless, piece of Catholic lunacy.

A much more dangerous view of the city was conceived in the summer of 1805 by Lieutenant General Karl Mack, the Emperor of Austria's excitable Chief of Staff. For Mack there was more to Ulm than snails. It was, he pronounced, 'the Queen of the Danube, the bulwark of the Tyrol, and the key to half of Germany'. He who controlled Ulm, controlled the destiny of the Continent. So *Helix pomatia*, the gastropod of Ulm, was slithering about in the strategic heart of Europe.

Which is why, at the beginning of September 1805, Mack sent his army of whitecoats over the River Inn and across

Bavaria. Their orders were to secure the town of Ulm for God, the Emperor Francis and the Third Coalition. The Bavarian army did not fight. For one thing it was only about 12,000 strong. For another it was officered by panicky young aristocrats who hardly knew one end of a musket from another. While the Elector Maximilian had not decided whose side he was on. So the pride of Bavaria were marched north out of harm's way to idle in the valley of the Main, while Maximilian pretended to negotiate with the Austrians, all the time waiting to see what Napoleon would do.

He did not have long to wait. Mack and his men were no sooner ensconced in Ulm than the French crossed the Rhine. I never did find out whether Napoleon agreed with Mack that Ulm was the queen, bulwark, key, etc., but the Corsican did spot an Austrian army a long way from home, surrounded by a disgruntled population and completely cut off from its powerful Russian allies. So he pounced.

The Grande Armée came across the Rhine in six huge army corps. While Maréchal Murat's cavalry squadrons poured into the forests west of Ulm to posture in front of the Austrians and draw off their left flank, Lannes and Ney headed straight for Ulm. Meanwhile Davout, Soult and Marmony wheeled round to envelop Ulm from the east, leaving Bernadotte to secure Munich. Mack had theorised himself into a strategic trap.

On the maps which Waldman and I had pored over in his study, Napoleon's move would have looked eminently rational and straightforward. But on the ground it looked very different. As I rode slowly (and, I admit, nervously) up the Danube to offer my services to the Emperor Napoleon, trailing behind me a wall-eyed mule called Heinrich loaded with my clothes, books and instruments, I ran into the eastern edges of the French columns.

The French were moving across the Bavarian countryside

like clouds of blue-backed locusts. But locusts struggling in mud. The autumn rain had turned the roads into a quagmire, through which struggled a ragged armada of weary men, exhausted horses, broken transport carts, slow-moving ammunition carts and limbered cannon. Men were shitting in every ditch and pissing against every tree that had not been hacked down for firewood.

I amused myself with a quick calculation. Every one of the 140,000 men (French and Austrian) eating their way across Bavaria and Württemberg had a stomach capacity of around half a litre. Which meant that the military beast had a 78,000-litre stomach that had to be filled every day to keep its 280,000 legs moving. I never did calculate how many cubic litres of shit would be produced by a stomach that size. But the roads and ditches stank like sewers.

I was only about ten miles west of Ingolstadt when I was hauled up by three Hussars scouting for the French. Their exotic-looking, fur-trimmed uniforms were spattered with mud. All three had long hair tied in straggling plaits from their temples. Two of them sported heavily waxed moustaches which their younger companion had tried to emulate by painting his face with a burnt cork which the rain was washing away.

But there was nothing bogus about the short-barrelled cavalry carbine which he was pointing at me. He would have shot me there and then as an Austrian spy if his older colleagues had not knocked his carbine aside. They then rode me a few miles west to their divisional headquarters where I was bundled off my horse and hauled in front of a one-eyed staff officer who was sitting in the doorway of a ruined farmhouse.

With as much dignity as I could muster I explained that I was a French-speaking citizen from the Republic of Geneva who had been studying anatomy and medicine at the

173

University of Ingolstadt in Bavaria, and now wanted to offer my services as a surgeon to the French army. I showed him my letters of introduction from Professors Krempe and Waldman. I assured him I was an enthusiastic opponent of despots. He was unimpressed.

'I am indifferent to your personal politics, Monsieur,' he told me. 'And papers can be forged. Why should I believe what is written here? The names Waldman and Krempe mean nothing to me. I have never heard of the University of Ingolstadt. And even if you are telling the truth, why should you assume that the Grande Armée is in need of surgeons? Have you decided that the Emperor's arrangements are inadequate?'

But I refused to be intimidated. 'There are *never* enough doctors, Monsieur,' I replied. 'And while I do not expect any respect for what you call my personal politics, I do expect some respect for my professional skills. Now if *you* have decided that the Emperor has no need of them, then I would be obliged if you would allow me to return to Ingolstadt.'

He looked at me coldly, told me to wait and disappeared into the farmhouse leaving me in the charge of the three suspicious troopers. I began to panic. Did they really think I was a spy? Did my Genevan French sound like an Austrian accent? And if they searched my pack mule, what would they make of the Cuthbertson electric generator and the Voltaic piles? Signalling gear? Bomb-making equipment? I could feel the firing squad's musketballs penetrating my sternum as the one-eyed officer emerged from the building.

'Very well, Monsieur Frankenstein,' he said, handing me back my papers. 'You will report to Surgeon General Larrey who is with the Imperial Guard somewhere near the town of Donauworth. That is west of here, as I'm sure you know.'

He gave me a letter with a military seal. 'This is a safe conduct. It *should* see you safely through the French army.'

174

He smiled for the first time. 'If you are a spy, then you'll be shot. If not, then good luck.'

By the time I reached Donauworth I was wishing I had never set out. I was exhausted, soaked, totally discouraged and weary of being questioned by suspicious Frenchmen. They quizzed me on the Danube bridge, they quizzed me at the Kapell-Strasse, they quizzed me twice as I made my way up the Reichstrasse and stopped me yet again outside the mansion the Fugger family had built at the top of the town.

When I finally walked my horse and mule into the old invalid barracks which the Imperial Guard Ambulance had commandeered, I had decided that Napoleon and his cut-throats could go to hell. I wanted nothing more than my warm study in Ingolstadt and the comfort of my books and instruments. My horse, my mule and myself were on the point of collapse.

After another couple of hours kicking my heels I was marched into a house opposite the barracks by a soldier in a black felt shako, pale-blue uniform and hussar boots. I took him to be some kind of cavalryman like the young hussar who wanted to shoot me, but he was a mounted medical orderly from the Imperial Guard Ambulance.

At which point things began to improve. Dominique Jean Larrey, Surgeon General of the Imperial Guard, came to meet me with a friendly grin, shook my hand warmly, thanked me for coming, ushered me into a chair in front of his paper-littered table and poured me a stiff measure of brandy. He was just under the age of forty, a short, dark, powerfully built man with hands like shovels. His sallow-skinned face was framed with long black hair and dominated by alert dark eyes. He spoke softly and with a strong southern accent.

I had expected a brief interview and a few impersonal questions before being either accepted or turned away. But

Larrey questioned me in a friendly but meticulous manner for more than half an hour. After satisfying himself that my credentials were worthwhile and that I had some knowledge of anatomy and surgery, he questioned me about my interest in electricity. He had read something of Priestley, Galvani and Volta, and recalled hearing about the Abbé Nollet and the electrical clinics of London. But he doubted whether much would come of it. Electricity would prove to be yet another of medicine's blind alleys where the quacks, frauds and charlatans lurk.

I was stung. 'You're mistaken, sir. The day is coming when every hospital in Europe will have its electrical instruments. For all kinds of treatments. The practice of medicine will be *unthinkable* without them. The advantages are . . .'

Larrey held up a hand to stop my tirade. 'All right, Monsieur Frankenstein,' he said. 'You'll just have to make allowances for an old army sawbones. Someday you must demonstrate to me the, ah, effectiveness of your electrical appliances. But not today. Nor tomorrow I fear. We have soldiers to patch and mend as best we can. I can offer you the rank of assistant surgeon major – third class – with the Imperial Guard Ambulance. It is a junior position, but I think we can promise you some interesting times.'

Larrey then put me under the wing of assistant surgeon major Émile Pascaud, a hunchbacked little man from the Creuse Valley, with a rasping voice, a bent nose and large pale eyes that glowered out under beetling brows. Pascaud was so short that his sabre trailed behind him in the mud. He was forever tripping over it. He was abrupt, caustic, foul-mouthed and unflaggingly rude. He was also, I was to learn later, an adroit surgeon, a compassionate doctor and a loyal friend.

'Frankenstein, eh,' were his first words to me. 'What kind

of name is that? You're not some kind of sausage-eater are you? Can't stand the sausage-eaters myself.'

'Genevan,' I told him. 'French speaking.'

He spat in the mud. 'Genevan, eh. Not a breed I care for very much. Too mealy-mouthed. How's your German? Good I suppose.'

'Pretty good,' I said. 'I've been living in Bavaria for the past ten years.'

'Can't speak a word of it myself,' he said proudly. 'Can't even stand the sound of it. All that barking and bow-wowing. It's the language of dogs. Austrians, Prussians, Saxons, Bavarians . . . Swiss. They're all the same.'

'No they're not,' I retorted.

He shrugged. 'If you say so. But we'll be cutting into a few of the bastards any day now. So your German should come in handy. If only to tell them to stop screaming.'

After stabling my horse and mule in the baroque splendour of the Heiligenkreuzkirche Pascaud found me a billet – or at least a straw pallet on the floor – next to his in the Fugger house. It was not much, but it was the best a junior surgeon could expect.

Donauworth was teeming with French. Every public building and most of the houses had been commandeered by the Grande Armée. There were Frenchmen everywhere: snoring in the pews of the Marienkirche, farting in the Spital Kirche, playing cards in the Rathaus, squabbling in the Tanzhaus, and drying their linen and breeches in the Kappell-Strasse which had been solemnly dedicated to the Knights of the Teutonic Order. Whores were everywhere; every decent woman over the age of twelve stayed indoors.

Over a meagre supper in the Fugger house, Pascaud explained to me how Larrey's ambulance system worked. Each army corps (and the Imperial Guard) had its own ambulance consisting of 340 men, divided into three separate divisions. Each division was headed by a surgeon major. The rest of the medical staff consisted of two assistant surgeon majors, second class and twelve assistant surgeon majors, third class. So, Pascaud and I were at the bottom of the medical pecking order. But we were supported by a full complement of quartermasters, military policemen, medical orderlies and farriers.

After our meal Pascaud showed me over some of the flying ambulances parked among the tombstones of the Heiligenkreuzkirche. They were at the heart of Larrey's system. They were light, well-sprung, two-wheeled carriages, with leather hoods and doors at the rear. The floor of the vehicle slid out on rollers and was upholstered with a mattress and bolster covered in leather. The sides of the carriages had capacious pockets for water bottles, medical dressings, blankets, food, brandy.

The ambulance was designed for two patients but could take three if necessary. It was pulled by two horses, one of which was ridden by a mounted orderly. Pascaud assured me that Larrey's flying ambulances were far advanced of anything the sausage-eaters or the Russians could put into the field. 'And Christ knows what the English do with *their* wounded,' he said. 'Probably eat them.'

The interesting times Larrey promised began early next morning when he called an anatomy lesson for all the medical officers of the Imperial Guard Ambulance. There were about forty of us crowded into a room in the round tower of the Invalid barracks. I was awkward in my new uniform: a pale-blue affair with high black boots, a black bicorn hat and a leather belt from which dangled a cavalry sabre. I had never used a sword in my life and had no intention of starting now. But Larrey insisted we wore them.

Larrey walked into the room, followed by two orderlies carrying the naked corpse of a young man. The corpse was placed on the table in the middle of the room. I judged from the loll of the head that its neck had been broken. Larrey put on a rubber apron and spoke: 'I'm about to deliver the little sermon I give at the start of every campaign. For those of you who have heard it before I apologise.'

He held up a bone saw and a long knife with a curved blade. 'These instruments, gentleman, are the weapons with which you'll wage this war. Nothing – I repeat nothing – saves more lives on the battlefield than the speedy removal of badly damaged limbs. Fast, clean, efficient amputation. That's the art that every one of you has to cultivate. Or you'll be no use to me. Or to the Imperial Guard. Or to the Emperor.'

He then launched into one of the most impressive surgical lessons I have ever attended. With astonishing speed he removed the corpse's left leg about six inches above the knee and dropped it into a basket under the table. The whole operation took no more than ninety seconds. Then he showed us on the right leg just how he had done it: three round, deep cuts, a few swift strokes of his bone saw and the leg was off.

'Speed, gentlemen, speed. That's the secret. Get the limb off as fast as possible. Do it on the battlefield if you can. Do it while the soldier is still in shock. That way he'll feel next to nothing. Do it before infection makes the limb rigid. That way it's easier. Do it while his pulse is feeble and his blood pressure is low. That way he won't bleed to death. Or shouldn't, anyway.'

Then he demonstrated how a stump should be bandaged. 'Don't smother it,' he told us. 'Don't cut it off from God's good air. Let the wound breathe. Wrap it in a square of linen that's been perforated, and tie it above the cut. That lets the air in and the discharges out. Then get the poor bastard off the battlefield.'

179

After that, Larrey said, the wounded man should be encouraged to get up and about as soon as possible. 'Let him forage for his own food,' he said. 'Let him gather his own firewood. Let him walk back to France if he can. That's the way to get his muscles in shape and his blood moving. It might sound brutal. But there's no better way. Pitch him back into his life.'

Compound fractures, he told us, were best dealt with by amputation. But for simple fractures Larrey had his own system of splints. With a heavy mallet he broke the corpse's left forearm and then demonstrated how it should be set. The broken arm was first wrapped in heavy linen and stiffened all round with bundles of straw bound together with twine. Pressure points were protected with pads of cotton filled with oat chaff. Then the limb was bound again and the outer wrap stiffened with the white of egg. The end result looked extremely effective.

'Right gentlemen,' he said. 'Any questions?' There were none. Newcomers such as myself were too overawed by Larrey's expertise and the veterans had seen it before.

'Very well. As you may have heard, tomorrow we start campaigning in earnest. The Emperor has ordered the Imperial Guard towards the town of Ulm which has been occupied by the Austrian army. The Emperor intends to change that state of affairs. So I suspect we'll all be kept busy. Keep your knives and scalpels sharp.'

In one of the rare breaks in the rain, Pascaud and I climbed the wooded hill of the Schellenberg, northeast of Donauworth, to inspect the battlefield where the Bavarians and the French had been routed in 1704 by the British. As he limped his way up the slope, Pascaud told me about himself. The son of a poor innkeeper from a village called Lascelles Dunois on the River Creuse, he had been slicing the limbs off Napoleon's soldiers ever since the battle at Castiglione near

Mantua in 1796. His father was dead – killed by a Royalist murder gang in the 1790s – but his ancient mother still ran the little inn on the Creuse.

The view from the Schellenberg was startling. Pale shafts of sunlight spiked through the huge dark clouds illuminating the red roofs and white spires of Donauworth. But the sight did nothing to improve Pascaud's mood. This was where Frenchmen had been defeated by the British. Like many Frenchmen he nursed an almost primitive hatred of the islanders. They were the source of all France's woes. The Austrians and the Russians were simply dancing to England's tune. He glared out over the battlefield muttering to himself.

'This time they're not dealing with some Bourbon half-wit,' he announced. 'This time they have Napoleon Bonaparte to contend with. This time we'll have the balls off the bastards as soon as they set foot in Europe. Or as soon as we set foot in England, which is more likely.' This tirade seemed to improve the little man's mood.

But the rain soon drove us off the hill. On the way back down we stumbled across the site the locals called the Kalvarienberg, a tableau of three life-sized crucifixes, a slender Christ flanked by two muscular thieves. I was intrigued that while the Christ figure's hands had been nailed to the cross-bar, the arms of the two thieves were roped. One of them had pulled his forearm free and seemed to be gesturing at heaven. All the figures were beautifully crafted.

'Primitive, isn't it?' Pascaud said, staring up at the three figures. 'Bogeymen to frighten peasants. Painted Catholic monsters to terrify the simple minded.'

'I'm not sure it would work either,' I said.

'How do you mean?' he asked.

I nodded to the Christ figure. 'How heavy would a man

that size be? Hundred and fifty pounds? Hundred and sixty?'

'Something like that,' Pascaud agreed.

'That's too much weight to hang on two points of iron. The bones of the metacarpus are too light to take that kind of weight. The spikes would dislocate the small bones and tear through the interossens tissue and the palmar fascia . . .'

'And so the body wouldn't hang long enough to kill it,' Pascaud concluded.

'Exactly,' I said.

'You might be right,' he conceded. 'So what *did* they do?'

'Probably what they did to the other two. Roped them to the cross-bar to keep them up on the cross. Then drove nails through their feet to add to their misery. Or maybe put the spikes through the wrists or forearms. That would do the trick. The ulna and radius would handle the weight all right. There would be enough big bone there to hold the body in place.'

'I can see you're a man given to speculation, Frankenstein,' Pascaud said with a grin. 'Well, if you're interested enough you could always try nailing a dead man to a tree to see how long he stays up. There'll be no shortage of corpses where we're going.'

As we made our way back down the hill to the walls of Donauworth we heard rough laughter and screams from the undergrowth. French soldiers raping local women.

Pascaud shrugged. 'The joys of war.'

ULM, BAVARIA: OCTOBER 1805

An army on the move is almost as devastating as an army in battle. The French were expert foragers. They were resourceful and ruthless. They stripped the fields of oats, potatoes, turnips, cabbages and anything that had not yet been harvested. They ransacked chicken coops, emptied goat pens and piggeries, they milked cows until the animals' teats bled. They commandeered horses, mules, donkeys. They broke into houses and stole wine, blankets, clothing, cooking pots, furniture, even crockery. They stripped the thatch off roofs to build fires.

But our progress towards Augsburg was a lengthy and miserable business. Some of the lumbering supply waggons were very slow indeed. The procedure was for the infantry and the cavalry to walk single file at the edges of the road, allowing the centre of the road to be taken up by the limbered cannon, ammunition wagons, supply train, ambulances and coaches of the generals and marshalls. It was a system that broke down every few miles as wagons lost their wheels or horses panicked into the ditch, or the roads became so mired as to be impassible.

Time after time we were forced off the roads and found ourselves ploughing our way across sodden water meadows and flooded fields, plundering as we went. Every village and hamlet that lay in our path was systematically ransacked: Mertingeh, Wardendorf, Meitingen, Gersthofen, then all the villages around Augsburg itself. After a few days billeted in Augsburg's florid seventeenth-century Rathaus we were on the move again, this time in the direction of Ulm itself.

The weather did not improve. I found myself lurching westwards through the rain on a *fougon* – one of the slow-moving wagons that were stuffed with medical supplies – while my mare walked behind on a rein. My wall-eyed mule Heinrich had been pressed into the Emperor's service elsewhere. I never saw him again. My medical books and electrical instruments were carefully stowed away in boxes buried in the *fougon*. My new pearl-handled surgical instruments (a present from Felix Waldman) I kept in the leather portmanteau we all carried.

In this military chaos, Pascaud rode beside me expounding on military matters. Many of the Guard's doctors and surgeons had a passing interest in warfare, but Pascaud was an expert. He knew more about Napoleon's thinking than the General Staff. He enthused about Bonaparte's way of dividing his forces into large corps and allowing their commanders to use their initiative. He pointed out that Napoleon owed much to the Royalist general Gribeauval who had made French artillery the best in Europe. But the most important weapons of war, he insisted, were the 'Charleville' muskets of the infantry.

'Good gun,' was his opinion. 'Reliable and fairly accurate up to sixty yards. A good musketeer can get off three or four shots a minute, although it does need cooling off after fifty shots. When you see a man pissing down his musket, that's what he's doing.' The short cavalry carbines, however, were useless. 'Couldn't hit a horse while sitting on its back,' he said. 'Stick the muzzle in its ear and you'd *still* miss.' He could not understand Napoleon's distaste for the new rifles which the British were now using in Spain and Portugal to great effect.

Pascaud intrigued me. He was plainly an intelligent and educated man. But he was irredeemably foul-mouthed. His epithets for Napoleon were endless: that Short-Arsed Corsican Bastard; Tsar of all the Corsicas; the Midget with the Map; Mother Bonaparte's Brat; Boney the Belligerent. And so on.

For all that, he was ready to die for his leader. His brutal manners and foul mouth seemed to be a carapace within which he fought his way through life. Underneath it all he seemed a decent man. But he was a strange mixture of the medical and the military. He was a skilled doctor and a humane man who was besotted with Napoleon's killing machine.

Most of the time I had no idea what he was talking about. But his enthusiasms were infectious. He was proud of the Imperial Guard, although he cursed it endlessly. I quickly learned that the Guard was a kind of army within the army. They were Napoleon's 'favourite children'. There were about 6,000 of them in 1805, and they were surprisingly diverse.

There were the tall, moustachioed infantrymen of the Grenadiers à Pied with their high bearskin caps; the Grenadiers à Cheval, heavy cavalry who called themselves 'The Gods'; the fast lightly armed Chasseurs à Cheval, the best of whom formed Napoleon's personal bodyguard; the Artillerie Marine, sea-going soldiers who were to have manned the barges for the invasion of England; and the

Sapeurs, engineers who sapped and dug for the glory of the Emperor.

But none interested me as much as the Imperial Guard's Mamelukes, the squadron of Egyptian horsemen who had been brought back to France after Napoleon's unsuccessful campaign on the Nile. They were an extraordinary sight. Their officers wore red turbans striped with gold and topped with white plumes. Their tunics were green, lavishly embroidered with silver lace. Their pantaloons were red, their cross belts were gold, their saddles green and their saddle blankets sky-blue.

Under the hot sun of Egypt they must have made a dazzling sight. But in the rain, fog and drizzle of a Danube autumn, these swarthy horsemen looked sadly out of place. Their silks and colours looked dingy and washed out, and many of the men were racked with coughs and fevers. Some had died in manoeuvres in the rain. Many of their superb horses were suffering from saddle lesions which stank terribly. A few of the beasts had succumbed to the cold and damp and had to be slaughtered by the Guard farriers.

'Mad nigger bastards,' is how Pascaud described the Mamelukes when I asked about them. 'Great horsemen, though. Even better than the Russian Cossacks, and that's saying something. But they've absolutely no idea of tactics or strategy. They've only one thought in their heads and that's to charge . . .'

'So what are they doing tramping about in the rain for Napoleon?' I asked.

'God only knows,' Pascaud said.

The Guard were still struggling the south bank of the Danube some miles to the east of Ulm when the Austrians tried to break out along the north bank. It was October 14, and it was still raining. The Guard Ambulance was despatched to the little township of Elchingen on the other side of the Danube. It was a stampede. I was riding side by side with Pascaud when the order came. Most of the units got there before the bridge across the Danube collapsed. But in the rush to cross the river we had outstripped most of our vehicles, flying ambulances and *fougons*. The only medical supplies we had were what we carried in our saddle bags and portmanteaus.

I was nauseous with fear and excitement as we scrambled, cursed and thrashed our way through the mired and sodden water meadows and up the steep hill towards Elchingen. My stomach heaved and bile rose in my mouth as we moved closer to the rattle of musketry and the screams of injured men.

Pascaud rode alongside me on his mud-spattered grey mare. 'It's never as bad as it sounds,' he yelled at me. 'You'll be all right once we start. Just keep a tight arsehole.'

Elchingen was not much of a place: a collection of red-tiled cottages, houses and barns perched on a hill overlooking the Danube and huddled round the Benedictine Abbey of Peter and Paul. Most of the village was surrounded by a high brick wall, which also enclosed the abbey's gardens, orchards and graveyards. It was the kind of small, orderly, township which are found everywhere in Bavaria – except that the orchards and allotments were littered with dead and dying men.

'Jesus Christ!' Pascaud said as we crashed through the rear door of the church, which Larrey had commandeered as a field hospital. 'Look at that?'

It was an extraordinary sight. The interior was an essay in white and gold Baroque which now echoed to the screams of damaged men. The polished marble floor was awash with blood, urine and spinal fluid. Sobbing soldiers were dying under the gaze of plaster saints, winged angels and seraphim. Religious pictures adorned every wall, as the battle-shocked men stared blankly at them.

Across the ceiling, saints and angels adored their God with extravagant piety, while below them men writhed in agony. The skeleton of a long-dead minor saint, dressed in faded red and gold cloth, lay in a glass-fronted case. A few feet below him a young Austrian was convulsed on the floor with a terrible chest wound. From the ceiling hung a huge crucifix on which a wooden Christ wore a painted gash on his side. Under it young men with real wounds breathed their last.

As the fighting raged outside, casualties from both sides were dragged into the Abbey church. Larrey had ordered that the wounded should be treated on a strictly medical basis. There was to be no priority for rank. For a student of practical anatomy like myself the lessons came thick and fast. At one stage the Austrians were skirmishing at the main door of the church, and the battle nearly spilled inside the building. It was an anatomy lesson conducted to the sound of musketry and screams.

There was much to study. Faces which had been sliced open by sabres displayed the gleaming white bone of maxilla, mandible and zygoma. Skulls which had been split open with shrapnel revealed the frontal and parietal lobes of the brain. One Austrian emptied his entrails onto the ground when I opened his coat. I was surprised. The tripes of the dead are dull and flaccid. Those of the living are a riot of colour. Pascaud ended the wretch's agony by slicing the arteries in his neck. The Austrian died quickly.

The little man from the Creuse was magnificient. Without ever ceasing to curse the inadequacy of our equipment, the Guard Ambulance and Napoleon Bonaparte he worked tirelessly. He wielded his bone saw, amputating knives and scalpels adroitly and with huge energy. My job was to help. I removed the severed limbs, held down the thrashing men and helped carry out the corpses. Pascaud looked like a blood-boltered minor demon, but he was a good doctor.

'A brisk business Monsieur Frankenstein,' Larrey said over my shoulder as I held down a shuddering infantryman whose leg Pascaud was sawing off. 'Nice cut Emil, nice cut.' He turned to me. 'If you can stand the company of this foul-mouthed little goat, Frankenstein, you'll learn a lot. But his company's a terrible price to pay.'

'Bastard,' Pascaud grunted as Larrey turned away.

Larrey prowled the Abbey incessantly. Time after time he took the bone saw from a weary assistant surgeon major's hand and ordered the man to rest. Larrey was extraordinary. He could have a man's leg off before he knew it was missing, extract a lance-head from a man's chest before he had time to scream, or pluck out a damaged eye with the ease of a man picking a cherry from a tree.

As the day wore on and the casualties piled up I was allowed to work on my own. Under a fading painting of the Virgin Mary in one of the side chapels, I removed arms and legs that had been wrecked by shot. I extracted bits of bayonet from intestines and musket balls from shoulders, thighs and buttocks. I cut out what was left of a Frenchman's genitals and patched him up as neatly as I could.

By the end I was exhausted in a way that I would never have believed possible. But I was also strangely exhilarated. And I learned more anatomy that day in the Abbey Church of St Peter and Paul in Elchingen than I would have done in a year in Ingolstadt.

'Not bad for a Genevan,' Pascaud admitted.

Later I learned that the battle had been close. The Austrians had made a determined effort to break out but the French ring held. The fighting raged from house to house, wall to wall and room to room, devastating the little town.

But at the end of the day the Austrians fell back in the direction of Ulm while the French infantry hunted them down in what was left of Elchingen and in the birch woods to the west. It was, according to Pascaud, a minor but significant victory. Quite satisfactory.

The next day we continued our move on Ulm. As the Austrians fled, the Grande Armée moved to take the Michelsberg, the high ground to the north of the city. There they unlimbered their guns, howitzers and mortars, and proceeded to lay waste Ulm. Pascaud and I followed, to see the fun as he put it. From the slopes of the Michelsberg the city lay below us, a confusion of steeply pitched red roofs, dominated by the squat bulk of the Cathedral. The rain had stopped, and in the sunlight the spires of the surrounding villages glinted white. Columns of black smoke rose out of the town.

Halfway up the Michelsberg we stopped to debride and bandage the injuries of an artillery officer with powder burns on his hand and arm. He was a handsome young Norman, with a glint in his blue eye. His injuries had done nothing to dampen his enthusiasm for his squat siege mortar. He was plainly enjoying himself, watching his well-drilled gun crew fire shot after shot into the streets of Ulm.

'Ugly isn't she?' he said fondly. 'Fat Maria I call her. Like a pregnant sow, and ten times as ugly. But *that*, gentlemen, is how wars are won.'

'It is, is it?' Pascaud said.

'Damn right it is,' the Norman replied. 'Fat Maria is the future of war. Forget your cavalry and their prancing and dancing and their pretty uniforms. It's the big guns that'll do it. Every time.'

'You'd fuck the thing if your member was big enough,' Pascaud suggested.

The young artilleryman grinned amiably. 'I would if I

thought she'd produce a litter,' he said. 'With a few thousand like Maria we could bring the whole of Europe to heel.'

The object of his affections was indeed an ugly thing. It was like a short, black-painted howitzer with a gaping mouth twelve inches in diameter, set on a wooden bed, and chocked to an elevation of forty-five degrees. It did not remind me of a sow so much as an iron toad.

'Give her four pounds of powder and she'll send a shell fifteen hundred yards,' the Norman told me. 'And right over the top of any wall known to man. A decent crew will get a rate of fire of about one round a minute. Slow, but it adds up.'

He then went on to elaborate Fat Maria's charms. Most of the time the howitzer fired mortar bombs, fused iron spheres packed with gunpowder which exploded in the air or on the ground. Now and again Maria was called on to lob incendiary 'carcases': canvas bags packed with a combustible mixture of saltpetre, sulphur and pitch. And very effective it was too, judging by the fires that were blazing in the city.

'You must be killing hundreds,' I told him as Fat Maria lobbed another incendiary.

'Maybe,' he said. 'But look at those fortifications down there. Moats, escarpments, firing platforms, ditches. Think what *our* casualties would be if we had to fight our way through that lot. Christ, there'd hardly be a man left in the Grande Armée.'

Pascaud agreed. 'He's right,' he said. 'Nobody builds these things better than the sausage-eaters. His way is better.'

'Damn right it is,' the artilleryman said. 'Old Mack can only take so much of this stuff raining down on his head, and he'll *have* to give up. He can't hold out much longer.'

191

The Norman gunner was proved right. After a few days of artillery fire, Mack had had enough. His problems were compounded when the Danube burst its banks and flooded Ulm. The water swept away many unburied Austrian corpses, and for days white-coated bodies bobbed in the swollen river and littered the banks.

Pascaud wondered aloud what the people of Vienna would think when half the Austrian army came floating home. 'They'll be fishing their sons out of the water like carp,' he muttered. 'Poor bastards.'

On October 25 Karl Mack surrendered. The surrender ceremony was pure theatre. In bright sunshine the Grande Armée arranged itself on the hills around Ulm in full battle order. Mack's Austrians marched out of the Frau-Tor in the North Wall, made their way along the side of the Michelsberg, stacked their muskets and cartridge belts, then marched back through the Neu-Tor. Many were weeping, some cursing defiantly. Napoleon stood brooding on an outcrop of rock, the Kienlesberg, that looked as if it had been put there for the purpose.

'Look at him,' Pascaud said pointing at Bonaparte watching the ranks of disconsolate Austrians. 'He loves it! He thinks he's Julius Caesar. That little Corsican is getting more than a bit above himself. If he goes on like this we'll all come a cropper.'

I was mildly shocked. 'That's sedition,' I told him.

'I'm an old-fashioned Republican', he said. And us old-fashioned Republicans do not believe in all this *imperial* flummery. He's good at what he does. He's probably the best there's ever been. But one day he'll come unstuck. It's bound to happen. And when he does, he'll take a lot of good Frenchmen with him. I just hope that I'm not one of them.'

After the theatricals some of us rode into Ulm to do what we could. The Queen of the Danube was a sorry sight. On the south side of the town anything that had not been wrecked by the bombardment had been flooded by the river. Pascaud, myself and two of our orderlies picked our way through the Münsterplatz among the corpses of horses, men, women and children. There were broken carts, ammunition boxes, spiked artillery pieces and gun limbers strewn everywhere. Houses which had been split by the shelling spilled their contents into the streets: bedding, tables, crockery, toys, books, pianos.

On the gallows in front of the Schwörhaus a recently hanged man was being tugged at by a pair of large dogs. Sullen Austrian infantrymen spat on the ground as we passed. One snarled at us and promised that he would be back. I could see that he meant it. I believed him. Winning a battle was one thing; winning a war was another.

But Napoleon and the fates had done their worst in the southwest corner of Ulm, the old, crowded, low-lying quarter where the River Blau runs into the Danube. This was where the town's fishermen, ferrymen and boatmen lived. The narrow lanes between the half-timbered buildings had turned into tributaries of the Blau, along which debris and corpses floated. In what had been the Fischerplatzle boatmen were using hooks to drag corpses out of the water.

The sight sent a surge of excitement through me. Here was a chance to try out the revival techniques which the English surgeon Kite had explained to me near the estuary of the Thames. I had the breathing tube he had given me among my instruments. Quickly I explained to Pascaud what I had in mind. He was sceptical, but agreed to accompany me. We left the horses with one of the orderlies, commandeered one of the Danube skiffs and a couple of boatmen, paddled around until we found a house equipped with a crane and block and tackle over an upper window, and climbed in.

Then began a bizarre operation. While the boatmen

plucked corpses out of the water, rowed them to our house and slipped a noose under their armpits, Pascaud and the orderly hauled the bodies up on the crane and manoeuvred them through the window. I stretched the bodies out on the floor and set to work. My technique was simple: I blocked one nostril with a wad of cotton, inserted the ivory nosepiece in the other, and blew, hard down the mouthpiece into the leather tube. It was an exhausting business, and mostly it was a waste of time.

But not entirely. I had two partial successes. One was an Austrian trooper whose chest heaved once or twice before he finally expired. The other was a young woman, no more than eighteen years old, and still wearing a head-dress of flowers and ribbons in her matted hair. Her skin was livid, her lips were blue and she was without pulse or heartbeat. She looked as dead as the rest, but after a few minutes of determined blowing down the tube into her nostrils I saw her chest and diaphragm expand and her lips begin to move.

In a state of some excitement I turned the girl on her side and she coughed up a large puddle of muddy water. Then she began to tremble and her limbs moved in little convulsions. A few seconds later her eyelids flickered and then opened. She was alive. Her heart was beating and she was breathing faintly. But she made no sound. She lay, wide-eyed, staring at the ceiling. I passed my hand in front of her eyes but she did not follow it. She was alive but inert.

I shouted to Pascaud who left his work at the crane and came over to study the girl. He did not share my excitement at the miracle I had wrought. He shook his head slowly. 'Something's happened to her brain,' he said. 'That's my suggestion. Maybe we've done the poor cow no favours. Maybe we should have left her to the Danube.'

I was irritated and grabbed his hand and placed it on the

girl's chest. 'Feel that,' I said. 'Her heart. She's alive. Give her time. She'll recover. She will.'

But he was unconvinced. 'Well if she does,' he said, 'I hope she thanks you for what you've done.'

We left the fishermen of Ulm to care for the girl and dispose of the dozen or so bodies we had plucked out of the Blau, and made our way back to the French lines.

As I surveyed the havoc, it occurred to me that the snails had probably survived well enough. The molluscs hibernate underground in winter, which was likely to have saved them from most of the artillery fire. And to protect themselves from the cold and wet they create diaphragms of slime and calceous matter over the openings to their shells, which would have kept out the Danube floods. So the chances were that the *Helix pomatia* of Ulm were safe, dry and sound asleep.

Which was just as well. The burghers of Ulm were going to need every snail they could lay their hands on to pay for the damage done to the town by Karl Mack and Napoleon Bonaparte. We left Ulm to handle its misery as best it could, and followed the Grande Armée east down the Danube. We were, I was told, in pursuit of the Russians.

AUSTRIA AND MORAVIA: NOVEMBER 1805

Émile Pascaud was one of the best surgeons I have ever met, but he had no taste for theory. Abstraction bored him. Unless he could feel it, taste it or stick a knife into it, it did not exist. Theoretical medicine bored him. The idea of electricity bored him. Nothing I said could convince him of its power and potential. There were times when he seemed to consist of bone from ear-to-ear above his neck.

'A load of shit,' was his considered judgement of Aldini's work in Bologna and London. 'Dancing corpses. What's the point?'

We argued all the way across the war-battered country-side of Bavaria and we had almost crossed the border into Austria before I could persuade him to co-operate with me in an experiment. 'Nothing major,' I told him. 'Nothing to worry about. Just a small demonstration. A few turns of the handle on the electric generator, that's all. A few incisions on a corpse.'

'Well, there will be plenty of those,' Pascaud said.

This proved true enough. As we lurched our way down

the Danube in pursuit of the Russian army the rain never let up. It just got colder. More and more men were falling victim to dysentry, pneumonia and various fevers. Accidents were common. More than one soldier met his end when a wagon toppled on him, or a limbered cannon fell over or a scrambling horse crushed his skull. Corpses were no problem.

Reluctantly Pascaud agreed to my experiment. So one night I dug my Cuthbertson's generator out of the *fougon* in which it had been travelling, while Pascaud and my orderly Marnier went in search of a corpse. They came back with the body of a slightly built cavalryman whose neck had snapped when his horse had thrown him. He was a light-boned youngster of nineteen. While Pascaud stripped the corpse and laid it out on some boards on the ground, I assembled the Cuthbertson machine.

I was not ambitious. What I had in mind was not so much an experiment as a demonstration to whet Pascaud's curiosity. I wanted to show him the possibilities. I simply repeated what I had seen Aldini do in London. I moistened each of the corpse's ears with salt water, attached a connection to each eartip, then cranked the handle vigorously. The effect was startling. The eyes shot open, the mouth worked vigorously and the face grimaced horribly.

I laughed as both Pascaud and Marnier jumped away from the corpse like frightened schoolgirls. Pascaud was taken aback, Marnier frankly terrified. The burly young orderly crossed himself two or three times. 'Dear Mother of God,' he wailed. 'The poor soul is alive. He's coming back. Dear Mother of God.'

Pascaud recovered his composure quickly. 'Don't be so stupid,' he swore at Marnier. 'It's just the electricity. Isn't it?'

'What do you mean *just* the electricity?' I asked. 'Can you think of any other way of doing what I've just done?'

He thought for a while and then said, 'No I cannot. Do it again.'

So I repeated the experiment with much the same result, although the trooper's face did not grimace with quite the same ferocity. And only one of the man's bright blue eyes opened.

'All right,' Pascaud said. 'I'm impressed. But what is going on exactly?'

I shook my head. 'All that we know is that electricity has the power to agitate the nerves that move the muscles.'

'And does it only work in the face?'

I told him to watch. With some difficulty I cut into the neck, removed part of the vertebrae and uncovered the spinal cord at the base of the man's skull. Then I made an incision on the biceps of the left arm and completed the arc between the arm and the spine. The wheel spun, the machine whined and the dead man's arm rose slowly from the ground.

'Bloody hell,' Pascaud said, awestruck. 'It really does seem to work.'

Marnier was growing fearful. 'It's unnatural,' he kept muttering. 'It's unnatural. Stop . . .'

I tried to reassure him. He was a hard working and conscientious orderly. I did not want to scare him off. 'There's nothing unnatural here Marnier,' I said. 'The man's as dead as he'll ever be. It's only the electricity from this machine that's making the muscles in his arm move. He doesn't know anything about it. Don't worry.'

I repeated the experiment but this time put a stone on the corpse's hand. Then I cranked the wheel vigorously and watched as the dead hand and arm lifted the stone until it fell off with a clatter that made Marnier jump.

'Uncanny,' was Pascaud's comment. 'Damnedst thing I've ever seen.'

198

I did consider breaking into the thorax and making an arc in the perocardium, but I thought that might be a bit more than Marnier could take. So we bundled the body up in a blanket and took him back to lie with the rest of the day's corpses awaiting burial. Marnier beat a hasty retreat to his sleeping quarters after promising not to tell any of his friends what he had seen.

My little demonstration had served its purpose. Pascaud was intrigued. As we walked back to our billet he bombarded me with questions. How long did it work after death? Did mortification affect the process? Were some muscles more susceptible to the electrical charge than others? What were the practical applications? Then his doubts began to resurface.

'Where does it get us to make a dead man's face twitch?' he asked. 'Or his eyes open? Or his arm move?'

'It gets us nowhere,' I said. 'But let me ask you this. What if we could use that Cuthbertson machine – or something like it – to agitate his *heart*? What's the heart but a big muscle? We know that the electricity works on other muscles. Why shouldn't it work on the heart? Why shouldn't it *restart* the heart?'

Pascaud looked at me with astonishment. 'I never thought of that,' he said. 'Get the heart going again. After it had stopped. Hell . . .'

The next day the Imperial Guard crossed the border into Austria and the rain changed to snow. Under the lowering sky and in the freezing weather the Guard cavalry's Mamelukes suffered grievously. The baggage train was ransacked for extra greatcoats and blankets for the Egyptians to wear over their bright silks. But still they shivered in misery, baffled by a climate that they had never encountered.

When one of them came to me with a gashed hand, I

struck up a conversation with him. His name was Ibrahim, and he told me in excellent French that his people were not Arabians, but originally came from the Caucasus mountains. The Mameluke Beys had ruled Egypt for hundreds of years, and that he was serving the army of France for the best of reasons.

'Because I want the *knowledge* of France for my own people,' he told me. 'Not just the knowledge of the gunners and the engineers. But knowledge such as yours, Doctor Frankenstein. Otherwise Egypt – and the rest of Araby – will be crushed under the Christian heel. The English are already telling my people what to do. So! I am here to learn.'

And he was as good as his word. Whenever he could, the young Mameluke left his column and rode with us in the ranks of the ambulance. His curiosity was insatiable. He quizzed us endlessly. At first Pascaud grumbled about being 'pestered by the little nigger' but he soon succumbed to Ibrahim's eager questioning and was generous with his advice. Ibrahim informed us that when his soldiering days were over he intended to return to Alexandria and become a surgeon 'just like Doctor Émile'. It was the only time I ever saw Pascaud blush.

The French columns worked their way down the Danube, bedraggled but confident after the Austrian collapse at Ulm. The officers of the Guard, and especially the younger ones, knew they had the beating of the world. Bonaparte had Europe in the palm of his hand. The campaign was now a simple matter of imposing the Emperor's will on the humiliated Austrians and chasing their primitive Russian allies back to their Asian wastelands.

One night our ambulance shared an abandoned farmhouse with a dozen young officers from the Guard Chasseurs and a few artillerymen. The talk round the fire was of grand strategy, battlefield tactics, and just *why* the

Grande Armée was now the finest army in the entire history of the world. One young Chasseur ascribed it all to the genius of the Emperor. One of the veteran gunners spat contemptuously into the fire.

'Rubbish!' he said. 'Bonaparte's got the best maps and the best map-makers in Europe. He spends half his life poring over maps. He knows every foot of ground between Brittany and China. That's how he can get idiots like you halfway across Europe before the Tsar or the Emperor Francis have got out of their beds. Good maps. Good information. Good planning. That's what Napoleon's about.'

But the horse soldiers would have none of it. Napoleon was their inspiration, their guiding star. Had not he turned Europe on its head? Had he not carved the name of France right across the world? Did not kings, emperors and tsars tremble at the sound of his name? Was he not the greatest strategist the world had ever seen? Was he not invincible?

At which point Pascaud butted in. 'Listen arseholes,' he said,' I might be just a bone-saw artist but I've known that Corsican bandit since he started beating the stuffing out of the Italians in 1796. And I'm still trailing around Europe after him. Even though he has been getting a bit above himself recently.'

There was some muttering at this but Pascaud pressed on. 'Take some advice from a medical man,' he told them. 'There's a condition called strategic idiocy. Our old Austrian friend Mack suffered badly from this. But Napoleon, he suffers from strategic genius. And as any doctor will tell you, it can be hard to tell the two apart. Genius and idiocy I mean. Genius can be very dangerous. Especially for the poor bastards who have to live with it. And that, gentlemen, is us . . .'

Pascaud's diagnosis brought cries of outrage from the young cavalrymen, but he held his ground. 'What I'm saying is that nobody – not even Napoleon Bonaparte – is that good. He'll win most of the battles, yes. But he can't win *all* the battles. People learn from their mistakes. Even Austrians. The bigger the mistake, the faster they learn. And you can't make a bigger mistake than the one the Austrians made at Ulm.'

'That's for sure,' one of the cavalrymen chipped in.

'So it was easy for us then,' Pascaud continued. 'It will be a bit harder the next time. Even harder the time after that. And it will go on getting harder until . . .'

'Until the Emperor prevails over the whole of Europe,' the noisiest of the Chasseurs said loudly. 'And then we can get on with the job of knocking in the heads of the English . . .'

There was noisy agreement, after which the young horsemen lapsed into the Frenchman's favourite pastime of downing England and describing the havoc they would wreak when they finally got there. London was to be plundered then levelled, the British royals were to be guillotined, the British army was to be disbanded and the British navy sent to the bottom of the sea. None of us knew that a few days earlier the British had destroyed the French and Spanish fleets at Cape Trafalgar. Napoleon's cross-channel invasion plans were off.

We knew all about the Russians, however. As the Russian army fell back eastwards they devastated the countryside behind them. The Russians burned down the wooden bridges, pulled down the stone ones, set fire to crops, poisoned wells (sometimes with their own dead) and stripped the country bare of farmyard animals. Whole villages and small towns were levelled to deprive the French of shelter. With winter at our elbow this was serious.

There was continual skirmishing between our light cavalry and the Russian rearguard. The Russian withdrawal was being covered by Prince Peter Ivanovich Bagration, one of the finest of the Tsar's officers. Again and again the French cavalry seethed on the bank of a river a few minutes after the Russians had pulled down the bridge. The most troublesome of Bagration's units was the Pavlograd Hussars, reckless horsemen led by an Irish Jacobite called Count Joseph O'Rourke. As many among the ranks of the Grande Armée were themselves descendants of Scots and Irish Jacobites, the irony was not unremarked.

Occasionally we came across a baggage train which had been abandoned by some slow-moving Russian unit. The French descended on such plunder with glee. The lucky ones emerged wearing sky-blue Hungarian pantaloons, warm Austrian greatcoats, or clutching good linen underclothing. One upturned cart yielded a regimental chaplain's vestments and sacred vessels. The Russian priest's heavy robes were seized by a big infantryman who wore them for the rest of the campaign. He swore they made a better job of keeping off the rain and cold than his army greatcoat.

As we moved east the snow got heavier. By the beginning of November the countryside and the forests were under a heavy white blanket. It deadened the noise of the rolling French columns and utterly transformed the scenery of the Danube forests and gorges. We progressed in near silence through a white wilderness. When the mists froze, millions of icicles formed and hung from the branches of the trees. It was if we were moving through tunnels of tinkling, whispering crystal.

But the Guard Ambulance was kept busy. Every five or six days the Russian rearguard would turn and fight. Then the snow would be spattered with blood. It happened at Lambach, not long after we had crossed the River Inn into Austria. Then there was a ferocious tussle near the village of Amstetten on November the 5th. Murat and two cavalry brigades emerged into a forest clearing to be confronted by lines of Russian infantry. The horsemen did a quick about face, but a young gunnery officer saved the Grande Armée's pride by bringing his eight-pounders into action. The first volley brought down slabs of snow from the trees and thousands of icicles rained down on the helmets and shakos of both sides.

Both sides then threw grenadiers and heavy infantry into the forest battle, and the casualties mounted. Pascaud and I spent a frantic day plucking casualties out of the snowy forest and racing them back to the field hospitals for treatment. The Grande Armée claimed that more than 2,000 Russians were killed. And every one of them died fighting.

A few days later Bagration's men turned on us yet again at the village of Durnstein on the north bank of the Danube. That was a terrifying business. There was some close-quarters artillery work, and many men, French as well as Russian, were trapped in blazing buildings and burned to death. The smell of roasting flesh hung over the countryside. Pascaud said it made his stomach heave, but in fact the smell was rather pleasant. Durnstein was a minor victory for Bagration. He battered a French column back across the River Danube, and gave Kutuzov's main force time to retreat northeast into Moravia.

After the carnage at Durnstein there was a plentiful supply of fresh corpses. At Pascaud's urging we hauled out the Cuthbertson machine and carried out another electrical experiment. This time our subject was a huge Russian who had been killed through the right eye by a musketball. The procedure was the same as before but the results were disappointing. When we made an arc from ear to ear and charged the machine, the facial muscles hardly flickered.

'We must be doing something wrong,' Pascaud said. 'What are we doing wrong?'

'Nothing that I can see,' I said. 'Let's try again.'

The result was the same. The Russian's face hardly twitched. There was a slight tremor of the eyelids and a tremulousness about the lips but that was all.

Pascaud was thoughtful, then brightened. 'How's this for an explanation? This man is a lot bigger and heavier than our last subject, isn't he?'

'A lot,' I replied.

'So. Maybe we just don't have enough electrical power for this big Russian ox? Big muscles need more moving. More moving needs more electricity. How does that sound?'

'Could be,' I said. 'In which case there must some kind of body-weight to electricity ratio which could be tabulated. We could do this, I suppose, if we had enough subjects to experiment on.'

'We'll have the subjects all right,' Pascaud said. 'But I doubt if we'll have the time to do any tabulating. The Corsican genius will see to that.'

Pascaud was right Bagration's rearguard action came to a halt at the end of November in the Moravian town of Olmütz, where Kutuzov's battered army was joined by fresh Russian troops under Count Buxhövden. A few days later 10,000 men of the Russian Imperial Guard entered the town, closely followed by an army of Austrians eager for revenge after their humiliation at Ulm. And the Austrian Archduke Charles was on his way up from Italy with another experienced force.

Suddenly Kutuzov had more than 80,000 men at his disposal. And suddenly Napoleon looked vulnerable. Unease ran through the French ranks. Had Bonaparte been outwitted by the Tsar Alexander and the Emperor Francis? Had he been lured into the kind of strategic trap he specialised in setting for others? It was possible. The killing ground, the *cognoscenti* said, would be somewhere between the Moravian towns of Brünn and Olmütz, probably at a place called Austerlitz.

BRÜNN, MORAVIA: NOVEMBER 1805

The Imperial Guard Ambulance rolled into Brünn one afternoon at the end of November. After the sodden, battered countryside of Bavaria and the Danube the town looked like paradise. In the winter sunshine it was neat, colourful, well-appointed. Built where the River Svratka runs into the Svatava the town nestled under a wooded hillside on top of which stood the Spielberg Castle. This edifice, Pascaud assured me, was one of the foulest prisons in the Austrian empire.

Although the Russians and the Austrians had been through Brünn before us, the town was more or less intact. In fact, the arsenals were still stacked with arms and ammunition which, for some astonishing reason, the Allies had failed to notice. It was an oversight for which the French were duly grateful, and for which the Allies were to pay.

While Napoleon and his marshals accepted the surrender of the town's dignitaries, Pascaud and I scouted for a decent billet. All we wanted was a dry bed under a solid roof. We struck lucky. We found ourselves some decent accommodation at the house of a large young widow, dumped our equipment, then went out into the streets of Brünn. The sights, sounds and smells went to my head.

Brünn was well-supplied with handsome women. But a few turns round the streets cooled my ardour. Each pretty lady was being besieged by at least two pretty Frenchmen in pretty uniforms. My chances were next to nothing. And as Brünn's whorehouses were overrun by French troops, most of whom had picked up every variety of pox known and unknown to medicine, Pascaud and I decided to make do with a hot meal and a few bottles of red wine.

'I might try to have a peep under the fat widow's skirts later on,' Pascaud told me. 'If that sounds ambitious, let me tell you I have a certain curosity value. You'd be amazed by the number of women who are happy to accommodate ugly old soldiers like me. Usually they're ugly bitches themselves, but not always. I've bagged a few beauties in my time. Maybe they do it out of pity. Maybe it's some kind of sexual patronage. Noblesse oblige. But whatever it is, I'm grateful, I can tell you.'

We found an inn, bolted down a bad meal, and then got rapidly drunk. We drank toasts to the Revolution, to medicine, to each other, to Dominique Larrey, to the wondrous power of electricity, to Napoleon, to the Guard Ambulance, to France, to the Republic of Geneva, to Pascaud's home village of Lascelles Dunois. 'And a special toast', he said, 'to all the poor bastards out there – French, Russian and Austrian – who are going to get their heads blown off. Let's just hope we're not among them.'

I left him lurching back to the billet, his ridiculous sword trailing behind him, to lay siege to the fat widow. I walked around the city walls. The French army were spread out for miles and the lights of their cooking fires seemed to vanish over the horizon. Just outside the walls vast pyres were blazing, around which hundreds of French soldiers were gathered. They had been plundering Brünn for fuel. Chairs, beds, picture frames, tapestries, cupboards and a piano were being pitched into the flames, while a few Moravian civilians looked on helplessly. I bumped into a trio of drunken dragoons who asked me if I realised that we were campaigning in the land of Moravia which translated into Mor-a-via, or Mort à Vie. Death to life.

I was superstitious enough for this thought to bother me. Reason has its limits. Thoroughly depressed, I retraced my steps to the fat widow's where an indignant Pascaud told me he had returned to find our hostess spread beneath a strapping young horseman from the Guard cavalry.

The following day Dominique Larrey began to prepare Brunn for the slaughter to come. One of Larrey's talents was an ability to estimate casualties. He called together the surgeon majors from every ambulance in the Grande Armée and gave them their instructions. Every sizeable building in Brünn was to be commandeered and converted into a hospital. Churches, schools, monasteries and nunneries were to be pressed into the Emperor's service.

Our own Surgeon Major came back from one of Larrey's conferences shaken by his casualty estimates. Austerlitz, he told us, was likely to be one of the bloodiest battles Europe had ever seen. Both armies were huge. Almost 200,000 men would be involved. Both sides had all the artillery they needed. We were deep into winter so battlefield injuries would be exacerbated by cold and wet. Dysentry and hospital fever were certain to follow.

Maybe Napoleon insisted on nothing but the best for his élite Guard. Maybe Larrey worked it in the Guard's favour. Maybe it was just the luck of the draw. But the Guard was assigned the Brünn almshouse for its hospital. This news was met by a collective sigh of relief. The almshouse was set amidst some greenery on the edge of the town, well away from the crowded centre.

'What's so good about that?' I asked Pascaud after the Surgeon Major's meeting.

'You must be joking,' he said, surprised at my ignorance. 'After this bout of fisticuffs, this town will be the fever capital of Europe. Believe me! The more space we can put between Brunn and us the better I will like it.'

When we moved into the almshouse Larrey told us what he wanted: 'Light, air and cleanliness.' So we took the place apart. Partition walls were ripped down and ceilings were ripped out to make the spaces bigger so that air could circulate. Closed stoves were carted away, and fireplaces which had been blocked were opened up.

Every rotting floorboard, window frame, door jamb and picture rail was pulled out and replaced by fresh timber. Patches of damp plaster were stripped out, replaced and painted. Wooden surfaces were scrubbed and coated with coat after coat of varnish until they gleamed like glass. Floors were honeystoned until they shone. Cracked window-panes were replaced. Every corner and cranny was scrubbed, scrubbed and scrubbed again. Then the whole interior was limewashed.

After more than a week of this drudgery the almshouse was ready for Larrey's inspection. The place was dazzling. Cold, perhaps, but awash with fresh air and the winter sunshine. It shone off the whitewashed walls, glinted on the new glass and gleamed on the newly varnished woodwork. All the surgical instruments had been carefully sharpened, washed in hot water, then wrapped in boiled linen. As Larrey walked around he gave little nods of satisfaction. Then he stopped to talk to Pascaud.

'Morning Émile,' he said.

'Morning sir,' Pascaud replied. 'Not a bad job eh?'

Larrey grinned. 'Not bad at all, Émile,' he said.

No sooner had we finished transforming the almshouse than the Guard was ordered out of Brunn into the country-side to the east. Napoleon wanted the Guard in reserve on his left flank, near the main road between the two towns. Larrey had identified the barns, mills and farm buildings he wanted for his field hospitals and set the ambulance divisions to work. They had to be capable of treating the injured before they were moved to the main hospitals in Brünn.

Next day we all rode over the ground with Larrey. As we were to man the flying ambulances, we had to know the geography. We rode south to north, north to south, east to west, west to east and then did it all over again. We established the best routes up onto the plateau known as the Pratzen and the best routes off again. We traced the most effective ways around the cluster of ice-bound lakes and marshes to the south. We tested the ice itself to see whether it could take the weight of our ambulances (and decided it could not).

Larrey's eye was unfailing. He spotted difficulties where I could see none. Slopes that looked easy turned out neverthe-less to be too steep for horse-drawn carriages. Plains of smooth grass revealed wheel-shattering boulders. Tracks that looked wide were pitted with deep potholes. Every outcrop of rock and patch of bog was carefully noted and transferred onto the maps prepared for us by Napoleon's headquarters staff. By the end of that day the topography of the killing ground was burned into my mind. I knew just where I could – and could not – take my ambulance.

The day before the battle was another misery of rain, sleet and wind. It chilled me and drove me into a melancholy which I tried to overcome by checking and rechecking each item of my equipment. Marnier and I went over every nut, bolt and cotter-pin on the ambulance. We tested wheels, springs, axles and traces. I scrubbed the leather upholstery until I almost wore it out. But I could not help wondering what, in the name of a God in which I did not believe, I was doing sitting in the freezing rain on the eastern edge of Europe, waiting to be pitched against the armies of two of Europe's most powerful empires.

All the battles which I had experienced – Echlingen, Ulm, Amstetten, Durnstein – had been sudden, brutal shocks. There had been little or no time to brood over the consequences. But this was different. This time I had had two weeks to consider which part of my anatomy I would miss most. Or how I would cope with the agony of a bayonet in the entrails. Or how it might feel in the split second before a three-pound cannonball removed your head.

'Scared witless' is how I described my feelings to Pascaud when he asked. 'I'm having serious trouble keeping a tight arsehole.'

'Me too,' he told me. 'Never fails. It's the same every time. The day before a Big One – and this is going to be a Big One – all I want is to be somewhere else. Preferably back in Lascelles Dunois, catching fish. Or sitting beside the fire in the inn with a bottle of wine at my elbow. This is the time when I think I just want to go home. I've had enough.'

'So why do you do it?' I asked.

'I'm French,' he said. 'Why in Christ's name are you here, Frankenstein.'

'God only knows. And he's not telling. It seemed like a good idea at the time,' I told him.

I was faintly comforted by the fact that I was not alone in my dread. A string of Guardsmen came to us with assorted pre-battle ailments. One soldier had accidentally shot himself in the foot. Another had gashed his right hand and wrist with a bayonet. Others complained of diarrhoea, vomiting, headaches and mysterious aching in the limbs. One elderly colonel was so badly stricken with gout he feared that he would not be able to mount his horse in the morning.

Napoleon spent that day on horseback. Bedraggled by the rain and trailing only his personal escort of Guard Chasseurs, he visited every unit in the Grande Armée. He inspected the field kitchens and questioned the quartermasters. He chatted with artillerymen about the condition of their guns, the weight of their shot and the consistency of their powder. The Mamelukes were solicited about their high-bred horses. The Marines were assured that after the Russians and Austrians had been disposed of, they would all be marched back to the invasion barges for England.

Late in the afternoon despatch riders distributed copies of Napoleon's pre-battle exhortation. The rhetoric seemed to amuse and irritate Pascaud more than inspire him.

'Listen to this,' he said, '"This victory will complete our campaign, and we can then resume our winter quarters, where we shall be joined by the new armies which are forming in France . . ." I hope he's right about that. We'll need some new blood after this lot.'

That night the weather changed. The rain stopped, the cloud cleared, the temperature sank and the night became clear, starlit, frosty. As Napoleon moved among his soldiers someone had the idea of lighting a torch to mark his passing. Within minutes the whole west flank of the Pratzen was ablaze with 60,000 waving torches as every man in the Grande Armée set light to a handful of straw or plucked a burning brand from the fire. It was one of the most extraordinary things I have ever seen. I heard that Napoleon declared it the greatest moment of his entire life.

'The Russians must think every man in the French army

has set fire to his drawers just to keep warm,' was Pascaud's comment on the spectacle. 'Oh, well. That's war.'

AUSTERLITZ, MORAVIA: DECEMBER 1805

The Battle of Austerlitz confirmed what I already knew: that there are many ways of dying. Some men died screaming or grappling with phantoms in the air. Others died whimpering or sobbing for their mothers. A few screamed for their sweethearts. Many died cursing Napoleon or the Tsar or the Emperor Francis. Others just cursed. I saw at least one man who died laughing hysterically. A few went smiling gently. Some were clearly glad to go. Others wailed in disappointment and loss. Most soldiers just died, unobserved and unnoticed.

I was constantly aware of lost opportunities. One Russian guardsman died on the ground in front of me, the top of his skull sliced off and most of his brain exposed. The grey tissue was still pulsing. What could I not have learnt from the effects of electricity on the brain of a newly dead young man?

I saw a Guard Chasseur's vertebral column that had been cut open by shrapnel such that most of the spinal cord was revealed. I itched to insert the poles of a pile into it and note the results. But in the chaos of battle nothing was possible. There was no time to do anything but saw, cut and run.

Everything I learnt about the battle itself, I learnt later. A man in a flying ambulance has no overview of events. From where he sits there are no patterns, no sense of thrust and counter-thrust. There is only bloody shambles. All he can do is find the quickest way to transfer damaged men from the chaos of the field to the confusion of the field hospitals, while at the same time trying to avoid taking a cannonball in the chest or a musketball between the eyes.

Pascaud, with his taste for strategy, explained it all to me afterwards. 'Every now and again that short-arsed Corsican bandit gets it right,' he said. 'This was one of those times. Old Kutuzov walked straight into a trap. He did *exactly* what Napoleon wanted him to do. He threw his regiments up onto the Pratzen and then along the top to attack Davout's veterans on our right flank. At the same time Bagration hit Lannes on our left. So their whole army was strung out over five, six miles. They were stretched far too thin.

'And that's when Napoleon hit them. Straight in the middle. Right in the solar plexus. He pitched Soult and his lads – all 24,000 of them – straight up the hill and cut them in two. Then Soult wheeled round to the south and trapped them between himself and Davout. The other half were pushed back down the hill to Austerlitz.

'Kutuzov tried to counter-attack by sending in his reserve, the Russian Imperial Guard. Big bastards they are. Good soldiers too. But the Corsican turned the Guard cavalry loose on them. They put up a good fight, but our cavalry did for them. Then he sent in the rest of the Guard. After that, well, it was all over. Except for the killing. What a day!'

I suppose that is what happened. I do not know. I do know it was the longest day of my life. It began in the dark, at four o'clock in the morning when the Russians made their

216

first move, and did not end until eight o'clock in the evening when the last of the Russians and Austrians were harried off the field. My own recollection is of smoke, gunfire and screaming men and horses. And lurid moments in the fog of war.

I remember Pascaud climbing awkwardly up onto his big grey mare and then turning to me. His coarse features were drawn and tense. 'Remember, Frankenstein,' he shouted. 'Cut 'em early, cut 'em fast, and get 'em out. And never forget the motto of the Guard Ambulance – keep a tight arsehole.'

I remember shouting back 'Too late!' and then cantering off to follow the Guard cavalry with my ambulance rattling behind me. My mounted orderlies were Marnier and a youngster from Alsace called Otto Beck who wanted to be a surgeon. They were both as white-faced and silent as I was.

I remember my first casualty, a huge trooper of the Horse Guard who lay on the wet ground howling like an outraged infant. His left leg was hanging on below the knee by a few strings of gristle and flesh, so slicing it off was simple. Then we slid the shocked man into the back of the ambulance and raced back down the hill.

I remember picking up a Guard Chasseur whose left shoulder had been pierced by a Cossack lance. His collar-bone had been broken in at least three places and he must have been in agony. But he was cheerful. 'I managed to pistol the bastard that did it,' he told me. 'Right in the face. Spoiled his day.'

I remember a fatally wounded Russian infantryman hauling himself a few yards to the east just to be that much nearer Mother Russia when he died. I rummaged through the Russian's knapsack and found some filthy foot rags, a few lumps of coarse bread, a handful of dry firewood and a little leather box containing a crude picture of St Christopher carrying the infant Christ.

When the Guard went into the battle, the Guard Ambulance never stopped. The procedure was the same every time: while Beck held the horses, Marnier would hold down a soldier while I sliced off his arm or leg. Then we would slide the patient into the back of the ambulance, wrap a blanket round him and career at high speed back to the field hospital. Larrey's survey of the ground on the eve of the battle proved invaluable.

I have no idea how many journeys we made. But we went wherever the fighting was, racing in under the cannon fire, case-shot and musketry. We were lucky. One three-pound ball went straight through the canvas hood of the ambulance without doing any damage. Long-range musketry rattled harmlessly off the sides of the carriage. Beck's horse had a close shave from some case-shot while a musketball nicked Marnier's bicorn hat. So far as I know nothing came close to me.

But I did see the final stages of the battle. We had followed the Guard to the south end of the Pratzen ridge, and watched the Russians and Austrians streaming away through the frozen marshes and lakes to the south. The French unlimbered their guns and turned them on the fleeing Allies. The shot broke the ice under the retreating columns and men; horses, guns and wagons floundered and sank in the freezing water. Most of the men struggled to the bank but some drowned. It was a miserable end for men who had fought all day.

There was more dead meat on that battlefield than I had ever thought to see. The soldiers had died in flocks. There were Russians and Austrians, French and Egyptians, Croats and Ukranians, Alsatians and Bavarians. Between them the three emperors – Napoleon, the Tsar Alexander and the

Emperor Joseph II – had contrived to kill off more than 40,000 of their fittest and most active subjects.

We spent that night on the battlefield searching for injured men. Larrey reminded us that the ambulance had two functions. One was to tend the injured. The other was to bury the French dead. That was the job of our foot orderlies. It was grisly work and military police dragooned local civilians into helping with the work, which they did willingly – dead soldiers make easy pickings.

That night packs of Moravians and French camp-followers moved across the battlefield plundering the dead. Local cobblers cut up cartridge pouches and leather webbing to make boots and shoes. Blacksmiths stripped the shoes off dead horses and the iron from powder-boxes. Squads of children collected lead musketballs and shot. Women ripped the silver braid and brass buttons off the uniforms of dead cavalry officers. Austerlitz produced the kind of bounty that most peasants see only once in their lifetimes.

That night was the only time I ever saw Napoleon Bonaparte close to. He swept into the Guard's field-dressing station as Pascaud and I were unloading casualties. Every soldier that could move tried to struggle to attention. The men lying on the floor propped themselves on one elbow and saluted. There was a feeble cheer. Napoleon looked around, touched his hat, then went from pallet to pallet exchanging words with the injured men. He recognised Émile and stopped to say a few words. Then he swept out, followed by his entourage.

'That', Pascaud said, 'in case you hadn't noticed, was Napoleon Bonaparte. Know why he always recognises me? Because I'm the only man in the whole army he can look down on.'

That evening we trundled back to Brünn to look to the injured who were piling up at the Guard hospital. Larrey had underestimated the casualties and many of the lightly wounded men were transported south to hospitals in Vienna. Dressings, instruments and medical supplies were distinctly hard to come by. Military medicine was not a priority with Napoleon's war department despite all Larrey's efforts. And the revolutionary notions of Liberty, Equality and Fraternity seemed to be fading fast.

Two days after Austerlitz I was changing the dressings on a Mameluke with a badly infected sabre gash in his side, when an orderly tapped me on the shoulder. The Lieutenant-General who had just been brought in wanted to talk to me. I finished dressing the Mameluke's wound then went to see the general. He was a youngish man in the uniform of a staff officer. He had a broken collar-bone, was in some pain, and was not pleased. He informed me that he was a general officer in the army of the Emperor of France and as such expected to be treated with some expedition. Was that understood?

I was not impressed. 'Sir, I take my orders from Surgeon General Larrey,' I told him, 'and those orders are that *all* patients are to be treated strictly in order of *medical* priority. You have no such priority. I will attend to your injury in due course. Now if you will excuse me . . .'

At which the young general exploded. His handsome face twisted with fury. He fumed and ranted. He threatened to have me court-martialled. He told the orderlies to lock me up. They were looking at one another uneasily when Larrey himself came into the room demanding to know why the peace of his patients was being disturbed. He then gave the young general a fearsome dressing down in front of grinning orderlies and guardsmen.

'Me, I blame Napoleon,' Pascaud said when I told him about the incident. 'Imperialism's contagious. Everybody wants to be a monarch. When the Corsican made himself an emperor every jumped-up little fool like that general started to prance about like some aristo. Bring back the Republic, I say. Otherwise it will all end in tears, I tell you.'

Napoleon had some strange ideas. He decided that the finest tribute he could pay to one of the heroes of Austerlitz, a colonel of the Guard Chasseurs called Louis Morland, was to have him embalmed, pickled in brandy and shipped back to France. Larrey was given the job, which he did with little grace. The dashing Chasseur was duly gutted, pumped full of chemicals then lowered into a cask of good brandy.

'Should have got the Mamelukes to do this,' Pascaud grumbled as we watched the mustachioed cavalryman disappear into the brandy keg. 'They've been at it for thousands of years. Their pyramids are full of pickled corpses.'

Not pickled, the Mameluke Ibrahim told us on one of his visits, but salted. The bodies were covered in blocks of salt which drew out the corrupting fluids. Then they were swathed in bandages which had been steeped in resins and gums. And where we closed the mouths and eyes of the dead, the Egyptians fixed them open. 'So that they can see where they go and speak the sacred passwords on their journey into eternity,' Ibrahim explained. At which Pascaud harrumphed.

Ibrahim was relentless in his pursuit of medical information. Whenever there was an amputation to be done, or wound to be debrided, or a dressing to be changed, Ibrahim was there at our elbows. Eventually Larrey got fed up and arranged to have the young Egyptian transferred to another ambulance as a medical orderly. Ibrahim was delighted and proved to be a tireless worker. Or so I heard. I never saw him again.

Pascaud's prediction that Brünn would become the hospital-fever capital of Europe proved true. Within a week hundreds were dying. The fever began among the Russian prisoners who were packed into the churches, and then spread through the town. Within ten days it was raging in every hospital in Brünn, with the exception of ours. Larrey's insistence on daylight, fresh air and total cleanliness had paid off.

As the fever tightened its grip Larrey called a meeting of the Guard Ambulance's medical officers. 'The army cannot afford to lose doctors,' he told us. 'So nobody – *nobody* – goes near a patient unless he's wearing a gown, hood and mask which have been dampened with vinegar and water. Boots will be taken off at the door and left outside. Every doctor and medical orderly will wear sabots which have been dipped in turpentine or spirit. Hands must be washed in vinegar and water. And all instruments are to be washed in brandy. There are to be no exceptions. Do you all understand?' Larrey's instructions were carried out to the letter. And the Guard hospital survived the epidemic unscathed.

But Émile Pascaud did not. One night the little crook-back got drunk and wandered away to offer his services in the worst of the fever-ravaged hospitals. He did not take his gown, hood and mask. A few days later he was found collapsed in a corner, sweating and shivering and complaining of pains in his joints and his twisted spine. He was bundled into a bed in a specially set aside room, where he spent the rest of that day retching and vomiting.

Next day he was worse. His skin burned, his eyelids swelled up, his expression slackened and dulled and he became delirious. In his ramblings he seemed to spend most of his time fishing in the River Creuse from the old bridge at Lascelles Dunois. He muttered about his mother, Father Jean, the Russians, Napoleon and someone called Éloise. He never mentioned my name. Then he seemed to go deaf.

'Try to keep him cool and comfortable,' Larrey told me on

one of his visits. 'Watch out for bed sores. With a spine like his, he's bound to lie awkwardly and suffer from them. Otherwise . . .' he shrugged, 'not much we can do for him. Except pray to a God we none of us believe in.'

But the God we did not believe in was not disposed to favour the irascible little atheist. Pascaud got steadily worse. On the fifth day rose-red papules emerged on his chest and spread across his body. They suppurated and bled. He suffered chronic diarrhoea, his pulse became fainter, his tongue became dry and coated, and sores sprouted around his mouth. As the disease raced through his body he seemed to shrink, until he looked like a broken child. My foul-mouthed little friend died at three o'clock in the afternoon.

The medical orderlies watched open-mouthed as I carted in my Voltaic pile to Pascaud's bedside and carefully assembled it. I built a pile of sixty plates of zinc and sixty plates of silver in a salt water solution. I quickly stripped off his linen and applied the terminals on either side of his chest. As the electricity from the Voltaic pile surged through him the little twisted body convulsed once, shuddered, then fell back. I tried again. This time the convulsion was weaker. I tried a third time. The movement was weaker still.

'What in God's name are you doing Frankenstein?' said a voice at my shoulder. It was Larrey, dressed like myself in the long vinegar-soaked hooded robe and mask. It struck me that we looked like members of some strange religious order. A species of scientific monk. Evil-smelling friars dedicated to the worship of medicine.

'I'm trying to restart his heart,' I snapped. 'But it's not working. It's just not working.'

Larrey brushed me aside and checked Pascaud's pulse. He shook his head, stepped back and watched silently as I reapplied the terminals to Pascaud's chest. Again the body convulsed, and I thought I saw a tremor ripple across the face. One eye almost opened. But again Pascaud fell back onto the bed, inert.

'Come on!' and I shouted at him turned to Larrey. 'I'm going to try to get in closer to his heart. Hand me that scalpel.' Larrey did as he was told. I made an incision on either side of his chest and inserted the terminals into the wounds. The little body heaved violently but once again fell back, dead. I tried again and again, but the reaction only got weaker and weaker. I was sweating with effort and almost sobbing with frustration.

Eventually Larrey hauled me away from the body, withdrew the terminals from Pascaud's chest and covered the little man's face. Then he studied me thoughtfully. 'I thought you'd gone mad, Frankenstein,' he said. 'But then ... dammit, I saw his chest move. I saw something happening. I don't know what the hell it was, but something was happening. Something important . . .'

But nothing seemed more important to me than the death of Émile Pascaud. I had known the little man from the Creuse Valley for less than three months, and in that time I had seen more men die than I care to remember, and in ways that I never wanted to see again. But now I was over-whelmed with loss. For reasons that I still do not understand I was overcome by my grief. I felt numb, bewildered and outraged. I stumbled out of the Guard hospital and walked into the streets of Brünn. Tears blinded me.

THE WANDERING

EUROPE: 1805–1812

To the religious and the credulous the number seven has a peculiar significance. Seven is special, seven is sacred, seven is mystical. There are seven days in creation, seven spirits before the throne of God, seven days in the week, seven graces, seven divisions in the Lord's Prayer and seven ages in the life of man. There are seven phases of the moon, seven churches of Asia, seven champions of Christendom. The seven deadly sins are countered by the seven joys of the Virgin. The ancient world had seven wonders; ancient Greece had seven sages.

Alchemical texts talk of the seven bodies of alchemy. The Apocalypse of St John is a book of sevens: the Lamb has seven eyes, there are seven horns, seven candlesticks, seven stars, seven trumpets. The God of the ancient Hebrews has seven names. The seven sleepers of Christian legend fled from the Roman persecution and hid in a cave on Mount Celion where they slept for 250 years. Why the number seven has such meaning I have never understood. Nor has anyone been able to enlighten me.

But for seven years I wandered. For seven years I was in a wilderness of the mind. For seven years I lived in a state of the direst confusion. For seven years I drifted around Europe from country to country like a ship cut loose from its moorings. They were the strangest seven years of my life.

The battle at Austerlitz dislocated me from myself. That great clash has been described as the culmination of Napoleon Bonaparte's genius. All I ever saw in it was the triumph of my old enemy Death. That day he stalked the Pratzen Heights, the icy Satschan marshes and the makeshift hospitals of Brünn smiling contentedly.

And so he should. His harvest was prodigious. Almost 40,000 men had died at Austerlitz. No one knew how many died of infected wounds and fevers in the months that followed. The corpses came from across Europe and beyond: Frenchmen, Italians, Russians, Austrians, Lithuanians, Ukranians, Bavarians, Egyptians, Württembergers, Hungarians. Most were young when Death took them.

Austerlitz became known as the Battle of the Three Emperors. After the killing was done, Emperor Francis of Austria shared a glass or two of wine with Napoleon while they discussed an armistice. Tsar Alexander of Russia sent Bonaparte a message congratulating him on his victory. They say that in London Prime Minister William Pitt ordered his officials to 'Roll up that map of Europe; it will not be wanted these ten years'. He was right. Most of Europe was under the boot of the little Corsican. His enemies were helpless.

One of the most persistent was the mistress of my imagination, Germaine de Stael. She made no effort to hide her view of him. Germaine infuriated Napoleon. Her writings drove him to fury. He described her trivial novel *Delphine* as 'wrong, anti-social, dangerous' After her second novel *Corinne*, a vapid tale of unrequited love, Napoleon banished her from Paris and back to Coppet. The Genevan authorities were instructed to watch her carefully and to report on her regularly.

But I was to see nothing of Germaine for years. In those seven years I drifted across the face of Europe. I wandered from country to country, city to city, university to university. Time after time I found myself in some obscure corner of Europe – Lithuania, Poland, Zurich, Slovenia – staring into a bottle of wine, trying to remember what I was doing, and what exactly I was looking for. It became a search without point, a pilgrimage with no destination. Often I feared for my sanity.

But Calvinism dies hard. I made some semblance of putting my affairs in order. I wrote to Waldman handing over to him my share of the St Moritz Clinic and wishing him well. I wrote separately to Erika relieving her of her obligation to me and hoping that the future would treat her with kindness.

I wrote to my father in Geneva, thanking him for the money he had settled on me and telling him that I could no longer be contacted in Ingolstadt. I wrote to my brother Ernest wishing him well in the Frankenstein business. I did not ask to be remembered to Elisabeth.

For seven years I kept no journal. I now rely entirely on my memory. I know that in 1807 I was in London pretending to study physiology with a touchy Scotsman called Charles Bell, who prided himself on his skill as an artist as well as his expertise as a physician. Bell had caused a stir when he combined his two interests in a tome entitled *Essays on the Anatomy of Expression in Painting*. Bell and I parted company when I told him that his ideas were as worthless as his canvases.

After falling out with Bell I headed north to the city of Worcester where one Alexander Wilson Philip was making a reputation as an electrician at the Worcester General Infirmary. I arrived in the city with high hopes, only to find that Wilson Philip was doing nothing that Felix Waldman and I had not done a thousand times before, usually more effectively. Nor did Philip take kindly to my criticism of his methods. Before long he asked me to leave.

That was the pattern. I would seek out one of Europe's eminent electricians, to find that they usually knew less than I did, and that very often their electrical equipment was out of date, or badly maintained, or both. A brief and very unhappy spell with Jean-Noël Hallé in Paris was followed by some unsatisfactory months with Karl Gradengeissen in Berlin.

I suppose I was looking for a mentor, a modern Paracelcus to guide me on the path to revelation. In 1809 I thought I had found the man in a youngish Silesian called Johann Ritter, then teaching and working in Munich. I knew something of Ritter. He had been a protégé of von Humboldt at the University of Jena where he had studied electricity. He then found a patron in the Duke of Gotha and Altenburg, who installed him at his court and funded his experiments. In 1805 – the year of Austerlitz – Ritter moved to Munich, a full member of the Bavarian Academy of Sciences.

There is no doubt that Ritter had been an original, energetic and hard-working scientist. By the time I found my way to Munich in the autumn of 1810 he had already published thirteen volumes of electrical experiments and scientific philosophy. At the age of thirty-three Ritter's reputation stretched across Europe. And it was, so far as I could tell, well deserved.

I had been told that Ritter had developed a dry cell, in which electricity could be stored for long periods. It could be moved about and tapped whenever and wherever it was needed. In short, Ritter had come up with a device that would replace the effective but cumbersome Voltaic pile. He seemed a man worth knowing.

But I was too late. Long before I joined him Ritter had succumbed to that appetite for the mystical that affects so many Germans. The hard-headed natural philosopher had become lost in a miasma of romantic and poetic notions. He had lost all interest in real work. All his attention was devoted to the power of what he termed a 'world soul' and the efficacy of water divining, crystal gazing, sword swinging and other such flummeries.

Ritter's guide through this strange darkness was a Bavarian mystic called Frederick von Baader. Von Baader was an odd, half-deranged man who nourished many a strange theory. He also wandered the streets, hostelries and even the churches of Munich telling anyone who would listen (and there were many) that all the ills of Bavaria and Europe should be laid at the door of the Jews, particularly rich Jews. His influence on Ritter was as profound as it was baffling.

'Mark his words, Frankenstein,' Ritter told me. 'Mark von Baader's words. The little synagogue on the corner is the root of all the evil in this continent of ours. The Jews are the only people to profit from the wars of Napoleon. They are an abomination – a cancer – on the world soul. I tell you, Frankenstein, the time is coming when we must arm ourselves against Judah, before it is too late and we are destroyed.'

But my time in Munich was crucial. Despite his obsessions, Johann Ritter served me well. His strange intellectual decay cleared my mind. Ritter was a lesson in how a good, perhaps even great, mind could lose its way. The realisation halted my drift towards the irrational into which Ritter had sunk and from which he would never escape.

I returned to science. I saw clearly that only facts, facts hard won and closely observed, would serve my purpose.

Knowledge was the only way ahead. I had to know more, much more, about the structure of bone, flesh, tissue and nerve which the Man of Light inhabited.

ANATOMIST

GLASGOW, SCOTLAND: 1813

Scotland was, I had decided, God's joke on Europe. He had filled this awful place with talented men, obliging the rest of us to seek them out. Its universities and medical schools were peppered with Dutchmen and Germans, Frenchmen and Americans sitting at the feet of Scots anatomists, chemists and surgeons. Just why the Lord populated this sodden corner of Europe with so much learning is one of His mysteries. Further proof, if proof were needed, that He does not exist. Only His malign counterpart. Many was the time I cursed the fate that brought me here.

No more than the cold and the weather did I like the Scots. They were as stiff-necked as Prussians, as volatile as Italians, as penny-pinching as the Swiss, as argumentative as the French, as drunken as Bavarians and as senselessly violent as Corsicans. They contained every miserable character trait Europe had to offer. They had no food, no music, no wine and no drink other than their throat-scalding whisky. They were both noisy and timid. They spoke either a guttural dialect of English or a species of Irish that not even the Irish can understand.

They were creatures of their foul weather. Night fell shortly after noon and the rain never stopped. It swept endlessly off the Atlantic, transforming Glasgow into dank cliffs of grey and black. The streets of the city were a perpetual quagmire. The pallid citizenry flitted from doorway to doorway in a vain attempt to avoid the weather. The poor, in their rags, seemed immune to the damp. Every bone in my body ached for the clear air and clean snow of a Bavarian winter.

The city of Glasgow was like no place I had ever known. I was a central European, a landlocked creature. I belonged in a universe of high grey mountains, clear lakes, dark forests and green meadows. But here I was, perched on the dark western edge of Europe, on a river that flowed into an ocean I had never seen, in a great, grim city that looked west to the Caribbean and the lands of America.

The quaysides reeked of rum and tobacco, sugar and whale oil, sealskins and timber. The river was lined with schooners and brigantines which shuttled backwards and forwards between Glasgow and Jamaica and Newfoundland, Nova Scotia and Saint Kitts, Grenada and Demerara. It was a world bounded by the sea. And these strange, unruly, sea-bound people were the most implacable of Napoleon's enemies.

I had arrived at the end of October and found myself a miserable room in Ingram Street, where dinner consisted of a dish of oaten porridge and plate of warmed-up mutton. There were no vegetables and the wine had been watered to extinction. The dishevelled servant told me that the owner – a Mr James Provan – had just dropped dead, so the premises were about to go on the auction block. He was, therefore, entirely indifferent to my comfort.

236

My heart was in my boots. I knew no one in Glasgow, not even by reputation. I had no letters of introduction. So I scanned the *Glasgow Herald* for some scientific soirée which might produce a few introductions. One notice caught my eye; Dr Andrew Ure's 'Course of Lectures on Experimental Philosophy' which promised a 'Variety of Splendid experiments and illustrations in the subjects of Astronomy, Optics, Magnetism, Galvanism, Hydrostatics and Mechanics . . .' It was to be held at the Andersonian Institute, founded, it seems, in 1796 'for promoting the study and diffusion of science'.

I found my way to the Andersonian Institute and joined the crowd in a gas-lit chamber to hear Dr Ure on the subject of Galvanism. He was a stocky, energetic man of about my own age, with a determined look about him. He delivered a fine lecture. He demonstrated the Voltaic pile and the Cruikshank trough. He electrified the head of a dummy so that the hair stood on end. He touched on the medical uses and electrical treatments for rheumatism, asthma and melancholy. Then he sent his audience out with the notion that the day was coming when every hospital in Europe would be equipped with electrical machines to the huge benefit of the sick. I was impressed.

After the lecture I introduced myself as an electrician from Bavaria. Ure, in a state of post-lecture euphoria, seemed pleased to make my acquaintance. He insisted on inviting me to his home in Glassford Street for a 'bite of supper' and a 'bit of a blether'. When he heard where I was staying he laughed and recommended the Commercial Tavern in Buchanan's Court just off the Trongate. I promised to take his advice. He seemed the soul of amiability.

'Mark my words, Frankenstein,' he told me, as we made our way through the darkness and rain. 'Mark my words. There's a day coming when every street in this toon – sorry town – will be lit by electricity. With one spark, we'll light the whole of Glasgow. Can you imagine that, eh? Every house in the land – even the poorest – lit by the power of electricity. Maybe even heated as well. Electrical fireplaces, eh. Hoo ... how does that fancy tak' ye? It's coming, Frankenstein. I tell ye, it's coming.

'Ye see,' he went on. 'Wi' the richt kind of electrical devices we'll send messages from one end o' this earth to the other. Imagine that if ye will. Messages. Frae here tae America. I tell you my friend, we're on the brink o' the Age of Electricity. That's the only name for it. It'll be the greatest boon that mankind has ever known. No' that mankind deserves any kind of boon if ye ask me. Nature's too good for mankind.'

But we had no sooner crossed his threshold into his house when another Ure emerged. Within minutes he had reduced a servant girl to tears for dropping his papers, shouted at a second for failing to clear some mud off the floor, demanded to see the cook for overdoing a 'gey expensive' piece of beef, and angrily banished both his children for some minor infraction of the house rules.

His wife Catherine – an amiable, round-faced woman with a bold eye – fled the room as soon as it was polite to do so. As she made her exit I noticed an agreeable backside. Ure caught my look and frowned. Servants, children, wives and particularly the working classes, he told me, were not to be coddled.

'The working man has got to be watched, Frankenstein,' he warned me. 'At least in this Scotland of ours. They drink ye see. There's the problem. They drink like thirst-maddened beasts. Well, I say that the man whose Saturday night is spent in drunkenness and riot will make a bad Christian on the Sabbath, an indifferent workman on Monday, and an unhappy husband and father through the week. If more folk minded these words we'd all be better off.'

I took polite exception. 'I fear I must speak up for the modest happiness to be found in a glass of good wine,' I told him. 'Or in a glass of your Scotch whisky.'

He grimaced at the word happiness. 'Happiness!' he snorted. 'There's far too much talk these days about happiness. A man must not expect his *chief* happiness in the present, but in a future state of existence. It's not happiness we need in this world. It is a store of moral capital, to be invested wisely, for our eternal futures.'

I soon discovered that Ure was reactionary to the point of mild lunacy. He was the kind of man who believed that there was nothing like stuffing a child up a chimney for improving its character, and that the factory system was in dire need of protection from the so-called humanitarian conscience. He was also a scientific visionary with a powerful sense of the world's future. A reactionary buffoon, with, nevertheless, a sinewy grip on the shape of things to come.

'So it's an anatomy school you're seeking efter is it?' he said. 'Well in my ain view you could do nae better, sorry no better, than Mister Granville Sharp Pattison's wee school in College Street. He's the coming man, they tell me. A maist handy surgeon. And he's got one of the best collections o' anatomical specimens in Scotland. Maybe even in Britain. And, maist important, he never seems to be short o' a corpse or twa tae dissect. There's aye *somebody* lying on his dissecting table. Or so they tell me.'

That interested me. Corpses were a scarce commodity in this civilisation of ours. It was the same everywhere. Scalpels were rusting all over Europe because of an irrational squeamishness over the dead. The best anatomy is learnt by hand and knife. 'Are they legally acquired?' I asked.

Ure shrugged. 'Who knows. Some of them, probably. But I hear that our Mister Sharp Pattison has certain sources of supply that are denied tae other anatomists. How I do nae know. Frankly, it's why the College Street school is such a nice wee business. That and his museum of anatomical specimens. They say there's mair than a thousand items in there.'

'He sounds just what I'm looking for,' I said.

'I'd say so,' Ure replied. 'Ye could do worse. Mind you, the mannie himsel' is no' tae everybody's taste.'

'Are there any alternatives?' I asked.

'Only James Jeffray's course at the university,' Ure said. 'But I'm no' sure I'd recommend it. Jeffray's a cantankerous devil, and no' exactly what ye'd call modern. No, for my money, Mister Sharp Pattison's your man. But then it's no' my money.'

Next day I took Ure's advice and transferred my luggage to the Commercial Tavern, which was short on luxury but was decent enough. After settling into my room I sought out Mr. Granville Sharp Pattison's anatomy school. I found it at Number Ten College Street, a modest two-storey house in a narrow thoroughfare at the end of which stood Glasgow's university. Granville Sharp Pattison took me by surprise. I found a tall, young man with a narrow hatchet of a face and vivid dark eyes. He was ten years younger than me and had a restless, combative look about him. He would not have been out of place in the Guard Cavalry.

'I'll be happy to take your money Mister Frankenstein,' Pattison said to me. 'And I'm sure you'll get value for it in return. But I must stress that in this establishment we specialise in *practical* anatomy, a business which is not without its slight, eh, hazards. If you want anatomical *theory*, then I suggest you look elsewhere. Such as Dr Jeffray's course at the university.'

240

'I can learn anatomical theory anywhere in Europe,' I told him. 'Even in Bavaria. But what you call practical anatomy is hard to come by. Which is why I am here. In this place.'

'In this God-forsaken country, you mean,' he grinned.

'In this God-forsaken *climate* I certainly mean,' I replied.

But there was an air of disdain about him that rankled. I decided that he should know of my history. I was not here to be lectured, I told him. I doubted whether he could teach me anything. I had studied with Waldman and Krempe at Ingolstadt, with Ritter in Munich, had worked with Aldini in London and conferred with Pringle and Cavallo in London. I had followed Napoleon's Imperial Guard down the Danube and been with Larrey at Austerlitz. While he was scribbling in his schoolbooks I was dismembering and stitching up soldiers all over central Europe.

So I had not come to Glasgow to sit at his feet or to bask in his reputation. I had come because I had heard he could provide the cadavers I needed for my studies. For this privilege I was prepared to pay, and pay well. But I had to be allowed to do my own work and in my own way. Those were my terms. He could take them or leave them.

It was a risky strategy. I could see he was a man with a large opinion of himself. I half expected him to show me the door. But he did not. I do not think I had intimidated him. But he was impressed and plainly curious as to my expertise. Maybe he thought he could learn a trick or two from me. Maybe he thought a foreigner would be good for the school's reputation. But whatever the reason, he studied me for a few seconds, then grinned broadly and stuck out his hand.

'Very well Mr Frankenstein from Bavaria and late of the Grand Army,' he said. 'We will accommodate you as best we can. Providing, that is, that your private studies do not disrupt our other students or the running of the school. That we could not tolerate.'

'I think I can promise you that,' I said shaking him by the hand. 'In fact I'm sure I can. Just give me a table and a corpse and leave me to it. You will never know I'm there.'

'What's your interest?'

'The heart, the lungs and the nervous system,' I replied.

'Brain and spine included?'

'If possible. Spine certainly.'

'So you want torsos?'

'Yes,' I said. 'The fresher the better.'

'Hmmmm,' he mused. 'Not so easy.'

'No, I didn't think it would be.'

'We might disappoint you,' he said. 'Good corpses are becoming harder and harder to come by. Prices are high and getting higher by the day. Every medical man in Scotland wants them. Demand outstrips supply. I fear we're having to resort to methods that are, well . . .'

'Unlawful?' I suggested.

'Possibly,' he said.

I shrugged.

'But we do what we can,' he said. 'I'm sure we'll manage to struggle along somehow. The good Lord willing.'

That night a general illumination between seven o'clock and ten o'clock had been ordered by the magistrates of Glasgow to celebrate the victory of the allies over Napoleon at Leipzig, news of which was beginning to fill the local newspapers. Any household which did not display a candle or a lantern in every window risked being showered with bricks and bottles by the celebrating crowds.

I went out into the streets to watch the festivities and found them brightly lit, crowded and loud with the sound of breaking glass. I suspect that many of Glasgow's less popular gentry and merchants had their windows broken that night. A few old scores were settled in that outburst of patriotism.

Meanwhile Pattison was as good as his word. I was given a dissecting table in the corner of one of the rooms and left to get on with my own work. I also had the full run of College Street's collection of anatomical specimens, and whenever I wanted I could attend the lectures given by Andrew Russel or Pattison himself.

Pattison was by far the better of the two. While he lacked the authority of Dominique Larrey, he was as good an anatomist as I had seen. Better than most of the clumsy fools who passed for anatomists in the great universities of Europe. He was as good, if not better, than Aldini, superior to anyone at Ingolstadt. He was hardly older than his students but they regarded him as the incarnation of medical science.

Pattison's system for providing the College Street anatomy school with usable corpses relied on a network of midwives, doctors, surgeons and students all over the city, who were paid to let the College Street anatomists know when someone was approaching the grave. The burial site was duly recorded and one of Pattison's snatch squads was sent out to the dig up the corpse.

The system was not perfect but it worked well enough to supply College Street with more dissecting material than any other establishment in the city. Certainly more than the university, which relied exclusively on executed murderers from the gallows. And turbulent as Glasgow undoubtedly was, there were never *quite* enough murderers to go round.

GLASGOW, SCOTLAND: 1814

Of all the corpses that passed through my hands at the College Street anatomy school none was as memorable as the one known as 'Cutchie's Uncle'. A midwife in the village of Mearns, south of Glasgow, had let us know that a healthy middle-aged man had dropped dead leading his family in prayers. His death had baffled the two local doctors but Pattison suspected that the man had been felled by a catastrophic failure of the heart.

I was intrigued by this case and badgered Pattison to let me have him. He told me that if I could resurrect the corpse I could have the torso. But he warned me that getting a dead man from Mearns into the centre of Glasgow could prove to be a chancy business. He advised me to seek the collaboration of a student called Rab Cutchie, one of the most audacious of his graveyard raiders.

I took his advice. I knew Rab Cutchie and liked him. He was a resourceful little man who knew every graveyard in and around Glasgow. If anyone could smuggle the corpse into College Street it was Cutchie. So Cutchie, Pattison and I struck an agreement: if we could get the body back successfully, Cutchie would take the legs (he was studying the articulation of the joints), I would have the torso and Pattison the rest.

'The problem will no' be at Mairns kirkyaird,' Cutchie told me as we sat down to plan the raid. 'The problem will be getting past the mannie at the toll-gate in the Gorbals. He's a richt auld scunner and he's yin o' the toon guard. He's death on resurrectionists like oorsels. Foreby, the magistrates have telt every watchman and toll-keeper in Glasgow tae keep an eye oot for the sack-'em-up lads. And that, Frankenstein, is us.'

But Cutchie was nothing if not resourceful. He was not about to be thwarted by the Gorbals toll-keeper. 'Twa respectable gentlemen will gang doon tae Mearns,' he announced after some thought, 'and *three* respectable gentlemen will drive back tae College Street. That's how we'll dae it.'

Next day we hired a horse and gig from Sandy Leith's establishment in the High Street, bought a suit of decent second-hand clothes and a hat from an Irishman in the Salt Market and set off early in the evening to the village of Mairns to resurrect our man.

Bagging him was no problem. Just as Cutchie predicted, there was no watchman, no prowling relatives. Within twenty minutes we had dug up the grave and cracked open the coffin. Then we stripped the corpse of its shroud, dressed it in the suit we had bought in the Salt Market, put the hat on its head, propped it up between us in the middle seat of the gig and set out back to College Street.

Cutchie was audacity itself when we got to the Gorbals toll-gate. As audacious as Murat at the Danube Bridge. 'Hurry up man,' he shouted at the lumbering gatekeeper. 'My auld uncle here is faintin' awa' for the want o' a doctor.

He's in a bad, bad way. If we dinna' get him tae the medical men soon we'll hae a corpse on oor hands.'

The gatekeeper lifted his lantern to study Cutchie's uncle. 'Oh, my God ye're richt,' he said. 'The puir mannie's at death's door by the look o' him. Awa' wi' ye afore the puir soul passes tae his maker. Drive canny noo, lads, see that ye drive canny . . .'

So, for the rest of its short existence, the cadaver was known as Cutchie's Uncle. It was quickly disassembled into its component parts: Cutchie's Uncle's brain, Cutchie's Uncle's liver, Cutchie's Uncle's eyes, Cutchie's Uncle's stomach and intestines, and so forth. Cutchie's Uncle achieved a kind of immortality when various of its bits and pieces were pickled and bottled to join Pattison's large and growing collection of anatomical specimens.

Pattison was true to his word: I was given Cutchie's Uncle's torso, minus the viscera. And when I broke into the thorax and sliced through the pericardium I found the heart as sound as a bell. There was no trace of disease or damage. Whatever part of his anatomy had killed Cutchie's Uncle it was not his heart. I was provided with one of the finest hearts I have ever dissected. It was a superb specimen.

And in the wall of the right atrium I laid bare a node of muscle, rich in nerves, which had obviously been very active in life. This, I decided without too much proof, was the device which regulated the beat of the heart, probably through the bundle of fibrous tissue that bridged the atria and the ventricles.

I painstakingly mapped the contours of the membranous sac of the pericardium, taking notes on its relation to the muscles of the diaphragm and the lungs. I examined its gleaming inner surface, glistening with a fluid which, I guessed, helped the heart to beat smoothly. I traced the

246

arteries and the nerves which seemed to be branches of the of the vagus, phrenic and sympathetic.

For some reason the nerves of that particular heart were well defined and traceable. I hunted them down through every tissue in the organ. Gradually, painstakingly, I began to understand how the heart worked. By the time I had finished I had a full notebook. There was little left of the heart but a pile of chopped meat, which I think I saw one of the College Street porters feed to his cat.

Pattison and Russel were both good anatomists and clever surgeons. But they were an odd pair. Pattison was the dominant one – tall sardonic and aggressive where Russel was stocky, diffident and usually polite. They were both, intrigued by my experience as a surgeon with the Grande Armée. But where Russel's curiosity was medical, Pattison wanted to know about the Imperial Guard and about Napoleon himself. Two of his brothers, he told me, were military men. One was a veteran of the Duke of Wellington's campaigns in Spain and Portugal.

Pattison was curious to know what I thought of the death of Jean Moreau who had changed sides. The event was well reported by the Glasgow newspapers. At Dresden a French cannonball had taken off one of Moreau's legs, before ploughing straight through his horse's belly to shatter his other leg. He survived the amputation but not the infection.

'One of the finest soldiers of the Revolution,' I told Pattison. 'At least that's what most of the officers of the Imperial Guard used to say.'

'They didn't see him as a traitor to Napoleon and France?' he asked.

I shrugged. 'Some did. But most were just sorry that he fell out with Napoleon. Some could see the reason for it. They're not all fanatical *Bonapartistes*, Pattison. Many of them believe

Napoleon should not have crowned himself Emperor. Old-fashioned republicans.'

'So why do they go on fighting and risking their necks for him?' he demanded to know.

'Why did your brothers go on fighting and risking their necks for the Hanoverian half-wit on the British throne?' I replied. 'And for the Prince of Wales who'll be King of England soon, unless he eats and drinks himself to death.'

My remark was not welcomed. Pattison bridled at this insult to British royalty. Russel tried to intervene and change the subject, but Pattison glared at me and walked away. He avoided me for a few days and there was a decided chill in the air between us for some time. From then on I tried to avoid the subject of France and its Emperor.

I worked long and hard. My only exercise was walking the damp streets of Glasgow or joining one of the snatch squads on a raid. I came to enjoy the sport. The Scots took a dim view of the activity. Their old law against 'disturbing the sepulchres of the dead' was still in place. Graveyards were patrolled by the City Guard and, sometimes, the relatives of the dead. In some places man-traps and spring-guns were set to discourage the resurrectionists.

In fact, I almost lost my life one wet and windy night in a graveyard near the village of Govan. I stumbled in the dark, triggered a spring-gun and felt the rush of air as a projectile hurtled past my left ear. I winced to think how my demise would have been explained to Noble Alphonse Frankenstein in Geneva. His oldest son, stone dead in a wet graveyard on the banks of a river of which he had never heard, in a land of which he was only dimly aware.

The resurrectionist's worst enemy was decomposition. A corpse that came apart in the hand was of no use to any anatomist. The art was to retrieve the body before the acid-like fluids released by death reduced the corpse to a heap of fleshy rubble. Unless we reached a cadaver within three or four days it was useless. This fact was well enough known and some relatives patrolled the graveyards at night for a week after a burial. Fortunately such dedication was rare. Most people seemed content to let their dead fend for themselves.

Our technique was simple enough. All a snatch squad needed were a couple of shovels, a crowbar, some rope and a roomy hessian sack. We never dug up the whole coffin: that would have taken too long. We simply exposed one third of the box, levered it open, slipped a noose around the corpse's shoulders, heaved it out and slipped it into the sack. Occasionally we went into a grave through a tunnel behind the headstone but that took longer and was much riskier.

A skilled team – and the College Street teams were all skilled – could usually have a body sacked up in less than half an hour. Rab Cutchie boasted that one of his squads had done it in ten minutes. 'Mind you, that was oot in country in guid saft grund,' he admitted, 'an' wi' naebody within a mile o' us.' The trickiest part of the operation was usually trundling the corpses through the streets. Fortunately for medical science, Glasgow's town guards preferred the shelter of their watch-huts and the comforts of a whisky bottle to tramping the streets. Most could be bribed with a few pieces of silver.

One way or another we kept the College Street anatomy school well supplied with torsos. I cracked thorax after thorax. Some had arms, legs and head attached; most did not. Some were male, some were female, some were old, some young. One belonged to a baby of five months and for the first time I cut through a sternum which had not ossified into bone.

The heart became familiar territory, a robust, cone-shaped pump, five inches long, three-and-a-half inches wide and weighing between ten and twelve ounces in men and eight to ten ounces in women. The heavy muscle intrigued me. It was at the centre of human existence. Everything depended on its power to pump blood into every cranny of the body.

Thanks to the bodies of dead Scots I gradually came to know every twist and turn of the chambers, channels, valves and pipes of that fleshy device.

GLASGOW, SCOTLAND: MAY 1814

I made a good friend of Rab Cutchie and got on well enough with the other College Street students. But most of them were a good ten years younger than I was, and some were distinctly wary of my foreign ways. A few were polite rather than friendly. The fact that I had wielded a bone saw and a scalpel for Napoleon Bonaparte did nothing to improve their opinion of me. I began to feel lonely, and vaguely homesick, although for what, I am not quite sure.

So I was pleased when a servant girl brought me a note from Andrew Ure inviting me to join him and his wife Catherine for an early supper to be followed by theatricals at the Theatre Royal. When I arrived at Ure's house in Glassford Street in what passed as my finery Ure was in an expansive mood. Catherine was waiting for us in the drawing room, comely enough in a dress of blue taffeta. Her grey eyes were bright with the prospect of an evening out.

All through dinner, Ure was cheerfully tedious. All he wanted to talk about was ways of making money. 'Now's the time Frankenstein,' he kept saying. 'There'll never be a better time. This toon's – this town – is aboot tae double in size. What do you think o' that? This'll be one of the biggest towns in Europe before long. And if a man invests wisely – wisely mind ye – he could do very well in this town of oors. I mean ours.'

'Shush Andrew,' Catherine said mildly. 'I'm sure that Mister Frankenstein didn't come to hear you talk business.'

'Tosh, woman,' he snapped. 'Every man worth his saut – salt I meant to say – is interested in business. Am I right, Frankenstein? There's some would say money is the measure of a man's worth.'

Baron Alphonse Frankenstein for one, I thought. And my younger brother Ernest. But I asked him what he had in mind.

'There's a number of nice wee – little – properties I'm keeping an eye on,' he told me. 'In the chemical industries. That's the future, ye see. I'm convinced o' that. The chemical industries. There'll never be enough chemicals. There's nothing more certain.'

The 'nice wee properties' Ure had in mind were a vitriol works in Carntyne, a soda works in Govan, a dye factory in Anderston. And he warbled on about them all the way to the Theatre Royal where Catherine sat between us through a dismal play, dismally acted entitled *John Bull, or an Englishman's Fireside*. Ure could hardly conceal his boredom, but Catherine was delighted with the proceedings and applauded enthusiastically.

After the play we were treated to a ballet by one Signor Montignani, Miss Malpas and Miss Parr. This seemed to excite Catherine to the point where she was pressing her thigh firmly against mine. Ure failed to notice. I suspect his mind was drifting among the vitriol vats of Carntyne and the soda pipes of Govan calculating the profit that could be scraped out of them.

Then, following a rousing version of the British national anthem we were decanted into the winter streets of Glasgow. I thanked them both profusely for a 'wonderful evening of theatre', kissed Catherine's hand – a gesture which made Ure scowl – bade them goodnight and made my way back to my lodgings at the Commercial Hotel. I scanned the *Glasgow Herald* to see which evenings Ure lectured at the Andersonian.

Three day's later Catherine Ure's sturdy legs were wrapped around my bare backside as I pounded her into the old *chaise longue* in a small basement room next to the kitchen. She was an enthusiastic copulator, energetic and inventive. She gave as good as she got, matching me thrust for thrust. She squealed, panted and grunted until I feared the servants would call out the Town Guard. By the time we had finished she was red-faced with effort and glassy-eyed with sexual delirium.

I'd called on the Ure house in Glassford Street on the flimsy pretext that I may have left a small notebook behind when I had dined. She immediately led me downstairs telling me that 'Andrew always moves his papers into this little room down here.' We were no sooner across the threshold when she closed the door with her rump, took my right hand and pressed it between her legs, and pushed her mouth against mine. Thirty seconds later I was into her and hard at work.

She proved to be an agreeable sort of mistress. I became very fond of her. She was an amiable, intelligent and straightforward young woman who wanted nothing more than to be appreciated. Her sexual appetites were strong but entirely conventional. She told me Ure could not be excited into action without elaborate theatricals involving strange clothes. But even that, she said sadly, was very rare. Most of the time he just left her alone, which was hard for a lusty young woman.

'He's a strange man my Andra' she told me between bouts. 'There are times I think him the strangest man I ever met. He's clever. He's successful. He's a good provider. He impresses folk. Yet he's full of, well, hate I suppose. He never has a good word for anybody. He hates the servants. I think he hates the children. And I'm sure he hates me. Which is hurtful, because I don't hate him. But he likes you, Victor. Or at least he respects you. A man of real scientific intelligence, he calls you.'

As Ure lectured at the Andersonian Institute most evenings I became a regular caller at twenty-one Glassford Street. Ure's servants knew what was happening but Catherine assured me that their loyalties lay with her and not with her husband, whose dislike for them they returned. So the faded little room next to the kitchen became the cockpit of our amours and the dingy *chaise longue* the scene of many a joust.

Mostly she was a considerate partner but from time to time she would go into a sexual frenzy which both drained and alarmed me. She would thrash, heave and sometimes bite with real violence. Afterwards she would apologise and sometimes weep for being 'a terrible wanton woman.'

The three of us – Ure, Catherine and myself – made a number of outings to the Theatre Royal to watch the theatricals she loved so much. She always sat between us, and invariably rubbed herself against me. Once she insisted we go to a 'ball' at the Assembly Rooms in Ingram Street, a notion that Ure resisted on the grounds that he was no 'damned prancer and dancer'. But Catherine prevailed and for a few hours we skipped about the brightly-lit room.

Afterwards we had a late supper of oysters at the Commercial Hotel. Her foot played with mine under the table throughout the meal.

One evening, Pattison decided to patch up our relationship by inviting me to dine with him at his family home in Calton Street, a newly-built terrace on the south bank of the River Clyde. The house was elegant without being too grand, with high ceilings, superb curved balustrades, beautiful carpentry. It had been built in that neo-classical style at which the Scots had become adept. Which, given their distance from Greece, or anywhere else for that matter, always struck me as odd.

Pattison ushered me into the drawing room and introduced me to his mother, a large, heavily-built old woman whose widow's black only emphasised her pugnacious expression. She greeted me politely enough but with a searching look that I found vaguely unsettling.

'Have we met afore this d'ye think Mister Frankenstein?' she asked me. She made no concessions to the English ways of speaking affected by so many Scots of her class.

'I'm sure I would have remembered if we had,' I said with what I thought was a flirtatious smile.

'Awa' wi' ye,' she said. 'Whit wey wid a young craitur like yersel' mind meeting an auld wummin like me?'

'Speak English, mother,' Pattison chipped in. 'Or poor Mister Frankenstein will never understand a word of what you say.'

'Then puir Mister Frankenstein will hae tae gang ignorant,' she replied. 'For the tongue in mah heid is the tongue that the guid Lord gi'ed me. An' it willna' speak ony other wey.'

'Ignore your son, madam,' I told her. 'I've been in Scotland quite long enough to understand you.'

'Ye see, Granville,' she declared triumphantly. 'Yer Mister

255

Frankenstein understan's me just fine. Ah've aye said that a' this Englishness was just so much flummery.'

'Aye, mother,' Pattison said wryly. 'That's whit ye've aye said. An' mair times nor ah care tae remember. Now will we gang tae the trough afore we fa' doon wi' hunger.'

I led Mrs Pattison into dinner and did my best to charm her. I praised the style of her house, the cut of her furniture, the lavishness of her silver, whiteness of her table linen, and even the paintings on the wall. But she was not to be impressed by such European blandishments. She was quiet throughout the meal and kept staring at me in a disconcerting way.

'Ah mind now,' she announced loudly in the middle of the badly-cooked fish. 'Ah mind where it was that ah've seen ye before.'

'Madam?' I said politely.

'You're the young gentleman that's been walkin' aboot Glasgow wi' Catherine Monteath. Her that's married on Andra Ure. Ah've seen ye at the Theatre Royal and ah've seen ye at the Assembly Rooms.'

'Your memory does you credit madam,' I said politely. 'I have indeed escorted Mistress Ure to these places. Along with her husband, of course.'

She snorted and threw down her napkin. 'Escorted is it? That's no' whit decent fowk ca' it. No' the wey that you an' her were gallivantin' aboot. Her that should have kent better. Na, na. There's mair tae this than escorting.'

Pattison tried to leap to my rescue. 'Mother,' he said in a pained voice. 'You have no right to say this. I'll remind you that Mister Frankenstein is my friend and colleague. And a guest in our house.'

But the old woman was not to be placated. She glowered and rose to her feet. 'As ye say Granville, this Mister Frankenstein is a guest in oor house. As sic ah canna' order him oot. But ah dinna hae tae sit at the same table as an adulterer. So, if ye wid excuse me, ah'll bid ye a guid nicht.'

With that, she walked away from the table. She turned at the door, her eyes sparking with indignation. 'Mister Frankenstein, ye wid oblige me if ye widna' cross mah threshold again. This has aye been a decent hoose. Ah'd like tae keep it that wey.'

Her outburst left Pattison aghast. 'What can I say Frankenstein,' he muttered after the old woman had marched out. 'It's a terrible thing when a man has to apologise for his own mother. I fear she's a bit old-fashioned. That was unforgiveable.'

'Not unforgiveable,' I said. 'Regrettable, perhaps.'

'As you can see she's a woman who's inclined to arrive at the wrong conclusion. Always has been.'

'We all do at times,' I said.

'Assuming that is,' he said staring at me thoughtfully 'that she has come to the wrong conclusion.'

I said nothing.

'Ye lucky wee bastard,' Pattison said, eventually.

GLASGOW, SCOTLAND: 1814

One of Glasgow's few delights was John Smith's reading room in Hutcheson Street. For an annual subscription of twelve shillings and sixpence, an enthusiastic reader could buy access to most of the newspapers published in Scotland and London, plus the *Journal de Paris*, the *Gazette de France*, the *Journal des Débats* the *Hamburg Korrespondent*, the *Frankfurt Gazette* and the *Bremen Altona Merkury*. For an exile like myself it was treasure trove. Through regular visits round to Hutcheson Street I attempted to keep up with events in Europe. But the feeling of being on the edge of things never ceased to unsettle me. I was on the periphery of the periphery.

I was still ruminating gloomily when I turned into College Street to find a large, angry crowd at the door of Number Ten. Pattison and two of his students – I recognised John McLean and Robert Monro – were being bundled through the mob by the town guard. It was an ugly scene. All three looked pale and miserable as they were jeered at, kicked, punched and spat upon.

'What's going on?' I asked Rab Cutchie, who was standing on the other side of the road looking worried.

'A bloody mess is what's going on,' he said. 'Let's get out of here, Frankenstein. I need a drink.'

Over a few glasses of heated brandy in a Trongate whisky den he told me what had happened. 'Monro and McLean did a wee job last night,' he explained. 'They lifted a wummin called McAllester oot o' the Ramshorn kirkyaird, just roon the corner. I've never liked that. Ower close tae hame. But she'd died o' consumption, and Monro was keen tae hae a look at the lungs. Ye ken whit he's like aboot lungs. So the pair o' them went oot and bagged her. But they made a richt mess o' pittin' the grave back. There was muck a' ower the place. And footprints leadin' straight tae College Street.'

'So it was noticed right away?' I asked.

'Richt awa',' he said. 'The Ramshorn gravedigger – a miserable body called Braid wha's no above a bit o' corpse baggin' himsel' – noticed it first thing in the morning. He tells the deid wummin's twa brothers, wha immediately ask the magistrates for a warrant tae search College Street.'

'Which they got?' I said.

'Oh aye,' Cutchie said. 'By half past one in the efternoon they were hammering like thunder on the door. Wi' half the toon guard at their back. It was pandemonium inside. We had a damn good idea whit they were efter, and there were bits and pieces o' Mrs McAllester a' ower the place. We spent half an hour trying tae hide her, ah, pairts, amang the ither corpses. Monro took the heid aff, whipped oot the jaw, nose, top lip, some teeth, and dumped it wi' twa other heids in one o' the tubs. But the dunder-heid wrapped her jaw in a handkerchief wi' his initials on it and stuck it in the pocket o' his apron.'

'Oh my God,' I groaned.

259

'Weel micht ye blaspheme,' Cutchie said. 'Of course Pattison had tae let them in eventually. But he's a cool one is Granville. He apologised maist politely for keeping them waiting, and told them he hadna' heard their banging because the bellows was going.' He smiled. 'One o' the toon guard said he didna believe him because they'd been banging loud enough tae waken the deid.'

'Did they identify the corpse?' I asked.

'They did their best. One o' the wummin's brothers, a man called McGregor I think, was wi' them. When Monro hauled the heid oot o' the tub, he took wan look at it, swore it was his puir deid sister's, and fainted. Oot like a snuffed candle, the puir bastard. I couldna' but feel sorry for him.'

'That's when they carted Granville and the other two off?' I asked.

'That's when they carted them aff,' Cutchie confirmed. 'Straight doon tae the Tollbooth, I suppose. Tae be charged by one o' the magistrates. Probably Archie Newbiggin.'

'What happens now?' I asked.

He shrugged. 'They'll get bail. It's no as if they're dangerous men, or thieves that are aboot tae mak' a run for the English border.'

'Will the magistrates close Number Ten?' I asked.

'Mebbe. Mebbe no',' Cutchie replied. Then he grinned. 'The only good thing is that when the story first got aroond, the folk in the street thocht that Jeffray and the university was to blame. So they marched roond tae his hoose and broke a' his windaes. He canna' go oot in the street noo withoot gettin' a dod o' muck in the lug. Serves him richt.'

Cutchie was right. The College Street trio were granted bail. At the end of the month Andrew Russel was also hauled in and charged. Their alarm was heightened when the Glasgow magistrates passed the case to the Crown Office in Edinburgh, where it became a matter for the Lord Advocate and the High Court of Justiciar.

Pattison put a brave face on it, but Russel and the others were frankly terrified. It was hard to blame them. The indictment which came from Edinburgh was a long and alarming document. All four of them were accused of 'violating the Sepulchres of the Dead, and the raising and carrying away dead bodies out of their graves . . .', a crime which, the indictment reminded them, was 'of a heinous nature and severely punishable'.

'What ye've got to remember Frankenstein,' Pattison said to me over a meal in Mrs Veitch's tripe-house in the Bridgegate, 'is that it's no' so long since we were burning witches and warlocks in this benighted land. There's a streak o' superstition among the Scots that all the science and literature in the world will never extirpate. They suffer every disease and ailment and injury on God's earth, and come running to us when they hurt. But when we seek out the knowledge that'll ease their pain, they see us as wicked ghouls. It's madness. Sheer bloody madness. The law will hae tae be changed.'

But there was no prospect of that before the College Street three came to trial. Pattison did his best to arrange things in their favour. He got the best lawyers his ample cash could afford, and they persuaded the court the trial would have to be held in Edinburgh. The population of Glasgow, they argued, was so hostile to Pattison, Russel, McLean and Monro that the court would never find fifteen jurors who would give them a fair hearing. Reluctantly, the Lord Advocate agreed. The trial date was set for the beginning of June 1814.

Meanwhile it was business as usual at the College Street anatomy school although the supply of corpses dwindled. But there were enough of them for the school to continue

261

functioning. I had the suspicion that at least one of the bodies we acquired – that of a bloated and dissipated young woman – had never seen the grave. Russel was inclined to inform the magistrates but Pattison told him to keep his head. Beggars could not afford to be choosers.

The resourceful Rab Cutchie tried to open up supply lines from Ireland. His father was a well-off merchant who ran (among many other things) a patent-medicine emporium in the Trongate. He travelled continually around Britain in pursuit of goods to sell in his various businesses. While he was in Dublin, Cutchie senior fell in with an Irish surgeon who told him that dead bodies were plentiful in Ireland.

When the son heard about this he was delighted. Here was opportunity. He would match Scotland's demand with Ireland's supply. He promptly booked himself a passage to Dublin where he made contact with a group of Irish students who were enthusiastic resurrectionists. For every corpse they bagged and delivered to the Glasgow-bound brigantine, Cutchie would pay them two pounds. They would be shipped into Scotland as rags bound for one of his father's trading companies. Once the Irish dead were in Scotland, Cutchie planned to sell them to the anatomists of Glasgow and Edinburgh for anything from ten to twenty pounds each.

It was a well-laid scheme but it fell apart with the first shipment. The Irish students omitted to tell Cutchie when the shipload was due, and Cutchie failed to inform his father that a curious cargo was on its way from Dublin. So when the captain of the brig demanded shipping dues Cutchie senior refused to pay up. The bags of rags were hauled off the ship and dumped in a shed in the Broomielaw, where they lay for days before they began to give off a powerful stench. When the excisemen opened them up they found dozens of putrifying corpses. In good condition they would have been worth a fortune.

'Not that the old man would have objected to me trying tae mak' a bit o' money,' Cutchie told me later. 'It's just that he didna' ken whit the hell the Irish captain was talking aboot. So he wisna' aboot tae pey up fifty pounds for them. I'm still kicking masel' for no' telling him a' aboot it. Mind you if I had, he'd have wanted his share, and I'd have grudged him that. Ach weel. We'll just hae tae mak' dae wi' the local sack-'em-up men.'

We did our best but the College Street anatomy school was not the place it was. As the trial of Pattison and his colleagues crept closer, unease and depression settled over the place. The supply of cadavers almost dried up, and nobody seemed to care. A lot of time was spent discussing the prosecution, and whether the British would ever accept that doctors and surgeons *needed* corpses on which to learn their trade.

'They widna' try to train carpenters withoot gien' them a bit wood tae saw,' Rab Cutchie observed sourly.

EDINBURGH, SCOTLAND: 1814

It was the bayonets that chilled me. There were eight of them, gleaming in the morning sunshine, carried by eight men of the Edinburgh town guard. The guardsmen sat in the dock one on either side of the College Street four. They were British infantry bayonets, flat like long knives or short swords. They were practical stabbing weapons, not so long as the triangular French bayonet, but more versatile. No doubt they were made from good steel and well honed.

Their meaning was clear. The Glasgow anatomists had been accused of heinous crimes. As such, they were danger-ous men. They were in the Edinburgh court-room to stand trial. Any attempt by them to thwart justice by escaping and they would be skewered. Even the self-possessed Granville Sharp Pattison was subdued and uneasy. The others – Andrew Russel, Robert Monro and John McLean – looked frankly terrified.

Nor did their spirits improve when, at ten o'clock precisely, five judges filed onto the bench. We learned from the clerk of the court that they were Lord Boyle, Lord

Hermand, Lord Meadowbank, Lord Pitmilly and Lord Gillies. They were impressive in their red robes and coarse horsehair wigs. They certainly intimidated the fifteen Edinburgh shopkeepers, merchants and gentlemen who made up the jury. The presiding judge was Lord Boyle, a smiling, kindly looking man who, I was told, had a reputation for handing down brutal sentences.

I was anxious for my friends, but fascinated by the process. His Majesty King George the Third was represented by a trio of advocates led by Alexander Maconochie, the Solicitor-General for Scotland. The brightest of them proved to be a young spark called Francis Jeffrey. The College Street four had two representatives: John Clerk, and a wiry, balding young man of enormous energy called Henry Cockburn.

The court-room was mobbed. People were lined against the walls and in the aisles. Hundreds had been turned away at the doors, and the square between the courts and the old church of Saint Giles was crowded. Half of Glasgow seemed to be there. I recognised faces from the University, the Andersonian and the Infirmary. Most of the College Street students had made the journey. Every Glasgow coach had been booked for days.

The court-room was seething with an excitement which John Clerk, one of the defence advocates, tried to spoil. He began by arguing that the court should be cleared of the public because the evidence was of a peculiarly indelicate nature. Too much so, he argued, for the sensibilities of the ladies and gentlemen of the Scottish public.

The judges rejected his request. Blood, bone and flesh were the human condition. Details were not likely to corrupt His Majesty's lieges. Their Lordships did, however, suggest to the reporters on the press bench that they might play down the more colourful details for fear of inflaming the curiosity of the lower orders. The press men nodded solemnly. Only the barest bones of the proceedings found their way into the *Edinburgh Evening Courant* and the *Glasgow Herald*.

Then the jousting between the advocates began. The chief prosecutor, Maconochie, was a man of rotund oratory but some skill. He led a string of witnesses to prove that the bits and pieces discovered at the College Street Anatomy School could have been reassembled into the body of Mrs McAllester, late of the Ramshorn churchyard.

The dead woman's brothers and sister-in-law confirmed that the hands found in College Street were those of their relative. A scarred left thumb and blackened thumbnail convinced them. A surgeon called John Gibson, who had attended Mrs McAllester in life, agreed that the mutilated head he had examined was that of the lady in question.

The most effective evidence was given by William Alexander, the Glasgow dentist who had made a set of false teeth for Mrs McAllester. Every set of custom-made teeth, he told the court, is unique. Teeth made for one mouth will not fit another. Then he proceeded to explain how Mrs McAllester's false teeth fitted precisely onto the mandible which had been found in the pocket of Monro's apron. At this I saw Monro blanche and bury his face in his hands. My colleagues were in despair.

But they were despairing too soon. Their advocates proved effective. John Clerk was particularly good. First he established beyond doubt that Sharp Pattison could not have been involved in the resurrection of Mrs McAllester. Three witnesses testified that he had been at a ball given by a Mrs Bell in Carswell Court. He never left the room all evening, saw a Miss Mary Copland home to her house in the Trongate and was back at his house in Carlton Place by 1.30 am. His silk and velvet party clothes were completely unsoiled.

266

Then Clerk set about demolishing the prosecution's medical evidence. His first witness was Dr Robert Watt, who told the court that he and doctors Cleghorn and Anderson had examined the torso retrieved from College Street which was supposed to have belonged to Mrs McAllester. There was no trace of the scar tissue that invariably follows pregnancy. And Mrs McAllester had borne no fewer than eight children.

Dr William Anderson confirmed Watt's finding that there was no way that the pelvis could have belonged to the late Mrs McAllester. In fact, it could only have belonged to a seventeen-year-old virgin. I could see what had happened. In the chaos of the raid on the College Street Anatomy School the court officers had picked up the wrong torso. With so many and such varied human remains lying about it was an easy enough mistake to make.

Dr Watt had ruined the Crown's case. I could see doubt sweep across the faces of the jury and the judges. If the prosecution had got that wrong what else had they got wrong? Could the rest of the prosecution evidence be relied on? Then when Clerk wheeled in a brace of dentists who briskly challenged the prosecution's dental evidence the jury's doubts grew even stronger.

And Clerk's final speech was a minor masterpiece. He did not dispute that Mrs McAllester's grave had been violated, only that the body found in College Street was *not* Mrs McAllester's. The fingers may have been, the teeth may have been, and the head may have been. But the trunk was definitely not. And as the College Street anatomists had been accused of carrying away the *whole* body, it followed that the indictment must 'fall to the ground'.

The jury were then asked to consider their verdict. They looked exhausted. They had been listening to the medical arguments for more than sixteen hours. It was three o'clock in the morning of Tuesday the 7th of June before they were finally dismissed with instructions to 'return their verdict in the same place this day at two o'clock in the afternoon'.

The next morning I breakfasted late. I had found a room in the Union Hotel in St Andrew's Square, the comfort of which surprised me. My only companion at the breakfast table was a florid-faced man of business from the town of Stirling.

'Up to the capital to do myself a bit of good, sir,' he said with a knowing wink. 'Timber's my line, sir, and Gibson's the name. Robert Gibson. A man wha's proud tae say he owns one of the most flourishing sawmills in Scotland. Living weel as a free man in a free land.'

The complacency of the British never ceased to astonish me. They were unshakeable in the belief that they were the freest people on earth. They were run by the most arrogant royals in Europe and burdened by an aristocracy and gentry which aspired to be even more obnoxious than their betters. Their churches danced to the government's tune and their working class lived in the most brutal squalor in Europe. But to the last man they believed that no finer system of government had ever been devised. Nor could be devised.

At two o'clock in the afternoon I was back in the court-room. Once again it was crowded and seething with anticipation. The fifteen men of the jury strutted their way into their seats. Every eye was on them, examining their solemn, foolish faces for signs of their verdict. Their chamberlain handed a slip of paper to the clerk, who handed it to Lord Boyle. Boyle looked at it, handed it back to the clerk, who read it out in a thin, reedy voice.

'We all in one voice find the said Andrew Russel and the said John McLean *not guilty* . . .' At this there was a gasp and a cheer from the court while Russel beamed. McLean almost fainted with relief. The clerk went on: '. . . and find the libel *not proven* against the other two accused, Granville Sharp Pattison and Robert Monro.' All four were free. Guilty as sin, but free as air. And surrounded by Glasgow medical men slapping their backs and anxious to shake them by the hand. McLean was sick in the street outside

The College Street anatomists spent the rest of the day in celebration. We went from drinking den to drinking den, ever drunker and noisier as we went. 'Damned close run thing,' Pattison bawled in my ear. 'I thought we were gone. Gaoled, never to practise again. Or transported to New South Wales to plant cabbages in the desert. I thought that the dentist and his false teeth had done for us.'

I raised my glass. 'Here's to the fallibility of dentists,' I said.

'And to the fallibility of Scottish justice,' Pattison said with a grin.

'What does a verdict of not proven mean, anyway?' I asked him.

'It means', Pattison told me, 'that we think you did it but we cannot prove it.'

'Sounds about right,' I said.

After which the rampage got serious. In one establishment Rab Cutchie picked a fight with an Edinburgh stonemason who flattened him with two punches. Cutchie spent the rest of the night with one eye closed, trying to drink through a swollen mouth and three loose teeth.

Later that evening we dined in a grubby tavern at the head of Fishmarket Close. We ate dish-loads of oysters, and sunk more bottles of Bordeaux wine. We were joined by a pair of sooty men from O'Neil's firework factory in the Canongate who were also celebrating. They were working day and night, they told us, to keep up with the demand for fireworks.

'A'body that's anybody wants their ain wee fireworks pairty,' said the firework packer called Rab. 'They've pit a smile on the face o' my wife for the first time in seventeen years. And we're mair than happy to oblige. So if you gentlemen wid like a wee, eh, event organised, Davie here and ma'sel' are yer men.'

When I quizzed Rab about his trade he fished a Bengal light out of his pocket, slit open the pasteboard cylinder, and spilt the contents onto the table. He separated the powder with a pocket knife. 'This is a red one,' he told me. 'So it's made oot o' a mix o' chlorate of potash, nitrate of strontia and sulphur. Oh and some lamp black. If it's a bonny-like green yer efter, then ye want nitrate of baryta, chloride of lead, a sulphur and some resin. Some if it is gey dear. Especially lithium carbonate.'

As he leant over the table to talk I studied him. Drunk as I was, I could see that his eyes were yellowish, bloodshot, and there was a pallor to his skin. I suspected Rab's liver and lungs were paying a heavy price for his ability to conjure fleeting beauty out of these obscure metals and chemicals. Edinburgh's enthusiasm for the Battle of Leipzig and Treaty of Paris had probably shortened Rab's life by ten years.

'Gie them a wee display Rab,' Davie said. 'Yin or twa Theatre Fires. That canna dae ony hairm. So long as we dinna set fire tae the place.'

Rab grinned, and hauled four Theatre Fires out of his coat, set them up on the oyster dishes and lit them. The fireworks burned with a fierce light and white smoke that cast an eerie glow over the packed tavern. The Glasgow anatomists were delighted and the crowd cheered wildly.

GLASGOW, SCOTLAND: NOVEMBER 1814

If I had a friend in Glasgow it was Rab Cutchie. We were kindred spirits. He reminded me of myself ten years previously. He was bright, enterprising and obsessively curious. He quizzed me endlessly about the German universities, the politics of Switzerland, Bavaria and Austria, Napoleon's strategy and the Imperial Guard's tactics. He was fascinated by the idea of Larrey's flying ambulances.

Cutchie once showed me around the family shop in Brunswick Place. Every patent medicine I had ever heard of was arranged on the shelves in alphabetical order: asthmatic candy, balsam of honey, Bolton's tincture, camomile drops, carbonic tooth powder, cephalic snuff, essence of mustard, essence of pearl, Fothergill's nervous cordial, Frake's tincture of bark, golden pills, Henry's calcined magnesia, James' analeptic pills, Jesuit drops, McSparan's cordial for the stone and gravel, Senate's steel lozenges. It was a cornucopia of placebo and panacea.

'Christ only kens whether any o' it does anybody any guid,' Cutchie said as we wandered up and down the shelves. 'Personally I hae my doots. We've probably killed mair fowk than we've cured. But a lot o' fowk swear by what they can swig oot o' one o' Cutchie's bottles. If nothing else it's made a wheen o' money for my faither and the rest o' the Cutchies. So I suppose I canna' complain.'

Meanwhile my affair with Catherine Ure continued. She had obviously taken her servant girl into her confidence, because almost every other evening the giggling girl arrived at my lodging with a note informing me that Ure was lecturing at the Andersonian, and I would be most welcome to call.

I rarely missed the opportunity. Catherine was eager and enthusiastic. Sometimes I would be shown into our little trysting room beside the kitchen to find her half dressed or completely naked. On other occasions she would affect a maidenly reluctance. This she abandoned as soon as I touched her, then resumed when she had taken her pleasure.

Very occasionally I would find her engrossed in a book, and we would spend an hour or two discussing literature, the progress of science or the affairs of Europe. I enjoyed these moments. She had a quick mind and soaked up information rapidly. Now and again she would be overcome with remorse. More than once she informed me tearfully that she could no longer go on meeting me. But her resolve lasted only as long as it took me to get my hand in her drawers.

She did, however, suffer from *post coital* guilt. 'You must think me a terrible woman,' she murmured into my chest as we lay, exhausted, on the *chaise longue*. 'I am. I know I am. It's just that Andrew has, well, no time for me. He's cruel . . .'

She had said all this before, but something in her tone that night conveyed the depth of her misery. She was a lively woman who had no way of penetrating the carapace of obsession and arrogance with which her husband surrounded himself. I was simply a source of warmth on a cold night. A voice in the dark. A body to rub herself against. If it had not been Victor Frankenstein it would have been somebody else.

But our consolation could not last. And it came to an end one night under the high, bony nose of the Duke of Wellington. Ure had invited me to join him and Catherine at a Grand Divertissement and Fancy Ball to be held at the Assembly Rooms, to celebrate the defeat of Napoleon at Leipzig. The fact that the British were absent at the battle seemed to be of no significance. The entire place was brightly lit and decked out in a profusion of red, white and blue ribbon and streamers.

And from one wall of the ballroom a full-length painting of Field Marshal, the Duke of Wellington, in full dress uniform gazed disdainfully down on the company. Ure took the view that the whole effect would have been improved immeasurably if the Assembly Room managers had taken his advice and installed coal-gas lanterns. But there was, it seems, 'Nae tellin' them'.

Before the dancing began, we submitted to a musical entertainment provided by Signor Rivolta and his dancers. Then we all stood to attention while Signor Rivolta played 'God Save the King' on no fewer than eight instruments – a virtuoso feat which did nothing to improve that mournful ditty. Only then could the ball begin.

Catherine was enjoying herself. Her face was flushed with pleasure and her eyes shone. Like every woman in the room she had been swept up by the fashionable enthusiasm for the Bourbons. Her ballgown of white lace was studded with pearls in the form of the fleur-de-lis. Her head-dress was a 'Wellington' wreath of white and green foil inset with crowns. 'Whole thing cost me mair than I make in a month,' Ure grumbled to me. 'Damned women.'

But Catherine was delighted with herself. In her new

273

finery she was lively and confident. She strutted and skipped, first on Ure's arm and then on mine, humming to the music, occasionally squealing with laughter. She pranced and danced and giggled with pleasure. She looked happier than I had ever seen her.

But the end was brutal. When she began to move among a little crowd of Glasgow matrons, some of whom she knew, she met icy stares, averted heads, turned backs, and whispers behind fans. None of them would speak to her. The women gently detached themselves, leaving her stranded, bewildered, devastated. As an exercise in refined cruelty it was impressive. Wild-eyed and shaking with humiliation she fled to Ure, pleaded illness and rushed him out of the room. I saw Pattison's mother watch them go, a look of satisfaction on her face. She turned to glare at me. I glared back.

I never saw Catherine Ure again. The next morning a red-eyed servant girl arrived at my lodging with a note from Catherine telling me that I was no longer welcome to call at the Ure household. I made no reply. There seemed little point. But I missed Catherine and our strenuous activities on the Glassford Street *chaise longue*.

The end of my affair with Catherine Ure depressed and saddened me. I began to long for the familiar voices and familiar sights of central Europe. I had had enough of Britain. This wet, dark land was no longer for me. Next day I said my farewells to the College Street anatomists and booked myself a berth on the London & Edinburgh Shipping Company's smack *Sprightly*. Two days after that at six o'clock on a fine evening, we slipped out of Leith harbour into the Firth of Forth, bound for Miller's Wharf in London.

From there I travelled on to a Europe that was at peace for the first time in twenty years. Or so it seemed.

ELECTRICIAN

LANDSHUT, BAVARIA: 1815

I returned to Bavaria but not to Ingolstadt. I had good reasons to stay away from that old walled town on the Danube. One of them was a simple reluctance to confront Erika Waldman. I knew that I had wronged her, but I also knew she was better off without me. She was now married to an affluent merchant whose Catholic piety almost matched her own. My second reason was practical. Ingolstadt's university and medical school had long since been closed and moved to Landshut on the River Isar some 60 kilometres to the southeast.

And it was in Landshut that I used some of the money that my father had settled on me to set up my own clinic. The Landshut Electrical Dispensary I called it. It was a modest establishment compared to the one that Felix Waldman and I had run in Ingolstadt, but it was big enough for a sole practitioner. I managed to rent a house on the steep slope leading up to the Trausnitz Castle, that collection of hill-top buildings which had first been built by one of Bavaria's Ludwigs.

I liked Landshut. The town suited me. It had something of the look of Ingolstadt but it was not so cloyingly Roman Catholic. The streets were spacious and pleasant. And the university housed enough atheists and erstwhile members of the illuminati to make intellectual life tolerable. I was allowed to use the university's well-stocked library, and as a few of the teachers were Ingolstadt graduates I was invited to give the occasional anatomy lecture.

Some of these teachers became friends and drinking companions. Three of them had been members of the Society of Ingolstadt Golemites. We spent agreeable evenings in Landshut beer houses reminiscing about student days in Ingolstadt: the brawls we had fought, the duels we avoided, the money we spent in Madame Hortense's whorehouse on the Paradenplatz.

The Landshut Electrical Dispensary did well enough. I never managed to repeat the success that Felix Waldman and I had had in Ingolstadt. But a sufficient number of damaged people came through the door of the clinic to cover my expenses. And I found enough free time to correspond with electricians all across Europe in an attempt to keep up with new thinking and new equipment. Hand-cranked generators of the kind I had carted from Ulm to Austerlitz were now relics of another age. Variations of the Voltaic pile were the machines of the day. They were becoming better known as batteries. In the year 1815 electricity came in boxes.

My only problem was the location of the Landshut Electrical Dispensary. It was a little too close to Trausnitz Castle from which Lower Bavaria had been ruled for generations. The Trausnitz had acquired a miserable reputation. Some of the minor royalty who had stalked its ramparts had been both mad and cruel. One had kept pens full of wild beasts and there were dark tales about what they had been fed.

278

Many Landshut folk looked up at the old schloss on its wooded hill and crossed themselves. To some of them I became the strange foreigner who did things with lightning – surely the province of God – in the shadow of the Trausnitz. But there were enough sensible folk in and around Landshut to keep me busy easing melancholia, freeing locked joints and trying to repair dimmed eyes.

Most evenings I wandered down the hill to one of the inns on the Neustadt near the university. Usually I was joined by some of the teachers and students from the medical school. One or two of them were intrigued by my work and wanted to learn what they could about medical electricity. Others clearly regarded it as a waste of time. It was an opinion which sparked many a noisy argument.

Good times in Ingolstadt were mulled over. Every now and again there was news of old friends. Once, when one or two of the Ingolstadt graduates were musing over student days, one of the university's Austrians asked me if I had heard about von Grafenberg. I had not.

'Killed at Leipzig,' he said. 'Taken down in the Grimm-gasse not far from the Grimma Gate. And by a Swedish sharpshooter who thought the Austrians were French. Killed by one of his own side. What a shambles. My brother was there. He says von Grafenberg was one of the maddest bastards who ever sat a horse. Always at the front of his men.'

I was not surprised, but I grieved for my old friend, and for the waste of his death. Francis II, Emperor of Austria, was one of the last men for whom I would want to die. One of my grudges against Napoleon was that he had failed to deliver Europe from Francis and all the other royal clowns. But the Corsican had climbed into their territory and then come badly undone. Now all he ruled was a few square miles of the island of Elba.

All of which changed in March that year, when Bonaparte sailed across the Mediterranean, reached the south of France and marched through the country to Paris to start the whole bloody business all over again. Or so it seemed to me, until news of Waterloo filtered through to Landshut. Between them, the British and the Prussians had destroyed this latest and last version of the Grande Armée. Even the Old Guard had broken and run under withering British fire. I could imagine the effect it would have on French morale. The slaughter was prodigious. Napoleon was led away, heart-sick, into his final exile.

The night I heard of Waterloo I dreamt again of my mother. She was lying in one of Larrey's two-wheeled flying ambulances, her face contorted in pain. Her left shoulder was hopelessly crushed, one of her feet had been shot off and her entrails were spilling out under her nightdress. Her blood was all across the interior. Larrey strolled up, looked at her briefly and shook his head. He ordered me to cut her throat to put her out of her misery. Which I did.

I woke trembling and sweating. Thunder was rumbling over Landshut, and through the bedroom window I could see lightning flickering over the Trausnitz Castle, lighting up the pale towers and turrets and casting the strangest of shadows.

GENEVA, SWITZERLAND: 1816

Alphonse Frankenstein finally gave up the ghost in June 1816, at the age of seventy-nine. His grip on life, like his grip on his money, was tenacious to the end. The cancer which killed him had invaded every corner of his tripes. He fought it with a grim and fruitless determination. His corpse was beginning to reek by the time I made the long journey from Landshut through the rain and mud of that wet summer. Another two days above ground and I swear the smell of Alphonse Frankenstein would have done for half the *haute ville*. But I surprised myself by shedding a tear as they lowered what was left of him into the grave beside my mother.

I never learnt what Alphonse Frankenstein thought about the decision of the Republic of Geneva to become a member of the Swiss Confederation. I have no idea whether he voted for or against. He never said so, but he gave me the impression that he had rather enjoyed being a leading citizen in the *Département du Leman* of Napoleon's empire. Like most men of business he valued stability more than freedom. And there was money to be made in the new French-run empire and colonies.

But Alphonse Frankenstein lived on in my younger brother. Ernest now presided over the Frankenstein business interests with the same careful eye. Now that Geneva had abandoned its independence to become the smallest of the Swiss cantons, Ernest knew he would never wield the same kind of political power as our father. But his ambitions were, if anything, even bigger. They were certainly wider ranging.

'America,' he told me. 'That's the place. Now that they've finally disposed of the English – and the French – that's the place to be. They'll not be long in seeing off the Spanish too. I tell you Victor, that's where we should be putting the Frankenstein money. Into buying land around the cities of America. New York, Philadelphia, Boston. That's the future. I plan to go there and look around.'

He told me that he had already been corresponding with Albert Gallatin, the Genevan-born financier who had just retired as Treasury Secretary of the United States. 'Gallatin assures me that there are any number of investments to be made in his adopted country,' Ernest said. 'He says good Protestants are always welcome in America. Especially if they have some money behind them.'

Watching the enthusiasm in Ernest's eyes it struck me that perhaps he and I were not so different. Maybe Ernest's passion for doing business was the mirror image of my passion for science. Perhaps we shared the same hunger, the same greed, only for different things. Both of us were driven men. Both dedicated to what we were doing. And whatever else might be said about Alphonse Frankenstein, he was no dilettante. Perhaps I was my father's son after all?

I knew Ernest feared that I, the oldest son, would return to Geneva and elbow my way into the Frankenstein businesses. The relief on his face when I told him I had no such intention was almost comical. I would be happy, I said, with just sufficient of the profits to keep me alive, travelling and working. That, he assured me, would be no problem. There was more than enough money to keep me more than content. And he agreed to have the family lawyers draw up the necessary papers for signature.

Over the next few days I wandered the big house in the Cour Saint-Pierre in a state of some confusion. I examined the paintings, fingered the tapestries and brocades, picked up ornaments and trinkets, leafed through books and ledgers, gazed out of windows into the rain. I seemed to hear the voices of my parents echoing in the rooms.

Then a note from Germaine restored me to my senses. She commiserated with me on Alphonse's death, told me how much she still missed her own father, and invited me out to Coppet to meet Lord Byron. 'The finest poet England has produced since Shakespeare,' she told me, 'and a most *intriguing* and fine-looking man.'

Germaine was clearly delighted with her new prize, so I made the journey out to Coppet to inspect the great man. She met me at the entrance to the château. She was wearing an outrageous sea-green dress which clashed abominably with her orange turban. No one ever accused Germaine of knowing anything about colour. As usual she carried a frond of greenery. As we walked upstairs to the long salon she was brimming with gossip from a France trying to reconstruct itself after the ruin of Napoleon at Waterloo.

'Incidentally, Victor,' she said as we made our way up the staircase, 'I heard the most remarkable story about one of your mentors.'

'Which one?' I asked.

'Baron Larrey,' she said.

I stopped. 'What about him? Is he dead?'

'No. But he almost was.'

'What happened?'

She told me that when Larrey was trying to flee the field of Waterloo he encountered a detachment of Prussian cavalry. They killed his escort, took him prisoner, stripped him of his valuables and placed him in front of a firing squad. Their muskets were cocked and ready, but when the Prussian surgeon went to blindfold Larrey, he recognised the baron. It seems he had sat through Larrey's lectures in Berlin and had been mightily impressed.

'So the execution was called off,' Germaine said with a laugh. 'The good doctor was not about to see Napoleon's great Surgeon-General shot. Larrey was taken to General Bulow who could not make suffcient apology. Then he was passed on to Blücher himself, who gave him dinner and promised to tell Madame Larrey, what is her name . . .?'

'Charlotte,' I said.

'Blücher promised to get word to Charlotte that her husband was alive and well. He then gave Larrey some money and a coach and sent him on his way to Paris. Isn't that a fine story?'

'Larrey always was a lucky bastard,' I said. 'Trailed about after Napoleon for decades, often in the thick of battle, and never so much as a scratch.'

Germaine's salon was crowded as usual and the largest group was around the guest of honour. When she introduced me to Milord Byron I found a plumpish man of middling height, about ten years younger than myself, who limped from a club foot. His pale skin and pale eyes were offset by dark curls which looked as if they had been carefully teased into poetic disarray. He had the mouth of a Moritzkirche cherub, but set in a sneer. It was a clever, arrogant kind of face. I disliked him on sight.

And a few minutes listening to him did nothing to improve my opinion. He mouthed equality and breathed privilege. He lamented the downfall of Bonaparte and behaved like the Duke of Wellington. He was arrogant, domineering and ignorant. His French was lamentable, he had no German and only a smattering of Italian. Out of politeness, the company spoke English. This seemed only to reinforce Milord Byron's sense of superiority.

His *forte* was to shock. In the heart of European Calvinism he announced that Roman Catholicism was the only true religion. Jean Calvin was a Christian who had 'somehow mislaid' Christ. The Reformation only served to 'muddle an already confused peasantry'. And Switzerland was 'a selfish country of brutes set down in the most romantic region of the world'.

I thought he was a humbug. There was nothing spontaneous about his aphorisms. He had plainly sweated over them. I could hear him repeating them in drawing rooms from London to Istanbul. He was the poet as outcast. The aesthete driven out by the grossness of the world. No doubt it was a line that had upended many a society hostess. Germaine among them, perhaps.

As all Geneva knew, Byron was living at the Diodati house in Cologny which had become the centre of a gaggle of English *littérateurs*. It seems that they spent their days floating around Lac Leman declaiming on the 'sublime' beauty of their surroundings and their evenings admiring one another's fairy stories. The gossip was that Byron, however, only had eyes for his half-sister Augusta.

Naturally, Milord Byron danced in the centre of the ring. He and Germaine sparred, while polite Geneva fluttered and cooed. Madame de Stael was well used to such bouts, and knew Byron well from her visits to London. But he baited her with some malice and I thought his fine flourishes did little to conceal a contempt she did not deserve. His game was to provoke her until she erupted into a torrent of talk which he dismissed as 'all show and sophistry'. Germaine was enjoying herself, but I found myself increasingly irritated by the Englishman.

'What's wrong with your foot?' I asked him in a lull in the conversation.

The blunt question took him aback.

'The folly of Scottish doctors when I was a child,' he answered, looking down at his twisted foot. 'Alas!'

'Ever tried having it straightened?' I asked.

'No. I haven't. Could it have been done?'

'Probably,' I said. 'But not without some pain.'

'You're familiar with pain?' he said coldly.

'I'm a surgeon.'

'Forgive me, but do Geneva surgeons see *much* pain?'

'Now and again,' I told him.

'Doctor Frankenstein was with the Grande Armée,' Germaine told him. 'On the Danube. And at Austerlitz.'

'Ah!' he said with some interest. 'Austerlitz. The affair of the Three Emperors. The great Napoleon's greatest triumph. Then you must have seen Bonaparte himself.'

'Close up, only once,' I told him. 'At a field hospital under the Pratzen Heights. He walked in, took one look at the men who'd nearly died for him and walked out. Never saw him again, though.'

'A Titan,' Byron said, 'if mightily flawed.'

'The Midget with the Map,' I said. 'That's what some of the Imperial Guard used to call him. That and the short-arsed Corsican bandit.'

'I've walked over the battlefield of Waterloo,' he told me gravely, struggling to add tone to the conversation. 'That sepulchre of France. I will admit to being moved. I sensed history. There was destiny in the dust under my feet. I've been writing about it.'

'What you sensed, Milord Byron, were the bones and

tripes of good men. If you'd been there a few months earlier you'd have smelled them as well. Maybe even got some of their shit on your shoes. Nothing like case-shot and musketry for loosening a man's bowels. As you'll find if you ever wander onto a battlefield before the battle is over.'

'I rather resent your tone Monsieur Frankenstein,' he told me. 'I knew men who died at Waterloo. I had a relative who died there.'

'Then he died shitting in his breeches,' I said. 'All men do. Which may be unpoetical of them, but that's the way it is.'

'The fate of Europe,' he said, trying to ignore my boorishness. 'Decided within a few fields.'

'Twenty years of slaughter and we're back where we started,' I retorted. 'Every petty king in Europe smirking under his crown. France damn near ruined, and the Bourbons lording it over Paris. Thanks to your hero Napoleon.'

'No hero of mine,' he announced. 'My politics are simple. I utterly detest all forms of government. All of them. If a universal republic were declared tomorrow, then I'd immediately advocate despotism. Of the harshest kind.'

'With a bit of luck your despot would stamp out bad poetry,' I said. 'And let the rest of us get on with our work.'

'I'm glad you disapprove of *bad* poetry,' Byron said. 'On that at least our views coincide.'

'I doubt it,' I said. 'My views on poetry are simple. I utterly detest all forms of poetry. All of them. If universal poetry were declared tomorrow, then I'd immediately advocate it's abolition. In the harshest way. I prefer politics.'

'Victor,' Germaine said. 'Please stop teasing Lord Byron. Whatever will he think of Genevan society?'

'He's already told us what he thinks of Genevan society,' I said. 'Not very much.'

'Can you blame me?' he asked.

'Certainly not,' I replied. 'We're the dullest of dull dogs here. Clockmakers and cheesemongers. Safe behind our Alpine ramparts. We wouldn't know a good poem – or even a good poet – if one climbed out of one of our cheeses.'

'And is that where Genevan poets usually emerge from?' he asked with a smile.

'Usually,' I replied. 'They're much less *fundamental* than the English variety.'

Germaine laughed and the grins and giggles around the salon told me I had won the round. Byron had the grace to dip his head in a slight bow.

'Gentlemen, gentlemen, please,' Germaine said with a straight face. 'This will never do. This will end in fisticuffs.'

'Oh, I hope not,' I said. 'Milord Byron is far too skilled an athlete for a Genevan sawbones. Even one who's won money betting on Molineux the black.'

'You've seen Molly fight?' he said. 'Where?'

'Glasgow,' I told him. 'Near the lake they call Lomond.'

'Good God! What were you doing in Scotland?'

'Stealing corpses. Cutting them up. Getting drunk on whisky. And watching prizefights.'

'I'm a Scotchman myself,' he told me.

'You don't sound like one,' I said.

He shrugged. 'Educated in England. Alas!'

'What's wrong with England?' I asked him.

His opinion of England was no higher than his opinion of Geneva. It was, he told us, a 'low, humdrum, lawsuit of a country'. It was a place where the winters 'ended in July and began again in August'. English society was now one of two tribes 'the bores and the bored'. No one with a spark of creativity lived there. English women were the dullest in Europe. Art was dead. Society was inert. Commerce ruled. Life itself was 'a mere affair of breath'.

'Well, I like England,' I told him. 'It may not be a paradise for poets and their admirers, but it's interesting. It's full of new ideas and clever people. If you know where to look.'

'And where is that?' Byron asked. 'Among the chemical retorts, steam engines and reeking chimneys, I suppose. And all the other places where poetry, art and beauty rot.'

'You mean the places where useful things are made,' I said. 'And where power and money grow. The very money that's needed to give people like you the comforts you enjoy. And the time to write your poetry.'

'You're being offensive, Monsieur Frankenstein.'

'No. Merely pointing out that there is more to life than rhymes and ruminations,' I said. 'No offence intended.'

He smiled. 'Men such as you frighten me. In your instrument cases and your laboratories I fear you carry the world's ruin. You give me dreams which are not all dreams. I have been writing about that too.'

'You surprise me,' I said.

'"The bright sun was extinguished",' he recited at me, with some defiance. '"And the stars did wander darkling in the eternal space, rayless and pathless, and the icy earth swung blind and blackening in the moonless air. Morn came and went, and came and brought no day. And men forgot their passions in their dread of this, their desolation. And all hearts . . ."'

'Very pretty,' I interrupted before the ladies could applaud. 'But if this world is ever ruined in the way you describe, it won't be men like me who'll do it. It will be done by irrational fools who cannot relate cause to effect. Men with their heads stuffed with poetry, panting after the world's luxuries.'

After which Milord Byron refused to speak to me. He averted his flushed face and directed his conversation at the ladies. Germaine was too accomplished a hostess to let him see it, but I had reduced him in her eyes. As the company

289

broke into little groups – the largest of which was around Byron – she came looking for me. She found me in the corner of the salon, leafing through a book.

'You've come a long way, Victor Frankenstein,' she said.

'The man's a fool, madam,' I said. 'He and his like will be the ruin of England one day.'

She stared at me. 'What happened to the awkward boy who stood in this very salon performing his electrical trickery?'

'The boy grew up, I suppose. And learnt a few things.'

She smiled and fixed me with her level gaze. 'I think you and I should continue this debate. But rather later in the evening.'

I inclined my head. 'I am at your pleasure, madam.'

She grinned amiably. 'I do hope so, sir.'

And so I finally bedded the mistress of my imagination. It was a mistake. She proved to be a sluggish lover. Her flesh was pale, over-abundant and creased. She was conscious of her sagging breasts and belly and plainly disliked me handling them. When I finally entered her she moaned and gasped dutifully but she was acting. She was a middle-aged woman pretending, to me and to herself.

When I was finished she turned away and wept quietly.

PARIS, FRANCE: JULY 1817

The note from Germaine had been brief, the handwriting feeble and spidery. 'Your old friend has been felled by a silly stroke,' she wrote, 'and is confined to her bed. The world's most active person now finds herself petrified. It is the punishment of heaven for uncountable, but surely minor, sins. If your pilgrimage of science ever brings you to the rue Neuve-des-Mathurins in Paris, then this frail old creature would welcome a visit. Germaine.'

After returning to Paris at the end of 1816 Germaine had thrown herself into a frenzy of writing, argument and entertaining, all laced with large quantities of good wine and bad opium. Her salon on the rue Royal became the centre of anti-Bourbon dissent. She believed that, at last, she was shaping the politics of her day. Perhaps she was.

Then one evening in February, at a reception given by Decaze, First Minister to the Bourbon king she had come to despise, Germaine was struck down by a stroke of apoplexy. Her powerful brain had turned on her. On the First Minister's staircase, under the glitter of the chandeliers and dressed in all her awkward finery, Germaine had fallen, paralysed and speechless. As they carried her into her coach only her eyes could move.

In the weeks that followed she improved, but not much. She remained helpless. Her loyal English maid, the stern, crop-haired Fanny Randall, fed her, bathed her and saw to her necessities. She never left her bedchamber unless carried or wheeled. She did gradually regain her speech, her mind was dimmed but still functioning. A string of visitors trooped into her bedroom to pay court.

It was some months before I was able to rearrange my affairs to make the long journey to Paris. So it was a sunlit evening in late June when a silent, and I thought disapproving, Fanny Randall showed me into Germaine's bedchamber. The room was filled with flowers and perfumes which did nothing to conceal the reek of sickness.

Time was never kind to Germaine. She had not aged well. She was too heavily boned, too fleshy, too coarse in the skin and hair. The long years of arduous travel, rich food and too much wine had sapped her physique. And her recent fondness for the opium bottle had cast a sickly pallor over her face. The old Germaine existed only in the sharp, dark eyes which glittered from the pillow.

'What do you think of me now, Victor Frankenstein?' she said with a wan smile as I approached her bed. 'A sad end for the great hostess of Coppet. The tormentor of Napoleon Bonaparte.'

'The end, Madame?' I said, lifting her hand and putting it to my mouth. Her flesh was cold, waxy. 'Surely not.'

'I think so,' she said.

'There are treatments,' I suggested.

She grinned, showing me yellowed teeth. 'Oh, yes, I have been treated. Abominably. The doctors of Paris seem to believe that my predicament is due to a failure of my liver.'

'Your liver?' I repeated, astonished. 'How did they come to that conclusion?'

'Who knows? But they are convinced that whatever ails me may be cured by forcing me to swallow a purée made from crushed woodlice, which tastes disgusting and makes me vomit. Cruel to me and even crueller to the woodlice. Thousands of the creatures must have perished in the cause of my raddled liver.'

'A dismal end for some of the earth's oldest and more interesting creatures,' I said with a smile.

'Ever the natural philosopher, Victor.'

'One of my many failings, Germaine.'

'And most of the other treatments that have been worked on this poor frame of mine are too distressing to discuss – even with a natural philosopher such as yourself.' Her eyes filled with tears and her voice shook. 'So I have told the doctors, no more. No more.'

'I know some fine surgeons, Germaine. Please, allow me to . . .'

She shook her head. 'It is too late, Victor. Believe me. Your old friend is approaching the end of her days. All that grieves me now are the sores on my body. And they can be made tolerable by my little bottles of opium, of which I have a regular supply, thank God. So, I lie here and drift in and out of my dreams.'

'Pleasant ones, I hope.'

She smiled again. 'Not always, but mostly. I often dream of Geneva, your mother and her *salon* in the Cour Saint-Pierre. She was a good woman Caroline Beaufort Frankenstein. And a good friend. Perhaps we'll meet again.'

'Do you believe that?' I could not resist asking.

'No,' she said. 'But one time I dreamt of that strange afternoon at Coppet when a young Victor Frankenstein played the part of Saussure's electrical apprentice. Do you remember that?'

'I do indeed,' I said. 'I also remember that every time you touched me I thought I would die from excitement.'

She laughed again. 'I do seem to recall a certain, shall we say, disturbance in your breeches. But then the leg of a table is enough to excite a boy of that age.'

'True,' I admitted.

'They were good days, Victor,' she said. 'When we all had so much to live for. And so much time to live it in.'

'Perhaps you are ready to abandon us all too soon,' I suggested.

She shook her head. 'No, Victor. My life is over. Not even the electrical wizardry of Victor Frankenstein could conjure up more years for this poor shell. And before you suggest it, I forbid you to try.'

I inclined my head. 'As you wish, madame.'

'I am in earnest, Victor.'

'You have my word.'

'The truth is, Victor, I think I shall be happy to join my father and mother in that little mausoleum in the garden of Coppet. I've asked to be placed at my father's feet.' She laughed again. 'He and I can spend eternity discussing the affairs and finances of the underworld while my mother admires our brilliance.'

'And so she should,' I said, lamely.

She smiled, but her words were becoming slow, faintly slurred. 'I can see you are sad, Victor. I am flattered that you are. But it comes to us all. You must know that more than anyone.'

'Knowing and accepting are different things, madam. I loathe and despise death.'

'Then I think you are being unkind to poor death. Many of us long for his embrace.'

'The great seducer,' I said, and was surprised by the bitterness in my voice.

'More than that, I think.'

And with those words, she closed her eyes and drifted off into unconsciousness. I stood staring down at the pale, heavy face with its ring of coarse black curls sticking out from under a white turban. Her full mouth was slightly agape. When I bent to kiss it her breath was rank but touched with the sweet scent of opium. I left the room knowing that I would never see her again.

Germaine died a few weeks later, on the 13th of July, the month that the revolutionaries called Germinal. By then her sores had turned gangrenous and her pain was acute. The day before she died she talked politics with the Duke of Orleans and told him she was expecting a visit from the Duke of Wellington. That night Fanny Randall made her a stronger than usual dose of opium and Germaine slipped into a deep sleep from which she never woke. She was fifty-one years old.

Fifteen days after she died a gang of workmen cracked open the walled-up Necker mausoleum at Coppet. They found old Jacques Necker and his wife still well preserved in the alcohol which filled their black marble coffins. Four municipal councillors from the village carried Germaine's coffin into the little chamber and laid her at her father's feet. Then they left the workmen to reseal the entrance to the tomb where the Necker family lay in the dark.

GLASGOW, SCOTLAND: OCTOBER 1818

The years had done nothing to improve Andrew Ure's temper. I had no sooner stepped off the London stage than he started to rant. 'Ye'll not be seeing the whore this time, Frankenstein,' he told me. 'She's gone. Gone to have a bairn. In some common lodging, or pig sty, or gutter for all I care. But she'll get not a penny from me. Not a penny. Not from Andrew Ure. She's made her own bed, and now she must lie on it. She'll never dirty my bed again, I can tell you that . . .'

Ure's rage was so incoherent that it took me some time to realise that he was talking about his wife Catherine. The same lively woman with whom I had whiled away many an afternoon. I was glad the afternoon was dark enough to hide my embarrassment. I mumbled something about being sorry for his troubles. But I do not think he heard me.

'Andrew Ure is not a man to be made a fool of,' he ranted on as we made our way to his house. 'By God he's not. Not by some raddled sow of a woman. The divorce is under way. The papers have been served. I'll be rid of her, by God I will. It'll all be decided at the Court of Session. Then, he's welcome to her. She's spoiled goods. He can have her, but he'll not take her. Not a man like that. Well that's her own affair. She can fend for herself. She can rot in hell for all I care.'

He stopped and stared accusingly at me. 'Her paramour is a *gentleman* of your own acquaintance,' he told me. 'Oh aye. None other than your former colleague and tutor *Mister* Granville Sharp Pattison.' He spat on the street. 'That disgrace to the name of doctor. That sham of a surgeon. That low-bellied apology for a dog that whined his way into my own house and seduced – *debauched* – my wife. I ask you Frankenstein? What kind of man is it that can stoop to such a thing?'

A man like myself, was the only honest answer. I could not remember how many times I had tumbled Mistress Ure. But I could well imagine how easily Catherine Ure would succumb to the panache of Granville Sharp Pattison. I was sure she was not the first Glasgow matron to be charmed by the handsome anatomist. But if this scandal took root, she might be the last. Meanwhile I muttered meaningless condolences which Ure did not want to hear.

'That adulterer is finished in Glasgow, I'll see to that,' he said grimly as we climbed the steps to his house in Glassford Street. 'And he's finished in Scotland as well if I have a hand in it. By God I'll see him off. He's finished. Mr Granville Sharp Pattison is finished. His doctoring days are done.'

It was a relief to escape to my room. The journey from Landshut had been long. The last thing I wanted was to listen to Ure rant about his adulterous wife. I was already wishing that I had declined his invitation to Glasgow to participate in a unique electrical experiment. All he had told me was that a convicted murderer was about to be hanged in Glasgow, and that he had persuaded the authorities to allow him to carry out a series of electrical experiments on the corpse instead of having it dissected.

He assured me that the condemned man was young, fit, healthy and unblemished, and promised to be a choice specimen for Ure's brand-new electrical equipment. It was certainly a combination of circumstances unusual enough to draw me rapidly across Europe.

But lying exhausted on my uncomfortable bed in the damp, draughty room, my imagination began to run away with itself. Was Ure's letter a ruse? Had Catherine confessed her involvement with me? Was Ure planning to humiliate me in public? Was he scheming to have me murdered in my bed? Or was he thinking to slip some untraceable poison into my food? He was certainly chemist enough to do it. With these dismal questions rattling around in my head I fell asleep, only to be woken later by a servant telling me that dinner was served.

I arrived at the table tired and depressed. The food was plain, underheated and overcooked, but the claret wine was surprisingly good. I had hoped Ure had exhausted the subject of Catherine and her paramour but I should have known better. Men like Ure have reservoirs of spite which do not drain easily. As we ate, the invective continued. He was clearly obsessed with Pattison who, he reminded me, had been branded 'Beau Fribble' by a local satirist.

'Not that the scoundrel has much of a reputation left,' he told me, sawing savagely at the blackened mutton on his plate. 'The man's a joke. He's been working at the toun's infirmary. Last year he hacked the arm off one patient and the leg off another. They both died of course. The woman in the most terrible agony. But when Hugh Miller the senior surgeon rebuked him – quite rightly in my opinion – for incompetence, d'ye know what Beau Fribble did?'

I shook my head, trying to conceal my weariness.

298

'He challenged Miller to a bloody *duel*, that's what he did. Imagine it! Challenging a fellow surgeon to a duel! The man's mad. He should be locked up. He's certainly not fit to practise. Not fit to walk the streets if you ask me.'

'So what happened?' I asked.

'Naturally, Miller declined,' Ure said. 'Told Pattison not to be so dim. To take his rebuke like an honest man. But that wasn't good enough for Beau Fribble. Oh no! He then posted a notice in the infirmary accusing Miller of *cowardice*. The fool!'

'And then?'

Ure shrugged. 'An inquiry by the hospital managers who made it plain that Beau Fribble's services were no longer required. Then, would you believe, they made him Professor of Anatomy and Surgery at Anderson's. My own institution. Of course I was obliged to welcome him as a colleague. I offered him the hospitality of my house. And that's when he started sniffing around the bitch, Catherine Monteath. My wife of ten years. They tell me that Beau Fribble is now hiding out in France. Which is not far enough for my liking.'

He lapsed into a brooding silence, then jumped to his feet. 'Come,' he said, beckoning me. 'Let me show you something.' He led me down the stairs to the basement where he threw open the door to the small room off the kitchen that I knew so well. All it contained was two upright chairs and a French-style *chaise longue* with a grubby cover. Nothing had changed since Catherine Ure and I idled away more afternoons than I can recall.

'*This* was their stew,' Ure said grimly. 'And *that* was their bed of lust. Elegant isn't it?' He walked into the room and rapped on the wall. It made a hollow sound. 'Timber partition,' he said. 'Timber and plaster. That's all there was between their miserable, ah, passion, and my own servants.

Who, of course, heard everything that was going on. Everything!'

Ure then called the cook and the kitchen maid and asked them to describe to me what they had seen and heard. The poor women were mortally embarrassed. They stood in front of us flushed and stammering. The kitchen maid was wringing her hands on her apron. Fortunately – for me anyway – neither had been in Ure's employment when it had been me pleasuring the mistress on the other side of the flimsy partition.

'Go on. Tell him,' Ure insisted. 'Tell Dr Frankenstein what your precious mistress was up to when I was out lecturing. When I was out earning enough to keep her in her finery. Let him hear what kind of sorry state the moral life of Scotland is in. How far the *ladies* of this land have sunk into degradation.'

The cook did the talking, but she refused to share Ure's hysteria. She admitted that Dr Pattison had been a regular visitor when Mrs Ure was alone, and that sometimes the couple had repaired to the little room from which she had heard laughing and stirrings. She had also seen them standing 'face to face and close together', and had once seen Pattison's arm around Mrs Ure. 'When I opened the door his arm fell from her shoulder and her face dyed up red – she was in confusion.'

But that was all. The honest woman refused to paint a more lurid picture. She had seen more, but was not about to gratify Ure. She plainly had much more regard for her disgraced mistress than she did for her outraged master. Which did not surprise me. Wanton she might be, but Catherine Ure was an amiable creature. Her husband, on the other hand, was a creature of pure malice. I had never disliked him more.

But showing me the actual scene of his wife's debauchery

seemed to purge Ure of his anger, to have satisfied him in some strange way. In fact, he mellowed enough to apologise for burdening me with his domestic problems when I had come all the way to Glasgow to talk science. We returned to the dining room where he explained the rare combination of circumstances that had prompted him to write to me urging me to participate in an experiment he had organised.

'Ye'll mind from your previous incarnation in Scotland', he said, 'that the only *legal* source of corpses for dissection is executed murderers?'

'I remember,' I said.

'Well up to now every one of them hanged in Glasgow has been handed over to James Jeffray, to be chopped up in the University's anatomy room by his hooligan medical students.'

'I know,' I said. 'I've seen them in action.'

'For years I've been badgering Jeffray to let *me* have a freshly killed corpse to experiment on. He's always refused. He doesn't believe in medical electricity. Thinks it's a waste of time, money and energy. And he's not the only one that thinks like that in this benighted town.'

'But you managed to change his mind,' I prompted, before he went off in a tirade against James Jeffray.

'Yes. After weeks – no months – of nagging and pestering various members of the university court to prevail on Jeffray. He's finally agreed. The next one to come off the rope is mine. To do with what I want. Under his supervision.'

'Good for you,' I said, imagining just how unpleasant it would be to suffer Andrew Ure's nagging for months on end. But I was impressed. I knew Jeffray's reputation for being stubborn and awkward. Ure must have intrigued endlessly to bring enough pressure to bear to bend that stiff neck.

'And he's a beauty,' he went on enthusiastically.' His

name's Clydesdale, Matthew Clydesdale. He's twenty-six years old, hacked an eighty-year-old collier man to death with his own pick. Probably killed his own brother a few years previously. Some folk say he murdered a widow woman in the town of Hamilton as well. A heart as black as the Earl of Hell's waistcoat.'

'It certainly sounds like it,' I said.

'Oh he's a bad one, believe me,' he said. 'Nae guid tae man nor beast. I promise you Frankenstein, if his corpse yields up the smallest piece of scientific information he'll have done more good dead than he ever did when he walked the earth.'

'When is the day?' I asked.

'Seven days time. November the fourth.'

'Is that time enough to prepare?'

'Everything's ready,' he said. 'And you and I are to call on Mr Clydesdale at his, ah, rooms tomorrow. I've arranged to meet the Glasgow hangman at the New Prison in the afternoon so we can run an eye over our subject. Some more port?'

I declined and we mused in silence.

'It's a funny business this,' he said staring into his port glass. 'I sat in the High Court all the way through Clydesdale's trial. Not that there was any doot about his guilt. At the end of it he seemed resigned enough to the thought of being *hanged*. But when the judge sentenced him to be dissected afterwards, he was reduced to a trembling ruin. If the guard hadnae been there tae catch him he'd have fainted clean away. The rope that would kill him didn't seem to bother him. But the knife he'd never feel terrified him witless. The lawyers tell me that's quite common. Now there's an odd thing is it not?'

GLASGOW, SCOTLAND: OCTOBER 1818

The next morning Urc and I met the Glasgow hangman – a remorselessly cheerful lout called Tam Young - on the steps of the city's gaol. He told us that he needed to see Matthew Clydesdale for himself just to make sure that everything went as it should. As he was one of the busiest hangmen in Britain we had no doubt that it would. He had enough practice. We were shown in to the condemned man's cell by the turnkey, a kindly looking man called MacGregor.

Our subject turned out to be a small, fierce-looking creature with a dull eye. He reminded me of the men who fought as the *voltigeurs* of the Grande Armée, nimble, fast-moving soldiers whose job was to shoot and run, and try to rag the edges of the enemy's formations. Some of Napoleon's élite hussars had the same agile menace. Clydesdale was the kind of little man that could rip the throat out of a larger one before the latter had time to bunch a fist.

When we approached the door he moved away, clanking his chains. He had made a fruitless attempt to escape, so was now destined to spend what was left of his life manacled hand and foot. There was an air of animal-like suffering about him. I had no doubt he deserved to hang, but I could not help but feel some sympathy for the wretch.

'He'll no' be hinging on his ain,' the hangman told us in that Scots dialect I still found hard to follow. 'There's a laddie called Simon Ross, a butcher tae trade, that's tae keep him company. Mister Ross took tae being a burglar. Broke intae a hoose in the village o' Rutherglen and stole some weemin's claes. His partner in crime gi'ed evidence against him. So he's tae hing for the sake o' a puckle petticoats and drawers. He should have stuck tae the butchering. He's tae gang tae meet his maker at the same time as Matt here. And may the guid Lord hae mercy on baith their souls.'

While Ure and the turnkey tried to extract information from Clydesdale about his age, family and state of health, I studied the man's physique with some care and made a few notes. He was almost twenty-six years old, about five foot two inches tall, but with a well-muscled body plainly used to hard physical work. The skin was tanned and leathery, and his hands calloused. I estimated his weight to be around nine stone. There was little sign of physical dissipation apart from a few broken blood vessels around the nose and eyes.

'Did you gentlemen ken that Matt here fancies himsel' as a runner?' Young said to us. 'Is that no' right Matt. Oh aye. He's won many a foot race has Matt. Mind you he'd have been an even better runner if he hadnae' spent a' his winnings on porter and whisky. He aye used to celebrate his victories by drinking himself intae a stupor. Efter he'd broken some puir bastard's heid. Is that no' right Matt? Is that no' right ye wicked wee craitur ye?'

'Awa' tae hell wi' ye Tam Young,' Clydesdale said harshly. 'Leave me alane.'

MacGregor agreed. 'Aye leave the puir mannie alane, Tam. Ye'll be botherin' him soon enough. Nae need tae mak' mock o' him. It's no' seemly. Now if you gentlemen have got whit ye came for, I think we should leave the man tae whatever peace he can muster, God help him.'

As we left the prison Ure surprised me by slipping MacGregor a few coins to buy some porter for Clydesdale. 'It's against the law, of course,' Ure told me. 'Nothing but water is supposed to pass his lips in the condemned cell. But where's the harm? Where's the harm?'

We parted company with the hangman and made our way back to Ure's house. We were in good spirits. Ure might be insufferable but he knew his business. And he was right about Clydesdale. He was an ideal subject for electrical experiments. He was young, fit and as strong as a horse. Every muscle in his body was in excellent working order. The tissue would be fresh, well charged with blood. The heart would be strong, the lungs healthy. The ganglia would be responsive and alert. He was perfect.

Ure and I spent the next day planning the experiments we would carry out on Clydesdale's corpse. It was a process which consumed sheet after sheet of paper, and involved some heated argument. We agreed that the most important experiment would be the one which infused the heart and lungs with electricity. But where Ure wanted to do this by galvanising the phrenic nerve above the clavicle I wanted to pass the charge through the great sympathetic and vagus nerves.

'Look Andrew,' I told the obdurate Scotchman, 'if we cut in through the sternomastoid muscle between the clavicle and the angle of the lower jaw, we could lay bare the vagus *and* the great sympathetic nerves. They're so close together we could pass the charge down through *two* main nerves and not just one. It would double the effect. Twice as much electricity bearing on the heart and lungs. Twice as much chance of some effect.'

But Ure would have none of it. 'Na, na,' he said. 'It's my firm belief that the phrenic nerve on the left side is the lad to go for. And we can get at him by going in through the sternomastoid about three above the clavicle. Then we make an incision into the cartilege just below the seventh rib to activate the diaphragm. Positive pole to the phrenic, negative to the diaphragm. And we'll see what happens.'

I was sure he was wrong, but nothing I could say would shake him. After a long tussle he asserted his proprietorial rights over the experiment, and that was an end to it. Then he took me completely by surprise.

'Of course, we cannot do this experiment first. That's out of the question. It'll have to come down the list somewhere.'

I protested noisily. The experiment on the heart and lungs was by far the most important one we had to do. Its success depended on the cadaver being in the best possible condition. We wanted the nervous system intact. The venous system undamaged.

But Ure just sat shaking his head. 'Think about it,' he said. 'Man, what would happen if we were successful? Where would we be if we restored to Matt Clydesdale his miserable life? For God's sake Frankenstein, the man's been sentenced to death by the High Court of Justiciar. Would he have to be hanged all over again? Or would we have to kill him ourselves after we'd brought him back tae life? I tell ye, there can be no prospect of Matt Clydesdale being hauled back from the grave.'

'But the law's finished with him,' I protested lamely.

'The law's never finished with anybody,' he replied grimly. 'At least not in this Scotland o' ours. Dead or alive, we're all subject to the law. And apart from the very good chance that you and I would find ourselves in Mr MacGregor's gaol for contempt of court – a serious business in Scotland – there would be such an uproar and scandal that we'd set back the cause of medical electricity a hundred years. Surely ye can see that?'

I had to concede the point. Matt Clydesdale was not the most deserving of causes. He was not the kind of citizen that anybody in his right mind would *want* to see re-suffused with the vital spark. Nor was there any chance of it being done in secret. We would be working in public, watched by a gallery of physicians, surgeons, medical students, experimental philosophers and the plain curious. Newspaper men too, no doubt.

'This is a real problem,' I said. 'If the body systems are too badly damaged, the most important part of the work could be made useless. We'd be wasting our time.'

It was a delicate balancing act. We were looking for some way of making *sure* that Clydesdale could not be revived, but without damaging the body so badly that it would yield no useful information. We wanted him dead, but not too dead. The man had to have crossed into eternity, but not so far as to be useless. It was easier said than done. I suggested decapitation, as in Aldini's experiments in Bologna, but Ure feared the effect of such a massive disruption of the spinal cord.

'How about this?' he suggested. 'We drain most of the blood out of him by baring the spinal marrow. We could then expose the sciatic nerve by cutting into the great gluteal muscle, and that will drain even more blood. Then we complete the arc between the spinal marrow and the sciatic, and see what happens.' He anticipated my objection. 'I agree it won't tell us much, but the man will be truly dead. And the damage shouldn't be too bad. And then we could carry out our real purpose.'

It was a neat solution. I agreed.

'There's another thing,' Ure said. 'It would be politic to have the actual incisions done by a man called Thomas

Marshall. He's Jeffray's nephew and one of his best assistants.'

This suggestion irritated me. I had planned to do the cutting myself. 'Whatever for?' I asked. 'Am I not to be trusted?'

He shrugged. 'It's not that,' he said. 'I just want to keep Jeffray happy. I want him to feel involved. I don't want him changing his mind and snatching Clydesdale away from us just because he feels left out. He's prickly and he carries a lot of weight in this town. But don't worry. Marshall's a good man with a knife. A lot better than I am. Maybe even as good as yourself.'

But it was not Jeffray who tried to cheat us of our subject, it was the subject himself. A few days before the hanging a messenger arrived from the New Gaol to tell us that Clydesdale had tried to cheat the hangman again. But not by escaping. This time he had cut his throat and wrists with shards of glass.

'Damn the man,' Ure grumbled as we rushed out of the house. 'What's his hurry? A few days wait wouldn't hurt him. Is he impatient for the fiery lakes o' hell?'

At the jail we found a little crowd of prison officials pressed into Clydesdale's cell. The felon himself lay on his cot, pale and silent but still very much alive. There were rough bandages around his throat and wrists. MacGregor the turnkey was almost as pale as his charge. He told us that Clydesdale had begged to be allowed to keep one of the bottles of porter for which Ure had paid. MacGregor had agreed, and shortly after Clydesdale had broken the bottle and used the glass to cut his wrists and throat. But he botched the job. The body flinches from such work. The gashes were not nearly deep enough to threaten his life.

I cleaned the man's wounds as best I could, and dressed them with fresh linen from Ure's medical bag. While I worked on him, Clydesdale stared sullenly at the wall. The little murderer's despair was almost tangible. He was not only facing the notion of his own death, but the knowledge that some of us would be playing tricks with his corpse. Before long his lights and tripes would be paraded before the amused stare of Glasgow's medical students. It was a profound helplessness. No wonder the poor brute had tried to cut short his time. It was his last act of free will.

Clydesdale's suicide attempt reinforced Ure's dismal view of the human species. 'It was my own fault,' he told me as we left the New Gaol. 'It could have cost us dear. Thoughtless charity is nearly always wrong, Frankenstein. It insults the beneficiary and inconveniences the benefactor. The prison rules are there for a reason, and now we know what that reason is. The charitable – and the pious – will drag us all down, see if they don't. Well, I'll know better the next time, by God I will.'

The day before the hanging kept us busy. In the forenoon Jeffray's assistant Thomas Marshall called on us to discuss the anatomical work. He was a small, brisk, bushy-haired man with a businesslike manner and a keen eye. He handed each of us his visiting-card, told me that he was 'mair than delighted' to make the acquaintance of 'the renowned Mister Frankelstein', and informed us that he was looking forward 'tae tomorrow's wark'. Then he attended to the diagrams which Ure and I had drawn up to show exactly where we wanted the cuts made.

'That's fine, that's fine,' he kept saying as we explained what we wanted. 'Nae trouble, Mister Ure. Nae bother, Mister Frankelstein. That'll be nae trouble at a'.' With a final glance down our list and a last 'nae trouble' Marshall shook both of us by the hand, trusted that I would enjoy my stay in Glasgow, bade us good day and marched out. His brisk energy reassured me. He knew his trade and I liked that.

After a heavy dinner, at which Ure compared a real anatomist like Marshall with a sham like Beau Fribble, we discussed just which of his Voltaic batteries we would use on Clydesdale. Ure's collection of electrical machines was small but more than adequate. He was all for using his largest, a huge pile of more than 400 pairs of zinc and copper discs. But I was able to persuade him that the effects on a light-boned man like Clydesdale might be disastrous.

After an hour of wrangling we settled for one of Ure's minor batteries. It was a beautiful piece of equipment, made in Glasgow to Ure's own specifications. The mahogany gleamed, the brass shone and every connection was solid. The pile consisted of 270 pairs of zinc and copper plates each four inches in diameter. The sharply pointed terminals were fitted with insulating handles and attached to the battery with strong metal wires. It was one of the finest batteries I had ever seen. After checking it over and satisfying himself that everything was working, Ure had the battery transported to the University's anatomy room.

'Great work in front of us tomorrow Frankenstein,' he said, swilling down his fifth glass of port. 'Original work. Work that'll make the whole of Scotland – maybe even the whole of Europe – sit up and take notice. By God it will! And work that'll show Beau Fribble for the paltry creature that he is. That'll make that *bitch* Catherine Monteath realise that there's more to a man than what swings between his legs . . .'

But his elation did not last. Before long he plunged into a brooding silence, staring into his port glass. His heavy features were set in a mask of rage and disappointment. There were tears in his eyes. 'There's a question I've got to ask you Frankenstein . . .'

I could see no point in adding to his misery *and* setting at risk tomorrow's experiment. So I held up a hand to stop him. 'I know what you're about to ask me Ure,' I said, with as much sincerity as I could muster. 'And the answer is no, I never did. Nor did she ever tempt me. You have that on my honour as a man of science.'

GLASGOW, SCOTLAND: DECEMBER 1818

If there is one thing the Scots enjoy it is sounding a pious note. Like the Jews, they regard themselves as one of God's elect people. Everything they do seems to be suffused with a kind of overweening piety. And hangings are no exception. Whereas the French and the English see their felons off with a cheerful brutality, the Scots invest their public executions with a sanctimoniousness that is more chilling than the hangman's rope.

I watched it work on Clydesdale and his partner-in-death, Simon Ross. Just before two o'clock in the afternoon the two men were hauled out of their fetid basement and led into the chapel of the New Gaol. They stood blinking in the daylight, their arms pinioned behind their backs, to confront the magistrates of Glasgow. They were solemnly told that they were to acknowledge both their own guilt and the justice of their sentences. This they did, if reluctantly. They were a sorry pair: Clydesdale a picture of sullen resentment, and the wretched young burglar witless with fear.

The men were flanked by two clergymen in their black

robes. Ure told me they were the Reverend John Lockhart and the Reverend Mr Mackenzie from the Gorbals. The latter was a renowned enthusiast and evangelical. Poor young Ross was in a constant state of agitation, as was his father who sobbed bitterly on the sidelines. But Clydesdale remained impassive. He just looked around with a cold stare that no one cared to meet.

The Reverend Mackenzie was in his element. He strutted and fluttered like a crow at the carcass of a rabbit. His high-pitched voice led the denunciations of the sinners and the singing of the psalms. While the Reverend Lockhart invoked God's mercy the Reverend Mackenzie preached only retribution. His breath was sulphur: his voice the crackle of hell fire. Mackenzie's pleasure rose in a crescendo as he led the singing of the fifty-eighth psalm which declared that 'The righteous one shall wash his feet/in blood of wicked men'.

Just before three o'clock, Clydesdale and Ross were led out of the building and across the street to the gallows. A huge crowd had gathered. Ure told me that Glasgow was alive with rumours that the Lanarkshire colliers – a fearsome crew apparently – were planning to storm the scaffold and rescue Clydesdale. This struck me as unlikely, if only because Clydesdale's victim had been a Lanarkshire collier himself.

But the Glasgow magistrates were taking no chances. They had called out the Fortieth Foot and the First Dragoon Guards. The foot soldiers were an unimpressive lot but the dragoons were big, hard-looking men, well equipped, well mounted and with the watchful air of veterans.

But there was no disruption. The colliers were, it seemed, content to let Clydesdale hang. At three o'clock Clydesdale and Ross were welcomed onto the scaffold by Tam Young. While Clydesdale stood watching, Ross dropped to his knees to pray until Young took him by the elbow and lifted him back to his feet. Then the hangman shook hands with both of them, placed white hoods over their heads, and despatched them at precisely five minutes past three. Clydesdale seemed to die instantly, but the unhappy Ross convulsed on the end of Tam Young's rope for many minutes.

While Clydesdale and Ross twisted in the wind, Ure and I fretted impatiently about the delay in transporting our man to the anatomy room. The longer Clydesdale dangled on the rope the less we liked it.

'Dammit!' I grumbled. 'If they don't get him off that rope soon the whole thing will be waste of time. He'll be too long gone. And we'll be a laughing stock.'

Ure shrugged. 'Nothing we can do,' he said. 'They'll both swing for a good half hour yet. As an example to the like-minded.'

'Jesus Christ!' I swore. 'Half an hour! In half an hour there'll not be a spark left in him. Everything will have shut down. Is there nobody you could *talk* to? A magistrate perhaps. Get him to speed things up a bit. Christ Jesus . . .'

In fact it was almost four o'clock before a cart, drawn by a huge white horse, pulled up under the gallows and Clydes-dale was cut down and inserted into a black-painted wooden box. By then I was beside myself with impatience, swearing loudly in French and German. A dragoon sergeant edged his horse towards me glaring at me as if I were Napoleon himself. I smiled ingratiatingly up at him and he moved on.

But the ceremonials had to be observed. With fatuous solemnity, ten officers of Glasgow's City Guard dressed in red coats, black beaver hats, blue breeches and white stockings, and carrying ancient battle-axes formed up on either side of the cart. And only when they were satisfied that their lines were straight did the procession move off, followed by most of the crowd who had watched the two men hang.

314

Ure and I hurried ahead, anxious to reach the anatomy room before our way was blocked by the mob. We beat the cart to the University by a good fifteen minutes. It was hard going. One irate citizen fetched me a clout in the ear which set my head ringing. Word was out that something unusual, and possibly spectacular, was about to happen to the notorious murderer. And most of Glasgow wanted to find out what it was.

The anatomy room was packed and buzzing. Every seat was taken and people were sitting on the steps and all over the floor. There was standing room only at the back. James Jeffray and Thomas Marshall were waiting for us. A tall, spare, ascetic-looking figure in long white robes, Jeffray looked more like a popish bishop than an anatomist. He oozed disapproval. But Marshall gave us a welcoming grin and wink.

As Ure and I quickly donned our medical smocks there was a series of loud 'huzzahs' from outside the building. The guest of honour had arrived. Ure quickly checked that the connections on the battery were sound and that the zinc and copper plates were in the correct sequence. Then he charged the pile with a quantity of dilute nitro-sulphuric acid which brought it into a state of intense action.

He had no sooner finished than the naked body of Clydesdale was carried into the room by four members of the town guard and strapped into an upright wooden chair. A ripple of anticipation swept round the room. There was nervous laughter from some of the younger students which was quickly stilled by Jeffray's cold eye.

'These *unusual* electrical experiments', Jeffray intoned to the hushed audience, 'are to be carried out, under my supervision, by Dr Andrew Ure. Dr Ure, as you know, is the Professor of Natural Philosophy at Anderson's Institution. He will be assisted by his colleague, Dr Victor Frankenstein of Landshut in Bavaria. The dissections will be carried out by Mr Thomas Marshall, a member of my staff at the Department of Anatomy of this university.'

After making this important point he paused, and then continued: 'The body is that of Matthew Clydesdale, aged twenty-six, who was hanged today after being convicted by the High Court of Justiciar of the crime of murder.' He stared at the younger members of the audience. 'I trust', he said solemnly, 'that the scientific gentlemen present will conduct themselves with suitable gravity.' Then he nodded to Ure. 'Dr Ure, you may begin.'

At which point the experiment started on its path into Glasgow legend. It was soon to take on the dimensions of myth and magic. With a wave of his electrical wand, Andrew Ure, the Glasgow warlock, conjured Matthew Clydesdale back into life. He undid the work of the hangman with a bolt of energy from his magical battery. According to at least one popular account (which seems to have originated with an excitable newspaperman called Peter Mackenzie), Clydesdale's eyes opened, his mouth worked, he groaned bitterly, rose slowly from his chair and stood upright.

Then his arm shot out to point accusingly at his tormentors, while the audience fled, howling in terror. The dead man would have followed them into the High Street had not brave Jeffray plunged his scalpel into the terrible figure's jugular, killing him all over again. Clydesdale fell to the floor with a crash, never to rise. Or so ran Mackenzie's story.

The truth, of course, was very different. Ure and I began by examining the body. I was surprised at its condition. The face looked oddly natural, neither livid nor tumefied. And there was no dislocation of the neck, which meant that the spinal marrow within the vertebrae was intact. The gashes on the throat and wrists had healed well. Satisfied, Ure nodded to Marshall who stepped forward and expertly cut a large incision in the nape of the neck. Immediately great gouts of blood spurted from the corpse and rained on the floor. The boards under foot became slippery, hard to stand on.

When the flow of blood ceased, Marshall used a bone forceps to reveal a portion of the spinal marrow. He then stooped, cut deeply into the great gluteal muscle on the left hip and laid bare the sciatic nerve. He made another incision on the heel of the left foot. Marshall was a neat worker. He wielded his scalpels with precision. The little Scotsman bore a passing resemblance to Émile Pascaud, now dead these thirteen years.

Ure then attached one terminal to the spinal marrow, and the other on the sciatic nerve. When the arc was completed the spectators gasped. Clydesdale's body shuddered and convulsed, gripped by a post-mortem seizure. After repeating the experiment a number of times, Ure removed the rod from the thigh and inserted it into the heel. There were shouts of alarm when it appeared to those watching that the corpse's leg was thrown out with enough violence to knock me over. In fact I lost my footing on the blood-slicked floor.

All of which was colourful, but predictable. Then we moved onto the crucial second experiment. While I held Clydesdale's head steady Marshall cut through the sterno-mastoid muscle about two inches above the clavicle. He then made a deep incision just below the seventh rib on the left side. This time the cries of astonishment were loud when Ure inserted his rods and completed the arc. Full breathing appeared to commence. The chest heaved and fell. The belly protruded and collapsed. The diaphragm rose and deflated. It looked as if the little murderer was trying to fight his way back to life.

Ure repeated the experiment while I took careful notes. It

317

was a remarkable sight. As I watched the chest inflate and deflate I felt exultant. We had almost done it! We had almost brought him back. If we had not drained the blood out of him with the initial cuts, we would have a live man on our hands. If the system had not been drained, then Ure's battery would have kicked the heart and the lungs into action, more than an hour after Clydesdale had died on the end of Tam Young's rope.

After that, the other two experiments were an anticlimax, although they impressed the audience. Marshall bared the supra-orbital nerve in the forehead and when Ure completed the arc to the heel, rage, anguish, delight, horror, despair and satisfaction all flitted across Clydesdale's features. At this point some of the spectators had had enough. One man was sick, another fainted, and yet another fled from the hall yelling 'Blasphemy! Blasphemy! A terrible blasphemy'.

Oddly it was the last, and least important, experiment which caused the most outrage. When Ure made the arc between the spinal marrow and the ulnar nerve in the left elbow, the fingers of the hand moved nimbly. It looked as if a dead hand was playing a melody on a ghostly violin from the abyss. When I tried to close the hand into a fist I found I could not.

Marshall then made a small incision in the forefinger of the left hand, and when Ure completed the arc with the spinal marrow, the finger extended and seemed to point accusingly at the audience. There were cries of 'God help us all' and 'He's come to life' and 'Make them stop' as yet more of our audience abandoned us. By the time we finished, shortly after five o'clock, the anatomy hall was looking less crowded. We left the corpse and the gore to be disposed of by the college servants.

It was an excited little crowd of medical men who met in Jeffray's rooms afterwards. They had all come to shake Ure's

318

hand, slap him on the back and quiz him. Jeffray did not look at all pleased. He made it plain, in a loud voice, that while Ure's work was doubtless extremely interesting, he could see little practical use in making corpses grin. But one of the Edinburgh doctors had seen the significance of the respiratory experiment and questioned me for fifteen minutes. I told him what I knew.

Ure and I spent the rest of that evening going over my notes and trying to sort out what we had learnt. We agreed on a number of points: that it was significant that Clydesdale's neck had not been dislocated by the hanging; that if the blood had not been drained out of him the second experiment might well have revitalised his heart and lungs; that electricity can, if anything can, restore the vital functions.

But I insisted that the phrenic nerve was *not* the most effective channel. 'I still think we'd have done better to go for the vagus and great sympathetic nerves,' I said. 'If only because laying them bare needs no great skill. Any half-decent physician could do it.'

'Maybe you're right,' Ure conceded. 'But perhaps we don't need any surgery at all. Maybe we could wrap the rods in cloth soaked in something like, oh, sal-ammoniac. Then just place them on the unbroken skin near whichever nerves we decide are the most effective, phrenic or vagus. The other on the diaphragm. And see what happens. It might work.'

But the exultation I felt during the experiments and immediately after had long gone. I felt mildly depressed. I could see that Ure also was descending into gloom. I wanted to avoid yet another rant against the iniquities of Beau Fribble and the 'whore', Catherine Monteath. So I told him I needed to clear my head with a brisk walk, and took myself out into the wet streets of Glasgow.

Later that evening I found myself in a High Street whisky

319

den talking to a brace of merchants' clerks. They told me their names were Davie and Tam and their only topic of conversation was the goings-on at the University that day. They were eager to tell a foreigner like myself all about it. Their's was a startling version of the events in the anatomy room.

'I wisnae there masel',' Davie told me, 'but I ken a man wha' was. He saw the whole thing. He telt me that when they put the electric bellows intae the deid man's nose, he opened his eyes, got tae his feet, stretched oot his airms, and said in a loud voice that he'd come back tae dae the wark o' his maister the devil.'

'That's whit I heard as weel,' Tam said. 'They say that maist o' the doctors just ran awa'. They say the deid man was halfway oot the door, his airms stretched oot in front o' him, when Dr Jeffray took a big sword and cut aff his heid. They say the sword had been specially blessed by the kirk ministers. They say that's the only way tae stop the deid fowk once they've been brocht back tae life.'

'Aye,' Davie said. 'That's richt. And then the body and the heid was pit in a special lead coffin and buried deep, deep in the grund. No' in a kirkyaird wi' decent fowk, but awa' oot on the hill. Somewhere at the back o' Dumbarton. Awa' doon in an auld coal mine. He's buried so deep that he'll never be able to climb oot again. No' even at the day o' judgement. Did ye ever hear o' sich a thing sir? In yer ain Germany I mean?'

I had to admit to Davie and Tam that that I never had.

Next morning Ure walked me to the London coach. The Glasgow Literary and Philosophical Society had invited him to read a paper on the subject of his electrical experiments. I asked him not to mention either my name or my contribution. He was surprised, but did not protest. He was cheerful enough, but yesterday's success had done nothing to drive out his demons.

'Beau Fribble will rue the day he ever tampered with Andrew Ure's wife,' he said suddenly. 'Aye, he will. I'll *extirpate* him from this city. Just like I did tae that whore Catherine Monteath. She's now moved to Edinburgh d'ye know. She's living in a lodging house and calling herself Mistress Thomson.' He spat in the street. 'The next time I see ye – if I ever see ye again – I'll be rid of her.'

Ure's obsession with his adulterous wife and her paramour depressed me. Ure may have been one of the best electricians in Europe but he was a miserable character. I was half tempted to tell him, there and then, that I had taken my pleasure with his wife under his own roof more times than I could recall.

But I held my tongue, shook his hand, thanked him for his hospitality, mounted the London coach, waved him goodbye and left him to stew in his own bile.

BRAUNAU-AM-INN, AUSTRIA:
NOVEMBER 1819

Braunau sat on the south bank of the River Inn at the end of a bridge which linked Bavaria with the Austrian Empire. It was a small town of pastel-coloured houses running south from the bank of the river. In the pale, slanting light of an autumn afternoon the bulk of the Stephanskirche, its high tower topped with an onion-dome steeple, looked almost grotesque. It was typical of the small towns which flourish in the southern reaches of the German-speaking world.

The eighty kilometres from Landshut had taken me a day longer than it should have. The rain was incessant and chilled me to the bone. My big black gelding picked its way through the mud well enough, but the mule I trailed behind me was weighed down with equipment. Every few hours the beast would come to a halt and have to be whipped and kicked into carrying on. By the time we clattered into Braunau, almost three days after we had set off, the animals and I were exhausted. I found them a decent stable and some fresh feed, then booked into an inn in the Stadtplatz. It would suffice until I found rooms to rent.

Not for the first time did I find myself bemused by my strange reasons for being in such a place. I was here, lying bone weary and unwashed, in a grubby inn in a small town on the Austrian border because the Bavarian legal authorities still preferred to cut off the heads of convicted felons. With a sword. Like almost everything else in Bavaria it was well-tried, old-fashioned and not about to change.

I had seen it done in Ingolstadt. The condemned man was strapped into a chair, an official held his hair to stretch his neck and then his head was severed from his body by a blow from the executioner's long, heavy sword. Usually there were a few pious lunatics waiting under the scaffold with cups to collect some blood. They believed the blood of an executed man was a cure for epilepsy. Provided, that is, he had repented of whatever sin he was being beheaded for.

But headless corpses were no good to me. Which is why I was here in Austria. Under the Empire of Francis II they hanged their criminals, just as they did in Scotland. My task was to track down the local hangman and persuade him to let me have the corpse of one of his healthier clients. And if the hangman of Braunau could not, or would not, oblige, then I would move further into Austria until I found an executioner who was open to persuasion and a purseful of silver.

I had no trouble finding Braunau's executioner. Such functionaries are usually well-known. An hour of asking around the inns and I knew all I needed to know about hangman Lothar Bitz. Like many men who spend their lives looking death in the eye Bitz was a modest fellow. He did his work with no fuss, some humanity and for a small wage. This he eked out by doing odd labouring jobs around the town. He was, I was told, a good gardener, a decent carpenter, a useful bricklayer and could turn his hand to plasterwork.

His wife was dead, trampled to death two years earlier by a runaway dray horse, leaving him to rear five children. Bitz drank a bit and whored hardly at all. In short, he was a quiet, decent, conscientious man. Everybody approved of him: nobody went near him. He ate and drank alone. He walked alone. He even prayed alone. It was said that the priests in the Cathedral arranged special masses for him and his children. A hangman is a hangman.

Bitz lived in a trim, little red-brick cottage just outside the Torturm at the south end of the town. I was told he spent his time cultivating his vegetables and making toys for his children, a boy and four girls. One of them was reputed to be very bright. Another was said to be sickly. The family was poor, but decent.

When I knocked at the house a red-haired girl of about twelve came to the door. She looked at me once and fled back inside. Bitz came to the door, wiping his hands on an apron. He was a slightly built man in his forties, whose balding pate was offset by a neat black beard flecked with grey. He eyed me warily.

'Lothar Bitz?' I enquired.

He nodded.

'My name is Frankenstein. Victor Frankenstein. I'm a doctor in the town of Landshut, across the river in . . .'

'In Bavaria. I know where Landshut is, doctor . . .'

'Frankenstein,' I repeated. 'Victor Frankenstein.'

'Doctor Frankenstein. What can I do for you?'

'May I come in?'

With some reluctance Bitz let me in and led me through the little house and into the kitchen. Five bright-eyed children sat around the table spooning soup into their mouths. They ranged from a little girl of three to the red-headed girl who had answered the door. When I entered the room the girls climbed down from their chairs and dropped curtsies. The boy just stared, soup all over his round face.

'Nice looking children,' I said smiling. 'You have been blessed.'

'I think so,' he said. 'Most of the time.'

I laughed. 'Difficult are they?'

He shook his head. 'If they had a mother they'd be just fine. We'd all be just fine. As it is . . .' He shrugged. 'I do my best. We get by. But what can I do for you Dr Frankenstein?'

I dropped my voice. 'I need a corpse. A body.'

Bitz silenced me with a frown and a raised hand. Then he turned to the children and shooed them out of the room. They went reluctantly with reproachful stares at me, the oldest girl holding the hand of the youngest. At the door the little one fell over and started to cry. Her sister picked her up and carried her out.

'I never discuss my business in front of them,' Bitz told me. 'It's hard enough for them. Being the hangman's brats.'

'I understand,' I said.

'Maybe,' he said. 'What do you want a corpse for?'

'Medical research,' I told him.

He was not surprised. It was a common request. Delivering up corpses to the anatomist's scalpel was against the law but the Austrian authorities turned a blind eye to the trade. I guessed that Lothar Bitz had provided the professors of the local medical school with many a cadaver for dissection.

'Well, maybe something can be arranged,' he said. 'At the right price, of course.'

'Good man. But I need a body in good condition. A healthy corpse, if you like.'

He thought for a while then shook his head. 'There's nobody at the moment. I've got two drunks, both of them pickled and one of them on his last legs. And an old whore who killed a soldier with his own bayonet. She said he had tried to ravish her.'

'How old is she?'

'Fifty if she's a day. Not a tooth in her head.'

'And that's all you've got?'

'The entire stock.'

'Hmmm . . .'

'But you'll not wait long,' he assured me. 'Folk being what they are.'

I spent the next day searching for a set of rooms that would serve as a workshop. After asking around the town, an overweight postmaster directed me to a narrow alley near the Stephanskirche, where a slatternly widow agreed to charge me too much money for a rundown outhouse at the end of her vegetable garden. I moved my instruments in, cleaned the place up, hammered a few scraps of wood into the roof to stop the rain coming through, lit a fire in the fireplace and installed a mattress in one corner.

Then I bought some planks of wood from a local sawmill, assembled them into a long workbench around which I arrayed my instruments and batteries. It was not the St Moritz Clinic or even my own little clinic in Landshut, but it would do. I now had to wait for Lothar Bitz.

I did not have long to wait. A few days later I saw him making his way down the widow's garden to my outhouse. 'I think I've got what you want,' he said, looking around the room at the glittering instruments. 'Jesus! What the hell is all this stuff for?'

'What have you got?' I asked.

'A big brute of a fellow,' he told me, still eyeing up the apparatus. 'Must be six and a half foot. Built like the side of a barn. But a simpleton, if you ask me. Can't speak. Doesn't know what day it is or what's happening to him. The brain of an infant. He's a sad case.'

326

'What did he do?'

'Killed a little girl. Ravished then strangled her. Or maybe he strangled and then ravished her. So the locals have told the court. Out in the Kosching woods near Beitbrunn. He tried to bury her body under a tree. She was found by a charcoal-burner and his dogs.'

'Age?'

'Six. Seven?'

'Not the girl, your man.'

'Late twenties by the look of him. Maybe less. It's hard to tell with somebody like that.'

'And in fair condition?'

'I'd say so.'

'What's his name?'

'Nobody knows. No family. No friends. He's been living for years in some hut in the woods on the other side of Kasing. The locals call him The Creature. They're terrified of him. They'll be glad to see him hang, just to be rid of him. The poor bastard. You can have a look at him if you like.'

The creature was even bigger than Bitz had suggested. As he rose, ragged and dishevelled, from the pile of stinking straw in the town gaol he seemed to fill the cell. He was huge. I estimated him to be almost seven foot high. He must have weighed nearly 300 pounds. The manacles on his hands and feet looked like flimsy bracelets. As he shuffled towards us, grinning and gesticulating, I backed away. But The Creature just pushed his hands through the bars of the cell. He wanted something but he had no way of telling us what it was.

'What do you think?' Bitz asked me.

'I don't know what to think,' I replied.

As The Creature stared out at us through small, blood-laced eyes I felt a tug of pity. Whatever is inside us that makes us grow, somehow this poor man had been given more than his share. And whatever chemical mechanism first prompts us to sprout up from infancy and then stop in adulthood had gone badly awry in this wretch's body.

Gazing at the cruelly ill-formed young man I was swept by a feeling of ignorance. After years of work and study, travel and reading, I realised I knew nothing. Standing in that loathsome place before this sad monster it seemed to me that another thousand years of learning were needed before we even began to understand our own bodies. But with some luck this creature might shed a flicker of light on my darkness.

'When's he due to drop?' I asked Bitz, who was scribbling in a notebook.

'Three days time,' he said. 'He'll take some hanging this one. I hope to God he doesn't fight. I'll have to call out the army. So, Dr Frankenstein. Will he do?'

I stared at The Creature long and hard. He stared back at me and tried to smile. I smiled back.

'He'll do,' I said.

BRAUNAU-AM-INN, AUSTRIA:
NOVEMBER 1819

The day before The Creature was due to hang I met Lothar Bitz in a beer house on the Stadtplatz. The place was crowded and noisy but the hangman was sitting on his own, nursing a tankard of beer. There was a distinct lowering of the noise as I walked in and sat down opposite him. Some of the drinkers stared at us. Most turned away their faces. Two men at a nearby table moved away and found other seats.

'I'm used to it,' Bitz said to me as I settled down.

'Doesn't it offend you?'

'Only when it happens to my children. Especially the girls. They can't help having the hangman as a father.'

I had already decided that I had to have The Creature in the town gaol. But I had to have him intact, with his neck unbroken. That was essential. That much I had learnt from Ure's experiment in Glasgow. Everything now depended on being able to persuade Bitz to go along with me. By the time I had ordered more beer from an ample but surly barmaid I knew what my strategy would be.

'Why do you do what you do?' I asked Bitz after the beers had arrived. 'I'd like to know.'

He stared at me for a long, chilly moment. 'For the money,' he said. 'Although there's little enough of that. And because my father did it before me. And his father before him. Runs in the family, you might say.'

'I'm told you do it well.'

'I do my best. To be merciful.'

'I can see you're a humane man,' I said. 'I need a humane man's help.'

He gave a sour laugh. 'How can the likes of me help the likes of you, sir?'

I changed my approach. 'What have you heard of medical electricity?' I asked him.

He shrugged and then surprised me. 'Is that what all these strange devices of yours are about?' he asked.

'Yes. That's what they're about.'

'I've heard a little,' he said. 'But not much. You give shocks to cure people of their ailments. Or *try* to cure them. It comes out of a bottle or a jar or a machine. Something like that.'

'As you say, something like that. The thing is, Bitz, many of us – and I'm one of them – see electricity as the medicine of the future. It's the way ahead. It's something that will stop people dying unnecessarily. Something that will give life back to people who appear to be dead.'

He raised his tankard in salute. 'Then I wish you well with your work, sir.'

'You can do more than that,' I said to him. 'You can deliver to me that man you showed me.'

'I said I would,' he replied.

'Hanged, yes. But with his neck unbroken.'

There was a long silence as he lowered his tankard and stared at me. I found Bitz's level gaze disconcerting.

330

'Do you know what you're asking me to do?' he said, with a trace of anger in his voice.

'Yes,' I replied. 'Yes I do.'

'You're asking me to make that poor wretch's end more miserable than it need be.'

'I understand that,' I told him.

'That is something I never do,' he said.

'I'm happy to pay you well for doing it.'

'Maybe. But I'm not happy to take your money. You can have the corpse, Dr Frankenstein, but his neck will be broken.'

'Then he's no use to me,' I said.

'I cannot help that.'

'Yes you can,' I argued. 'By just doing what you are paid to do, and letting him hang.'

'God, man, do you know how long that can take?'

'Bitz, look at it this way. If that wretched creature can help me understand more about life and death, then maybe he won't have died for nothing. His death might be of more value than his life.'

'That's one way to look at it,' he replied. 'The other is that he'll have gone through God knows what kind of hell to make you an even bigger doctor – a more famous doctor – than you are already.'

I changed tack by feigning indignation. 'Oh, for God's sake, man. Think! He killed a little girl. An innocent child. Somebody's daughter. The wretched man deserves to die. And if he takes a few more minutes to do so, does it matter? I'll wager that the child's parents would be more than happy to see him dance on the end of your rope all day.'

'That's neither here nor there,' he said.

'And that's exactly what you'd want if it was your little girl he'd butchered.'

At that thought his eyes shuttered in distress. I could sense him weakening, so I pressed home my advantage. 'What's her name,' I asked. 'Your little girl, the youngest one?'

'Kirsten,' he said.

'And what does she call you?'

'Papa,' he replied.

'What if it was your Kirsten who had her life throttled out of her by that creature? What if it was your little Kirsten who had wandered into the paws of that thing? What if it had been Kirsten who was lifted by the neck, her legs thrashing, her throat crushed, after he'd done God knows what to her. Trying to scream for her Papa, but not able to. Imagine that . . .'

'I cannot,' he replied.

'Then try,' I said harshly. 'Try to imagine the sheer terror she would have felt when she realised that her Papa was not going to help her. That her Papa was not going to make this go away. Not this time. She would have died feeling betrayed. Betrayed by you. Because when she needed her Papa most, you were not there. Imagine all that, Lothar Bitz.'

He was silent, staring at me. I pressed on.

'Now put yourself in the place of the father of the child that died. He probably hates himself more than he hates The Creature that killed his little girl. Why, because he was not there. The mother, Christ, the mother will feel even worse. They'll both hate themselves for the rest of their lives. Long after the murderer is dead and gone and at peace. They'll die with broken hearts.'

I could see from Bitz's face that my words were striking home. 'Think man. A whole family ruined. Decent people destroyed. And all because of that wretch you want to save from a few extra minutes of distress. Let The Creature serve some useful purpose, Bitz. Do him a favour. Don't let his whole life go for nothing. Let him give *something* back in exchange for the life he took.'

There was another long silence as the hangman drained the beer from his tankard. Then he stood up. 'You're a persuasive man, Dr Frankenstein,' he said.

'Then we have an arrangement?' I asked, offering him my hand.

He ignored it. 'I'll think about it,' he said, and walked out of the room. Many eyes watched him as he left the beer house. Some of them turned to stare curiously at me. I finished my beer and then pushed my way through the crowd.

The day that The Creature was due to be hanged I spent in a state of some anxiety. I busied myself with useless work. I scrubbed and rescrubbed the rough workbench I had made for myself. I cleaned and recleaned, checked and then rechecked all my instruments, particularly the battery I had modelled on the one used by Andrew Ure. The principle was the same but mine was much bigger. I made sure all my notes were in order and that my inkwells were filled. And then I waited.

Late that evening I heard hooves outside my lodgings. There was the sound of voices and a soft knock on the door. It was Bitz and two of his associates. The huge corpse of the hanged man was lying under a pile of sacks on the back of a cart. It took the four of us to carry The Creature into my workshop and lay him out on the long bench. The three Austrians crossed themselves as they looked around the room.

'When did he hang?' I asked Bitz.

'Less than an hour ago,' he replied.

'Did he make a fight of it?'

Bitz shook his head. 'Like a lamb,' he said with some bitterness. 'He had no idea what was happening to him. Poor soul.'

333

But when I went to hand Bitz a purse of coins he looked at me with cold disdain. Then he gestured to his colleagues.

'Give it to them, Doctor Frankenstein,' he said, turning away. 'I have enough on my conscience.'

BRAUNAU-AM-INN, AUSTRIA:
NOVEMBER 1819

It was with a mixture of excitement and trepidation that I viewed the corpse laid in front of me. The creature was huge. The great body stretched from one end of my makeshift workbench to the other. His feet – one boot was missing – dangled over the end. He was dressed in ill-fitting rags and the stench from his voided bowels was prodigious. For the first time I felt a surge of misgiving. Did I have the expertise and the electrical equipment to revitalise a man of this size?

But I shrugged off my doubts and set to work. Working quickly, I began by stripping the cadaver of its soiled rags, which I threw into the open stove. When I measured him I found him to be three inches short of seven feet, smaller than my original estimate. I had no way of calculating his weight, but my experience told me he was around 275 pounds, perhaps more. Big enough to require a substantial jolt of electricity. The pile that almost revived little Matthew Clydesdale would never work on this massive creature.

I examined my subject closely, taking notes as I went. His head was a huge, a wide skull topped by coarse black hair.

Small pale eyes, half closed in death, peered out under a grossly thickened brow ridge. That ridge under a high forehead dominated the face. The whites of the eyes had a yellow tinge to them, flecked with blood.

The nose was large, wide and with capacious nostrils. The mouth was oddly formed, with thin lips drawn back in a grin to reveal yellowed, widely spaced teeth. The jaw was long and heavy. The skin was very pale, coarse and studded with pustules. It felt oily, almost greasy to the touch. To judge from the moisture tracks in the grime on his face, the man had been sweating heavily before he was hanged.

His limbs were long and bulky and oddly jointed. For some reason the bones in his shoulders, elbows, knees and ankles had become – or perhaps had always been – ill fitting, badly articulated. And there were signs on the elbows and wrists of the same thickening that had disfigured his skull. With joints like these movement could never have been easy. This man must have dragged himself around for most of his life, probably in pain.

And his hands were strange. They were massive, the fingers puffy and oddly splayed, and the finger joints were swollen. But the skin was remarkably soft for a creature who survived by foraging around the Braunau countryside. I had expected them to be calloused but they were not. The feet, like the hands, were huge, with swollen joints on the splayed toes.

After washing the body down with the hot water which had been simmering on the stove, I set about organising my batteries, the design of which I had copied from Ure's, adding a few refinements of my own. One was a mahogany-clad pile of 250 zinc and copper discs which I dubbed 'minor'. The other I knew as 'major', a large 450-disc pile, by far the biggest in my armoury. There was no question about which of the two I would use.

336

It was now one in the morning and a heavy rain was battering at the windows of my ramshackle laboratory. Working quickly I dragged my big battery close to the table, checked the connections for the fiftieth time and then collected my surgical instruments from the water in which they had been boiling.

With a newly sharpened scalpel I cut through the sternomastoid muscle just above the left clavicle and laid bare the vagus and sympathetic nerves. Another incision under the seventh rib exposed the sympathetic nerve near the diaphragm. In both locations The Creature's skin seemed strangely thickened.

It was with mounting excitement, mixed with trepidation, that I inserted the terminals into the two incisions and completed the arc. The creature's body lurched and the back arched. I cursed as one of my candles guttered and then died. But by the glimmer of the half-extinguished light, I saw the dull yellow eye of The Creature open. The huge chest rose and fell. He breathed hard and a convulsive motion agitated his limbs.

DRAMATIS PERSONAE

Aldini (Giovanni), 1762–1834
Italian physician and surgeon. Aldini was a professor at the University of Bologna where he spent most of his working life. He toured Europe promoting the cause of his uncle Luigi Galvani against the claims of Volta. Aldini experimented extensively with corpses in the hospitals of Bologna. In the winter of 1802 to 1803 he was in London where he carried out the well-publicised experiments at Newgate Prison on the hanged murderer Foster. Like many of his contemporaries, Aldini was a practical scientist. In later life he turned his attention to quarrying, fire fighting and the design of lighthouses.

Kite (Charles), dates unknown
English physician and surgeon who practised in the town of Gravesend on the Thames. He was also an officer in the local militia. He is best known for his 1788 paper *On the Recovery of the Apparently Dead*, which won a silver medal from the Royal Humane Society.

Larrey (Dominique Jean), 1766–1842
French surgeon who became Surgeon-General to Napoleon's Imperial Guard. He was also one of Napoleon's favourites, although Bonaparte never gave him charge of the Grande Armée's medical services. Larrey was arguably the greatest military surgeon of his time. He is credited with inventing the system of 'flying ambulances', the purpose of which was to get casualties off the battlefield as quickly as possible. This is now known as 'casevac'. He also advocated amputation of damaged limbs while the patient was in shock, and then getting him back on his feet as soon as possible. As a result of Larrey's methods the Imperial Guard suffered fewer deaths from infection and disease than any other unit in the Grande Armée.

Paracelcus (a name coined for himself by Theophrastus Philippus Aureolus Bombastus Von Hohenheim), 1494–1591.
Swiss-born scientist and practical philosopher who acquired a reputation as an alchemist. In many respects he was the first 'modern' scientist. Paracelcus was a wandering scholar who denounced the 'high asses' of the universities of Europe, the clergy of the Roman Catholic Church and the medical orthodoxy of the Greek physician Galen and the Arab Ibn Sina. He was among the first to identify disease as the result of an external agent and to describe ailments like silicosis and tuberculosis as occupational hazards, rather than the work of evil spirits. Similarly he preached that mental illness was a natural condition and not the work of demons. Paracelcus identified the universe as a chemical crucible from which life emerged and argued that all forms of life were interlinked. Thirty years after his death (he was assassinated in Austria) a strong Paracelsian movement grew up among physicians, naturalist and chemists all over

Europe. That movement was influential into the eighteenth century, and was revived, to some extent, in the twentieth.

Pattison (Granville Sharp), 1791–1851.
Scots anatomist and proprietor of the College Street anatomy school, Glasgow, which had one of the finest collections of anatomical specimens in Europe. Described as a brilliant surgeon and anatomist but irascible and quick-tempered, Pattison's adultery with Andrew Ure's wife Catherine Monteath led in 1819 to divorce and the birth of an illegitimate daughter. The scandal obliged Pattison to flee Scotland for the United States. In Philadelphia he fell foul of the local establishment and fought a pistol duel with General Thomas Cadwalader which he won. After a spell in Baltimore he returned to Britain in 1826 as Professor of Anatomy at London University. He was not a success. In 1832 he returned to the USA where he joined the staff of the Jefferson Medical College before taking to lecturing at the Stuyvesant Institute in New York, where his lectures were a runaway success. After he died in 1851 his body was shipped back to Scotland and buried in Glasgow.

Saussure (Horace-Benédict de), 1740–99
Citizen of Geneva and one of the foremost scientists of his day. Saussure was Professor of Philosophy at the University of Geneva and researched and wrote on geology, physics and meteorology. He travelled extensively throughout Europe and had a wide circle of correspondents. Saussure's expedition in 1787 to the top of Mont Blanc, the highest mountain in Europe, was one of the first mountaineering expeditions with a scientific purpose. Part of that purpose was to study magnetism and lightning. His enthusiasm for the mountains is credited with starting Switzerland's tourist industry. He was a political reformer who abandoned

radical politics after the violent popular uprising in Geneva in 1794. His son Nicolas and his grandson Henri carried on the family tradition by becoming renowned scientists.

Stael (Anne Louise Germaine de), 1766–1817
Daughter of Jacques Necker, finance minister to Louis XVI, wife of the Swedish minister to revolutionary France and one of the period's most influential hostesses. Although she and her family made their fortune in France, they were Genevans by birth, with a mansion in the *haute ville* and a large château in the village of Coppet on Lac Leman. Politically liberal, Germaine de Stael quickly got the measure of the ambitious Napoleon Bonaparte and became one of his most outspoken critics. She was exiled by Napoleon and did not return to France until after the fall of his empire in 1815.

Ure (Andrew), 1778–1857
Scots chemist, philosopher and entrepreneur. Scientifically advanced but politically reactionary, Ure is described by Karl Marx in *Capital* as an 'enemy of society'. He was Professor of Natural Philosophy and Chemistry at the Andersonian Institute in Glasgow, now the University of Strathclyde. In 1816 Ure travelled in France, meeting, among others, Berthollet and Gay-Lussac. His electrical experiment on the hanged murderer Matthew Clydesdale became notorious and sensationalised by Glasgow journalist Peter Mackenzie. But his own, very accurate, account is contained in his *Dictionary of Chemistry* published in 1821.